W9-BFN-613

"Just when you think there's nothing new to be done with the serial-killer novel . . ."
—Ed Gorman, *Mystery Scene*

"ROBERT W. WALKER HAS ARRIVED"*

Killer Instinct
The stunning debut of Dr. Jessica Coran, an FBI pathologist tracking the blood-drinking "Vampire Killer" . . .

"Chilling and unflinching."　　　—*Fort Lauderdale Sun-Sentinel*

Fatal Instinct
Jessica Coran faces a cunning, modern-day Jack the Ripper nicknamed "The Claw" . . .

"A taut, dense thriller. An immensely entertaining novel filled with surprises, clever twists, and wonderfully drawn characters."　　　—**Daytona Beach News-Journal*

Primal Instinct
The Hawaiian beaches are awash in blood. The relentless "Trade Winds Killer" is loose . . .

"A bone-chilling page-turner."　　　—*Publishers Weekly*

Pure Instinct
New Orleans plays host to the notorious "Queen of Hearts" killer . . .

"Walker takes you into a world of suspense, thrills and psychological gamesmanship."　　　—*Daytona Beach News-Journal*

continued . . .

Darkest Instinct

From Florida to London, a copycat killer strikes, as Jessica Coran faces double jeopardy . . .

Extreme Instinct

A psychopath on a Satanic mission is terrorizing the American west . . .

Bitter Instinct

Beware the message of the Poet—for human flesh is his parchment . . .

And don't miss Robert W. Walker's series of thrillers starring Native American police detective Lucas Stonecoat . . .

Cutting Edge

An on-line computer game leads Stonecoat and psychiatrist Meredyth Sanger into a literal Web of intrigue, murder and mutilation . . .

Double Edge

Stonecoat and Sanger follow the snatcher, a psychopath who preys on the ideal victim: young teens—vulnerable, willing, and nameless . . .

BLIND INSTINCT

ROBERT W. WALKER

JOVE BOOKS, NEW YORK

This is a work of fiction. Names, characters, places, and incidents are either the product of the author's imagination or are used fictitiously, and any resemblance to actual persons, living or dead, business establishments, events, or locales is entirely coincidental.

BLIND INSTINCT

A Jove Book / published by arrangement with the author

PRINTING HISTORY
Berkley hardcover edition / March 2000
Jove edition / September 2001

Visit our website at
www.penguinputnam.com

ISBN: 0-515-13150-4

A JOVE BOOK®
Jove Books are published by The Berkley Publishing Group,
a division of Penguin Putnam Inc.,
375 Hudson Street, New York, New York 10014.
JOVE and the "J" design
are trademarks belonging to Penguin Putnam Inc.

PRINTED IN THE UNITED STATES OF AMERICA

10 9 8 7 6 5 4 3 2 1

*This book is affectionately dedicated to
John Schline
who has kept the vision of
the Instinct books intact and whole.
Thanks, John.*

Acknowledgments

My most sincere thanks to Marianne Norsesian for editorial help and encouragement on the final drafts of this book. My sincere thanks also to Ann Turner for help on British-isms and Great Britain in general (no one knows the territory like a native). My equally sincere thanks must go to Jean Jamison Leibig Prickett, whose editorial assistance on the book proved invaluable in its early stages. Many thanks to Lara M. Robbins for an excellent job copyediting this book. The many maps and books on England consulted would prove too long a list to tally here, but I will say that *British English from A to Zed* became my bible.

· PROLOGUE ·

*All that most maddens and torments; all that
stirs up the lees of things; all truth with malice
in it; all that cracks the sinews and cakes the
brain; all the subtle demonisms of life and
thought; all evil to crazy Ahab were visibly
personified and made practically assailable . . .*

—HERMAN MELVILLE,
MOBY DICK

*Below London, England, in an underground catacomb
September 4, 2000—Approaching true millennium*

She could not remember her own name, not even when the
man who'd brought her to this excruciating moment—to die
here—chanted her name in her bleeding ears. Neither could
she recall her very sex, age, race, or religion, for the burning,
searing pain washed so completely over her mind and blotted
out all clarity of thought. Clarity ran before this blinding pain,
banished from the realm of consciousness, sending the angels
of specificity and nouns and adjectives spiraling away from
this place. Now on the brink of death, she felt utter disappointment, having all her life believed that when she looked
into the eye of death, that she'd find some answers to life's
grandest questions: Who am I? What am I? Where am I?
Where have I been, and where do I go?

If there were answers, they remained blurred, dulled, and
finally lost to the pain of this death—the pain of a crucifixion
death. . . . *Not even St. Michael and all his legion can help
me now,* she realized. Or had he said that in her ear? Bile and
spit and gall. *I must prepare myself to sleep, prepare to sleep
forever.* Answers and resolutions all blurred. . . .

Crucifixion does that to you, to me, she told herself, here in this cold, dank coffin of "consecrated ground," as he'd called this place. Now, she realized this was no dream, no nightmare she might claw herself out of. In that realization her mind cleared for one crystal moment to tell her, *Yes . . . yes, you are actually dangling on a cross about to greet your Maker.*

She had been tied and staked to a cross, and she would soon die Katherine O'Donahue, at fifty years and some odd months—either a saint or a wretched fool, she knew not anymore. Part of her cared not; part of her simply wanted the pain to go away, to sleep eternal.

She'd reached a plateau in the agony; she no longer felt the pain at the bloodied feet—feet held together first by coarse hemp and next a large stake hammered through them and into the splintering massive cross. Nor did she any longer feel the stinging pain at the core of each palm where bone and flesh had made peace with each great stake sent through each hand where they'd been held against the crossbar. No, the pain in her hands and feet had mercifully ceased, but that suffering now stood replaced by a worse pain, the pain of a slow suffocation she hadn't expected.

The drug given her hadn't been potent enough to send her into merciful peace, and so she'd felt the three stakes as each had been driven through the flesh, cartilage, and bone.

She'd yelped at the flinty, striking blows caused by hammerhead against stake and its resultant rending of flesh. The man with the hammer had been startled. She feared making any further outcries would only bring on more pain and loss of breath and consciousness, only to hasten her crossing over. . . . Yet she wanted to cross over, didn't she?

Crossing over, her schoolteacher's mind mused. How lovely the euphemism, and how apropos to her unbelievable situation: her life ending in such a manner.

She wanted a last look at his face before she died; she wanted to implant it on her memory. Take it into the next life—take it to her God.

Her arms, flung out on each side of her, remained immovable, save for the incremental, steady pull of gravity that brought her chest caving in on itself. Trying to breathe had become a laborious effort. Her own weight snatched her breath from her like a ravenous animal, devouring it before she could have even a slight taste. The oxygen deprivation caused dizziness and a ringing in her ears.

Still, little snatches of inhaled air also fought like clawing animals to get through to her lungs.

No, she no longer felt any pain in her hands, bleed as they might into the ancient wood, wood that *he* said, "Has the advantage of having been blessed by the Holy Roman Church." Her mind screamed *Evil liar!* But there came no breath of air, which would be necessary to mold and fashion a word, much less a serviceable curse. She'd spent a lifetime fashioning words in diaries and in private poetry, but now her words, like a ship on a windless sea, had no life force to propel her stranded thought.

Her body gasped again and again for her life's breath, while her mind insisted, "Give it up." At once she wondered at the depth of her faith, matched as it was by her killer's own. At the same time, she remained unsure of the soundness or brokenness, fragmented-ness, frag-men-ta-tion—*which was it?*— of her own mind, or even if her mind remained *hers* anymore, if it had not somehow already transmutated into the pure soul? She mused about the evil man's faith—whether it was perhaps the most beautiful or the most twisted faith she'd ever encountered, or whether the very sincerity with which he now practiced it made the fact of it undeniable.

She felt certain of one fact alone: *His* faith and not her own had everything to do with why she was being literally crucified by him. She wondered if his commitment meant anything to God, who allowed so much suffering in the world. But even these, her private, final thoughts, she could not be sure of. She could not be sure they were cogent—were they driven by hallucination or the torturous agony or the numbness now in her soul? How could she even trust her own mind with her body involved in a concerted attempt to destroy what remained of her . . . *her?*

What is my name? she mentally asked again, having no breath left to form the question aloud.

However, at the moment, the war continued to rage, the

war for life coming down to a slow and painful fight for
breath due to the gravitational pull. *Gravity kills,* she thought.
My own weight is pushing the life from me. That's intense,
overpowering, excruciating, literally heartrending, and mind
numbing. *But the numbing is good,* she told herself—a blessing in horrid disguise. It must soon be over. *Through such
pain and such a death, perhaps I shall find final peace, even
redemption.* He had said so even as the stakes were driven
in. *Redemption in a place alongside my Maker, an end to all
suffering in this life.*

And for the moment, this hope sustained her soul, representing, as it did, her only reprieve.

She clutched at it.

Tearfully she decided, despite all pretense, that she had
little or nothing to show for all the years she'd put in. Nothing
beyond a pension amounting to so little she couldn't make
her monthly rent. No children of her own; no family. Even
at fifty, she had never been with a man, had never known any
real, true desire or passion. Until now. Now she passionately
wanted to either live or mercifully die.

Against the advice of her doctor, against the wishes of a
neighbor in St. Edmunds, she'd uprooted and gone fishing in
search of something—anything—to give her life new meaning. She'd thought to find it in London. So, she'd moved to
London, from the cottage community of Bury St. Edmunds.
Taking a flat, her schoolteacher retirement pounds helped out
along with her life's savings, but only so far. She had a few
stocks and bonds, and while only the rare commoner held
ownership to land in England, she had managed to make some
money on real-estate exchanges over the years—all quite
modest.

All having led to what? To this. Meant to be, perhaps.
Fated, perhaps. Her only and just karma?

Had she remained in Bury St. Edmunds, she surely would
have lived out her years to be buried there. Everything would
have ended differently—unless he had come there for her,
and that she could not say would not have happened. The
man she'd put her fleeting hopes into, after all claimed he'd
seen her death on the cross in a vision, and had since been

driven to find her and execute this death. So perhaps he would have sought her out in St. Edmunds had she remained there. She only knew he was a driven, determined being, no matter where he may be lurking.

She wished for a quick end to her life spent in the service of others. Her thoughts spiraled, revolved, circled, and came round and round on themselves, coiling snakelike, repeating themselves until she knew not how many times she'd had the same thought or memory or hope or tear.

Gasp . . . no breath . . . gaps in time . . . gasps in time. Gasp . . . no breath.

Mentally, she still lived her life. Regardless of her inability to recall her name or the fact that she was hanging like an insect pinned to a wall, she relived every detail of her life. It must mean something. She told herself that a life lived must mean something. Even *he* had to respect that. Then she wondered if she was making any sense at all. And if she couldn't make sense, would God Himself understand her? Would He make sense of her senselessness, of her death? Did her death make sense?

Inhaling without result, unable to exhale whatsoever, yet feeling the need to do so, Katherine O'Donahue smiled, recalling having signed over all her holdings to Mother Church. This much pleased her.

The fact that she was being crucified, the fact of its being witnessed by a man who whispered promises of a better life in the hereafter, none of it any longer got past the unfeeling, uncaring, unhearing, and inert body that now could not sustain itself. None of it, not even her own death, held any more meaning for . . . Again she'd lost all trace of her name. Perhaps that was part of death, to let go of such earthly ties as names, language, home, religion, beads, wishes, bread, needs, wine, flesh, bone, appearances, and such. *Who am I?* The suffering stopped. This life and this world held no more meaning or allure. Slowly, as with her breath, all thought drifted off like smoke over the railing of a cruise ship, until her last breath caught and died with her.

· ONE ·

*. . . For the detectives, the most appalling visions
have always demanded the greatest detachment.*

—DAVID SIMON,
HOMICIDE

Charing Cross Pier, River Thames, London
September 5, 2000

"Elderly woman, I warrant fifty if she's a day," said Inspector
Sharpe to his partner Copperwaite. "Looks like someone's
mum. Looks local."

"Then you don't make her out a whore, Sharpe? Killed
possibly because she'd gotten too old to draw in enough shillings?"

"I shouldn't assume her a whore, Coppers."

"Looks like someone's mum actually," Copperwaite
agreed. "Still doesn't rule her out as an old whore. Lots of
mums are whores, you know."

The dead woman's body had no identifying marks, no
clothing and so no ID. "Nothing whatever to inform us of a
bloody thing," muttered Sharpe. "And I resent your summing
her up as a whore, Stuart."

Lieutenant Inspector Stuart Copperwaite, working his way
up to full inspector status, felt compelled to agree with his
superior. "You're right, of course, Sharpie. Just *Another-
nother.*"

Sharpe thought of the sad term law enforcement in the
United States used: *Jane Doe*, and its British equivalent *A.N.*

Other. Murdered, but murdered in an unmistakably brutal and bizarre fashion. "Something altogether unique about this *nobody*," said the Scotland Yard inspector. "This poor, wretched woman has died the most horrid death, *staked* to a tree, Stuart."

Sharpe stepped away from the body and walked in little circles, ever-widening the breech between himself and the other authorities on hand. "Each time I look on such unconscionable, and despicable acts as this, I begin to believe that no new evil can ever rival what I must deal with before me. Yet . . . yet some fiend always finds a new twist, a new evil beyond anything you or I might ever have imagined possible, and this certainly proves the case here. *Something evil this way comes. . . .*"

Sharpe's feet, hands, and lungs ached from the thought of how this elderly woman had died literally crucified. He imagined the hours it had taken for her to suffer this tormenting death. The same agony faced by Christ.

"I've interviewed the bridgeman. He's of no use," Copperwaite said in Sharpe's ear. "The man called us about the body after sobering up. Discovered it physically 'in his way' as it were. In fact, he . . . ahh had ran over the body with the Volkswagen Jetta now parked below the bridge. 'An accident,' he called it, believing he had killed the woman. At the same time, an early morning American tourist, using a zoom lens, also spied the bridgeman with the body and reported a murder in progress."

Oddly, the body lay close but not quite in the River Thames. It appeared to glisten as if washed, yet leaves, grass, and dirt adhered to it due to some sticky substance that it— *she*—had been bathed in. "Smells awful, doesn't she?" commented Sharpe's younger partner. "Like a salad that's set too long." He covered his nose with a handkerchief.

As if unsure which element to choose, water or land, the killer had dumped her below the bridge. On a day when the wind proved right, a passerby might be treated to the sound of Bow Bells—the bells of Bow Church on Bow Street in the city of London. Since the location of the body itself proved of interest—so near the tourist circuit, within walking distance of Westminster—no doubt, the press would play it up; but the place also represented Sharpe's home. He'd been born within the sound of Bow Bells himself, and as the locals in London said of anyone actually *born* within this geographical area, "You're then born true Cockney."

Sharpe had worked hard, however, to lose his Cockney accent. He had aspired to a more military and even genteel-sounding professional voice, although he called upon his former speech pattern when occasion warranted.

Now full circle, Inspector Richard Sharpe, Criminal Investigation Division (CID) of the New Scotland Yard, looked over the result of a most horrid crime. He returned from his walkabout to again crouch over the pained face of the dead, squatting and wondering if the victim had also been a true Cockney.

"You think she's from here about?" asked Stuart.

For Sharpe the geography mattered for two reasons. One, he felt a sense of kinship with anyone born in the district. Two, and perhaps more important, it mattered in that if she were local, she'd be easy to identify down the road, perhaps at the first bar or restaurant he came to. However, if she were not from the Bow Bells district, she could prove difficult to name, and the investigation might drag on until he retired and after, perhaps falling into the category of a cold file, a case that relentlessly went on, unsolved forever. And the number of such cases already staggered the imagination.

Sharpe again lifted from his haunches to his full height, rivaling a signpost that warned of no swimming in the Thames. Methodically he stepped away from the body and peered out across the dirty river, taking in what he could amid the fog of Charring Cross Pier where one of the many water buses plied its trade back and forth across the wide, winding way. In the water boat's infrequent wail he heard the victim's voice crying for vengeance and retribution.

Through the fog, Sharpe could make out Westminster Bridge. To his left he could easily find Waterloo Bridge. He was surrounded by beauty on all sides, near Somerset House and King's College on the Victoria Gardens Embankment and the newly erected replica of Shakespeare's Globe Theatre loomed nearby. It seemed an ill-fit, dumping the tortured, murdered victim's remains here amid the flower gardens, which blanketed the Thames on either side. Sharpe wondered if this said something about the killer, about his relationship to his victim, about his last thoughts for her, or if the bastard simply wanted to be splashy.

The killer must know the businesspeople and the early morning tourists would be going by on the river ferries, and that someone would spot the body lying so near the water's edge. Yes, the body appeared to have been purposefully placed here with loving attention and concern. Always a twist in such strange cases, Sharpe thought, that so brutal a killer could be so gentle with the body afterward—after she could feel no pain. "Bastard," he muttered aloud to the soft fog overhead. "Perhaps he meant to place her in the river but his plans were spoiled by our drunken bridgeman."

"You think so, Sharpie?" asked his young partner, but Sharpe ignored the silly question.

When officials had first arrived on scene, everyone expected the usual floater—some poor slob victim of a domestic dispute gone bad, or a whore whose badly beaten body had been thrown into the river and had washed to the embankment. No one could for a moment have suspected the woman to be the victim of crucifixion, least of all Sharpe.

Young Inspector Stuart Copperwaite, Sharpe's assistant, now ruminated over the hideous and grisly wounds they'd found, pleading for some meaning to surface, asking his superior to help him make sense of it all. Copperwaite's pained questions floated out over the nearby river: *"Why? Why kill someone in so gruesome and complicated a fashion? Why bloody crucify her?"*

Sharpe, his stern gaze having returned to the body, matter-of-factly replied, "Cruelty's really little different than any other vice, Stuart."

"Say that again, sir?"

"Cruelty requires no motive outside itself. It merely requires opportunity."

"My God but that's profound. Better put that up over my

desk," Copperwaite said, trying to make light of the heavy moment.

When Sharpe and Copperwaite had first arrived, the London constables stood horrified around the body. Each in turn gaping over the ugly crucifix scars and the wound to the side, like that of a knife or spear. The wounds to hands and feet could only have been caused by three grim and hefty spikes— one to each palm and a third to the crossed feet. The local authorities had eagerly stepped aside for the men of the Criminal Investigation Division. No one truly wanted this case. Sharpe thought it unlikely that there would be any special claims of jurisdictional boundaries or a dispute of any sort over where the deceased's body had fallen, as had been the case in the politically charged murder of a parliamentarian a few weeks before. No such concerns for what appeared to be a woman of simple means.

Inspector Sharpe at fifty-four had seen great cruelty in his thirty-four-year-long career. Police agencies all over England, Scotland, and Wales, who were more than relieved to turn the strangest, most inhumane and bizarre cases over to England's elite detective agency, had no idea the extent of horror the average CID man saw. The sight of a crucified woman certainly qualified.

In the muffled stillness of the fog, somewhere off in the distance, another Thames River ferry blew out its mournful anthem. Both Copperwaite and Sharpe looked across the river for the boat, but the distracting noisemaker remained a phantom. "Likely the only send-off she'll receive, wouldn't you say, Stuart?"

" 'Less we uncover a relative."

"Pray we do. Perhaps with more information about the victim, we might start to uncover the kind of animal that she ran into. The kind of animal who could nail another human being to a cross."

"Where do you suppose it happened? In the forest? Where do you find a cross aside from a church these days?" asked Copperwaite. "Perhaps an old tree grown into the shape of a cross?"

"Telephone pole perhaps . . . long way to come from the nearest forest to Bow Bells."

Charring Cross Pier bustled at daybreak. Again Sharpe thought it an unlikely place for a killer to dump a body, what with the two nearby river bus depots looking on. Unless the killer meant to weigh her down and dispose of the body beneath the surface. Still, why so busy a place as this? Even in the fog, a killer wasn't likely to be so brash, unless he blended in with his surroundings to the point that no one took notice?

Likely having similar thoughts to Sharpe's own, one of the uniformed bobbies had come forward to say, "I wager the body was put in upriver somewhere and floated to this spot."

"Aye, now that makes all the sense in the world. Makes all the sense that the Thames—rough as she is this morning— could lift this body three feet, or four, up the bank and leave not a trace of water in her hair or mouth." Sharpe pulled forth a pipe and began chewing on the stem.

The officer, taking the sting of his superior's remarks, bit back a reply and found himself relieved when Sharpe added, "What say we hold judgment till we've scanned the ground around here. All you men! Have a search. The body does look . . . washed in oils, not in the waters of the Thames."

Everyone joined in the grounds search while Sharpe again stepped away. At odds with young Copperwaite and perhaps his colleague's entire generation, Sharpe thought of the irony of having been born and raised not too far from where they stood. Copperwaite by comparison hailed from Harrogate, a seaport city in Yorkshire summed up by Copperwaite as a place where "They've nothing but bails of quaint."

This time Stuart Copperwaite pursued his superior and walked about the embankment beside him, saying, "The victim could be difficult to identify, having no distinguishing marks and nothing whatever to pinpoint her identity."

"You state the obvious, Stuart. The fact of it weighs heavily," agreed Sharpe, who had seen his share of faceless, nameless victims, their killings going unresolved here in London. He resignedly muttered, "Stuart, get a sketch artist on hand at the morgue to make a likeness of Mum. Make the bloody *Sun*'s morning edition. See what comes of it. Perhaps some-

12   ROBERT W. WALKER

one will recognize her. Have a run at Missing Persons, all that."

"Yes, of course . . . Perhaps someone's looking for Mum as we speak." Copperwaite took studious notes and added, "Consider it done, Richard."

Both men felt the cold, nibbling presence of death as it hovered about the body like some primordial creature living just beyond sight, deep in the fog, a creature in search of more souls to take.

"She really isn't your usual age for a streetwalker," Copperwaite said, breaking the stillness between them.

"Three or four I've known have lived to the ripe old age of fifty, even sixty, Stuart, so we won't completely discount the possibility. It's *possible* she was plying the trade, being smeared all over with oil, being nude as she is. . . . Hard to say really. We won't know anything for certain until someone steps forward with some information about her."

"As for now?"

Sharpe returned to the body. He again removed the sheet to stare at the naked body, drained of all color save her purple, puckering wounds. The dead woman's feet remained stiff and overlying one another where they'd been nailed together, rigor mortis having set in, telling Sharpe that she had not been lying here long before her discovery, since rigor released its grip after four or five hours. Yes, indeed, something evil this way had come.

The trinity of nail wounds told the story of how some madman had pinned her to his idea of a cross at some other, remote location—possibly a forest somewhere as Stuart surmised. Now the gashes resembled three dead eyes. The viscosity of the flesh having been thoroughly compromised, the holes puckered in on themselves like oversized, gaping, purple gunshot wounds.

"Doesn't require Karl Schuller or any autopsiest to tell us—nor any man here—that this woman's death began with the slow, agonizing torture of having her hands and feet nailed to somebody's idea of a resurrection cross. Likely some religious fanatic," Sharpe guessed aloud but did not speculate further.

"Is that what you make of it, Sharpie?" asked Copperwaite, a look of intense pain fluttering on and off his countenance where he stood in the glow of a streetlamp. Nearby on the recently completed London to Essex motorway, automobiles whined and zipped and occasionally called out with their horns like mewing, mildly annoyed cattle.

Sharpe said no more, keeping silent counsel for as long as he might possibly do so.

Copperwaite, an exasperated breath of air flowing from him, bit back an urge to again verbally prod his senior partner for words. He felt a powerful need to hear something—anything—from the worldly, former army colonel.

Finally, Sharpe turned and shouted at them all, his voice sounding like a drill sergeant who'd missed a meal. "Anyone locate a scintilla of information, evidence, identifying item about the ground? Anyone? Anything?"

" 'Fraid not, Inspector," replied one of the Charring Cross district bobbies.

"Aye and not aught of ye've seen the like of her before today?" Sharpe blurted out in his native Cockney, raising the eyebrows of several of the uniformed men milling about.

"Sorry, sir . . . She's a stone cold mystery, this one. Not from the district so far as we know," came the answer.

"Perhaps new to the area then? Have a check with housing authority and what-do-you-call-them? Housewarming people. D'ya know any Warm Welcoming groups in the area?"

Sharpe then snorted into a handkerchief, bent down over the prone dead and once more examined her features with the care of a man preparing to paint in oil. With a gentle, gloved hand, he turned her cheek from side to side, studying the hard-etched, weary, worn features, his pipe still dangling, unlit.

Sharpe finally asked, "What do you really make of her, Coppers?"

Copperwaite pushed closer, kneeling in over the other side of the body, pleased that his senior had used his nickname. He and Sharpe now formed a kind of human arboretum about the deceased, their eyes intent on the dark results of the morning's find. "She's likely in the wrong place at the wrong time. . . . Like, as I assumed, out here hooking, I suppose, when this madman with spikes and a cross grabbed her up?"

"Then you suppose too much, but tell me why."

"I don't know. . . ."

"Exactly. You do not know, so you rush in with words to fill empty space, Coppers. CID men can't work that way. Now tell me why you suspect her to be a common whore? Certainly not the way she dresses? Come on, man! Why do you make her out a whore?"

"I can't rightly say. . . ."

"Yes, you bloody well can. Go on." Sharpe's frustration gave way to a flood of anger. "It's because of the district we're in, and perhaps the killer knew full well we'd take her for a whore, dumping her here."

Copperwaite, some ten years Sharpe's junior, looked more closely at the body and announced, "Look at her veins. Recently popped. They're not exactly shot, but she's done drugs. Not the most beautiful creature I've ever seen," he added with a grim shrug. "Most all of your street tramps're real hags, wouldn't you agree?"

"Virtual witches, but this woman, she's hardly a hag, Coppers. Somethin' *overweight*, surely, but hardly more than what, in Bow Bells, you'd call wholesome and—"

Copperwaite laughed at the use of Bow Bells' "wholesome"—another word for a fat woman.

Sharpe thundered on, adding, "And as for her features, she might be the picture of a British maiden in her youth: comely, rather proper and staid, if you're asking me. Like we earlier agreed, someone's mum or a bloody librarian, perhaps, but I see no whore before me. And one thing I've learned to trust on this job is my first impressions, my first instinct."

"Aye, I suppose you might say so, something pleasant about her demeanor. Maybe she's more Irish than English. . . ."

"Now you be looking for a fight! How would you be tellin' that?" Sharpe put on an Irish accent.

"I'm just supposing."

"Suppose? Suppose her age for me then."

"I'd say somewhere 'bout in her early to mid-fifties."

"Agreed. And that fact is—while not average for your typ-

ical girl working the Bow Bells as a hooker—making her easy
prey for the bloody bastard who's done her up this way, or
so you're supposing?"

"Exactly."

"Christ, man, you'll never make full inspector if you think
like . . . like one of those bobbies over there," Sharpe muttered
under his breath. "You're a Scotland Yard lieutenant now,
Coppers. No ordinary bobby." Sharpe gave a quick glance to
the men and women in uniform, and the few detectives that'd
come on scene from nearby district boroughs.

Copperwaite gritted his teeth, his young eyes flashing over
the body once again. "She's no prostitute in your estimation,
Colonel Sharpe?"

"I'll not be mocked with my own hard-won military rank,
Copperwaite," returned Sharpe, edgy now.

"I meant no disrespect, Richard."

"Look here . . . The moment we place her"—he stopped for
emphasis, pointing to the corpse—"in that ill line of business.
Indeed, the moment we place her in *any* category of people,
without evidence, we are merely labeling her—"

"But Richard—"

"—and thinking less of her as a human being with a right
to life like any other. We start in on the typical and useless
procedures that ultimately lead to yet another unsolved case,
of which I've had my bloody fill."

"Still, we only have what our eyes tell us, and we've got
to go by what our eyes tell us," Copperwaite weakly countered.

Sharpe managed not to laugh, suppressing all but the smile.
"The eye alone will be your downfall, Stuart. All right, suppose the needle marks you've perceived are there because the
woman was, in life, diabetic?"

"I see, of course. . . . Then we locate her doctor."

"We can't assume a bloody thing. If we do, we're lost from
the start. We can know or not know, but we cannot *assume*
and work from assumptions."

"Well, I should think we can assume she died of being
nailed to a cross."

"Perhaps . . . but it will take an autopsy to be certain even of that, and I suspect there's far more to this singular death than meets the eye, Stuart." Sharpe fell silent once more while Copperwaite tightened his own jaw, his body stiffening.

Sharpe, having seen enough of the victim's vacant, pained eyes, gently closed the lids, and then he looked into his partner's fervid eyes where a deep and youthful fire burned. "Suppose the killer is *himself* a priest?"

"Shall we begin our inquiries with priests then?"

"No, of course not."

"But why not if—"

"It's *assuming* too bloody much, Stuart."

"But now you . . . just now yourself, you just now said—" the younger man sputtered.

"To bait you, ol' boy, to bait you, and you took it like a mouse on the scent. Shame on you." Sharpe laughed loudly, sending his voice sluicing through the fog and upsetting the silent crowd of local officials who saw no humor whatsoever in this most grotesque, fantastic, eccentric, and bizarre of killings.

"Let's turn the body," suggested Copperwaite.

"Why? What for?"

"But we always turn the body, Richard, always. It's part of the protocol."

"But it's already been turned by men who found her earlier, some of these men standing about."

"How can you know that? Now *you're* assuming, Sharpie!"

"Look at the grass beside her, Stuart. Use your eyes, man, and again, quit assuming that all things are as they appear. They seldom are.

"We know the bridgeman ran her over, yet we see no tire marks. The marks are on her backside then. The first bobbies on scene turned her over to have a look at her front side, her features, but no one wants to own up to that, Stuart."

Copperwaite looked at the men standing nearby, nodding appreciatively to his wise mentor. Sharpe stared up at the recently completed bridge spanning the Thames.

Copperwaite pointed to the bridge and said, "The motorist who called it in was looking through a camera lens, a zoom camera, when he saw the bridgeman trying to right things after hitting the body. I'm told."

"Saw it from up there, while crossing over the bridge. Actually, only after he stopped illegally to snap a photograph," Richard calmly agreed. "He and his family were gaining an early start out toward Sussex, to see a bit o' the countryside, I understand. Anyway, after taking the name, they sent 'em all on their way. Or so I was told, Stuart."

Sharpe now stared down the high-fashioned, fieldstone wall, which held the Thames in check. For a moment, his eyes fell on nearby Jubilee Gardens and Queen Elizabeth Hall. For some years now, the city had been attempting to run out the vagrants from this area of the embankment. Officialdom threw money at it, hoping to improve it as a tourist walkway, but efforts had gone wanting. Wise city officials had actually thought that it might help if they planted new, exotic trees. Rather, it had added lush locations for the homeless to curl up by night and from which to fend for shillings by day.

Sharpe stood and stepped away, shouting, his order sounding more harsh than he'd wanted. "You men standing about with nothing to do, scour the area for homeless who might have seen something."

The body had been deposited in a busy area. Someone had taken a dreadful chance at discovery. Had the killer hoped for discovery? Perhaps unconsciously so?

From here it was some distance to the motorway from which the body presumably had been spotted by the American motorist. The roadway overhead, which the killer must turn off from to get down here, led north and south. By now, the killer might be anywhere in the enormous maw of the city or the London suburbs.

Sharpe stepped back from the embankment and returned to where Copperwaite remained kneeling beside the body. Seeing Sharpe, Copperwaite muttered, "Bloody awful hell, this. Can you imagine the depth of suffering this woman endured? Jesus . . ."

Both men pictured the torturous image in their minds once again.

"Yes, well, that's one item you can assume, Stuart," said Sharpe.

Stuart replied, a hint of confusion in his voice, "What one item can I assume, Sharpie?"

"That the killer knew she'd die like Christ if he did her up this way. . . ."

"Why the oil? It's still sticky to the touch."

"I haven't a clue, but I know the bastard knew she'd die an agonizing death."

Sharpe again kneeled beside his junior partner and pointed to the water's edge, saying, "Wonder why the body wasn't thrown in for 'cleansing of the wounds' before the killer disappeared. Perhaps caught in the act of *preparing* to dispose of the body in the river."

"The bridgeman unknowingly startled him, run him off prematurely."

"It would appear so, Stuart. But they tell us the bridgeman saw no one?"

The chief bobby, overhearing this, stepped closer to be discreet. "The man had been at his bottle early, sir. Saw no one, sir, not even the dead woman until he . . . Well, sir, he run the dead woman over."

"Yes, ran over the body, so we've heard."

"His first thought was it was *him* what killed her, sir."

"Of course. In his drunken state, he would."

"She was facedown when he hit her with the car, sir. We . . . some of us took liberty to turn her faceup," the man confessed, fearful not to do so.

Copperwaite found his voice. "Shall we roll her and have a look, Richard?"

They rolled the body to the sound of Richard Sharpe's curses. "Gore . . . Gore blime!" Sharpe muttered the Cockney vulgarism for *God blind me*, while staring at the unmistakable blistering of tire treads from a lightweight vehicle running the length of Mum's back and buttocks. "Yes, of course," began Sharpe, "add to the indignity of having been tormented to death and having to lie out here in the elements, the rummy bridgeman must find a way to thump over her body in the dark with his Jetta!"

Copperwaite gnashed his teeth over the gruesome image. Sharpe in turn released some of the pent up emotion he felt in a small explosion of exhaled air. "We'll have to examine the car," he told Copperwaite.

Copperwaite, pointing, replied, "Parked over there, at the base of the bridge."

Sharpe had seen the vehicle below a stone ladder that wound its way to the man's stone turret high overhead, from which perch he currently looked down on the scene, no doubt trembling still.

While staring at the damage done, two clear tire tread marks well tattooed onto the woman's back and backside for her to take to eternity along with the wounds inflicted by the killer, Sharpe groused, "Likely the only useful forensic evidence and it's from the wrong source."

Copperwaite and the others watched as Sharpe found a matchbox and finally lit his pipe tobacco.

"Can we assume that, Colonel Sharpe?" asked Copperwaite, using Sharpe's military salutation for the men all round to hear.

"Will you stop calling me 'Colonel.' Makes me out to be an old fart in front of the chaps."

"Sure, Sharpie, sorry."

"Not so sorry as that bridgeman when I get my hooks into him." Sharpe stormed off to climb the spiraling ladder that would take him to the only so-called eyewitness left to deal with. He snatched his now-lit pipe from his mouth and shouted from the third rung of the ladder, "Stuart, see what you can do to locate that bloody American tourist. We must question him." He silently cursed the bobbie beside Stuart for having allowed the tourist to continue on his merry way. Then he concentrated on what remained of the ladder, grateful that he had worked out at the gym the day before.

FBI Headquarters, Quantico, Virginia
Two days later

Dr. Jessica Coran, FBI forensic pathologist for the Behavioral Science Unit at Quantico, Virginia, paced her office, staring at the crime-scene photos of a particularly gruesome murder in which a man had been literally torn to death by rabid dogs. Police in New Jersey believed that the man was a murder victim, that the dogs had been the weapon. She and her team awaited shipment of the body, a man with full-body tattoos but not a trace of identification, having been stripped of wallet and clothing after the attack. The victim *had no pockets*, as the street cops would say.

Jessica, her hazel eyes dancing with the soft office light, had loosened her auburn hair to let it flow. She now studied the photos of the dead man, holding them up to the light when her phone beeped. Her secretary's voice followed. "Dr. Coran, I have a call that you really must—"

"I left word I wasn't to be disturbed, Gloria!" Jessica firmly replied. "I need a couple of hours."

"But . . . but this is a call from New Scotland Yard, an Inspector Sharpe, something to do with a . . . a crucifixion murder over there?"

"A crucifixion murder?" Jessica flashed on a newspaper account of a body discovered in some park in England, a woman whose body had shown the unmistakable signs of having been literally crucified. She realized the call must have something to do with that. "All right, put it through," she relented.

Inspector Richard Sharpe introduced himself, asking if she might inform him what she knew of murder by crucifixion. "We're still waiting on a final autopsy protocol on the murder, and as yet the victim has not been identified, you see."

Jessica loved the accented words, and his voice. "I see, and how might . . . What do you wish from me?"

"I am seeking your expertise and any information you can share on death by crucifixion."

"Ahhh, I see, now it's come to this, *Dial-an-Autopsy*."

"I've read that you are an extraordinary medical examiner. I'm fishing, as you Yanks would say. At this point all we know is that the woman died of her wounds, sustained from what appears a ritualistic killing."

"Then you are already wrong."

"Pardon? But that much is obvious," railed Sharpe.

Jessica Coran countered, saying, "If she hung from a cross for any length of time, and from the sound of her wounds— I've heard talk over the Internet about the case and the gaps where gravity did its work around the spikes—then I must assume she died of asphyxiation, not her crucifixion wounds."

Sharpe, taken so much aback that he now fumbled for words, finally replied, "Asphyxia? How do you bloody get that from her wounds?"

"Any postmortem man worth his salt will tell you that crucifixion means great stress placed on the breathing apparatus."

"Breathing apparatus?"

Jessica allowed a short, annoyed breath to escape into the receiver. "It has to do with the weight placed against the lungs until the victim can no longer support the effort it takes to breathe."

"Is that so? I never knew it."

"It has to do with the arms having been extended over the head for so long a period, and gravity's downward pull on the body, until the chest literally crushes in on its own vital organs."

"My God, then it's worse still than we've believed."

"You know how the infamous Elephant Man died when they found him in bed, unable any longer to support the weight of his own enormous head? He could not lift the weight from his chest as he slept, so he died of asphyxiation."

"Yes, of course every schoolchild in London knows the story."

"Then imagine crucifixion as infinitely worse and infinitely slower in killing the victim."

"And the killer . . . Whoever did this to her? You suppose he knows precisely . . . how she . . . that is, what killed her . . . How much distress she must have experienced?"

"I should think he knows all there is to know about crucifixion. Why else choose such an unusual and torturous method of disposing of your Jane Doe?"

"Out of some sense of outrage, perhaps? Perhaps she cheated on him with . . . a priest?"

"Yes, well there is that possibility. There are all manner of possibilities."

"Would you, Dr. Coran, be interested in consulting on the case?"

"Absolutely. Anything I can do, don't hesitate. I'll give you my E-mail address. Obviously you have my phone number."

"That would be superb, and look for me to contact you again soon. Thank you, Dr. Coran, for the information. I've already gleaned more from you than our own death investigator here."

"Karl Schuller," she said.

"You know Dr. Schuller?"

"Only by reputation."

"Aye, he has that."

Jessica sensed a touch of sarcasm in the inspector's final remarks. She hung up, giving thought to New Scotland Yard's strange case of the crucified woman. However, she had a lab full of problems and issues this side of the Atlantic to deal with, and she promptly returned to them.

London underground
Same day

Through the crucifixion and the resurrection, he and the collective would come to find Christ on His return in the year 2001 during the true millennium, which hovered over all of life, time, and space now. Poised now, the coming end of life on Earth as mankind had come to know it, accept it, and to generally assume it.

The crucifixion lived vividly in their collective mind. They were all of one mind now and forever. This pleased the mind they shared, and it pleased him, their leader.

They found—and rightly so—that even with failed resurrections, after each new crucifixion, they had grown in strength, resolve, and a sense of power and well-being, and so the collective marched onward as if to war in the battle as Christ's good and stalwart soldiers, shoulder to shoulder, hand to hand, will to will.

"In the name of the Father," they chanted their mantra, "and in the name of the Son, and the Holy Ghost."

They longed to complete what they'd begun, realizing that

all must step cautiously; but when the time came, all would be revealed to everyone, indeed to the world.

After all, the true millennium cometh . . . The year 2001 loomed before all of mankind, and with it the Second Coming as prophesied by the Bible itself and by God Himself. Soon they would be among *Them*—Father, Son, and Holy Ghost. For He and His Son would return to smite the insidious evil of the species.

The collective meant to be part of the glorious Second Coming. They had been told—a whisper from God and His legion of saints—to do His bidding. They need only to find the Chosen One, see to His crucifixion, and watch for the dead to rise. Again the Kingdom of Heaven would be proved to be the mightiest of all powers in the universe, and thus the blood of the world would fuse into a single, great ocean from which new life would come—reborn, rejuvenated, revitalized, all sin at ground zero.

It meant the Rapture and the end of the world as mankind knew it. But first they must find Him, the Son of God, in whatever guise He chose.

Of one thing the collective mind was certain, that however He came—whether it be in the form of a woman, a man, or a child—He would make Himself known to the Chosen few who worshipped Him as none other on Earth had ever worshipped Him before. He would show Himself by once again ascending the cross and rising again in a glorious new resurrection.

God had told their leader so, and their leader exuded purity, piety, honesty, accuracy, correctness, and absolute power—so much so that he could not be questioned in his motives. Nor could he ever be denied, nor ever be accused of wrongdoing or unjust or unholy thoughts.

His thoughts, channeled as they were from God the Father, could not be denied. His thoughts were pure, his motive was to combat evil as he found it, where he found it.

This life stood for something. This man lived the exemplary life of pure goodness.

The fact that the first choice for crucifixion hadn't resulted in resurrection did not deter either him or his followers. They together stood in the shadow of God, and God made it clear that, while they could not fully comprehend or fathom His plan, a plan for Katherine O'Donahue and a plan for them all did indeed exist. He promised that Katherine's sacrifice must lead to more such sacrifices until the purest of heart stepped forward to accept the cross as reward and redemption for all mankind.

Their leader reminded them that what they'd done to Katherine O'Donahue was preordained, that despite the fact that her resurrection hadn't come about, they had succeeded in following the wishes and whispers of the Supreme Being. Katherine remained part of a larger plan. They were told they mustn't for a moment think that they worked for God out of primordial fear but rather from a timeless, ageless, and untainted faith.

· TWO ·

Cave ab homine unius libri—Beware the man of one book.

—ISAAC D'ISRAELI,
CURIOSITIES OF LITERATURE

**FBI Crime Lab, Quantico, Virginia
September 21, 2000**

When Dr. Jessica Coran first heard of the body in the Chesterfield, New Jersey, junkyard she'd had no idea that it would hold so much fascination for her and her team. Nor did she anticipate the red tape and confusion in shipping the body that would delay its arrival for ten days. But here it lay now on her cutting slab, the most intriguing and colorful body she had ever cut into. Even after the rents and tears, even in death, and even after freezing—the body had been shipped in a refrigerated truck along with an array of needed supplies and chemicals—even after all this, she found the complete, head-to-toe tattoo artwork covering the murder victim mesmerizing.

Indeed, this utter fascination with the intricate detail and artistic lines depicting a myriad of symbols, animals, plants, and teeming insect life, as well as bizarre, alien life-forms, all went toward Jessica's dilemma. She hated destroying the artwork that was this "body electric" any further than it had already been obliterated by some hundred-plus gaping wounds, *dog bites*. The vicious dogs, long since destroyed by local New Jersey police, had torn away whole patches of the masterwork. One of the man's arms had been completely chewed off, the limb having been packed in the ice-coffin that John Doe traveled in.

Initially the dice-up work had been fast and easy because the body remained bricklike, and a frozen cadaver made for easier sectioning for microscopic analysis, be it the brain or any other major organ.

Jessica and John Thorpe—J. T. to his friends—both found it difficult to hold back, to allow their two young assistants, Kenneth Holbrook and Yon Chen to do the precision work with the new laser technology that allowed for efficient sections to be cut from the major organs. Both Holbrook and Chen eagerly passed the laser—connected to the latest computer-imaging software available—between them. Each assistant took separate organ cuts with mouths agape, both learning as the laser dissected John Doe's internal organs.

They soon finished the laser work, and J. T. instantly quizzed the neophytes, asking, "All right, now that you have sections of every major organ, Holbrook, Chen, what's next?" J. T. held the laser in his hand now, gently returning the wand back to its cradle attachment on the computer monitor.

Almost in tandem, like cartoon characters, Holbrook stammered an "I think . . . I think . . ." while Chen immediately said, "Blood and seminal fluid workup, I think."

"Excellent, but none of that *I think* stuff. Every time anyone says those two words, it means they don't really know what they think. It's both a qualifying of your answer and a stalling tactic. It also makes you sound stupid. 'I think,' 'in my opinion,' 'it is my feeling.' Forget it. Simply state your facts without all the introductory stammering. Right, Holbrook?" replied J. T.

"I think so."

"Damnit," muttered J. T. as Jessica helplessly laughed behind her mask.

J. T. frowned, recalling how he'd earlier had the same discussion with Jessica because he'd seen and heard the president of the United States sounding silly by prefacing every damned remark at a news conference on NATO with *I think*.

Jessica, for the benefit of the tape recording, loudly ordered a complete fluid workup, from semen to sweat, along with blood toxicology, all dissection and section work on the rack of organs called the viscera having been completed. Holbrook had logged in weight and appearance of each viscus as it had been surgically removed. Now with every laser cut, each slice coming off like a thin, large portion of salami, Chen bagged and labeled John Doe's specimens, using the number given her by the computer: case # 348-119-2000.

As they worked and time ticked by, day turning to night, Jessica and J. T. discussed the recent frozen body of a prison inmate who had wanted to give something back to society, and so he had left his body to science—to the science of forensic medicine in particular. Out of this had come phenomenal new computer software, already proving invaluable to physicians everywhere.

The young interns had also heard the news, but they had no idea that the computer-imaging software they'd just used was the result of that unselfish act on the part of one lone prison inmate, a man named Albert Lawrence Kurlandinsky. Kurlandinsky had made headlines initially by one day walking calmly into his place of work—a JCPenney distribution warehouse—with a high-powered rifle. He opened fire on fellow employees and bosses, a spree murderer with sixteen maimed and seven deaths on his head.

"The software was created when Kurlandinsky's body experienced postmortem freezing in a cryogenics chamber. Frozen rock-hard solid in order that every inch of his body—from crown to toe—could be cut into cross sections," explained Jessica. "Then each section was scanned into the computer."

"The entire body?" young, petite Chen chirped, birdlike.

"Like a stack of large, oddly shaped poker chips," supplied J. T.

Flashing on their ill-fated trip to Las Vegas a few years back, Jessica thought it just like J. T. to use a gambling metaphor. She continued saying, "Now that each section of an entire human body is filmed and on computer, scientists and autopsiests, such as we, benefit by seeing, for the first time in history, the human organs in three-dimensional form from top to bottom in successive sections."

"All in 'living' color," J. T. happily added, "so now you can call up any organ, and the computer will give you a full three-dimensional look at it."

Today's John Doe autopsy benefited from the inmate's generosity, and certainly Jessica did, as the new imaging software saved hours in the lab. A simple, straightforward autopsy could be completed in an hour, but one faced untold complications whenever opening a cadaver and rummaging about in the cranium and below the breastplate. With the new technology, she didn't have to cut so many sections; she could use the templates created by the software to see if the victim's organs proved oversized, overweight, distended, ballooned up, too small, shriveled or lacking in proper color, texture, diseased or healthy. If an organ checked out against the software, then there was no need to cut any sections, because the computer wand had just told the computer brain that the measurements figured accurately. But whenever an organ didn't fit the profile as determined by the computer, a cute little Daffy Duck *who-who* laugh sounded an alarm. The alarm notified the people doing the autopsy that sections of a given organ absolutely had to be taken.

In John Doe's case, the Daffy Duck alarm had gone off repeatedly, signaling a hard life, despite his relatively young age.

Jessica had fought long and hard to finally persuade Quantico that the new technology must be had for their labs and teaching theaters here in Virginia, if the FBI wished to stay current with new advances in medical procedures. And she'd been absolutely right. Today alone, six hours of guesswork and searching about the body, rooting around in the "rack"— as the professionals called the organs below the rib cage— had been saved due to the new imaging wonder. And now she tried to imagine how they had ever gotten by without it.

But now a new mystery presented itself—today's cadaver. The strange case of Mr. John Doe—*Horace*, J. T. had taken to calling him because he "looked like a Horace"—whose body had gone unclaimed, whose identity remained a mystery, and whose unruly hair, from ponytail to thickly bearded chin, kept falling out and clogging the drain below the slab. The man's wild hair, black with streaks of gray throughout, gave him the appearance of a modern-day mountain man; his clothing marked him as both a biker and a gang member. But the gang jacket emblem, *The Flesheaters,* didn't exist according to the FBI's extensive records on outlaw biker gangs. They surmised that Horace had begun his own new club, and perhaps some rival had killed him for his trouble. It was all rank speculation.

All the same, someone with extreme patience had set this Tattoo Man up for murder. Someone with access to a rabid animal and time enough to infect five other canines and thus had introduced that unfortunate to six mad dogs. Someone had set those killing dogs in motion. The evidence pointed to a strong hand or two working the strings.

"Think of the sheer amount of planning that had to go into this killing." Jessica clenched her teeth. *"G'damnit."*

"It'd take months to set up, maybe a year," agreed J. T.

Young Holbrook, one of her protégés, stared openmouthed at Jessica, having never heard her swear before. The Chinese intern, Chen, her nose dimpled and curled, offered an agreeing frown.

Jessica half-smiled to lighten the moment as much as possible and said, "The skin-art and hairiness of the victim presents you interns with a good lesson. We're not in the business of prejudging the victim from the evidence of the way he led his life. We don't write a body off just because of the chosen lifestyle, which often dictates the deathstyle, if you follow me." Jessica half-joked, but it remained a serious point. The foul-of-the-earth issue raged as hot debate among medical people in the U.S. and elsewhere. Whom to serve first and foremost, those who live a clean life, or those who live a foul life? Jessica saw that while Holbrook accepted the notion on its face, that Yon Chen appeared to mentally grapple with it. *Good*, Jessica thought.

She decided to go on. "Well, it represents only one of a multiple set of problems surrounding Horace. This stone-cold John Doe represents a mystery. He's died with absolutely no distinguishing or identifying marks or papers on him, no wallet, no cards, very few teeth—the assumption already having been made that his killer took his dental plates to retard identification efforts. Somebody somewhere went to a great deal of trouble to confuse any efforts we make to identify Tattoo Man."

J. T. had returned from the intercom where he'd shouted at maintenance, as he believed the temperature, and thus the odors in the room, was on the rise. He returned just in time to dovetail on Jessica's words for the benefit of the interning students. "No explanations as to who Horace had been in life, save the largest calling card Dr. Coran and I have ever seen on a body—the full-body tattoos that he accumulated over a lifetime of what one might assume—"

"Assume at one's own risk," Jessica cautioned.

"—to be the result of hard and fast living, a lifestyle which may well have contributed to his untimely death."

"The body's age, according to bone structure and what few teeth he has in his head, puts him at between fifty-five and sixty years of age," Jessica estimated. "I'd take the conservative path, guess the lower end of the scale more accurate."

"Whatever his age, he's lived the life of a hard-bitten, crusty old salt," J. T. put in.

Jessica immediately replied, "And the man appears to have had a 'hard-bitten' death as well."

Only young Chen remained silent as the other three laughed aloud. "Hard-bitten?" she asked.

"Later," Holbrook assured her. "I'll explain it to you later."

Still, Jessica hated the typical cop mentality that the deceased had probably brought on himself. In some ways, maybe so, but Jessica knew only a handful of men—serial killers she had hunted down—whom she honestly felt deserved a death as heinous as that which Horace had met, to be mauled to death by animals starved and made rabid by someone Horace knew.

"Horace's murder, and indeed it is murder," Jessica said for the record and the interns, "represents a particularly brutal one."

Jessica's sense of awe at the flamboyant needle etchings

and delightful, multicolored designs covering Horace's form only grew as she worked. She had to keep reminding herself to focus on the autopsy and to stop "reading" the illustrated man lying like an open book before her, but this proved impossible.

One set of images spiraled into a depiction of hell, while another displayed a rose garden that looked as peaceful and virginal as any heaven. Overall, Horace the Tattoo Man preferred dark and sinister themes in his body art, even incestuous scenes of twisted family life and child abuse. She wondered if such scenes meant a *graduation* from skeletons swallowing snakes and women whole, and eyeballs with all manner of terrible instruments plunged through them. Chains and peculiarly designed machines held people in limbo all about Horace's body. Torture all mixed up with sex appeared his main theme.

She wondered if his choice of artwork reflected anything of the man himself, or if the raw artwork with its undisguised themes of hatred toward women and lust for sexual power over them and children amounted to simple affectations taken on to make the man *appear* more sinister than he actually was. Either way, the artwork itself proved, by anyone's standard, superb. The artist was a master at his craft, likely at the apex of his career when he did John Doe's body. What year would that have been?

"We need to get an ink expert down here to make some estimation of how old the tattoos are," she said to J. T., who nodded appreciatively.

"Sure, it would tell us a lot to know when the most recent tattoo was applied."

"Exactly. Maybe after the when, we can begin to hone in on the where and the who."

"The artist, sure."

"Maybe he'll have a record or at least a recollection of the client. Either that or perhaps someone in the *know* about tattoos might recognize the artist's work. Lead us to the artist, and perhaps we're in Horace's neighborhood."

The body, gone rotting and decomposing over a weekend and discovered under a harsh sun, had been discovered in a

New Jersey junkyard by a couple who had come in search of some used auto part.

Having learned of the dead man's much mutilated and torn body, Chesterfield police proceeded to the scene, only to find six hungry and nasty pit bulls in various, eerily posed stances on and around the body—white, foaming slaver dripping from each muzzle. The animals, standing guard about the body, protective of their kill, had prompted the elderly couple to call 911 immediately.

Each of the starved and rabid dogs continued to take additional strips of meat from the carcass from time to time until the arrival of the infamous Pet Patrol police. They came armed with their dart guns. Six of the dogs by this time, lying over the body, were in the throes of paralysis, the rabies overtaking them completely. They were easily put down, one shot after the next, but the seventh—only recently infected and in the first stages of the disease—proved more difficult to target, hiding in the recesses of the yard. The seventh dog belonged to the junkyard owner, who professed no knowledge of the other dogs or Horace.

The junk dealer, it was reported, had been more upset about the loss of his dog than the fact a man had died on his premises.

The police could not identify the dead man. He remained a person the junkyard dealer claimed not to know, or to ever have done business with in the past.

Business had been bad, the junk man told police, so he had shut down for a couple of weeks and had taken a long-needed vacation. He claimed not to know how six additional pit bulls and a dead guy wound up inside his fence without any apparent break-in. Somebody lied somewhere, somehow, to someone. Either that or the killer knew not only how to make rabid dogs but how to pick expensive locks and subdue a junkyard dog on hand.

Regardless, Jessica Coran, having dissected hundreds of corpses, hadn't been so amazed by a body in years. J. T., her male counterpart in the lab and her most trusted friend, pointed out that she really ought to at least attempt to contain her amazement over Horace.

J. T. had jokingly told her, "I fear that the young and impressionable interns might get the wrong idea—that maybe you like seeing unknown victims of brutal attacks by vicious pit bulls come rolling through the door."

"Short of a bear attack or an attack by a wolf pack," Jessica retorted, "I imagine Horace's end to be the worst way to go out of this world, the pain absolutely excruciating."

J. T. nodded, bit on his lower lip, and replied, "I can't imagine a worse way to die."

"Maybe one," she countered. "Did you read that horrible story in the *Post* about the woman's body discovered in a park someplace in London in which the victim had been staked to some sort of cross and actually *crucified*?"

"Oh, yeah . . . how awful. Suffocation, slow and painful. Still, I think the rabid dog attack even worse."

"You really think so?" Jessica had her doubts.

"Oh, absolutely. I mean these dogs were hungry, mad, and vicious."

The dogs, all but the junkyard dog, had been rabid. They'd not only killed John Doe, aka Horace, their mindless attack had filled his body with the rabies virus. The neurological toxin commonly referred to as rabies did not kill Horace, as it had not the time to incubate in his wounds as yet. Given the number of bites and tears to his flesh, and the fact he'd been attacked by not one but six rabid animals who had ripped at one another as well, meant that the level of neurotoxin in his system would begin to work in half the normal three days to three months.

In time, the poison would have reached its full deadly power. His killers, banking on getting away, meant to leave him with a little something extra.

"Someone desperately wanted Horace dead."

Their eyes had met over the autopsy a hundred times, matching the number of punctures to the body. Each realizing that Horace could not have lived long even *had* he somehow miraculously been able to find an escape route from the gang of starved and rabid animals that'd repeatedly bitten and torn away at him. In fact, Horace's corpse remained riddled with the rabies virus, frozen in place. Perhaps his killers believed it a fitting gift to leave him with in the hereafter, a kind of forged chain for his ghost to rattle for eternity.

J. T. said, "Police in Chesterfield, New Jersey, tell us by all indications that Horace had put up a hell of a fight. He broke some doggy legs and bit off a couple of ears during the struggle."

This made Holbrook and Chen gulp in unison.

Jessica continued the assault on the young interns by saying, "They also surmise from cigarette butts, chewing tobacco wrappers, and a woman's cosmetic case dropped at the gate where Horace's final moments of agony ended, that his killers had had a front-row party, applauding the man's death even as he must have begged their mercy."

"Still," cautioned J. T., "all the speculation remains circumstantial with the consistency of candlewick smoke, nothing that can hold a DA's attention. The most interesting element about the case, aside from the full-body tattoos, so far as Jessica and I are concerned, is the total lack of identification save the tattoos. Perhaps our only hope of ever IDing this brutalized man is here in his skin-art." J. T. punctuated by jabbing his ballpoint at Horace.

Jessica felt a great pang of remorse for the unidentified man, telling the others in the room that "Horace, here, suffered a death as no one should, in a trap from which he could not survive even if he had managed to somehow claw his way free of the dog attack. Given the remoteness of the area and the time of death, which the New Jersey coroner placed at between two and three in the A.M., what hope did he have for survival? His blood loss alone was massive."

J. T. fielded the question with a question, replying, "Short of stumbling over a ten-foot-high fence and then stumbling on a medical team, what chance did poor Horace have?"

"He . . . he had no hope whatsoever," replied young Holbrook, who then bit back his lower lip.

"What kind of devious mind could concoct so heinous a murder and so pitiable a death?" Jessica now asked, as much to herself as her two interns. "Six dogs, each one infected, the dogs themselves at the slavering stage of the rabid animal. All timed perfectly. The dogs had to've belonged to someone—or to more than someone; they had to have had a sales history, a past of their own."

"Needle marks screamed out, located after the hair on each dog carcass had been shaved and the skin microscopically examined, revealing the puncture wounds where the rabies had been introduced to the dogs," explained J. T., who lifted a set of photos from a nearby table, adding, "We have photos of the dog autopsies. If we solve this case, believe me, it will be one for the books."

Jessica continued, using her scalpel like an index finger and saying, "Whoever the killer or killers are, they knew about animal venoms, and how to handle them. The doctor in Jersey who examined the executed dogs knew her stuff as well. She was said to have once been a veterinarian before becoming an autopsy specialist. This helped tremendously. Any other well-meaning autopsiest might not have taken as much time and care with the executed animals."

"Meanwhile," added J. T., "local authorities scoured every pet shop and animal shelter and anyone with a license to raise dogs, and anyone with a history of killing or brutalizing animals. For the dogs, too, are victims in this crime."

The two young people stood dumbfounded at such intentional brutality. Jessica feared for both that the first case involving them, even peripherally, could prove their last if their stomachs gave out. Still, Jessica believed in throwing the young who dared enter the field of death investigation into the deep end of the cesspool.

When neither student had anything to add, and it became painfully obvious that this was so, Jessica nearly shouted at her young Asian intern, Yon Chen, "Get a lot of photos, rolls and rolls of photos. And I want close-ups of every tattoo remaining intact."

"You mean? Effery wound, jes?"

"That, too, but I want clear and large shots of the tattoos, understand? And I want them blown up to eight by tens, got it?"

"Got it?" Yon Chen bit back another question, letting it slide.

"No, Yon . . . Don't ask me if I've got it, do you got—have it? Do you know what I want?"

"Jes, got it."

Jessica gnashed her teeth, hoping nothing was lost in the translation, and went on. "Then we're finished here, Yon, except for those photos. See to it they're on my desk by tomorrow morning."

"Yes, Doctor. First thing 'morrow on your desk."

Jessica looked dubiously at the girl whose big, innocent, black marble eyes seemed to mark her as entirely wrong for this profession, yet she'd never had a more enthusiastic intern. Despite her frail refugee appearance, she possessed an enormous capacity to learn. She seemed to feed on knowledge, reminding Jessica of herself at that age.

Jessica asked, "J. T., will you please oversee our two young interns from here alone."

"Sure, sure, Jess. Get out of here for a while."

Jessica stripped off her blood-smeared gloves and lab coat, preparing to exit the room. Glancing at her watch, she saw that 5:40 P.M. had crept up on them. She shouted over her shoulder at J. T. and the others, "Time to get a life, people. Have a nice night. What's left of it. . . ."

· THREE ·

There is no neutral ground in the universe:
Every square inch, every split second is claimed
by God and counterclaimed by Satan.

—C.S. LEWIS

Exhausted, Jessica stepped into her office, only to find her
divisional chief, Eriq Santiva, waiting there with two distinctly unfamiliar, well-dressed gentlemen. The men with their
rumpled London Fog coats, equally rumpled three-piece suits,
and inexpensive ties hanging limp about their necks, looked
the part of a pair of weary travelers—*two wise men from afar,*
she flashed—*who have come not bearing gifts but bad news.*

Santiva forced a smile while still fondling the female skull
which Jessica used as one half of a pair of bookends—the
other a male skull—from her bookshelf. He stood just behind
her desk with the visitors, one sitting and the taller, more
good-looking one, staring out the window. It appeared Santiva
had timed her arrival fairly closely to meet with the visitors.
Obviously, Gloria had kept him informed of her movements.
She'd called down to the autopsy room for Jessica's estimated
time of arrival, and Jessica had told Gloria to go home for
the night.

"Dr. Coran!" Eriq began, bouncing the skull in his hands
as if it were a Nerf ball. "I want you to meet our guests from
New Scotland Yard. They are here on an unusual mission."

Jessica immediately reclaimed her skull and space. Eriq
Santiva, inching from behind the desk now, gave ground to
Jessica. "Afternoon, gentlemen," she said, replacing the skull

against the books Santiva had disturbed. She noticed that DiMaio's *Forensic Science* and Helpern's *Autopsy* had their spines upside down. "I'm afraid you have me at a disadvantage," she continued while straightening the books, making a show of it for Eriq's sake.

"Please, forgive me. This is Inspector Richard Sharpe, CID, New Scotland Yard and—"

The tall one at the window eagerly stepped to her desk, reached across it, took her hand, and firmly shook it. His eyes were alight with energy but something darting and mysterious hid there as well. Something dangerous unless left alone. She loved the salt-and-pepper look of his thick, short, and unruly hair. "I believe we've met, or rather had words, a couple of weeks ago. . . . When I rang you up," he crisply said to her. "Richard Sharpe."

"It's an honor."

"No, I am honored to meet you, Dr. Coran. I've read a great deal about your successes in forensic investigation. I know we can learn much from you—at the Yard, that is."

"And this is Lieutenant Inspector Stuart Copperwaite," Eriq completed the introductions. "Also of New Scotland Yard." Eriq had managed to master his Cuban accent to the point that no one could tell where he was from. The only remaining giveaway was his dark features.

The one with the charming name, Copperwaite, had an equally firm handshake, Jessica thought.

"So, you're visiting from England?" she asked, returning Copperwaite's smile, turning her eyes again to Sharpe.

"Yes," Copperwaite readily replied, eyes beaming, "come to learn what we might from your famous profiling division."

"Looking for help?" she asked. "Then you've come to the right place. Our experts are the best," Jessica assured, dropping into her desk chair thinking, *My feet are killing me*, not realizing until now that the Britons, unlike Santiva, had remained standing until she sat. *How awfully British of them*, she thought with a touch of disdain, but finding that she actually liked the affectation.

Santiva asked, "How goes it with Horace, our Tattoo Man?"

"Tattoo Man's become quite the celeb corpse since arriving at Quantico. Everyone wants a look at him. I peeled a section of his skin for ink and tattoo experts to have a look at." She now fingered some of the books on her shelf, still reclaiming her invaded space. "You wouldn't believe the lineup outside the autopsy room to get a look at this guy's skin."

Santiva laughed heartily in response. "Speaking of horror, gentlemen, Dr. Coran is currently involved in a most interesting and weird case of murder, and a particularly brutal one at that."

Jessica picked it up from there, adding, "The man died of rabid dog bites to sixty percent of his body, and he was conscious the whole time. I see no blunt trauma, inconsequential organ disease, and I rather doubt that toxicology will report anything but inconsequential blood alcohol and barbiturate levels."

Santiva grimaced. "So the man was both alive and lucid when the animals attacked him."

"Unfortunately, yes. Prelim autopsy report will indicate that he died of the attack, the shock setting in before the rabies could take him out. But believe me, it was one slow, agonizing death."

"So then, it's true that someone actually set him up to die in this gruesome fashion?" asked Eriq, shaking his head over the image.

"No longer just possible, highly probable," she replied, pushing back in her chair, working out the autopsy kinks. "Someone loaded those dogs with the disease and used them as lethal weapons, turning them into voracious, mad wolves. After having been bitten ninety to one hundred times, escaping over that junkyard fence, Mr. Tattoo Man would've been paralyzed with pain. There was no way out, no escape."

"I've had any number of peculiar cases over the years myself," put in Sharpe, who now sat alongside Copperwaite, "but such a death . . . horrible."

Copperwaite tried on a smile for Jessica, adding, "We can match your American horror stories horror for horror over the centuries. We've been at it a great deal longer."

"Is that so?" She looked at Sharpe for an answer. While

Sharpe's penetrating gaze engaged her, the other man fiddled with a notepad and pen as if trying to learn their use for the first time. He flipped through the pad, obviously searching for some questions he'd meant to pose. *Stuart Copperwaite, Inspector Sharpe's right hand, as you Yanks would say,* she thought she heard him thinking.

"So, you gentlemen of the Yard have come calling on the colonies for help," she quipped.

"Stuart and I have come a distance on this crucifixion case, you see. Awful business."

"Indeed, you've come a great distance."

"To ask for your assistance, Dr. Coran."

"But you have it already."

Sharpe, obviously a man of few words, tossed a manila file folder he'd been holding close to his chest since she'd walked in the room. The file came cascading across her already cluttered desk, crime-scene photos spilling from it, crime-scene shots of crucifixion victims—three in all.

"Three bodies? There've been *three* now?" she asked, her quick perusal of the photos confirming the answer.

"Two men and a woman," said Sharpe.

"And you're certain it's the same killer at work in all three deaths?"

"Same MO."

"Precisely," added Copperwaite, "detail for detail."

Jessica's whiskey voice took on a tone of doom. "Then it's a serial killer you're after, one who crucifies his victims. I knew about the woman found in the park, but I thought it a freak thing, a onetime incident, not likely to be repeated."

Copperwaite lamented, "So hoped everyone."

"Would you have a concerted look?" asked Sharpe, his finger jabbing at the file folder filled with pictures of the victims.

"Yes, let's have a look," she replied, bracing herself for the crime-scene and autopsy photos, for even though she'd studied thousands, such images still caused her stomach to grip and her throat to go dry.

The crucifixion-death autopsy photos proved no exception, each more ghastly than the one before it. Obviously, no crosses in the photos, no shots of the primary crime scene, only the remains of the victims, which had been left at various dump sites.

Sharpe now added another file for Jessica to look over, this one displaying full-body shots and facial features of each victim, the Christ-wounds, including the side wounds clearly visible in these shots which detailed the wounds to each extremity as well. Jessica now put aside the horrid photos of the crucified victims, saying, "Your killer seems to prefer a more mature victim, I'd say."

"Yes, average age comes in around fifty," agreed Sharpe.

"And he's not particular as to the victim's sex." Jessica stood and paced to the window. "During my career, gentlemen," she began. Her eyes fixed on a troop of young and energetic FBI cadets doing evening calisthenics out on the lawn to the barking ,rhythm of a drill instructor. "I've seen asphyxia death in all its myriad forms, from asphyxiation by water to choking by hand to autoerotica and old-fashioned self-inflicted hangings, but this . . . This is absolutely unusual and rare: murder by crucifixion."

"Exactly how rare is it, Jess?" asked Santiva.

She pointed to the books he'd been thumbing through. "I'm willing to bet my pension you found nothing in your research, Eriq."

Jessica looked out across her office. It had recently been enlarged as a kind of thank-you from Quantico's powers that be, a rare FBI reward—an office rivaling the size of Santiva's own. Hers looked out across several partitioned laboratories where practitioners of the forensic arts worked like so many alchemists each day and night.

Jessica leaned forward in her chair, one hand on her pulsating temple. With the other she lifted another book from the shelf, doing her own quick reference, then held it up and said, "Nothing . . . not a word on death by crucifixion. It just isn't in the modern literature of death investigation. It's rare, quite rare in the long history of murder and homicide annals, yes." She continued, waving an arm. "Extremely rare business, especially since the Dark Ages. So few cases in fact, most books on forensics and pathology say not a word about it, as you found in rummaging around through my books, no doubt."

"Rare indeed," replied Sharpe, "but it would appear, Dr. Coran, that someone the other side of the Atlantic is in dire straits to change all that, perhaps make it a bit less than rare?" The man's commanding voice, filled with bell-like resonance, along with his British accent, fell soft and pleasant on her ears.

"Tell me, Dr. Coran," continued Sharpe, "what have you learned about crucifixion death since we last spoke on the phone?"

"Interesting thing about crucifixion, gentlemen . . ."

"Yes?" asked Sharpe.

"The weight of the body on the outstretched arms interferes with exhaling, due to the intercostal muscles which—well, suffice it to say that in a hanging state such as crucifixion breathing would become impossible. The normal rhythm of inhaling and exhaling would painfully and slowly cease due to the exertion of pressure on the lungs and the inability to lift the rib cage."

"Rib cage?" asked Copperwaite, fingering his own ribs.

"In normal breathing, we lift our rib cage to bring in air. A man on a cross, arms overhead, he can't do this. Exhalation is impaired as well, given that it's passive and due to gravity pulling at the body."

"Meaning the death occurs because you're unable to exhale properly?" asked Sharpe.

"Inhale, unable to inhale, so as to make the counterpoint of exhalation work. It's a tandem operation. Can't inhale, can't exhale, simple as that."

"Now I have it."

Jessica leaned forward in her seat, contemplating for a moment before going on, thumping the pen extended before her. "Any labored exhalation at all would become diaphragmatic, useless you see . . ."

No, they didn't see. She saw that in their eyes, not unlike the vacant black stare so often given to her by young Yon Chen.

She stepped to a chart of the human muscles and pointed,

pinpointing the exact location within the intercostal muscles of the chest to which she'd referred. She added, "Over a prolonged time, this undue pressure, pressure the muscles were never designed to withstand . . . Well, this would lead to impaired respiration and finally asphyxia."

"I would've thought the pain, shock, and trauma"—Santiva's Cuban features winced with the words as he spoke—"from the nails driven through your hands and feet alone would kill a man."

"A good Catholic boy like yourself, Eriq, and you don't remember how long Christ took to expire on that cross?"

"Guess it slipped my mind. Maybe I didn't want to know."

"Some say three hours, some say three days and nights." She turned to face their guests. She felt a bit like a female Sherlock Holmes, knowing the men wanted her to wave some sort of magic wand and instantly tell them their case represented an easy and simple matter to be cleared up in no time at all.

"Have you any leads whatsoever on the first crucifixion killing?"

Copperwaite bit his lip. Sharpe definitively shook his head and said, "We're in a dark closet."

Jessica said, "It sounds like an interesting case. And of course, if there's any assistance I can lend, why, you have it, of course."

Eriq told her, "Scotland Yard is requesting our—rather, your—assistance on this troubling case."

"Then you will take on the case, Dr. Coran?" asked Sharpe directly.

Jessica looked from Sharpe to Santiva who said, "I promised these gentlemen our best, Jessica. And I promised you a trip to London some time back, if you recall. This is your opportunity to work with Scotland Yard on the biggest case since . . . well, since Jack-the-Ripper."

"I suppose you've already sent two burly Secret Service men to my apartment to pack my unmentionables for me," she quipped.

"No, but I gave it some thought. It's an excellent opportunity for the bureau and the Yard to work hand-in-hand, something both agencies need more of, especially since the success you had taking out the Night Crawler with Scotland Yard's help."

Jessica remembered the case only too well.

Copperwaite said, "Everyone's seen reports on how you tracked down that Night Crawler monster in international waters off the Cayman Islands."

Richard Sharpe bit his lip and nodded. A long sigh like a memory escaped him before he added, "And two years ago when you cornered that madman in your famous National Park, how you brought an end to that terror. Disgusting fellow, that one, torching his victims after locating you on the phone to treat you to their screams for mercy."

Jessica looked quizzically across at the two Britons, saying, "I had no idea that British law enforcement paid so much attention to my cases."

"Your cases have been taught at the Yard," Copperwaite stated. "Every copper in London knows about you, and how you defeated Mad Matthew Matisak, and some of them other maniacs you've brought to justice. Some of your cases read like a . . . a Geoffrey Caine horror novel, I daresay."

Eriq now laughed and asked, "So, Jess, how soon can you be packed?"

"Packed for London? Me?" She stared off into empty space. A smile colored her features as she wondered how she might get her long-distance lover in Hawaii, Special Agent James Parry, to meet her in London. They had continued their relationship against all odds far longer now than anyone imagined possible, until their last spat. London might be the answer to rejuvenate their passion.

Sharpe remarked, "It's a serious problem we have on our hands, no doubting that, Dr. Coran. We've put it out on the wires, Interpol, CIA, your FBI, anyone anywhere who might have seen the like of it. . . . Well, as you see, we're anxious for help from any quarter, and if you can see your way clear to helping out the Queen, you see . . ."

"The Queen?" It sounded so quaint, she thought. "You mean I should go to London for God and Country?" she asked.

"And the Crown," added Copperwaite in deadpan.

"One hell of a case," repeated Santiva. "Think of it, Jessica. Serial murder by crucifixion. You know anyone else in our organization ripe for this kind of case?"

"No . . . no, I don't." She nodded and said, "I'll do it, and I hope your trust in me, gentlemen, is not misplaced."

"Not at all likely," countered Sharpe, whose grin brightened his dour countenance and the room, making him look like the quintessential father figure. Something most pleasing in his manner, something she found appealing, attractive.

Together they took Santiva's private car to the airport, and along the way, Santiva kept assuring Jessica from his front passenger seat that J. T. could handle the Tattoo Man case. The Britons, as if abducting her, crushed her between them in the backseat. They'd stopped at her apartment only long enough for her to throw a single bag together. She'd forgotten her umbrella.

"Three deaths so far, and silence for a time?" she asked Sharpe.

"Yes, that's the state of it," replied Sharpe.

"Perhaps the number three is significant to the killer?" She raised a hand to her head, running fingers through her hair, biting the inside of her cheek in thought. "So, you've come for a forensic profiler."

"That and all the advice and information your Behavioral Science Unit can provide," Sharpe replied. Sharpe had thick, graying hair, once a deep, reddish black. He appeared a man who kept a strict regimen, his tall frame and hard body rivaled Sean Connery, Jessica thought. That's who he reminded her of, the actor and Otto Boutine, a kind of combination of the two. Otto had been her first mentor in the FBI Behavioral Science Unit. They'd fallen in love, and Otto had died saving Jessica when he threw himself between her and Mad Matthew Matisak. It had been in Chicago, Illinois, the first major case she'd ever worked, thanks to Otto, and now it seemed like forever ago.

As the car made its way to Dulles International Airport, Jessica wondered what specifically about Richard Sharpe there was to compare to Otto, and quickly decided it must merely be the man's physical appearance.

Copperwaite, while younger, had slicked down hair and carried a hefty, stocky man's girth and barrel chest, thick hands and fingers, his eyes like melons with the seeds clear and alert, while Sharpe appeared his opposite, a man of height, who wore his hair in a shaggy but comfortable mess, his hands and fingers gracefully long, making her wonder if he didn't play a musical instrument. His eyes held a deep sadness, that of the wounded. There was certainly some misery and mystery there, but he rarely met her eye to be so examined.

Her gaze challenged Sharpe's to meet her own. He did not. In fact, the man's broad shoulders and stone-sculptured physique notwithstanding, his eyes seemed hardly able to hold her look, perhaps out of some almost boyish shyness that might have been cute in another context.

"So as it sums up, we know precious little about crucifixion deaths," commented Sharpe, "but there must be some literature, even if ancient, somewhere on the subject."

"No one I know has had any experience with it ever, at all," she replied, "not my father, or my old teacher, Asa Holcraft, no one."

"That's just it. No one, obviously, either side of the Atlantic."

"Well, I do know that Jesus died of dehydration and asphyxiation brought on by the weight of his body collapsing in on his windpipe and lungs during the most well-known of all crucifixions," Jessica stated, trying to make right her earlier, lame response. "I know a bit about crucifixion motifs in art, Raphael and all that. Took Art Appreciation 101 in college, you see, and well, even Picasso's little known, dark work. . . . Well, I guess that's of little consequence here. You didn't happen to find a tau cross or depictions of angels, the sun, or the moon anywhere near the body, did you? There was that gash at the ribs on his left side."

Sharpe's naturally narrow eyes widened. "In point of fact, yes. Each body had been bled like Christ with something the coroner suspects to be a spearhead. Just as in the Bible."

"You needn't think me psychic. I caught a glimpse of the wounds in the photos." Frowning, Jessica pushed on. "The question becomes: *Why* crucify the victim when drowning or simple strangulation would accomplish the task more efficiently and certainly more easily? Unless . . ."

"Yes?" Sharpe eagerly encouraged.

"Unless the bastard wants to enjoy a prolonged kill, or the ritual of the crucifixion itself. It might take hours, even days before a person would expire, depending on the stamina and perhaps the weight of the individual as the most important variables here. Age, of course, is a major factor."

"We've had three victims, all nailed to makeshift crosses, or a single cross, somewhere hidden. One cannot say with any degree of certainty which it might be, of course," said Sharpe in a tone so level, he might have been referring to tea and crumpets. Jessica at once admired his detachment, the man's bearing and professional sureness, his professional sense. At the same time, she understood the veneer of jaded cynicism and cold aloofness essential to maintaining one's own safety net in such matters, one's own wall of defense. Most people found her own professional air a "bitch act"— both officious and off-putting—when in fact, she required the necessarily stout and impenetrable wall of detachment to go about the business of death investigations every day. *If* she were to get by with the same dignity and bravado of her male counterparts, she knew detachment to be the only cure-all.

"So, I take it we do not have the crosses to work with, only the dumped bodies," Jessica said as the car entered the airport grounds. "At this point in my career, having seen so much human suffering and brutality, little remains to truly shock me. However, these crucifixion deaths do, even from this distance."

Sharpe shook his head. "We're scouring for the cross, but frankly, we don't know where to look."

"And the nails or spikes used?"

"No, the bodies are dumped with the spikes removed, but we've sized up the weapon, that is the spikes, through calculations made against the wounds."

"Nails driven through the palms and into the crossbar,

here," added Copperwaite, indicating exactly where on his own left hand, pointing and saying, "precisely in the center of each palm. At each wrist and the ankles, rope burns occur where the victims were anchored before the spikes were driven."

"No messages on or around the body?"

"Not a word, not a clue, nothing, no."

She nodded. "I see. Perhaps the killer believes his message is quite clear enough."

"Perhaps."

It hurt Jessica's hands to even think of a huge spike going through them, although she realized that the pain of the spike through hands and feet in a true crucifixion hardly began to tell the story of the excruciating manner of death brought on by this torturous end.

"There'd be frequent pass outs, simulating death. With each blackout, the killer may well rejoice, might even ejaculate," she informed the detectives. "Any semen or other foreign fluids found on the bodies?"

"Matter of fact, olive oil."

"Olive oil?" she asked.

"Smeared over the body with a mixture of wine and blood, yes. Kind of bathed in it, according to our lab people, up the anus, everywhere. Forensics also tells us that blood alcohol levels were high. And from stomach contents, it was determined the victims had consumed a lot of wine just before each died."

"And that's it?" she asked.

Copperwaite added, "That and the signs of crucifixion is all we've got."

Sharpe was quick to add, "Our experts tell us that olive oil is thought to have regenerative powers."

She sighed heavily and leaned back, trying to imagine the kind of madman behind such torturous killings. "Sounds ritualistic in nature. The blood is the wine, the wine is the blood, and olives have magical properties. . . ."

Copperwaite added some gruesome details, "Forensics has splinters pulled from wounds on palms and feet. Old, wooden cross, oak . . . well-aged . . . rarely found anymore."

"Bathed in blood, oil, and wine . . ." said Jessica, thinking
it over, made curious by the men from England. "Three victims found in this similar state already."

"Perhaps you're right, Dr. Coran," began Copperwaite.
"Perhaps three will satisfy the fiend. Maybe three has some
significant or symbolic meaning for him."

The others merely looked from one to the other, none of
them believing Copperwaite's hopeful wish. Jessica broke the
awkward silence with, "And you say two male victims, one
female?"

"Quite right," Sharpe responded.

"All of the same race . . ."

"All three have absolutely nothing in common," replied
Copperwaite, "save skin color, pale like all Londoners."

"One is of Irish extraction, the woman. She was born in
Cardiff but spent the better part of her life in Bury St. Edmunds. She was a schoolteacher there," began Sharpe. "We
learned of her identity when her landlord in London sent word
he recognized her from a sketch in the *Times*. She'd gone
missing."

Copperwaite added, "Another is a white male butcher
turned used automobile salesman."

"The third," concluded Sharpe, "renounced his Jewish faith
live on his radio talk show, for which the BBC took great
exception—doing it as he chose. Bad form, all that. And afterward, some years afterward, he converted to Catholicism.
He lost all favor with his listeners, lost his radio show, everything—a prime candidate for suicide for a time, or so asso-
ciates say."

"The victims were killed in that order?"

"Yes. The woman first."

"I see."

As fascinating as Tattoo Man's cadaver had been for Jessica, she must admit that this madman in London, England,
needed full attention. Besides, the prospect of traveling to
London to catch a killer of such obvious theatrical panache
could not be denied. The monster across the sea had already

proved to be ghastly even from this safe distance.

"The plane has been held for your boarding, Jessica, gentlemen," Eriq Santiva announced when the car stopped before
the delayed flight on the runway. "Keep me informed!"

· FOUR ·

*Juries want bleeding bullet holes, sucking chest
wounds with steak knives or hot pokers still attached to the victim of violent crime. Anything
less—such as scientific evidence—leaves room
for a junior high school definition of reasonable
doubt. . . .*

—STEPHEN ROBERTSON,
DECOY

In the back of her mind all the way to Dulles International
Airport in Fairfax, Virginia, Jessica had worried about J. T.
and her having dropped Tattoo Man's case in his lap.

Concern over Tattoo Man faded quickly, however, when
she looked out on the runway at Dulles International to see
the final preparations for takeoff of their nonstop to London.

With Scotland Yard paying the freight this time, Eriq Santiva displayed even greater pleasure at the combining of his
FBI personnel with that of the famous Scotland Yard. The
only downside: no ride on the Concorde. Perhaps on her return, Sharpe had promised, but not today since the Concorde
only flew into JFK, in New York, and they would be depart-
ing from Fairfax.

They'd been the last to board the plane, which had indeed
been held up for Dr. Jessica Coran, by order of the FBI and
Scotland Yard on behalf of Her Majesty the Queen. It was
enough to make Jessica blush at their boarding when the stew-
ardess had said, "Dr. Coran, I presume?"

Once settled in their seats on the commercial flight, Inspector Sharpe wasted no time, asking her even before she
had the opportunity to order a drink, "Shall I fill you in further
on the three crime scenes that we have thus far?"

She loved his mastery of language, the little touches that

made his culture bubble forth with each word, not to mention his melodic voice and lovely accent.

"Yes, I would like to see all that you have on each case, actually. Another look at the crime-scene photos and any forensic reports coming out of each case."

"Good, then be my guest." Sharpe snapped open his thin, black briefcase and produced several files. Each was marked with a victim's name scrawled in large, red marker across its label: *O'Donahue, Katherine; Coibby, Lawrence; Burton, Theodore.* No strange-sounding, exotic names with origins from faraway places, nothing to *die* for, she thought, simply homespun, middle-of-the-road, run-of-the-mill names that appeared as scattered as the victims themselves. Jessica read of a schoolteacher in retirement; a British used-car salesman with a mortgage, alimony, and child support to pay; and finally a stockbroker turned radio personality who'd strayed from his Jewish roots to embrace Catholicism, all in that order.

The victims appeared to share nothing in common save that they were all British subjects, the Irish schoolmarm having adopted Britain as her home in her youth, someplace called Bury St. Edmunds.

One of the crime-scene photos in O'Donahue's file gave Jessica a start. She hadn't seen it before. She helplessly stared at the tire marks, which were quite visible, like large tattoos across her back and shoulders where the skin had absorbed the impact of the automobile going over her. The tread marks shimmered beneath the lights in a perfect pattern, reminding her of Tattoo Man back in her lab at Quantico. "Did the killer run her over before or after crucifying her?"

"Neither." Sharpe explained the sad origin of the tread marks.

The plane sped down the runway, lifting like an ancient bird of prey, ponderous at first but suddenly light and airy, free of all restraint.

Settling in, Jessica released her seat belt to relax more comfortably, and said to Sharpe, "Tell me more about how you found the first victim: when, where, and the condition of the body at the time."

"That'd be the schoolteacher, O'Donahue. In her early to mid-fifties. Not your typical serial-killer bait, I'd say."

"No, although it's not unheard of."

"Well, as I said, we found her run over by the fool that discovered the body, tire marks over her back. She'd been dumped facedown near the Thames on the Victoria Gardens Embankment, along a dirty stretch of levy along the parkway below a bridge."

Copperwaite, who'd begun to listen in earnest, added, "We can take you to the scene if you like."

"Yes, I would like to have a look . . . give it the once-over."

"We suspect that body and perpetrator were en route to the Thames," suggested Sharpe. "That the killer fully intended to dump it into the river when he was frightened off."

"Points to the possibility it may've been his first-ever kill. Since he was so easily frightened off, you might look for a younger person," she countered.

"Good thought." Sharpe sat back heavily in his chair to consider this.

Copperwaite, from the other side of Sharpe, added as an afterthought, "We find a great deal floating in the Thames."

"Her hands and feet had been spiked with three-quarter-inch thick nails. Like bloody railway spikes, but not quite. Still, large enough to make you wince." Sharpe's matter-of-fact tone did battle with the content of his words. He paused for her benefit, fearing she might become alarmed.

"Go on," she dictated.

"We didn't know what to make of it at the time, of course, and only later were we made absolutely certain—"

"Certain of what?" she impatiently prodded him.

"—certain that the holes in hands and feet had been part of a crucifixion murder, you see. Accepting the fact at the time, I tell you, we wanted to deny it."

"I see, of course. Were the others similarly disposed of, the killer using water?"

"As a matter of fact, yes. Do you think there's significance in that? Because I do."

"Perhaps, perhaps not. Tell me about the other discoveries."

"Very well, as you like . . ." Sharpe launched into a typical police description of the scene, the body, the surrounding area—a small lake in a park frequented by families on a daily basis where children saw the body floating like a balloon toy in Coibby's case.

Copperwaite interjected here and there, adding a bit of detail and color, the two detectives complimenting one another in rounding out the description of how Lawrence Coibby's body—victim number two—had been discovered.

"Any defensive marks on hands, forearms? Any blood or tissue, not his own, found under his nails?"

"Like the woman, no sign of any violence done to the body save the slight cut to the side, the spikes driven into palms and feet," replied Sharpe. "No fight put up whatsoever."

Copperwaite added, "Nor the third victim. Perfectly untouched save for the crucifixion marks. And don't forget the needle marks, Sharpie—Inspector Sharpe."

"Then there were drugs found in the system?" she pressed.

"Trace elements of a barbiturate," replied Sharpe. "M.E.'s report is . . ." He paused, shuffled papers about the file, and finally pointed to a line on the M.E.'s protocol sheet—a form that appeared up-to-date and quaint at the same time, Jessica thought. She read the logo: *Coroner for the Crown.*

" 'Brevital,' " Jessica read aloud.

"That mean anything to you?" asked Sharpe, sensing her reaction to the word.

She let out a breath of air and shrugged. "Methohexital, used in sedating patients . . . barbiturate, short-acting."

"Short-acting?" asked Copperwaite, his youthful eyes alight with eager interest.

"As opposed to long-acting. In other words, your victims, injected with Brevital, would have dozed just long enough for the killer—"

"Or killers," corrected Sharpe.

"—to hoist the prone victims' bodies onto whatever makeshift cross he—or they—concocted for the sacrificial lambs."

"Just enough to put them under, then?"

"Exactly. And each victim must've awakened when the killer drove home the stakes at the palms and feet, most likely having already been secured by some other means. Rope, hemp, rawhide perhaps? Yes, the body would need lashing to the cross in addition to the stakes."

Copperwaite ground his teeth at the image.

Jessica added, "That would be my guesstimate, but don't quote me." She paused, all of them allowing the image to sink in. "Rope burns at both wrists and about the feet, right? To take the weight," pursued Jessica.

"Precisely," Sharpe said at once.

"The body weight on the victims," Jessica began. "Can you give me a ballpark figure?"

"Ballpark figure?" asked Copperwaite, confused by her language.

"She means an estimated guess, Stuart. How about a precise number, Doctor?"

"That'll do."

"You see, I've had the same thoughts," returned Sharpe. "The men each weighed over 190 stones, while the woman weighed 155 of your American pounds."

Jessica smiled at the use of the word "stones." "So, the ropes were enough to hold the body in place, so the stakes could be driven in. Certainly sounds like the work of more than one man, possibly a deadly pair, given the deadweight of the drugged victims."

"Once again, our thought also," replied Sharpe with a narrowed gaze. "Given how long we've had to study the cases, your deductions are positively . . . preternatural. Are you sure you're not a psychic to boot?"

While Jessica answered with a thoughtful smile, Copperwaite added, "Unless this bugger is bigger than Arnold Schwarzenegger, he'd have to be two men."

Everyone sat back, allowing the gravity of this fact to sink in. It was hard to envision not one but two men, working in tandem, crucifying random, innocent people. The why of it hung in the air thick and choking.

Jessica had brought along some light reading for the long plane trip, her volume of *Medical and Legal Procedures Related to Death* written some years earlier by her now deceased mentor Dr. Asa Holcraft. She'd long been wanting to reread Dr. Holcraft's work to, in a sense, be in his presence once again. She needed his firm grounding, if for no other reason than the sheer monstrosity this crucifixion evil represented.

Jessica had never known a finer scientific mind than that of Asa Holcraft. She now quickly scanned Holcraft's words for any information relative to crucifixion deaths—half knowing she'd find nothing specific to crucifixion. Still, a quick glance at the enormous index was in order. This only confirmed what she knew: His huge opus didn't touch on death by crucifixion. The topic simply didn't appear in any of the forensics books she owned—and she owned them all. Save for a paragraph here or there, Jessica had found no help in the literature of forensic medicine.

She was working on blind instinct here . . .

Even an electronic search of the World Wide Web had turned up more reams of religious-oriented material dealing with the death of Jesus Christ than anything else, and nothing substantive regarding the medical intricacies of dying in such a manner. Death of this manner being so extremely rare, no studies or treatises had ever been done on it.

She shared this information, or lack thereof, with Sharpe and Copperwaite. Her news met a pair of glum frowns. Sharpe said, "Not surprising, really."

She halfheartedly searched Holcraft for his remarks on asphyxia, as he remained the foremost authority on asphyxia deaths. She located the pages and placed a bookmark there.

She looked up at Richard Sharpe and asked, "Why don't you describe the scene of the third discovery, the body which ostensibly sent you scurrying in earnest to the FBI for profiling assistance."

"That would be Burtie Burton, Theodore Burton. Rather well-known chap at one time—known for his views, for his late-night radio talk program a year or so back. A rare breed indeed, both a stockbroker and a rebel-rouser as some call—called him. Rather enjoyed his program myself. Man made a lot of sense as well as money. Tore into our Tories mostly, roughed them up a bit before he got into trouble with the BBC."

Jessica imagined someone saying in such mild tones how Howard Stern upset Middle America, and she momentarily wondered at the British in general—their history of social gentility and blood beneath the carpet. She likewise wondered aloud for the benefit of the men, "I wonder if the man's profession, radio talk show host, had anything remotely to do with his dying so dreaded a death—after a used-car salesman and a teacher. What might that connection be? On the surface of it, perhaps the victims have nothing whatever in common. I'm sure you've dug for connections."

"Pile on the agony," muttered Sharpe.

"What?" asked Jessica.

Copperwaite translated, saying, "Old English for don't spare the gory details, Doctor."

"I mean *iffffff* that's so, then we're really scrambled as you Americans say," Sharpe announced. "With nothing tying the victims together."

"All I'm saying is that perhaps the selection of victims has been absolutely random. If the killer or killers 'saw the mark of Christ' on the foreheads of each of their victims, that might well be what the victims had in common—*everything* but *nothing*."

Sharpe fell silent. Copperwaite sensed his partner wanted silence for a time. Finally, Sharpe began telling Jessica more about victim number three: Theodore Burton.

"It was a few days after number two—Coibby—that Burtie Burton's body came to our attention. He'd gone missing, but people who knew him said that he'd do that, you know, disappear for weeks at a time—"

"Go on holiday without the slightest provocation or warning to others. Queer fellow, really," added Copperwaite. "And we knew the bloody moment we came on scene that it was him, but it was rather shocking to discover he was yet another victim of the Crucifier."

"The 'Crucifier'? Is that what you're calling the killer?"

"Press picked it up somehow," Sharpe apologetically replied.

"All Burton's wounds were the same, then?" she asked.

"Identical. Actually Stuart saw it immediately, before I wanted to believe it. We looked at the hands, and then to the feet of the naked body. Poor chap lay outstretched before us, and there once again—for the third time—we found the tell-tale marks of a murder by crucifixion."

As Sharpe continued to describe the murdered victim and the scene, Jessica allowed her imagination to flow, picturing the exact moment, trying to climb into Sharpe's world, to know the exact words and gestures exchanged between Copperwaite and the more experienced Richard Sharpe. In a waking dream, she saw Sharpe at the murder scene and heard him there, but his voice was muffled. She somehow found herself in a cold, cavernous well, the clamminess and absolute stillness like a coffin, when she realized that she lay inside the body of one of the crucifixion victims.

She felt memories bombard her, memories of her own near execution so many years before at the hand of a maniac named Matisak. She saw dark, featureless faces looking on, watching in gleeful exhaltation as one man held her against a huge wooden cross and another began to drive nails into her palms, finishing with her feet. Suddenly they let go, and her weight became her worst enemy. Gaining breath became an impossible labor.

All things around her became a blur as she struggled like a pinned butterfly, the struggle useless. All around her she felt the coldness closing in, and only when she blacked out did she feel any comfort. But she didn't black out; rather she woke to the voices of two Scotland Yard detectives seated beside her.

"And rather tidy, for a serial killer, wouldn't you say, Stuart? Concerns himself with washing the wounds."

"Washing the wounds, yes?"

"So to speak, what with disposing of the bodies in water. Wouldn't you say?"

"That just makes him all the more oddly weird, if that's his intention."

"His or theirs, either way, we're bloody sure to spend out that budget given us for calling international help. In any case, to whom do we turn now? How best to spend our money on this situation, Stuart? You know if we don't spend it, they'll find another use for the funds elsewhere."

"Interpol, the French, yes . . . If anybody's had any experience with something so gruesome as this, it'd have to be the French, French law enforcement, right?"

"Coran will do, Coppers. I've read her casebooks. And if the bulletins can be believed, and they generally don't go in for hyperbole, she's just the sort we need on this case."

"You're sure it's not just another way to piss off the boss, Sharpie?"

"That, too, of course," joked Sharpe.

"Then we've done well to get her this far."

"She has a great investigative mind. She'll do as Sherlock to my Holmes, what? Whatever the cost to the division, these dreadful murders can't continue . . ."

"I suspect Boulte will see the wisdom of it in the end," suggested Copperwaite. "Else the gentlemen of the *Times*'ll have us all for breakfast, my friend, but if they see we've taken the extreme step of calling Coran on board, why then. . . ."

"Now you're thinking like a bureaucrat, Coppers."

Jessica only half heard their conversation. Long hours in the lab, the excitement of the evening, and a bout with insomnia had taken their toll. She fell asleep beside Sharpe.

Two figments of Jessica's imagination now gathered fog-laden air into their "land of nod" lungs. The sun had as yet to show itself, and the darkness clutched their shoulders where they knelt over Jessica's body, her dream self, which had been laid out at a kind of watery crossroads here—below a trellis train-track bridge, a sign reading Grosvenor Bridge, someone saying it wasn't far to Battersea Park from here. Jessica's body, snatched now from the water, lay in a dirty sand beach that saw little to no traffic save for young teens in search of a place to drink, shoot up, and neck.

"I wager we know what the M.E.'s going to say. It'll be like the rest," moaned Copperwaite's dream personae.

Sharpe's soothing voice took hold again, lulling her back to dream, a silly dream actually, in which they examined her dead body, dead by the hand of the Crucifier.

"We can't overlook anything, Stuart. Suppose this isn't a fourth victim but a first, a copycat killing? Toxicology tests have to be made to rule out every contingency."

"Wretched business . . . So, what do we do? Wait for results until a fifth victim bobs up at yet another body of water somewhere?"

"We're in a rather awkward position, which often dictates a man do nothing. But I rather fancy we must act and act now."

"How so?"

"We go find this Dr. Coran, and we bring her back to England with us. We begin with *her* superiors."

"We've a problem with that, Sharpie."

"Oh? And what's that?"

"Dr. Jessica Coran is already here. This is her body, Richard! Don't you recognize her?"

Suddenly, Jessica started at the full sight of her face at their feet, and she instantly felt the weight of Holcraft's book on her lap back here in the plane, in the real world. Her dream was instantly replaced when she opened her eyes and focused on the pages opened to asphyxia deaths.

Jessica couldn't recall having opened the book to these pages, only marking them for later reading. But she also realized that she had been lulled into sleep by the sound of wind over a wing at her ear; an airplane-induced sleep on one side, Richard Sharpe's voice on the other.

She felt awful, having fallen asleep to the sound of Sharpe's tale. She'd been battling and failing miserably, with an ongoing case of insomnia using every cure known to modern science.

Now she wondered how much of her dream of Copperwaite and Sharpe had come of their words and how much her imagination. Either way, they had a most fascinating case on their hands, and she hoped to play a major role in its resolution.

"So, Doctor, you're back with us," Sharpe said matter-of-factly.

"Please, accept my sincerest apology. I haven't had much sleep lately, and the plane hum and your voices conspired to lull me to sleep. I do feel awful."

"Not at all."

She wondered how much she had injured his pride. He

pretended that nothing of consequence had happened, while she wondered what he and Copperwaite had said of her while she'd dozed.

"Coibby's and Burton's bodies were snatched from the water," Copperwaite ventured.

Sharpe glared at his partner.

"That's where Richard left off with you," Copperwaite explained himself.

Sharpe frowned and gave in. "Katherine O'Donahue was meant to be left in water. We surmised that the killer was interrupted, frightened off, really, before he could complete the job, you understand."

She nodded. "I see."

"That's when the bridgeman hit the body."

"Poor chap thought *he* had killed the woman," Copperwaite added with a bit of a snicker.

Sharpe finished with, "New Scotland Yard forensics has determined that our first victim had the same toxic level of barbiturates, and that she was long dead before the Jetta ever touched her."

Fatigue born of insomnia stalked Jessica.

She had once kiddingly told her psychic friend and fellow FBI agent, Dr. Kim Desinor, "I fear that I am *insomnia-stalked*."

Kim, quick to remind Jessica of their work together in New Orleans some years back, had replied, "Better stalked by insomnia than some human monstrosity like Mad Matthew Matisak."

True enough, Jessica now thought. Still, as a result of her insomnia, at times when she least expected, the fatigue washed floodlike over her, and Jessica found her mind and body shutting down with her tired eyes.

It—the fatigue that wouldn't be denied—came on her again like some pixie-dust–laden gnome. The jet engines, the monotony of aircraft against air current, the battering of the hull created the same lulling sound as a ship at sea . . . It all conspired like shadowy alchemy to make it impossible to keep her eyes open.

"I'm going to sleep on it now, gentlemen, if you don't mind," she announced in a slurred tone before placing Holcraft's volume aside altogether and closing her eyes again. She nodded off to visions of crucifixions and tattoos.

· FIVE ·

*. . . he who finds a certain proportion of pain
and evil inseparably woven up in the life of the
very worms, will bear his own share with more
courage and submission.*

—THOMAS H. HUXLEY,
ON EDUCATION.

Somewhere in a dark place in London

He paced before the cross. He knelt at the altar in the gloom
of this place and the far deeper gloom of his soul. He stood,
paced more, as if pacing might focus thought. He pondered
the situation. Pondered on—had pondered for hours on end
now: how to present his truth to them, and eventually to every
man.

His compatriot in the crucifixions watched him, watched
the emotional turmoil, and he tried to ease his friend and
mentor's soul, saying, "You tear at yourself with the talons
of self-recrimination and perplexity. You should not have any
doubts. We are doing the right thing."

"Self-doubt? Try self-loathing and despair, wonder and wa-
ver, ponder and stagger, vacillate and hesitate, distrust and
mistrust, suspect and question every step, so unsure of the
whether-or-nots, the *ifs, ands, ors, nors, yets, fors, sos,* and
buts of self-recrimination and doubt."

"You are the right man at the right time to perform God's
work here on Earth," replied the other. "You must not doubt
yourself."

"I doubt my ability to hold the others, to spread the word.

I doubt I have any ability with fact, and whether or not I can convey God's truth."

"Perhaps such truth cannot be conveyed to others, that truth, like God and Christ, lives beyond human understanding and perception."

"Still we must try to penetrate the obstinate others, to show them the way. Sometimes I dare ask the crucial question: Do the others even matter? Were they really a part of the grand scheme? Were they even real in the sense of reality as being truth, if indeed reality was never the truth to begin with? Perhaps the others have even less corporeal existence than the voices in my head. Perhaps the others *are* the voices in my head. No one, not even those who purport to understand and follow me, my dear friend, really know what lives are led inside the *Crucifier's* head." He laughed and shook his head. "That's what the London press calls me now, the Crucifier. The fools could not be further from the truth."

The friend agreed. "None of the fools of this Earth know that you were born fated and ordained, selected as the Chosen One. Born an archangel, really, someday to be known as both a prophet and a saint."

"I know this much to be so. For God, and not the many other voices of doubt and dissension, has said so."

"Perhaps in reliving the crucifixions that have gone before, in submitting each to the microscope of your keen mind, you could then explain to the others. Let them know, bring them to the same realization we hold dear—that failure is part of the process in getting from here to eternity."

"Well said! Not one single soul has been wasted. Every single one who has gone before us to be crucified, has cleansed his or her soul in the bargain. It has been so with the O'Donahue woman and Lawrence Coibby."

Lawrence Coibby had been given a more potent dosage of the drug, Brevital. He hadn't squirmed or moaned or whined so much as did Katherine. She'd been a big disappointment. She'd also been half conscious when the stakes were driven in, but Coibby was better about enduring the pain of it all, the drugs having dulled the sting, the suffering discomfort, the ultimate agonizing anguish that must be part of the path toward the ultimate pleasure, delight, joy, and rapture.

The drugs dulled the mind to all fearful sense of imminent danger. Coibby had died without pain, or so they all wanted to believe.

He recalled the exact moment of Coibby's passing. Coibby had simply expired, and not with his last painful breath as everyone would wish to believe. Coibby couldn't capture a last breath to have a last breath. When the man's last breath could not be taken, at the moment when one's breath became God's own breath, *that* was when he died.

Everyone agreed that Coibby's was a near perfect crucifixion.

Certainly, he flailed some at the end, but he never fully regained consciousness. And the inner peace brought on by the drug—and the knowledge he must go on to a better place—helped ease him over so that his spirit might imbue the dead corpse with a renewed source of power and strength, the strength that comes from knowing Jesus and the resurrection of the soul.

But again, Jesus failed to put in an appearance, and Lawrence's body had remained still and lifeless, as inert as the cross upon which he'd been sacrificed. So there was no corporeal proof of Coibby's resurrection, as there should have been, but then God tested men in mysterious ways.

Once again the all-night vigil grew long and unproductive, and the collective—*they*—became further disillusioned.

As director and choreographer of the Second Coming, he had much to answer for. His constituents and followers would soon abandon him if they learned the truth about him, that he hardly knew if what he searched for could ever be found in this or another millennium.

He'd been so sure with the schoolteacher.

He'd been equally sure with the car salesman, Coibby. And for a moment, he was absolutely sure it must be Coibby. But all hope failed when Coibby's corpse could not be enticed to show signs of resurrection after death, despite all prayer and all the power and life force coming from the collective.

They had simply miscalculated. All of them, including their leader.

"Too many voices in your head?" asked one follower.

"How is it possible that the Chosen One is not to be the Chosen One?" queried another.

"We must absolutely not become disillusioned," he cautioned the others. "We must! Absolutely *must* continue to look elsewhere . . ."

"Look elsewhere?"

"Indeed."

"For what, exactly, pray tell?" rallied the voices.

"For answers . . . enlightenment, of course. Holy enlightenment, indeed . . . exactly . . . pray tell . . ."

The Crucifier thought of that night when Coibby had gone over. He reviewed it in his head again and again, trying to get it right. Then he thought of the third Chosen One, Burton, and he again felt the doubts crowding into his mind, as he reexamined every step, every ritualistic moment of Burton's agonizing time on the cross. He heaved with the heavy burden on his shoulders and collapsed against a natural stone chair in this dark place where they must hide away their deeds until the world should come to enlightenment. His comforting friend placed an arm around his shoulders, gave him a warm hug, and said, "You must, like all the rest, be patient. The accurate millennium marks the Second Coming. We will see Christ resurrected through our combined will."

Jessica awakened just as the plane came in sight of what appeared to be a mammoth island lying just off the coast of mainland Europe: Great Britain—England, Scotland, and Wales. From her window seat, Jessica could make out the Isle of Wight. The coastline, jagged and steep, gave the appearance of a great plateau rising from the ocean like some bloated giant's clenched fist. Small English villages rose out of the landscape as the plane descended, each looking like the small Christmas villages found in novelty shops, Jessica thought, delighting in the beauty of this place as the plane floated over moors and marshes toward the spirals of London, making her feel like a modern-day Peter Pan.

The plane descended further, now over an area known as the Whitleyern Highlands where fertile valleys alternated with chalk and limestone hills. Jessica knew that by any standard, Great Britain's overcrowded population had begun to bulge at the seams, and that ninety percent or more of its people lived in cities and towns. She'd read somewhere that in all of Europe, only tiny Belgium had a higher percentage of people in urban areas. The lowlands, especially in southeastern, central, and northern England, by comparison remained among the most thickly populated places on the globe, and nothing bred crime and murder like overpopulation. Yet, at the same time, the cemeteries of England were filled to capacity even stacked tier upon tier and there was no more room for the dead.

Jessica's insomnia awakened her while the cabin remained dark and everyone else asleep. Her insomnia had her reading facts from guidebooks she'd shoved in her overnight bag. Now Jessica, fully "up" on the country, knew that Great Britain had 232 persons per square kilometer as opposed to France's 100 per square kilometer, the USA's 26 per square kilometer, and Australia's 2 per square kilometer.

She had found Copperwaite dozing while Sharpe, like her, sat upright, having come awake some time before her. Both of them fully awake, she engaged Sharpe in conversation, telling him bits of her recently acquired knowledge of his homeland.

He instantly wanted to hear what she'd learned, and so she plied him with the facts most tourists received every day on incoming flights. She finished with a dark twist, however, saying, "I hate to be the pessimist, but there's no doubt that England, and London in particular, will see growing crime of the heinous kind most people think reserved only for America in the coming years and through the coming decades, millennium wishes to the contrary or not. . . ."

He nodded appreciatively. "I have no doubt of it."

"I believe it inevitable and unavoidable, that perhaps the overwhelming crime rate of America is, after all, linked to the growing numbers who feel alienated in an increasingly technological age."

"Hmmm, interesting theory. I've heard it before, in fact."

"Do you doubt it?" she pressed.

"Not in the least, as one of many contributing factors, of course." He then ruminated about England's growth and progress, slurring the two words as if they were dirty, saying, "Greater London has—the last I looked at figures—a population of 6,775,000."

"As I said, crowded, most in ghettos."

He ignored her, going on, "Birmingham has 1,004,000, Leeds 711,000, Sheffield 534,000, Glasgow 725,000, and Scotland's capital, Edinburgh 438,000; while the capital and largest city in Wales, Cardiff, has a population of 280,000."

"You must have a photographic memory," she replied.

"I'm good with numbers. Photographic, I'm not so sure. At any rate," he continued, "in between these larger urban areas, a host of small towns and villages—all having one main street and one main shopping area—now flourish and grow."

Again the emphasis on "grow," the way it rolled bitterly from his throat, seemed a sure sign of how Sharpe felt about urban sprawl. Jessica said, "I take it, you don't care for progress as it is typically defined?"

"Look at it this way. Since the late forties, say about 1946, some twenty-one new towns were established in England, five in Scotland, and two in Wales. Some two million live in these small communities. In Great Britain alone, some six million dogs and almost as many cats also live as household pets, all with little or no room to scratch much less grow. So you can well imagine how the people feel about one another."

Jessica was about to reiterate her fear that violent crime in England would only increase when she found herself becoming lost in his powerful, potent, green-eyed stare, so instead she turned and studied the rolling green landscape below. The airplane began passing over great expanses of wheat fields, the number one crop in all of England. She marveled at the beauty unfolding beneath them.

Jessica could just make out the small white dots along all the hillsides, the countryside peppered with sheep and cattle. The land rose up a deep, plush carpet of green, a startlingly deep, abiding green that Jessica had never before seen.

They were above and to the right of Southhampton, and

soon after, they reached sight of the enormous city that had begun as a Roman seaport.

As they came within view of London's cathedrals, Jessica immediately made out the gargoyles. The cathedrals were littered with phallic-shaped gargoyles hanging far out over the pinnacles, some at heights no doubt impossible to make out from the ground. The whole effect made the city below appear almost hostile to those flying over, like a kingdom ever vigilant, ever expectant of enemies from without, ever ready for war. The buildings, taken as a whole, crafted a giant bed of nails in the gloom of twilight. Government buildings, castles, Westminster Abbey, St. Paul's Cathedral, St. George's Cathedral, St. Martin's and others, all jutting skyward with their arrowlike turrets, shone beautiful in the fresh morning light. The River Thames ran through the city like a huge, lacy ribbon or like an uncoiled snake, depending upon one's mood.

Jessica's mood had come full circle. Her arrival in London filled her soul with excitement. From Heathrow Airport to downtown London, she had an opportunity to see the choking pollution, congested roads, ugly factories, and blighted areas of the city—the necessary evils upon which all bustling, great cities rest. Far from the splendid, rolling, and majestic hills of England she'd witnessed by air. However, in forty minutes, she and the others entered the frenetic downtown city, which was filled with history and cemeteries. It had been the home of such notables as Rudyard Kipling, Samuel and Ben Johnson, Charles Dickens, Daniel Defoe, Tennyson, Blake, Byron, Keats, Shelley, Carroll, Shakespeare, Disraeli, Churchill, Shaw, Newton, and Darwin—all men who had shed light onto the world. It had also been home to Jack-the-Ripper and other infamous killers.

She was "on the old sod" so to speak, and the official New Scotland Yard car, sent to greet them, traveled lanes that had been traveled by Boswell and Bacon, Raleigh and Drake, kings and queens, and so many others in history and literature. The place swept her imagination and played games with her heart.

"We're nearing the York at York's Gate, where you will be staying, Dr. Coran," Richard Sharpe informed her. "We've got you a room there. It's central, close to the Yard, and coincidentally looks out over the Victoria Gardens Embankment where the first body was discovered."

"All rather a neat package, all in the City," added Copperwaite.

"The business district," Sharpe clarified for her. "We will drop you at your hotel, allow you to settle in, and motor round to pick you up, say at eleven?"

"Where are you going?"

"As officers of Scotland Yard, we're duty-bound to report in before all else." Sharpe then requested that the driver take Dr. Coran to the York by way of Savoy Place where a room awaited her arrival. But Jessica, seeing the now-famous revolving square sign that signaled New Scotland Yard headquarters, the modern structure at odds with all its ancient surroundings such as the Royal Horseguard and the Ministry of Defence, balked at separating so soon, saying, "No, I'd like to see what you have so far in your ready room before I go on to the hotel."

"Ready room? Ahh, you mean our operations room—the ops! But really, we have so very little there," apologized Copperwaite.

"You've seen the bulk of what we have in the files," assured Sharpe.

"I want to have a look at the bodies as soon as possible, then."

"It's rather early," countered Sharpe, "and you must take into account jet lag. It was a long crossing. You may wish to acclimate to our—"

"I rested on the plane!"

"So you did. Yes, of course, then if you're sure . . ."

"I'm sure. Take me to your corpse," she said, trying a joke to loosen Sharpe up a bit.

"That would be Chief Inspector Boulte." Copperwaite quickly plugged into her joke with his own. "He's likely white as a corpse by now."

Even the driver laughed at Copperwaite's remark.

"Well, yes," agreed Sharpe, amused. "Likely pulled the few remaining hairs from his head since we left."

There was some disturbance at the parking lot entrance leading to the rear of the Yard, so Sharpe told the driver to let them off where they waited before the building. "Shall we alight here?" he suggested to Jessica, opening her car door.

Jessica wondered if the man had a rude bone in his body. He behaved far more like a choirboy than a cop. "So your Chief Inspector Boulte, I take is as his name implies—rather tightly wound? And from what I gather, he isn't so sure of my joining forces with the investigative team? Is that it?"

Copperwaite came around and joined them on the curb. "Wasn't all for it, calling in help from the *colonies*, you know," he conspiratorially told Jessica.

"Has a hard time accepting the fact we lost the war to you Yanks. Asking for outside help, especially from Yanks, well, there you have it," added Sharpe. " 'Fraid I played a bit of a game with him. Gave the newshounds the impression he meant to seek out your help, you see, rather than it being my idea. He didn't care for the gesture, but it did assure us of getting you in on the case."

She could not help but wonder about the twists and turns that had placed her here beside Richard Sharpe. Copperwaite added over her thoughts, "You can well imagine the sum total of collar work on Richard's part to bring this about, Dr. Coran." Copperwaite then addressed his senior partner directly, adding, "Got your bloody neck in the harness now for it, Sharpie, and that's likely the only reason Boulte ever came round to the idea. Wants to tighten his reins on you, he does."

"Quiet now, Stuart."

"The man can be an absolute sticky wicket."

"I said stuff it, Coppers."

Copperwaite bit back his lip, his features taking on a more serious appearance, his hair still disheveled from the plane ride.

"Chief Inspector Boulte simply thinks of himself as above the salt," Sharpe said in near apologetic tone to his partner.

"Aye, true."

Jessica had no idea what they meant, and her eyes registered this fact with Sharpe, who added, "In olden days, the salt cellar at the dinner table was a huge affair, as tall as a pedestal, the size of a typical vase, you see, and it marked where the upper- and lower-class citizens sat at the table. Old stout Boulte is somewhat highborn."

Copperwaite added, "He's no alehouse politician."

"Don't know that I've ever seen him take a drop."

"Sounds like what we in the States call a tight-ass," Jessica said, joining them.

"Oh, that he is," agreed Copperwaite, now openly laughing. "And that thing he does, talking about how he gives charitably to all the poor—*all my eye and Betty Martin*, he does! The man's as cold as false charity, that's what!"

"Coppers, you're as near to the man as *damnit* is to swearing. Your skills of observation have improved tremendously to be sure, but to be fair, the man's facing an all-rounder here—a triple homicide," cautioned Sharpe.

"Oh, I've got 'im down, I do. As near as makes no odds. And the man's personality, well, it's all the fun of the fair, right Sharpie?" Copperwaite continued in levity. "And if I hear the man say, 'It won't answer' once more, I shall bloody run from the building screaming."

"And how is that the answer?" joked Sharpe. "Still, you do yourself a sad disservice speaking ill of superiors before such as the driver. Some in the department are paid bonuses to repeat what you and I have to say, Stuart. Believe me."

Jessica studied the modern edifice before them, staring at the entranceway to the famous Scotland Yard, and she asked, "Will your Chief Inspector Boulte be on duty this early?"

"He's lost a good deal of sleep over the Crucifier thing, and he knows we're returning. So yes, he'll likely be here. He'll want a full report. Very proper chap, as they say. Strictly by the book, you see."

"Really?" asked Jessica in a lilting tone. "More so than you?"

"Why, I'm not at all proper, not once you get to know me. Under the right conditions, some would call me a hell-raiser."

"Really?"

London bustled with life all around them, people on the street passing them, cars and double-decker buses blaring anger and resentment, making Jessica wonder if the cops here had as much difficulty with traffic quarrels as those in major cities in America. She guessed they must.

Looking about, Jessica found herself feeling downright naked without an umbrella. Everyone on the street carried a proper umbrella, it appeared. And everywhere, in shops, in doorways, in windows, in the hands of men and women, she saw flowers. Flowers simply abounded here.

"Shall we?" asked Sharpe, indicating the way.

Jessica followed Sharpe through an archway that led to the gleaming glass doors of the modern facility. As in America, the British taxpayer must pay dearly for crime, she thought; her understanding of the tax structure had the average Britisher paying three times as much as the American taxpayer. Back home, she herself paid enough in taxes to finance most third world countries; she felt some pity for the British taxpayer.

They went through a series of brightly lit corridors, down which the *blip-blip-buzz* and drone of noisy offices careened, as if manic to escape the building. They next passed through a door, past cubicles and several glassed in partitions where suspects in various crimes were being rigorously interrogated. Sharpe quipped, "We call that *assisting the police*. Problem is, most of these back-enders speak only back-slang, you know, that peculiarly British pastime of making words up by turning them round, like *ecilop* for police. It's how the term *slop* for police came to be."

Finally they stepped into a larger, open area in which ongoing murder cases were "displayed" to anyone in official capacity and interested in the cases set forth. Each case had its own "booth"—not unlike the booths set up at state fairs and in state capitals to display the work of Jaycee and Booster clubs. But here the subject matter presented a grim portrait of the various horrors dreamed up by mankind, so that the Scotland Yard operations room took on the quality of a house of horrors. The walls were papered with gory crime-scene photos, the tables were littered with the paraphernalia of murder—any and all clues to the identity of the victim, the killer, and the murder weapon. All of it lay before her like the artifacts dug from a recently unearthed archaeological site.

Sharpe and Copperwaite left Jessica and went on to Chief Inspector Boulte's office down the hall. Left alone for the first time since leaving America, Jessica studied the objects on a table below the heading of Crucifixion Murders.

The Scotland Yard detectives hadn't exaggerated. They had nothing to go on. As Copperwaite had put it the day before, "We've nothing, down to the bloody heirs and assigns who stood to gain from the deaths of these three victims, nothing *what-bloody-ever!*"

Victim number one had no living relatives. Victim number two had been estranged from his family, and despite child support and alimony payments, none of the family had heard a word from him in over eleven years. Number three had children, but like number two, he had had nothing to do with his children after a particularly nasty divorce, save sending the assistance checks, which he did like clockwork until his sons came of age and the money dried up.

Obviously, the usual methods, such as following the money trail, proved fruitless in the case of the Crucifier. All money leads had led the detectives nowhere, since in each case the only parties to benefit were each victim's favorite charitable organization. Each left explicit directions, in wills found in their bank vaults, as to how their estates were to be divvied up.

Jessica briefly wondered if, on the whole, Britons took more care with such postmortem matters than did the average American. Victim number one left her meager savings, amounting to 24,000 pounds, to the Church of Christ's Divination; number two left his entire savings, amounting to 36,000 pounds, to the Church of Our Lady of Merciful Tears, while number three ironically left a far greater sum, 170,000 pounds, ironically to the First Church of the Crucifixion.

According to records, each church benefactor had been closely scrutinized, but no collusion or duress raised its ugly head with respect to the various churches to benefit from the deaths of the victims.

The monies all being nontaxable, as they'd gone to charitable organizations, no one in government was interested save the watchdogs who saw to it that the organizations actually did charitable work.

So there appeared no money motive for killing these three individuals. *Unless,* Jessica facetiously thought, *you just happened to be a mad priest capable of knowing what a person's last wishes might be, or capable of accessing their records, say electronically.* After a mild, inward laugh, Jessica dismissed money as a motive, just as Copperwaite and Sharpe had done before her. Her eyes went over the minutia of murder laid out before her. Each item was labeled with a crime-scene number that corresponded to each victim.

Since the bodies were all found nude, early identification of the first two had been nearly impossible; while the third, a relatively well-known radio commentator, had been easier. The bodies *had no pockets*, a phrase in police parlance that meant IDing the victim would require great effort; this also meant that anything lying about the body had either been there before the body was dumped or had belonged to the killer.

As she stared down at the objects lying before her, Jessica realized that the killer may or may not have dropped a lapel button, may or may not have left a cigarette packet found at the scene, may or may not have left prints on the discarded candy-bar wrapper, or on the Essex Hotel ballpoint pen found near one of the bodies. A railway spike labeled "possible" murder weapon lay alongside the items found at the scene, but this had been introduced by the coroner whose guesswork led him to believe the hands and feet were pinned to the cross with something similar in size and weight. The railway spike then had not been recouped from the crime-scene area at all.

Jessica lifted the hefty, metal stake and imagined for a moment what it must feel like as it penetrated flesh and bone at the extremities. The thought gave her a chill. She imagined a helpless victim with three such stakes hammered in to pinion her body to some rough-hewn, splintery surface.

"Unfortunately, we don't have the actual murder weapons used by the killer or killers in this case. They seem cagey, these two. Not so stupid as to leave their prints on the stakes lying about for us to find." It was Chief Inspector Paul Boulte,

Jessica assumed since he'd come in the company of Richard Sharpe.

Boulte stood huge and round, a white James Earl Jones: broad-shouldered, full-faced, a painted grin, and he stood a head taller than Jessica. He appeared to like looking down on her—perhaps all women—from his high eyeball perch. *Gargoyle eyes*, she registered.

"Tidy killers, actually," the big man continued. "Very little blood involved, naturally, given the method of murder, but then that might say something about the prissiness of the killers, mightn't it?"

"Perhaps, but I hardly call staking someone to a cross prissy."

"I merely meant the killer or killers might feel squeamish about blood, that's all," continued the man Jessica had assumed to be Chief Inspector Boulte. He stood fingering some of the artifacts on the death table and quietly introduced himself, shaking her hand.

"Then you gentlemen are of the opinion there is more than one Crucifier?"

"That has become, we feel, apparent."

The Chief Inspector spoke in circles, Jessica realized. "But you are still surmising. No hard evidence of two DNA trails, two hair samples—nothing of a forensic nature to back your suppositions, I take it."

"No, not as yet. But then, that's what you're here for, isn't it?"

Jessica nodded and said, "You won't be disappointed Chief Boulte, not by the FBI." She was, after all, here on his buck. Still, forensic science did not set out to prove a previously established theory; it set out to prove the truth without any taint of preconceived notions. "I suspect that with each new kill, if he follows the pattern of most serial killers, our Crucifier will become more and more brash," she suggested. "Stupid mistakes will follow, I assure you, Chief Inspector."

Impressed by her assuredness, the man extended his hand once again, saying, "And when the killer's big mistake appears, you will be on him, or them, like a terrier, I'm sure."

"You know me better than I'd thought. When it comes to murder I can be a Jack bull terrier, sir."

The frank response took Boulte by surprise, forcing a nervous laugh from him, while Sharpe hid his own amusement. Jessica realized that Sharpe, who had stood aside to watch the sparks, had brought his superior to meet her here in order to show Boulte that Dr. Coran was already earning her keep.

Chief Inspector Boulte now smiled at her, finding her aggressive response to his liking, enough to take her hand hostage again amid his sweaty palms. He said, "I certainly meant no disrespect, nor to imply, Doctor, anything unsavory. Pardon my clumsiness with words. Are you finding London to your liking, Dr. Coran?"

"I hope to see a good deal more of it. I've only just come from the plane."

"So Sharpe here tells me how eager you are to see the results of the Crucifier's maiming. Perhaps you will be my guest tonight for dinner? Allow me to show you the fairer side of our beautiful city, get your mind off this horrid business for a time, once you've finished up with Burton's body, of course."

"Sorry, not tonight," she said automatically. "I'm going to be quite busy tonight. I want to do my own examination of all three of the victims right away."

"Burton, perhaps, but not the other victims, I'm afraid," he replied. "Two of them have been released. We don't like to hold on to them too long. Public opinion, PR, all that, you understand."

"I thought they were pretty much without family."

"Well, the first one, yes, but our freezer compartments are jammed this time of year, and she was getting fairly . . . ripe, if you follow." He brought a guttural laugh from his larynx to spill out over his lips, but he didn't, thank God, drag it out.

Almost in apology for his superior, Sharpe said, "We do have limited space, and Whitehall hasn't seen fit to improve the situation for the past several years now, not to mention the problem with burial plot space, and true to form, division tells us that if we fail to use what space we have left, we shall lose it. The commonwealth will seize it, as it were."

"Where did the body go for burial?"

"She was buried in a potter's field, ancient place in South-hampton owned by the city of London," began Sharpe, his apologetic tone getting much work this morning. "Not one of your more exotic London walking tour cemeteries, I assure you."

"We've got them buried in potter's fields here in layers," added Chief Inspector Boulte. "Some burial plots house as many as four and five residences, one atop the other."

Sharpe, paying little heed to Boulte's attempted thunderbolt of information, continued, saying, "Most A.N. Others are cre-mated, to save on space in the cemetery." She liked the way he pronounced cemetery as *cemet-tree*. "Still, as chief inves-tigator, I did insist we at least keep O'Donahue's body intact for the time being in case we need to review anything later."

"Probably a wise move, Inspector," she told him, holding the railway stake up to the men. "I'd really like to see what kind of a hole this made in her flesh. But, of course, we'll need more than my curiosity to get an exhumation order. I'm sure your government bureaucracy is at least as prickly as ours in America."

"I'm sure we've got you Yanks won on that tally," Boulte replied.

"Second victim's family had a burial plot in Hempstead," explained Sharpe. "Took the body there."

She allowed her surprise to color her features. "Really? I thought the family was estranged from him."

Again, Sharpe clarified for her, saying, "Funny how a crisis of this magnitude can break down those artificial barriers peo-ple impose on one another. Besides, the tabloid press gets interested and all sorts of roaches crawl out of the woodwork. The Coibbys were no different than the usual run of the mill. Still, blood is thicker than water, they say. And for having not seen the man in so long, the members of the family I spoke with were extremely and understandably shaken at *how* he met his end, dying as he did, you see."

"So, do you have victim number three for me to look at, or has someone carted him off, too?" she asked point-blank.

"He's here," assured Sharpe. Then he looked at Boulte for reassurance of the fact. "Right?"

"Yes, of course, as I said earlier to Dr. Coran," Boulte replied to Jessica even though he answered Sharpe, his eyes lingering as his hand had earlier done. "Knowing that you were on your way, we held tight to Mr. Burton, 'The Mole.' " Boulte laughed again, annoying her. Then he feebly explained, "That's what the lab guys are calling him, not me."

"And why are they calling him a mole?"

"His features suggest something of a cross between a ferret, a blind mouse, and a mole."

"I see, then he was, as they say, a plain man?"

"In every respect, yes . . . Quite ordinary, really."

"Take me to see your Mole Man, then, please."

· SIX ·

Evil sleeps and awakes at the tip of the human tongue, often benign, often not, but always present, in a place where deceit has found refuge over the centuries.

—DR. ASA HOLCRAFT, M.E.

They were each and all clothed in robes, their faces shrouded in the manner of supplicating monks. They'd gathered to hear their leader and to determine their next move toward bringing on Christ's new Kingdom on Earth.

The walls were as dark and dingy as their robes; they might have blended into their surroundings had they not been animate. Nearby, the sound of trickling water beat a rhythm, and torches only created glowing circles of light that reached but did not penetrate the blackness of the tunnels all round them.

Like the approach of the year 2001 itself—so terribly long in coming—they shambled nearer, ever nearer with each passing day, hour, *ticktock*. They feared they'd begun this quest far too late, that there simply would not be time enough to complete the task and bask in the afterglow of accomplishment.

Still they held out hope—faith really—hopeful faith instilled on a daily basis through prayer and their leadership. For hope was ever extended to them, and all of mankind, by God the Father and the Son and the Holy Ghost.

Their leader also in deep cowl, now gripped the enormous pulpit which stood in the foreground of an ancient wooden cross standing upright, fixed and waiting, a cross empty and waiting for a new Chosen One to take the place of Christ.

Some twenty-six followers paid rapt attention to the man at the pulpit, hoping his words would console and lift them up.

He cleared his throat and the sound of it echoed off the weeping walls here. Then he said, "The number four, my children, think of it. Four. That is the number—four. Four represents accomplishment, finality, wholeness. That is the belief of the cabalists and alchemists—religions lost in time, before Christ himself. Yet it holds true, in Christian teaching, that this number is a highly charged, holy number and has been since time's beginning. It represents the four elements, the four stages of life: infancy, youth, midlife, and old age. And so we believe—*and so we all believe as one mind*—that our fourth crucifixion will provide the answers sought by all: all the answers ever asked by all mankind. The mysteries of the universe revealed to those who believe, and they alone. *For it came to pass that they alone sought true and utter purity and rapture.* That all others were made blind and dumb to the sound of His voice."

But dissension, inevitable among even Jesus' followers, invaded the temple. One of their number pointed out, "But we have chosen badly and wrongly."

A second angry voice cried out, "None of those targeted to die on the cross have been a *right and righteous* choice."

"Wrong," their leader insisted.

"How so, wrong?" pressed a follower, another doubting voice.

He clearly, calmly, evenly pointed out, "In order to find and make the right choice, wrong choices are a necessary part of the process of getting from here to there. God is testing us one and all, my friends. Only through adversity does the spirit enter this world. So only through mistakes and pain and suffering can Christ come to us at this the time of the actual millennium. We were all made fools by thinking it was 2000, but as we now know 2001 is our true millennium."

Another of their number pointed out, "If the integer four means accomplishment, then the integer eight would mean accomplishment twofold, would it not?"

"If it is God's will that we crucify eight whom we choose to go before us, then so be it," their leader replied sharply.

"If it take a hundred, then so be it." The battlelike discussion inside and out of the mosque of mind and the synagogue of soul within their leader had raged now for days.

In the meantime, they'd crucified no one. "We must stop getting in the way," he told them in simple terms, "in our own way, slowing progress toward *any* completion. Now, I tell you that the number four is, after all, special, any way we may look at it."

"So, we look for number four . . ."

"Number four . . ."

"Number four," they took up the chant.

Their leader breathed a bit easier, seeing that his persuasive hold on them and his struggle to maintain control had, for the time being, won out.

"Number four!" he shouted to the earthen ceiling of this place, his enormous voice seeming to shake the huge cross behind him.

Scotland Yard Crime Lab and Postmortem Room

Theodore Burton's body, still as glass, a fishy underbelly-white hue overall, lavender with touches of purple—where bruises had formed—spoke nothing to Jessica. It lay before Jessica hard as linoleum from its time in the cooler, shriveled, and now the sheetlike skin with multiple folds looked back at her as if to say, *Go ahead, I challenge you to read anything from this body.*

Certainly the body stood in stark contrast to Tattoo Man back in the States. Not a mark on Burton save those obvious and horrid wounds to hands and feet that spoke volumes about exactly how Theodore Burton—the Mole—met his end: stark death via crucifixion.

Standing about the postmortem room, ostensibly to watch over Jessica's shoulder, Boulte and Sharpe showed signs of restlessness. More so Boulte than Sharpe, but Jessica had long stopped paying heed to either man. She did a mental Houdini, making them vanish from both the room and her focus.

Burton had once been heavy, but the thin frame looked as if he'd suffered some debilitating disease late in life, causing both body and face to wither. The punishment to the features seemed obvious to Jessica, and this also contributed to his ferretlike features. One certainty: He'd been completely out of shape, that much the body assured her. Certainly, he was in no shape to withstand the rigors of a crucifixion of many hours. He likely succumbed early to the torturous stress placed on his muscles and lungs.

Jessica found herself staring across the body at a dark-skinned doctor whose height challenged Jessica not to look down on him. His small head and beaky nose gave him the appearance of a rodent, yet his smile appeared genuine. He tried to put her at ease with his name by pronouncing it slowly and carefully as, "Al . . . just call me Al. It's easier than Al-Zay-don Ray-hill."

"And I'm Jessica," she replied, reading his nameplate: DR. AL-ZADAN RAEHAEL.

They shook hands and Jessica asked, "Did you check for any signs of cancer, Dr. Raehael?"

"I am assistant M.E. for Dr. Karl Schuller, the attending autopsiest here at Scotland Yard crime lab. Such an order must come from him, unless I have the body. That is, unless it comes to my attention first. Rules, but to answer your question, I rather doubt it."

"So, no general interest in disease prior to death?"

"Ahhh, no, we did not search for that. I did not, not specifically, no. Dr. Schuller saw no need for that. Mr. Burton died of asphyxiation from hanging for hours on a cross, Doctor." The last came out in a derisive tone that the genteel Egyptian accent could not mask.

"Hours," she chorused. "Exactly how many hours did Dr. Schuller surmise?"

"What difference?"

"I merely wondered if he'd been suffering from any malady *before* his death. If so, perhaps Mr. Burton thwarted the killer."

"How is it do you mean?"

"Any abnormality may have contributed to a curtailing of the Crucifier's fun and games, as well as to a lessening of the victim's suffering."

On the defensive now, Dr. Schuller's assistant replied, "What good does that information do in circumstances of this nature?"

Jessica examined the assistant more carefully. He was a black-eyed, black-haired little man. Somewhat round, his skin was pockmarked and rough, his attitude both subservient and challenging all at once. The small man's eyes bore into her, watching her every move, suspicious perhaps, and from his tone of voice, obviously unimpressed with her.

Sharpe wanted to hear more on this matter. "We brought Dr. Coran from America because of her reputation, Dr. Raehael."

"Yes, we have all heard at Scotland Yard how attention to detail is your trademark, Dr. Coran. However, the man's illnesses or lack of illnesses—had we done tests to ascertain either—hardly contributed to his slow, heinous, and torturous death. Does your FBI still rank the degree of torture to the victim as the most important fact in prosecuting offenders?"

Evasive fellow, Jessica thought even as she replied. "We still have a torture chart with levels to plot out the extent of torture endured by a victim, yes. This would—given the amount of time the victim suffered—be calculated in the upper levels, something of a *tort nine,* perhaps even a *ten.*"

Sharpe directed the conversation back on course, telling Raehael, "Dr. Coran didn't say that Burton's condition and health before his crucifixion would have contributed to his death, quite the contrary," corrected Sharpe. "What Dr. Coran is suggesting, if I'm hearing her correctly, is that Burton may have died a *less* torturous death—at least in terms of time in suffering—*if* he were in a weakened condition to begin with."

"That about sums it up," Jessica agreed.

Sharpe continued for Raehael's sake while the small, dark man nodded appreciatively and in silence. "The healthier our victim, in this case, the more time on the cross. Is that not what you're saying, Dr. Coran?"

"Precisely." Jessica bit back her anger at the complacency of the assistant M.E. and turned her attention back to the deceased, wondering why the dead man spoke to her—even in his serene and solemn silence—more intelligently than the living man standing across from her. Still, the body, like a ship with a hardened outer shell now, defied the scalpel—defied her as well—to unlock its secrets. Secrets locked away in a dark chamber called death. Nothing new in and of itself, but something more seemed at play here. Something grimly pleasant about the dead man's expression also defied logic; he appeared at absolute peace.

As if reading her thoughts, Sharpe broke in with, "Odd, that expression on his face, wouldn't you say, Doctor?"

"Death wears any number of masks," she replied, reminding herself of a favored Holcraft quote: *"Even bodies with the rictus smile—that ugly, snakelike crease—had nothing whatever to do with the victim's frame of mind, as it was a natural alignment of the muscles of the jaw that occurred in not all but many cases of death."*

So why should a pleasant smile be questioned any more than a horrid smile?

She almost heard the long-silenced voice of her old teacher and mentor, Dr. Asa Holcraft, mimicking her thoughts as if standing alongside her. Now she knew she needed to get more sleep.

Still, like a persistent hologram, Holcraft's apparition stood nodding his pleasure at her concern. He agreed with her, up to a point, but then he had also always staunchly maintained, *"A strong spiritual element, a filamentlike thread of spirit, remains even in the decaying corpse."*

Asa had always believed that spirit resided not only in the living but also in the dead. He had felt that at least some semblance of the spirit remained, and this spirit remnant could be found, perhaps understood, if only the doctor gave enough of himself or herself over to the task. Holcraft had even believed that it was the job of the M.E. to hold firm and seek out all spiritual connection between medical examiner and corpse, even in severe cases of fire, bombings, and explosive airplane crashes.

"So what of the crucified?" she muttered aloud.

"What?" asked Sharpe.

"Oh, nothing." Jessica also believed that some spirit element hovered about the body, doing all it could to communicate with the pathologist. She believed it the key element in so many of her instinctual leaps of faith in discerning the true nature of a crime. She owed a great deal to Asa for that.

She recalled just how good Holcraft had been as a teacher and as a medical examiner. He had had her looking for spirits in every cadaver she handled. *"Some of the spirits you'll find not to your liking, others tender,"* he had once confided with a Kriss Kringle twinkle in his eyes, his white beard bobbing up and down.

She focused in again on the body itself, seeing the familiar, large, Y-shaped scar from each shoulder to the groin area, the universal Y-cut, understood by every mortician and pathologist and medical examiner. Dr. Schuller's work greeted Jessica every step of the way; the autopsiest had already taken samples and weights of all the major organs during the initial autopsy, but the toxicological and medical tests that Schuller ran had been, by Dr. Schuller's own admission, limited to a few serum and toxicology reports. No one had run a full workup on the cadaver. Such tests ran up bills . . . and Burton was no member of the Royal elite. No going the extra mile for Burtie.

Dr. Karl Schuller, while not present, made his presence felt throughout this crime lab like a well hung, saturated blanket. The paperwork on Burton felt rushed. She wondered if he had any prejudice against Burton, if it at all entered into the man's work over the body of Theodore Burton, who had been born Emil Burlinstein. She feared that Dr. Karl Schuller hadn't been as thorough as he might have been in such a capital murder case. Still, Jessica doubted that raising such questions could be of any possible use at this late date. It might be best at this point to leave it alone. If she did pursue the issue of shoddy work in the Scotland Yard crime lab, she would do so vigorously, as Holcraft whispered in her ear: *"Order a full toxicological and tissue mapping of the cadaver to determine the condition of the man's body, health, and well-being. Frequently, what is central to the cause of death, existed before death.* Often, such total, complete, and expensive measures added some nuggets of information otherwise lost to an investigation, and just as often the effort netted nothing.

"Something troubling you, Doctor?" asked Sharpe near her ear.

"Yes, something is nagging at me about the sudden loss of weight signaled by the folds of loose skin."

"I see."

"A forensic profiler often begins with the physical as well as the mental health of the victim."

"So, you surmise that perhaps Burton's state of mind had something to do with the way in which he met his end?"

"And if his body had been in a shutdown mode, then perhaps this led him to some extreme measures in search of a cure. Perhaps in search of miracles and miracle drugs, the man reached out in desperation."

"Which led him down a particularly nasty lane."

"As perhaps it did in the cases of Lawrence Coibby and the Crucifier's first victim, the woman."

"O'Donahue."

"Maybe all three, for instance, sought out medical help at the same clinic or pharmacy. If each had been lured into some sort of web, partially of the victim's own spinning due to ill health or depression, then perhaps somewhere along the complex of each life-web, they crossed paths, and if I—or we, rather—can find some interconnecting thread . . ."

Schuller, the man who'd prepared all the slides and gathered all the minutia on Theodore Burton's body, had been notified of Dr. Coran's interest. He now came belatedly through the door from his Kensington address to confer with the famous American medical examiner.

Dr. Karl Schuller, nodding familiarly to Dr. Raehael, Chief Inspector Boulte, and Inspector Sharpe, now introduced himself to Jessica. His eyes were unblinking as he buoyantly proclaimed, "Welcome to the lab of the Nazi death-master." He added, "That's what they call me upstairs. Behind my back, of course, right Inspector Sharpe? Chief Boulte, right?" He waited for no answer from either Sharpe or Boulte who fumbled with words to reply. Schuller continued on instead with, "Yes, I am the official 'death-master' here, you will find. All responsibility for this lab falls on my shoulders." He smiled cordially at Jessica, and with a slight bow and a slight edge to his German accent—an accent he'd worked hard to master—he said for her benefit, "If there is anything at all I can do for you to make your investigation simpler, please do not hesitate to ask."

"Thank you, Dr. Schuller. I'll certainly avail myself of your hospitality." Jessica summed him up as he spoke: stiff, uncompromising, proud, angry at her having been called in on *his* case to lend *him* assistance and not at all wishing to be in the least help to her, his mildly German accent masked by his British tongue.

The cadaver had been washed clean, the wounds hardly as ghastly as those seen in the crime-scene photos, now that the crucifixion holes had had time to sink in on themselves. The holes in the hands and feet, however, were large enough and gruesome and strange enough to warrant Jessica's undivided attention. She snatched a large magnifying glass on a swivel arm and placed it between her eyes and the crucifixion wound to the right hand.

Soon her silence, her intense scrutiny, made Schuller and Boulte particularly uneasy. She *felt* Schuller stiffen even more, and she felt Boulte's body language behind her where he rocked nervously from his heels to the balls of his feet and back again, clearing his throat, and finally excusing himself, telling Richard Sharpe in a tone loud enough for all, "I have bushels of ancient paperwork awaiting upstairs."

Jessica guessed that Boulte must be thinking better of ever having asked her out, and that there would likely be no second attempt. For this she felt grateful.

Boulte promptly said, "I'll leave you four to it then, Richard, Doctors. Oh, and Richard, do keep me informed, please."

Jessica quickly, efficiently moved on with her investigation, reading notes into a small tape recorder she'd used on many such errands. "Noting the otherwise unhealthy appearance of the deceased, and having read Dr. Schuller's detailed autopsy report on the victim, Theodore Burton, it appears the victim died of asphyxia due to crucifixion torture. Holes in hands and feet measuring three-fourths to an inch in diameter were fitted with stakes recovered from railroad yard rail ties. My own findings are consistent with Dr. Schuller's findings."

She knew that her final remarks put Schuller somewhat at ease. Even Sharpe seemed to relax his stiff posture. Her words were designed for that effect.

"Are you quite satisfied, then?" asked Schuller. "Of my diagnosis?"

Jessica continued to probe the body with the movable magnifying glass, the arm outstretched like the leg of a robotic praying mantis. She searched for the telltale signs of puncture marks mentioned in the reports. She found them in both thighs, the abdomen, and the rump.

"He appears to have been shooting up pretty regularly. Diabetic, you think?"

"No, he wasn't shooting insulin. He was shooting up drugs—a wide variety from the look of his blood scan."

"So he was an addict?"

"Exactly."

"Did anyone check for diabetes?"

"There was no need after the drug findings and the gaping wounds to the hands and feet," countered Schuller, his guard up again like a shield.

Jessica dropped the subject of the obvious oversight. "What about the other two victims? Any evidence of drugs other than Brevital used in subduing them?"

"Matter-of-fact, yes. It's the one common denominator found in all three cases, but then, given the pervasive presence of drugs in London society nowadays. . . . Well, there you have it. No great shock. Rather think it should come as no surprise to an experienced forensics person like yourself," Schuller said, his tone turned slightly condescending.

"You think a lifestyle of habitual drug use had anything to do with their becoming victims?" On either side of the Atlantic the thinking was the same—most victims of violent death lived lives that courted such disasters. For the most part she couldn't deny that it held true, but the argument also lost in the end like blaming the rape on the raped woman. No one deserved murder or to be scammed out of their life's savings because they acted out of a desperation brought on by illness or old age. Still no one, coroners, pathologists, and medical examiners included, was without his or her prejudices. It sounded to Jessica, if she accurately read between the lines, that Schuller had an aversion to druggies.

Despite the choice of lifestyle, she maintained silently in her head that the victim did not nail himself to a cross. He did not kill himself. The victims were killed by someone of superior strength and cunning, possibly someone taking full advantage of the victims' weakest of weaknesses.

"Those who live by the needle, you know," Schuller added, confirming Jessica's assessment of the good doctor. "Inspector Sharpe can attest to it. We've all seen it. An addict necessarily must associate with the dregs of society, those even lower on the food chain than the addict.... The slightest something goes wrong and it's *execution time.*"

"I can't see a drug dealer crucifying addicts for nonpayment of debt, sorry," Jessica replied, unable to listen to Schuller's nonsense any longer without comment. "Did you examine the female victim for signs of diabetes or other life-threatening diseases?"

"I urged you to do exactly that," Sharpe said to Schuller.

Schuller shook his head. "All of them died not of disease but of evil mishandling. Someone cut off their oxygen supply to watch them die slowly and torturously. End of forensic story."

"Did you check the woman for signs of sexual battery?" asked Jessica.

"Yes, and there were none."

"Small favors," she muttered, her hands now lifting Burton's punctured left foot closer to the magnifying glass. "What about souvenirs? Did the killer or killers take anything from the woman's body? Anything cut off and gone missing from *any* of the three bodies?"

"Nothing of the sort," replied Schuller.

"I see, and the men, both intact."

"Nothing stolen, save the breath of life."

"So unusual," she murmured thoughtfully.

"What's that?" asked Sharpe.

"That the killer should not retain something of his conquests, something of a souvenir. A token to memorialize the moment, a keepsake, say like some of the hair, a hand, a sex organ, an internal organ, the heart, something to mark the occasion, to lift from his box of memorabilia to relive the moment at some later date."

Schuller lifted his chin high and said, "I assure you that Burton and the others were totally and wholly intact, not so much as a hair disturbed, other than the brutality done them as you see before you, Dr. Coran."

She nodded and addressed Sharpe. "Could be part of the killer's fantasy, to send them over whole and intact . . . as pure as he can make them, perhaps. Still, the killer may've made videotapes to commemorate their—"

"Videotapes?" Raehael was aghast.

"A perfectly awful thought," said Sharpe. "You do think like a killer, don't you, Dr. Coran?"

"Tapes of their deaths," she repeated. "Remember, Christ hung on the cross for what, minimum three hours before he expired? Lot of time for photographs and videotape. Many serial killers collect pictures of the event."

"If we imagine it all had to do with some sort of religious fantasy, involving the crucifixion—the blood, oil, and the water, all having rejuvenative powers, according to biblical symbolism—then any mutilation of the body, such as taking of a body part, might well interfere with the reanimation, the resurrection as it were. Do you suppose the killer or killers think they have the power to resurrect the dead?"

"It's a possibility, yes. Nothing's too fantastic for the fevered, psychotic mind."

Richard nodded. "All sounds logical in a twisted way, of course."

"If that is the case, it must've hurt the killer's sense of order and cleanliness to see the O'Donahue woman's body run over," she commented.

"I'm sure," agreed Sharpe. "However, I do hope we can hurt the bastard in more places than his sensibilities."

"I suppose it does sound foolish to speak of a killer's sense of order. But a killer like this one who premeditates, prescribes, stalks, plans out his kill, Inspector, is certainly concerned with a sense of orderliness and conduct in what he does." She momentarily wondered whether or not J. T. back at home was having any luck with Tattoo Man's case. Now there was a case involving a deadly planning out of every detail. She wondered what, if anything, the two disparate cases might have in common.

Sharpe near-whispered, "Do you think we can catch this madman anytime soon?"

"In time. All in due time, Inspector."

He set his jaw and nodded. "Are we finished here?"

She considered the pros and cons of asking that Burton's body be tested for disease of every sort. What might it net, what problems would it cause between the British doctors and herself? She finally said, "Yes, all done. These gentlemen have done a thorough job of it."

But the spirit in the corpse didn't think so, for slowly, almost imperceptibly, the swollen dead tongue, bloated to near bursting, parted the smiling lips and peeked out like a cautious gray gecko. The tongue kept moving now that it had parted the lips, moving as if independent of the body, as if it remained somehow alive. Forward it came, of its own accord, to lie over the lower lip where it stopped.

"What in God's name?" whispered Sharpe.

"Never seen anything like it," added young Dr. Raehael.

"Not unusual in my experience," Jessica said, albeit unnerved. Such artificial life movements in the dead always caused a ripple of fear in anyone looking on. The tongue made Burton's already distorted features an impious gargoyle's snicker. The overall effect made Burton a macabre clown poking fun to both startle and taunt all in the room.

Schuller, although curious, kept a straight face, while Jessica grabbed for the large magnifying glass on its swivel arm and focused it on the tongue, asking, "Had you seen this swelling before?" She wondered if it were not indicative of some exotic disease.

"Yes, it was mentioned as an addendum to my report," countered Schuller.

Jessica, not knowing why, found a pair of large forceps and pulled the tongue as far as the corpse would allow her, staring at the decaying, bloated thing for some time before she lifted it to stare at the underside, and there she found something that made them all gasp—some sort of brand.

"Son-of-a Bristol whore," said Sharpe. "Oh, pardon, Dr. Coran, but what the deuce is it?"

Schuller couldn't hide his confusion, nor the shakiness where he stood on the balls of his feet across from Jessica, staring at the blackened flesh. He finally asked, "Is it some sort of emblem?"

"Lettering . . ."

"What's that?"

"It appears to be lettering of some sort, but I can't make it out. Was there anything of the sort on the other two bodies?"

"No, some swelling of the tongue, but no . . . no branded letters on the underside of the tongues, no," replied Schuller. "But then . . ."

"But," Jessica finished for him, "there'd been no reason to look below the tongue, right?"

"Exactly, and what with the understaffing here and the overworked help . . ."

Sharpe, more interested in the message than the verbal jousting between doctors, firmly asked, "Can you make out what it says?"

"Small lettering. Guy had to use jeweler's tools or tattoo parlor tools or a hot brand to make this happen," Jessica replied, again thinking there may well be some connections unforeseen between Tattoo Man and the crucified dead here in London.

Sharpe, craning to see, demanded, "You can read it with the glass, can't you, Dr. Coran?"

"It's partially obliterated from where the integrity of the skin has collapsed in on itself, but the first letter appears to be *M*."

"Anything else?"

"*M-i-h-i*," she slowly read, each letter qualified by her tentative tone, like someone reading a chart in an optometrist's office. "I think, but don't hold me to it. And the message goes on."

"Saying what?" Sharpe bent over her shoulder now, trying

desperately to have a look, pushing against her, close enough that she could smell his cologne.

"Can't say without closer examination."

"What will that require?"

"What I really must do is cut out the tongue, strip the skin, and place it beneath electron microscope magnifica—"

"Ironic . . . Cut out his tongue? The man made a living with that tongue," said Dr. Schuller, sounding disturbed.

"There's more to the message, Doctor," she countered.

"I realize that, but suppose it's a mere affectation, say as you suggest, like a tattoo or tongue piercing, and all your time in cutting and searching for linguistic evidence is all a blind corridor?"

"Sharpe, it's your investigation," she said. "Tell us what you want."

"You're certain there's more to the message?"

"Absolutely, but the only way to get at it is to remove the tongue, spray it with a fixative and fillet it flat, and skin the portion with the message. It's the only way we can tell the age of the brand and whether or not it came about when he was still alive or after death."

"What the bloody hell does *Mihi* mean?" Sharpe wondered aloud.

No one in the room knew the answer.

"Sounds kinda Hawaiian to me," Jessica said. "Have you a linguistics expert on call?"

"We do. Father Luc Sante. He's a Catholic priest as well."

"Get him in here, then. I think Mr. Burton has made one thing clear. He wants to tell us something after all, and here I'd judged him wrong, thinking him stonily silent."

"I caution you not to rush headlong into this decision, Richard," Schuller said, putting a hand on Sharpe's shoulder and stepping him aside to huddle and whisper like boys playing football.

Schuller's assistant—the marble black eyes appearing a bit droopy and unfocused from a definite lack of sleep or no lack of drugs—nervously swallowed and tried to find anywhere to look but into Jessica's eyes. His demeanor said, "Yes, we royally screwed up here," but he kept the words to himself.

Sharpe suddenly walked away from Schuller, his teeth set, his jaw squared. Then he announced in clear defiance of Schuller, "Fillet the damned tongue."

This made the other men laugh nervously. Jessica snatched out her scalpel case. Using the stainless-steel scalpel her father had given her when she graduated from medical school, she tugged at the tongue with forceps in one hand and worked to slice it off with the other. As usual, removing a tongue proved no easy task, as the last fibrous threads stubbornly held on. Finally, with two quick flicks of her wrist, Burton's tongue lay in her hand like a baby trout.

"Short of peeling the skin, I'll try filleting the tongue and sectioning it as thinly as possible to fit below the eyepiece of the largest microscope you have, Dr. Schuller. I don't think we'll need to bombard it with electrons, so we won't need the electron microscope. That would only destroy the physical evidence anyway."

"Evidence of what?" Schuller remained skeptical.

Jessica went about the business of sectioning. She examined the other words of the small, cryptic message below the lens of a huge microscope that Schuller's assistant had pointed out to her. She read aloud what she saw before her. "*P*—no, it's a *b*—followed by *e-a-t* something *mater*." She then read aloud the entire message, "*Mihi be eat a mater.*"

"Sounds like Greek," said the Egyptian assistant.

"More likely Latin," replied Sharpe. "Something about beautiful or blessed mother, *mater* being mother, and if you put the *b* and the *eat* and an *a* together, it's *beata*, beautiful or quite possibly blessed. Blessed mother, which pertains, of course, to Mary, Mother of Christ," explained Sharpe, qualifying with, "But don't quote me. Father Luc Sante . . . he would know, most certainly. We've used him in cases before, often cases involving psychotics. He's a psychotherapist as well."

Stuart Copperwaite appeared from nowhere at Jessica's shoulder, asking, "What's this?"

Jessica was startled into dropping the portion of slippery tongue she'd balanced beneath the microscope lens, only to further obliterate the message. "Sonofabitch," she muttered under her breath. "Damnit," she more clearly cursed and stared at Stuart Copperwaite whose shoulders lifted like those of a puppet on a string.

"I am sorry," he pleaded, trying to help her lift the slippery fish from the floor, but managing only to cause more havoc.

"Will you just back off?" she shouted.

Copperwaite gasped and backed away as she had asked.

The message had been ripped and torn and parts of it were down the drain on the floor where it had splattered.

"We may have to exhume the other bodies to have a clearer look at this," she pointedly said to Sharpe. Then Jessica turned to Dr. Raehael and said, "Take a few photos of what remains of the wording, Doctor."

The little Egyptian nodded, his mouth agape, displaying good teeth.

"O'Donahue's tongue can't be intact after all this time. Maybe Coibby, but I doubt it," Schuller thought openly and loudly. "Soft tissue decay."

"Coibby then!" Jessica firmly replied. "We've got to know what we're chasing after in the dark, and this, gentlemen, is the first bit of light we've had. It may prove a false light, but for now, it behooves us to treat it as a divine light, a gift."

"Right you are, Doctor," agreed Sharpe. "If the others have this same mark on their tongues, then it originated, most likely, with the killer. I shall see to the exhumation order personally."

Shouldn't have released the damned bodies to begin with, Jessica thought. The thought colored her features, but she withstood the desire to throw it into Schuller's now less than smug face. "As for me, I'd like to find that hotel room you promised, Inspector Sharpe. Get some rest, maybe a bite."

"Absolutely. I'll see a car is waiting for you, Doctor."

With that, Jessica tore from the postmortem room, ripping her surgical mask and gown away, tossing them into a large, green hamper. Her mind played over the possible single clue left them by the killer. The words *Mihi beata mater* reverberated in a chant, a tight, enticing, rhythmic chant.

· SEVEN ·

Evil originates not in the absence of guilt but in the attempt to escape from it.

—M. SCOTT PECK,
PEOPLE OF THE LIE

The walls dulled all reverberation of the aboveground evening traffic that filtered down to them as a strange lilting chant resonating through the ancient stones, creating its own tone, pitch, note, and timbre. Even the walls chanted, remembering the words *Mihi beata mater. . . .* Theirs was a cave below the beleaguered city of London, a rat's den, yet a holy place where they might practice their special brand of religion unharmed and unrestrained. They were in complete safety from blind humanity above who went about their regimented lives like ants without question of time or space or God or soul. It was a place cool in summer and warm in winter, a place where only the sacred tred, where nothing profane nor evil could step one single foot before being smote into ash, so predicted their leader who had painstakingly sought out and found this place.

"Hear the walls?" he often asked. For here, the walls spoke a clear *oommmmmm, oommmmmm, oommmmmm* that never stopped, no more than the trickling water sounds could be stopped. Lately, the walls reverberated with the three words *Mihi beata mater, Mihi beata mater, Mihi beata mater. . . .*

The walls bled water that seeped in from the streets of London above the ancient, Roman-built catacombs where they met in secret ceremony. The walls became slick and mirror-like in their wetness, the evening rains above finding them. The ancient walls told stories, spoke of Roman conquest, of debauchery and defilement, of a time when Christians had been slaughtered here, further making this place sacrosanct. The walls might as well run with blood as with God's tears, their leader had more than once declared.

"Why are we beseeched so? Why are we tested so? Why, Oh Precious One? Why do You make me blind that I will not know, but must accept all Holy Writ on faith and faith alone?" he preached aloud to those who followed him, in the makeshift chapel, where an ancient altar of thick, coarse oak, and an equally ancient cross of the same wood, stood as sturdy props—the only holy props aside from the torches and the branding fire that awaited use again. "Why are we tested so?" he repeated, his words like thunder.

"Offer us hope!" cried out one among the congregation.

Their leader looked out on his small following, which was dwindling with each new meeting. There appeared less than forty who would step over into the true millennium with him and the newfound Christ.

"Send Thy divine message through this wretched vessel, so that others might also accept Your grace and reckoning," he continued. "Be not dismayed at our weaknesses, our failings, and give us Thy strength. If not in numbers then give it to us in power—the divine power that is You, Lord Jehovah." He slavered at the mouth with his pronouncement.

The others wore the robes of monks—robes he had secured for them—their faces covered in hoods like cowls, and each looked up in solemn wonder at the depth of their leader's passion, his compassion and his faith. Each thought: He must know. He must indeed have the ear of God as no man else.

It made perfect sense, even if on the surface of it they did appear to have failed three times in their attempts at the resurrection of a life, a life which the Son would inveigh with His very own divine presence in the Second Coming, to mark the second millennium—the true millennium. Their leader, a man of worldly knowledge and otherworldly passion, of outward and inward beauty, had said so. He had explained it entirely and utterly to their satisfaction, more than once.

The message went forth clear and concise, a kind of soliloquy in which their humble leader lamented again his choice for the Messiah. "As spiritual father of the collective, believing in all that we do and have done in the name of the Father, I cannot now unbelieve anymore than I can undo the steps we have taken. I accept the wisdom of the Son and the Holy Ghost, believing in all that we have put our blessed trust into. . . . In Your name, Lord Jehovah, we beseech Thee to guide our darkened path."

"It is dark indeed!" cried out one of the many.

"Show us the way!" pleaded another from behind closed eyelids.

Their leader had, after Coibby, turned to the well-to-do, born-again radio personality, Theodore "Ted" Burton. He had believed beyond any doubt that the man was the Messiah walking. . . . The Messiah, walking the Earth incognito, begging to be brought out into the light of recognition for all to see. For a time, Burton had looked like, felt like, sounded like, smelled like, and appeared to be God's Son—the Jew who had renounced Judaism in the name of Christ the Lord.

"Who better than a Jew to become Jesus, who was, after all, a Jew?" he'd instructed them back then.

"We all did love Burton for the part," he reminded his congregation now. "For his having renounced Judaism and his embracing the true church. But in the end, Burton proved an even greater disappointment than the two previous sacrifices. What say you, my followers? Is it not time to select a new Messiah?"

He looked out over his diminished flock, and it—they—seemed to be disappearing, vanishing before his eyes. One here, one there . . . They appeared defeated, tired, shriveled, atrophied as a group. They looked old, worn, frustrated, yet wanting guidance and reassurances. A fleeting thought beamed through the electrochemical network of his brain: He wondered if he were not they, and if they were not he, all in all, one in the same? Mannequins in a mindless world of chance and hallucination, smoke and mirrors, none of it real, none of it under the control of any universal power, more chaotic than Alice's Wonderland. But even as the thought formed in his head, he banished it with a more pious and self-recriminating one: How dare I exhault myself above the others, to stand here at this altar over their heads while they keep dropping off? Dying from view. I can't walk among them anymore, can't truly touch them ever again, so separate have I become. I, too, have vanished, and I, too, am weary of this tired world, but I have been called on, and I must heed His call to find the fourth Messiah.

Then it occurred to him: as a sea washes a lovely starfish to one's feet, so the idea came floating from an unseen hand. And it fit. It made perfect sense that God's Son would be a matrix of human qualities, that no single human posssessed them all. That in crucifying the others they had in fact created a kind of bank, a holding place, for all of the virtues Christ must have for the Second Coming.

Now he must determine when, where, and how to best explain this new revelation to his followers. The simple poetic vision, the simplicity of the truth alone, must be seen by the others as Divine Intervention. He raised the blood of Christ to his lips and drank a toast to the beauty of it all, the perfect syncopation of a plan that he'd taken on blind faith but was now coming into full-blown focus.

The York proved absolutely gorgeous, a fabulous place to stay, and the plush bed that Jessica slept in had allowed for a good night's rest. Dining in the breakfast nook overlooking the Victoria Gardens proved so relaxing that she almost forgot why she had come to London. She cursed the fact that she did not have time to see the sights, to breathe in the history and romance of this ancient city. Her limited time here would be wrapped up with the dark underbelly of London and the bleakness of forensic work, the evil at hand, the evil destroying the peace, an evil staining all the beauty.

On arriving at the hotel in late afternoon the day before, after her Burton autopsy, she'd walked out to the spot where Copperwaite and Sharpe had first encountered Katherine O'Donahue's naked body. In fact, Stuart Copperwaite, who had gallantly escorted her to the York Hotel, had offered to also accompany her to the Victoria Gardens Embankment.

Below the bridge stumbled the same drunken bridgeman, who had frightened off the Crucifier and had run over the "evidence." He foolishly waved at them as they searched the crime scene.

Jessica walked the path most likely taken by the Crucifier. Copperwaite and Sharpe had shrewdly assessed where the killer's "transport"—as they called his car—had most likely been parked so as to draw no attention. Copperwaite pointed out the spot. He also pointed out the likely trail where the body was carried toward water's edge before being dropped when the bridgeman's headlights surprised and frightened the killer or killers. No footprint impressions had been found as just enough rain fell in those hours before dawn to obliterate human tracks. Copperwaite explained, "But tire tracks were found and impressions taken that night. Unfortunately, the impressions matched literally hundreds of thousands of tires used in England, and so long as there remains no suspect, we have no suspect car to match impressions to."

As she'd walked with Copperwaite last night, Jessica had asked, "How long have you and Sharpe been partners?"

"Not long at all, actually." Copperwaite reminded her of Hugh Grant with some girth. He wore a perpetual, sly grin. "Sharpie lost his last partner in a gun battle over some drugs filtering in from Algiers. Nasty bit of luck. Then I come on with him, almost a month after. It's been two years now."

"You seem awfully—I don't know—alike?"

"Alike? Sharp and me? Ha! As different as chalk and cheese, we are."

"Close, then. You seem *close.*"

"Aye, that we are. Have to be close in every way, now don't we? Have to know the habits, the good and bad of one another to put your life in another's hands, you see. Isn't it done the same in your country?"

"Yes, very much so."

"Sharpie's one of the best, if not the best. Ought to have had Boulte's job, you see, but then, you know how it goes. Over here, we have a saying 'bout that."

She smiled knowingly but said, "Oh? And what's that?"

"*Buggin's turn*, we call it."

"Meaning?"

"Meaning every fool is given a turn at a job until all the fools have been exhausted. Meaning Sharpe was unfairly treated, and Boulte was promoted in order to demonstrate the height of stupidity in the Yard, to demonstrate Boulte's special brand of awe-inspiring incompetence."

"I get your meaning."

"You read what the *Times* had to say about our flaming Boulte? They're right on, they are. The man's a clot, a bloody, blinking, ballying, flipping, flaming, ruddy bastard! And he's a clawback as well, he is."

"A 'clawback'?"

"Toady, I suppose you'd say. Claw at your backside as it were."

She wondered what Boulte had done to deserve Copperwaite's total disdain. "Can you say that again, in its entirety, from the beginning?" she asked. "About Boulte. It sounded so resonant."

They laughed. Jessica turned to stare out across at the majestic Thames that wound its shimmering, ribbonlike self about the palacelike structures on either embankment. Sightseeing boats and ferries dotted the water. The sunshine and surroundings defied the fact of anyone's having been murdered here, and she said as much to Stuart. Copperwaite handily replied, "Curly it was, awfully curly that dark morning we come on her."

"Curly?"

"Awful gruesome, mum, Doctor. You can't imagine, seeing those bloodied hands, the gaping holes through 'em."

Jessica and Copperwaite walked back to the York where he had tea and she coffee with crumpets. Tired, she had said good night to Stuart in the lobby.

That had been last night. This morning, Jessica had taken the *London Times*, left at her door, down to breakfast with her, and read the lambasting given the Yard for having done nothing *visible* about the murdering Crucifier and for *allowing* the monster to roam freely through the streets of London. In a scathing attack on the steps—or lack of steps—taken by Scotland Yard, sidebar photos of the dead victims posed in life and in death framed the story. A reporter named Culbertson tore into Chief Inspector Paul Boulte as being unable to "rise to the level of competence." She thought the quote sounded suspiciously like something that might have come out of Copperwaite's mouth.

"The only ray of hope in all of this horror," wrote Erin Culbertson, "is that Inspector Richard Sharpe is leading the investigation and has wisely brought on a well-known forensic specialist, Dr. Jessica Coran, from the FBI, America." After this, Culbertson listed Jessica's previous wins, ignoring all the losses, many of which were supremely personal losses accumulated over a life given to chasing such abhorrent creatures as the Crucifier.

She walked the short distance to the Yard, enjoying the beauty of London along the way, feeling somewhat overwhelmed and yet fulfilled here on her second day at Scotland Yard.

On entering the building, Jessica found herself immediately besieged by the duty sergeant with a message. Having left an overseas E-mail address for the Yard with J. T., she felt not at all surprised to electronically hear from John Thorpe. Informed of the transmission and directed where to go in order to read her E-mail and respond, she found herself alone in a vast array of computers manned by computer drones.

J. T.'s transmission read:

Wish you all the best of British luck over there, and you know how lucky the British are, right? Right. Currently, having some difficulty tracking down the artist who did the fantastic artwork on our dear friend Horace the Tattoo Man, but have found someone who actually recognizes the art and artist, a so-called cutting-edge artist in the field, a fellow named Jurgen Dykes, who takes his inspiration from a mentor named Kyle Winterborne, who takes his inspiration from H. R. Giger, whom everyone knows from the Alien trilogy of movies, his artwork famous the world over. Fantastic stuff in every sense of the word.

She electronically replied:

> *At least now you know the name of the artist. You*
> *can begin to track him down. Have you a location on*
> *Dykes?*

She didn't expect a ready answer, realizing that J. T. was
not likely out of bed yet, given the hour in America, much
less at his computer terminal awaiting a reply from her.
She continued to read the remainder of his message:

> *Last known location of the artist somewhere in*
> *upstate New York and Florida before that, but he*
> *appears to have vanished off the face of the Earth.*
> *Will continue to investigate. Have plenty of help from*
> *division.*

Jessica typed in an addendum to her earlier question, and
then she looked it over for correctness and clarity. It read:

> *So far, here, J. T., it's not going so well with the*
> *Crucifier case, either. Please, keep me informed of*
> *your progress there, and I will do the same from here*
> *regarding our case at the Yard.*

Jessica took in a great breath of air and signed off, hoping
the best for J. T. and the strange case of Tattoo Man, when
she looked up to find Inspector Richard Sharpe coming directly for her. He held an enervating glint in his eye and a
sly turn to his lip.

"They told me I'd find you here. Is all well in the States?
Hope you found the York to your liking."

"Yes to all three questions, and how are you this morning?"
He seemed in a fantastic mood. She wondered what had
brought it about.

"I've been better. The *Times* article has Boulte on my backside, I'm afraid. The least of my worries, however, the least."

Jessica guessed that seeing Boulte made red in the face had
done the job for Sharpe, and that even as Boulte lit into him

for lack of progress on the case, Sharpe enjoyed seeing the man out of control.

Sharpe continued, almost chipper. "I understand you had a go-round the O'Donahue site with Stuart last evening?"

"Yes, I had . . . a go-round, yes."

"Anything strike you?"

"Nothing that will change the opinion of the *Times*, or help you with Boulte, no."

He shook his head and frowned. "Politics, really. Has no bloody place in the Yard, but then it's endemic now, actually. They wouldn't know how to run the place without politics."

"The press pushes buttons here like they do in America. A strong force."

He shrugged this off. "Culbertson's a friend. She rather prints what I feed her, rather dislikes Boulte for good reason. He treats her like an anaconda."

"Is she?"

"In some sense, yes, she is."

"How well do you know her?"

"Too well, some would suggest."

"Boulte, you mean?" She wondered if the reporter woman had slept with Sharpe, either figuratively or literally.

His half smile answered her unasked question. "You are a quick study, aren't you, Doctor?"

"I've been called quick, yes. I think it time you called me Jessica."

"Right-o, and you must call me Richard."

"Well done," she said, mocking his British accent.

He smiled in return.

"Come on, let's have at it. We've got work to do," he said, strolling ahead of her.

Jessica shut the terminal down and got up from the computer, following after Sharpe.

"What sort of work?" she asked, catching up and walking alongside him down the institutional-gray corridor.

"Luc Sante has had time to examine your tongue—Burton's tongue, rather."

"Thank you for that clarification," she jested.

He confided, "You'll find Father Jerrard Luc Sante an interesting old bird, I should think."

"Oh? And why is that?"

"Boulte thinks him certifiable because he can't understand a word the man says. Quite the intellectual where life, death, murder, and psychopathology are concerned. He is, besides a priest, a psychotherapist, and he's working on a book."

"Really? All that?" she replied, curious. "What is the book about?"

"His notes mostly, on clients in therapy. Says it's a book that will begin a great debate over the nature of evil as we know it, or as we think we know it. That's Luc Sante altogether. Sometimes I think he talks just to hear the sound of it all, the sound of his voice, the choice of his words, always entertaining and usually of great help in understanding the most aberrant deviates among us."

"Hmmm. Yes, indeed. Sounds like my kind of guy."

Inspector Richard Sharpe introduced Jessica to Father Jerrard Luc Sante, who flew from the chair like a witch to take her hand in his. He'd been sitting behind Sharpe's desk, studying the hard copy of the message left at the base of the tongue, presumably by Burton's killer.

Luc Sante stood rigidly stiff, a man in obvious physical pain, holding himself together through sheer willpower and defiance. His vivid, mesmerizing, stark blue eyes shone clear and icily lucid. Even in his handshake, she could feel the virtual wince that coursed through his body at her touch.

Sharpe had promised an ancient man, but he had said nothing of the man's infirmity, his demeanor, the folds of skin, the rutted wrinkles of a face that had seen too many evils in one lifetime.

"I have heard so much about you, Dr. Coran," his voice, unlike the body, came forth with ease, free of any hacking or cough or wracking pain. The wispy hair, like cotton candy, made angel-like push-ups atop his head.

Jessica wondered if he'd live long enough to actually see a book written much less printed. "And I have heard a great deal about you, sir."

"From Sharpe here, no doubt. We have worked a number of cases together, have we not, Sharpe?"

Sharpe cleared his throat and said, "Dr. Luc Sante has helped clarify a number of certifiables for us over the years. He's had a long association with the Yard."

"How long now, Richard? Tell the young doctor."

"Thirty some odd years, Dr. Coran."

"Remarkable."

"And in that time, tell her what I've done for Scotland Yard."

"Father Luc Sante, as Dr. Luc Sante, has helped tremendously in our understanding of both killers and their victims over the years."

Luc Sante muttered something under his breath, unhappy with Sharpe's brief and general reply, now taking up for himself. "I have helped solve over seven hundred cases, thanks to my knowledge of how evil works through men, my dear."

"Indeed a grand history, sir."

"Of course, I haven't the reputation you have, and in most cases, I'm well behind the scenes, acting as a psychotherapist, you see."

"Father Luc Sante also knows Latin. What would you translate this little message to mean, Father?" asked Sharpe.

Jerrard, some sixty plus years of age, Jessica guessed, debilitated through some disease he likely kept at bay with prescription drugs, swallowed hard before replying and said, "Well, Richard, it's fairly straightforward. No mystery here. It simply reads, 'Grant unto me, Blessed Mother.' "

"What does that mean?" she asked.

"It is a supplication, a prayer."

"What kind of prayer winds up as a brand beneath the tongue?"

"It is a supplication to the Virgin Mary to bestow special honor on the deceased."

"Special honor?"

"Quite . . ."

"I'd say it looks like a fairly twisted honor, from where I stand."

"Read my book! And Richard, you must purchase a copy.

You owe me as much!" He held up a copy of *Twisted Faiths: A Jungian Examination of Wrongful and Harmful Beliefs Throughout the Ages*, which had been lying on Richard's desk. "Finally just had the damn thing bound—self-published. No more time to waste with wretched and incompetent people in the publishing world."

"Rejected, huh?" asked Richard.

"Like a two-shilling whore, Richard, but I tell you the publishing world is one colossal whore, a giant bitch! All of them, merely interested in the almighty pound and what some teenaged Hollywood brat has for breakfast. Who or what Fergie is feeling today, or whether the Queen's ass is held too high, or if her hair will be allowed to go white this season or not—shameless twaddle!"

Jessica took the book from him and fingered through the opening pages, seeing an introduction by the famous psychotherapist guru, Dr. Phillip Deacre.

Meanwhile, Luc Sante, like a fount, continued to talk. "There've been twisted beliefs and twisted awards bestowed for those very beliefs for . . . well, for countless generations."

Sharpe broke in, asking, "So, Dr. Luc Sante, what do you make of this tongue branding? Has it . . . Have you ever come across it before?"

"A cult of St. Michael, originated as early as the resurrection, you might say, revived during the Dark to Middle Ages, yes, and never fully extinguished. Believed to inspire both the recipient and those in audience to cling a bit closer to God, you see."

"Inspire? But how does the cult inspire?"

"By driving out Satan, all his minions, including but not limited to the mental hellions."

"By driving out evil?"

"Combating evil as defined by the cult, of course—exorcisms, all that, which can include arresting sickness and boils and all manner of physical demonics, you see, as well as mental demonics."

"I see."

"Nothing really new under the sun in religion, actually, Dr. Coran, merely new twists on old tales, most rather predictable

at best. Not unlike your American cinema, really. Save these
followers, these fans, believe what they do constitutes the salvation of their souls."

"What are you saying? That Burton may have been a member of a cult?"

"Quite possibly, or their unwitting sacrifice. Either way, it
bears looking into, wouldn't you agree?"

"Well, yes, absolutely," replied Richard, as excited as Jessica had seen him.

Jessica closed the book and looked from Sharpe to Luc
Sante who declared, "Don't you see, Richard, my boy? If
Burton accepted the emblem of a cult, then perhaps his death
leads directly back to this very cult activity."

"Luc Sante, you are a genius."

"I did not find the markings. She did," he replied, pointing
a shaking, shriveled finger at Jessica who felt the finger pierce
a spot between her eyes. "She's your hero this time round,
me boy." He then glanced at his watch. "It's half past ten!
I've already missed one appointment. I must run, Richard.
Keep me apprised, and as always, I will do whatever in my
power."

"Let us give you a lift, Father," suggested Sharpe. "Get you
there in half the time."

"Run the siren?" he asked with a glint in the eye.

"If you like."

"You well know I love it."

Jessica and Richard exchanged a smile at the old man's
expense. Jessica thought him lovely.

As they made their way to the motor pool, Jessica asked
Luc Sante, "The words the ancients used in their tongue
branding, Father . . ."

"Yes?" he replied.

"Would they have been the same as those we've found here
today?"

"Actually, they would have been quite close, indeed. But
not likely identical, no."

"Perhaps we are dealing with someone who knows about
this ancient cult or similar cults in early Christianity."

"That is a likely possibility, yes, my dear, yes. However,

coincidence is also an enormous force in the universe, controlled at the hand of Puck, the devilishly sneaky orphan of Satan who enjoys a good laugh at our expense."

"Puck?"

"Of course, Puck. What? You do not believe in evil spirits or mischievous spirits aloft in the world?"

"I believe in a palpable evil."

"That finds its mark and inhabits a man's heart."

"Or a woman's, yes."

"Agreed then we are."

She thought he spoke like the *Star Wars* character of Yoda.

The siren wail all the way to his church and office delighted the wizened old man. "How like a banshee wail it is," he said repeatedly, a smile gracing his weathered features.

Father Luc Sante's church stood amid the squalor of a run-down neighborhood, looking like a castle under siege, held hostage by its surroundings. The church, built on the order of a small cathedral, had seen better days. It hardly measured up to the great cathedrals abounding in London. Still it displayed magnificent oak doors with huge metal hinges and a beautiful cupola, graced on all sides by wide-eyed, curious gargoyles staring down on them as they entered, making Jessica wonder if stone could think.

A light rain had driven them to rush from car to entrance-way rather quickly and hurriedly. Once inside, the priest quickly found himself on familiar ground and moved with more fervor than before, going straight for the office he maintained at one end of the rectory. A pleasant-looking, mild-appearing, gray-haired secretary named Janet, her gray skin like that of the gargoyles outside, greeted Luc Sante with a stern warning. With gritted teeth, as if meaning to bite him when finished, she said, "I won't be made the fool for you, Father."

"Whatever can be troubling you, my dear Miss Eeadna?" asked Luc Sante, taking both her hands in his in a protective gesture.

"I won't stand and lie for you, not here, not in eternity, not anywhere, Father."

"Ahhh, my patients, is it?"

"Will you tell me what I'm to say when you fail to meet with one of your . . . so-called *patients*?"

"Keep patience, my dear Janet. Always keep patience in your heart, dear."

A younger man in vestments came from a second office, hushing Miss Janet Eeadna, as her desk nameplate had her. The younger priest asked if Miss Eeadna would care to take tea with him. She beamed, delighted, taking the young priest's arm and sauntering out with him.

"That's Martin, soon to replace me here. Good man, really. 'Fraid the bishop won't be calling me out of retirement, no. But what I shall do in retirement, I don't know, Richard. I pray the police keep me active."

"We will call on you, Father, no doubt," assured Richard. "Look, we must be getting back. Much to do today, you see, so—"

"Oh, no! You must stay to meet Martin. He'll be right back, I'm sure. Oh, here he is now! Martin!"

The younger minister beamed, grasping hands all around, shaking vigorously and apologizing just as vigorously for "poor Miss Eeadna" whose mind, it seemed, wasn't at all what it once was. "I shall have to clean house once you've retired, Father," he chided the old man, "but I do appreciate your leaving the old parish picture up," he finished, pointing to a pastoral little parish in a wooded area in a painting behind the desk which Jessica thought beautiful.

"My first parish, painted it myself," explained Luc Sante with a shrug. "Once dabbled in art but gave it up." He then said to Jessica, "Dear Miss Eeadna needs rest, and the church will most certainly see to her getting a fair pension."

The two men seemed most agreeable about the changing of the guard, Jessica thought.

"Allow me, Richard and Jessica, to introduce my young protégé, who will be taking over my duties when I retire in a few weeks, Father Martin Christian Strand."

Sharpe introduced himself and Dr. Coran to the younger man whose blond haired ponytail marked him as of a new generation of clerics.

"Saint Martin, we call him round here," said Luc Sante, a twinge of bitterness in his tone. "Such a do-gooder, Richard, you've not seen the like before! Has no business in this business, and certainly no future in it, going at it the way he does!" He roared at his own joke. Strand joined in the laughter, Richard following suit. Jessica managed a smile.

The room felt darker than it actually was, what with the old, darkly stained wood bookcases all around and the huge, oak furniture with anthropomorphic legs.

Strand modestly declined the sainthood, explaining, "We don't need any more saints in the church. What we desperately need here in the community center is a new toaster and a microwave!"

Suddenly, a door burst open and from within Dr. Luc Sante's inner office stepped a man with a wild shock of hair and eyes both bloodshot and bloodthirsty, shouting, "I need to talk to you, Luc Sante! Now!"

"Jessica, Richard, go with Martin, and he will show you around St. Albans. I must see to Mr. Hargrove here who has been so very patiently awaiting my arrival."

" 'Fraid I can't stay, but you go ahead, Jessica," Sharpe told her. "I'll leave the car and driver for you outside."

Sharpe's departure came so suddenly, Jessica hadn't time to protest. She and Strand took to the massive corridor. Strand pointed out the paintings adorning the walls and the Italian marble floors as they moved along.

He explained what they did by way of helping the homeless and helpless of the neighborhood around the old cathedral located near one of London's most notorious bazaars where anything from drugs to an honest to God medieval table and chairs set could be had for the right price.

Strand appeared a devoted disciple of Luc Sante's, and was most obviously devoted to the old man's causes. Strand showed her a room where local children played at games and made things with leather and hemp. He showed her the soup kitchen where she saw the poor being fed.

They walked back toward Strand's and Luc Sante's offices afterward. Martin Strand—handsome, tall, powerfully built, remarked on how sad it sometimes became. "Toiling here in

relative obscurity, it pains me to see Father Luc Sante's work
going ignored. He is rather a genius, after all," finished
Strand.

"So, you've read his book?" she asked.

"Every word he's ever committed to paper, yes."

Jessica saw Luc Sante's red-eyed, wild-haired patient am-
bling fast away from the office and out the oak doors, the
sunlight pouring into the corridor as a result. The aberrant
thought that Dr. Luc Sante had just been murdered by one of
his own patients crossed her mind like a fleeing bird before
it escaped on seeing the old man in his office doorway, waving them to return.

When they reentered there was no Miss Janet Eeadna to
disrupt them, and no more patients to see for the day, according to the old man who looked pleased.

"And how is it with Mr. Hargrove today, Father?"

"He is a man plagued with as thorny a bush of perplexing
problems as I've seen in years. Still hearing the voices, I'm
afraid."

"Surely, they're no longer telling him to kill his wife?"

"No, they've quaffed that issue it would seem."

"But 'ave grown shrill on other issues, is it?"

"By my word, Martin! Have you placed one of those bug-
ging devices in me office?"

"I 'ave not, but I will if you wish it so."

"Can you imagine that, Dr. Coran, every word a patient
says in there"—he stopped to point to his psychotherapy office—"heard at some remote location by any and all who
happen along? It would be the ruin of me, but perhaps it might
also enlighten some otherwise intelligent folk who still have
not one flimsy idea that evil walks into my office every day."

Before Jessica could reply Strand cautioned her, saying,
"You'd best watch this old magician, Dr. Coran."

"And why is that?"

"Do you know what we in England call a psychiatrist, Doctor?"

"Inform me."

"A *trick cyclist* is what."

She laughed at this and Luc Sante sneered. "Go on with

your duties, Saint Martin. And if you haven't enough to keep you busy about here . . ." he threatened.

"I'm gone, I'm gone, and how very pleasant to've met you, Dr. Coran."

"Out! Get out!" The old man ended near tears of laughter. Jessica thought him sweet; obviously a man who lived every single moment to the fullest.

Father Strand and Doctor Luc Sante's relationship was charming, and Jessica felt the latter was an extremely likable, knowledgeable Renaissance man, quite up on criminal psychology. He had quickly won Jessica's confidence and friendship.

"I wish to thank you for the tour of the cathedral, Dr. Luc Sante, and for deciphering the mysterious words found under Burton's tongue."

"You are leaving so soon?"

"There's a great deal waiting back at the Yard for me, yes."

"At least keep this and read it," he said, lifting the copy of his book that Jessica had skimmed in the car coming over.

"Let me pay for the book," she insisted. And while he began to protest, in the end, he willingly took the British currency amounting to $24.95 American.

"It barely covers the printing costs, Dr. Coran," he apologetically added. "But I'm pleased, in the end, that you have taken a copy of my self-published treatise on the subject of the ultimate evil."

Jessica read the book's abbreviated title, without the Jungian preface, giving pause to the words: *Twisted Faiths*. A tagline read: *A History of Fetishism and Cultism in Middle Europe and Great Britain 1400 to Present Day.*

Jessica said her good-byes and Strand returned in time to usher her to the door where he smiled and said, "He's a wonderful soul, that man."

"Yes, I think we can well agree on that."

"I could do nothing to harm him. Yet here I am taking his one love, St. Albans, from him in a matter of weeks."

"He seems to have made his peace with it, and he . . . Well, I daresay he couldn't have selected a better successor. Will you also be doing the trick cyclist's work?" she quipped.

"I have some certification papers to finish up, but yes, as a matter of fact, I will. Regardless of what some think, the Vatican is interested in our carrying on as usual here at St. Albans."

"Good luck to you then, and I'm sure we'll see one another again."

"I'm sure."

He waved her off, the handsome *Billy Budd* of the place, looking like Richard Chamberlain in his youth, a regal and muscular young turk, she thought. The man was at extreme odds with the old man of St. Albans, so filled was Strand with rich life, earthy color, vigor, and power. He waved to her as she dashed down the walk doing her best to remain dry without an umbrella.

The midday drizzle had turned the sky a gunmetal gray, and the gargoyles far up overhead, guarding St. Albans as it were, wept under the steady drenching they stoically took. Yet, many of the gargoyles enjoyed the wet, even ciphoned off water from the roof, their tubular interiors acting as waterspouts, a utilitarian use of art if Jessica had ever seen it. On the one hand, the statuary stood as sentinels between two worlds, on the other, as sediment-filled drainpipes—quite the concrete opposite of the otherworldly symbolism attaching to the grim-faced stone monsters, and an oddly disproportionate thing to behold, she thought. But then, each day she discovered something new and queer and fascinating about London, England, and with this final thought on the matter, she climbed into the police car left behind for her "transport needs" by the ever thoughtful Inspector Sharpe.

· EIGHT ·

*Evil is not only a presence; it infiltrates mankind
as the ultimate disease.*

—FATHER JERRARD LUC SANTE,
FROM *TWISTED FAITHS*

Jessica and Sharpe spent the rest of the day in a frustrating
effort to gain access to the recently buried Frank Coibby.
When they were finally able to get the paperwork, it was
learned that Coibby's body had been misplaced. "By order of
the Crown that no bodies be buried in the realm," due to the
terrible overcrowding in British cemeteries. It had been for
this reason that O'Donahue's body had been cremated into
uselessness. Now Coibby simply appeared misplaced, as mortuary after mortuary was being checked.

"I thought you said there'd be no problem with this," Jessica asked, her rising voice telegraphing frustration.

Frowning, Sharpe replied, "I ordered the body be held intact, funeral service or no, and—"

"Funeral service?"

"Thrown together affair by the estranged family, out of a
sense of duty, I suppose. In any case, the mortuary paid by
the family for services rendered, such as they were, simply
shipped the body out to another mortuary, I am now told."

"Odd, isn't it?" Jessica wondered if there might not be
some hidden agenda in all this.

"A falling out over the billing costs, I'm told, caused the
second mortuary to return the body here, but they have limited
storage facilities, just as we do at the Yard."

"And so?"

"The mortician here has the body at his . . . home."

"His *home*?"

"In a full-sized freezer there. Bugger figured to leave it there until such a time as someone came asking for it back."

"Well, now we're asking," she huffed.

"Mr. Coibby's body will be returned to the mortuary by 8 A.M. tomorrow," came back the promise from the mortician, a Mr. Littelle.

And for tonight, Jessica found herself having dinner with Richard Sharpe at the Trafalgar Square's famous Rules restaurant, known for having fortified English stomachs since 1798. They ate quickly so that Sharpe could show her some of the sights and the famous area within walking distance of her hotel room at the York. Richard offered to take her to see Soho by night as well, and that invitation she found far too enticing to turn down. She planned to return another day to take in the nearby National Gallery.

"We will have to motor to West End, but my car is close at hand," he informed Jessica.

"Yes, wonderful . . . Soho. I've heard so much about the area."

Soho didn't disappoint. Jessica was delighted when she found herself on Oxford Street, London's number one shopping street, which history told her had been a road since Roman times. From there, Richard took her through Soho Square, a brooding place, laid out in the 1680s. "See the church there?" asked Richard, pointing to a spiraling steeple.

"Yes."

"French Protestant. French Huguenots formed the first wave to settle the district, followed by a melting pot of other nationalities, giving the place its international flair while maintaining a villagelike appearance."

"Much like Greenwich Village in New York," she replied.

"Exactly. That cosmopolitan flavor."

They strolled Frifth Street to Old Compton Street and on to Charring Cross Road, a place lined with fascinating and quaint bookshops. At Cambridge Circus, Richard pointed out the restored Palace Theatre, a fascinating sight, and soon they were on Gerrard Street, a pedestrian-only area in the heart of China Town. Richard asked if she cared for anything to drink as they stood outside the Dragon Inn.

"Yes, a drink would do me well," she agreeably replied. "But only one."

"My limit as well," he warned with a smile. "What would you like?"

"A whiskey sour, perhaps?"

"Hmmm . . . lovely. My preference as well."

Richard waved to the bartender, someone he knew from past visits, the moment they stepped through the red doors and into the dark interior. The Asian bartender smiled and nodded, knowing what Richard meant by his two fingers in the air. They found a table where Jessica put down the few small bags, her purchases amassed during their trek.

"I trust you found some real treasures to take back to the States with you," he commented on the bags.

"Yes, in fact, I have."

"Good. I'm glad you're enjoying yourself in my city."

He said *my city* as if he'd given birth to it; he stated it with pride and passion.

Jessica had never felt so passionate about a place as this man obviously felt toward London, but she could well understand it.

Along their stroll, he'd pointed out places of historical significance and interest, such as the House of St. Barnabas, a 1746 structure that reminded all Londoners of Soho's aristocratic beginnings. He had also pointed out a now charming small hotel named the Hazlitt on Frifth Street, where essayist William Hazlitt died. Richard noted a nearby inn where once Karl Marx and his family lived in abject poverty as well. The area, now cleaned up for the tourist trade, still somehow conveyed the feeling of a place where starving artists and idealists came to die. This lent a melancholy mood to the place, like that found in a cemetery, despite the modern veneer.

When Jessica voiced her feelings, Richard laughed and said, "Are you interested in visiting Soho Cemetery? Quite a few famous chaps buried there."

Their drinks had arrived, and seeing no ice in either of

them, Jessica recalled the custom. Liquor in London was
taken at room temperature. She stirred her drink with a swiz-
zle stick, staring into the brown liquid. "Truth be known, I
do enjoy a good cemetery search," she confided, "but—"

"Cemeteries abound in London, some with quite impressive
permanent Londoners as we call them."

"Which do you suggest as the best, if I've only time for
one?" she asked.

"That's difficult to say. St. Marylebone, perhaps. Westminster and the Tower of London have, of course, the most to
see, but they've become such traps for the tourists. Although
there are magnificent carved stones and statues to see. But for
the real enthusiasts, they should see Bunhill Fields."

"Bunhill Fields?"

"Probably a bastardization of bone field." He laughed
lightly and sipped at his drink.

"No doubt," she agreed with his assessment.

"John Wesley's buried there. An enormous likeness of him
as you enter the gates. John Bunyan, Daniel Defoe, William
Blake—"

"A regular writers' colony!"

"John Milton is entered at nearby St. Giles Cripplegate."

"Charming name, *Cripple*-gate?"

He raised his shoulders. "Not sure how a gate can be crippled, you mean? Likely as not a *busted* affair."

The terms *busted affair* and *Cripplegate* made Jessica again
think of James Parry and her crippled relationship with him.
Their busted affair.

"Is there anything wrong?" he asked.

She realized he'd read the dark shadow that'd eclipsed her
features as she'd given thought to James and their beleaguered
love, a love beset and plagued by problems of distance and
practicalities, a love tormented and besieged by loneliness.
When last she'd spoken to Jim Parry, he wanted her to mull
over the idea that they begin to see other people. He had needs
that she could not fulfill from half a globe away, he'd complained. To Richard now, she simply said, "Nothing, really.
Just . . . a memory."

"I see. Yes, I have a few bad memories of my own."

She forced a smile, realizing that he must be well-attuned to people to be the inspector that he was.

"I'm not one to pry, but should you wish to talk about it, about anything at all, you'll find me a good listener."

She smiled in return. "Thank you, Richard. I may take you up on that someday."

They parted at Jessica's door with an exchange of hand-shakes, eye contact, and smiles, Richard ever the gentleman. Jessica spent the rest of the evening alone with her longing to telephone James Parry. Her emotions ran the gamut from wanting to rub Parry's face in the fact that she had just spent the day with a wonderful British gentleman to whom she felt attracted, to hoping against hope that James had had a change of heart, that he would reconsider their relationship and the decision to end it. Richard Sharpe had awakened feelings in her she had suppressed for too long now. She needed James's reassurance that all between them would and could be worked out. But her analytical side, her unemotional scientific side knew that any reconciliation with James Parry was unlikely at this point.

Sometime later—in a nightgown that James had purchased for her in an exotic little shop their last time on Maui—Jessica lay on her back, unable to sleep, thinking intently about the last time she had heard James's voice. She wondered if it would prove to be the very last time she would ever hear his voice. That telephone call had been a connection made be-tween Quantico, Virginia, and Honolulu, Hawaii, during a rushed moment before the trip to London—typical of her life-style. Even in the midst of trying to hold on to James, she was packing and racing away.

She thought now of Hawaii, where they had first met in 1994, six years ago, and where they had continued a long-distance love affair since. It had been a good run, she now told herself, knowing that the intensity and passion of their feelings had waned to the point of estrangement, the kind of deeply sad estrangement only former lovers who still felt warmth for one another could know. Through no fault of Jim's or her own, things had gone the way of so many rela-tionships. Given the distance between them, given their egos, given their high-powered careers—he a field chief special agent with the Bureau, she a much-in-demand medical examiner—the oddsmakers in the FBI family had them down for a year, two at best. But such people didn't know James Parry, nor did they know Jessica Coran, not really.

Even so . . . Even accepting the fact that their love had cooled, creating an emotional chasm between them larger than the miles separating them, Jessica found herself in a quandary. She didn't know whether to cherish or to fend off all the myriad and power-filled memories of this love, the memories of this man, memories of them together. She still battled with the feeling of abandonment and emptiness, so bitter and gut-wrenching; still fought the needs, the tugging pull like an invisible cord in her abdomen somehow still connected between them.

"Talk about physical pain," she told herself and the empty room. She still felt—if she allowed herself to feel—his breath in hers whenever they had made passionate love. She still closed her eyes and saw the patterned beauty of his salt-and-pepper hair up close, while her chin lay against his forehead. She still felt the soft warmth of his gentle touch against her skin, the sweet smell of him lingering in her mind along with the way his laughter filled her with a giddiness she'd not known since childhood, and the thousand other small memories that went into building the whole memory of him that she so cherished. Let it go? Give it over to the grave? Bury it? Put it by with mourning? The sad irony in such intense passion remained at once to hold firm to that rarity, and at the same time control it. "So it does not destroy you," she pleaded with herself again. *Control it, control it, control it*— proved an internal memo she had to resend to her heart, back to her brain, then relay again to her soul, with the intent of gaining acceptance and balance in the trio of spirit.

Try as she might, it all came crashing back. She recalled that last, unfulfilling conversation. . . .

Jim came on, asking, "Jessica? Is that you? How are you? Where are you calling from?" He sounded groggy as if climbing from sleep. She realized too late the time difference between them.

"I'm home, but I'm off to London. I was hoping that perhaps you could join me there for a few days?"

"I'm actually in the midst of one hell of a political shakeup in the islands at the moment, and to add to my troubles, we've got a serial killer stalking striptease dancers over here."

"I see."

"He's already killed four without any sign of giving himself away. Uses a garrote to practically cut their heads off. Full of rage, this one."

"A garrote? Rather a specialized weapon. Have you considered the possibility it's a woman doing the killing?"

"Why do you say so?"

"Garroting is a backdoor approach, and one has to gain the near total acceptance of the victim, make her feel there's nothing whatever to fear. Of course, a Ted Bundy could talk a victim into completely relaxing around him, but the Bundy type is rare. Most women do not feel threatened by other women."

"Well, there's no sexual contact, no lust-murder elements, merely a clean, thin, cut line around the entire throat."

"It's entirely possible the murder weapon could appear as a harmless necklace. Garrotes are as thin as wire."

"Amazing," he muttered. "Some of us here have given thought to the possibility it's a woman doing the killing."

"No signs of struggle? Nothing under the victim's nails? No way to get at the killer if he or she approached from behind," she said.

"That's exactly what we've got. The killer leaves a scented handkerchief at every scene, a feminine touch."

The conversation shifted to their relationship and to precisely what they both knew they must talk about.

"All right, James. Time for the truth. Truth is we aren't talking about what's really on our minds anymore. Not like we used to talk . . ."

He had agreed, saying, "Truth is, we're . . . we've drifted apart, Jess, and I . . . I've become involved."

"Involved? With someone else?"

"You know how it is. Working late hours on an intense

case. Only natural to turn to someone, someone close at hand, not thousands of miles away."

"I can't say that you didn't warn me." She dared not ask how long Parry had been seeing this new person in his life.

James finally admitted, "I could no longer maintain our— my—side of our relationship, despite all my attempts to make it work."

"Greece, the Mediterranean, that was a beautiful attempt, James."

"It's over, Jess. You made the choice for us, not me."

"What choice are you talking about? I've had no . . . It seems to me that you're the one who has made the choices here, James."

"You chose your work over everything, Jessica. Over me, over us, over your own happiness. And that's where it's at for you, isn't it? Isn't it?" He'd begun to shout.

"I've done all I could to maintain an exclusive, long-distance relationship with you, James. I've done that and more. I have committed to you."

"Well, Jess, you have a funny definition of commitment. I can't accept what you call a commitment any longer. I'm forty-eight years old, Jessica, and one day I want to have children. I'm sorry, but I can't do this anymore. Not anymore."

"James, let's hold on, all right? Give me time to come over. We'll talk. We'll work something out, we'll—"

"No, I'm sorry, Jess, but—"

"What's the harm in giving it more time, so that we can discuss it like two intelligent adults faced with a problem. So we can find a solution?"

"Jess, you made a choice—your career over me. It's that simple. Problem resolved."

"You want me to give up everything—my job, my friends, everything I know—to join you in Hawaii, but you're not willing to give up a single thing." *Love makes fools of us all*, she thought.

"We've had this argument before, Jess." He spoke in a near-whisper. She could feel his pain coming through.

She whispered in return, "What are you willing to give up for me, James?"

"What we had . . . while beautiful, Jess, it's now clearly . . . over."

Jessica had felt all her inner resolve and strength drain from her body through bare-knuckled hands and fingertips that wrapped themselves tightly about the solid phone receiver, as if they could hold back James's determination. Her fingers lingered over the phone as if independent of her. Her hands felt and looked like someone else's. She calmly studied the flawless white skin and hardly noticed when her right hand simply dropped the phone on its cradle, her eyes filling with remorse and bittersweet tears. She was apart from herself, unable to feel a thing.

She hadn't even said good-bye; nor had he. Fitting ending. She felt angry and frustrated. There seemed no pleasing him. While he offered no compromise, Jim expected her to completely overhaul her life and lifestyle on the altar of their spoken bond. It would be easier to give into mad emotions now. Make demands of her own. Simply to say *Fuck Jim Parry*, and to hell with all his ultimatums. She was no one's property, goods, assets, belongings. "I'm no man's belongings, nor will I ever be," she told herself.

She could live without Jim, she rationalized now, and then she cried more deeply, not believing a word of it.

And now here she lay in a London suite paid for by Scotland Yard. Gulping back her grief at the loss of her lover, Jessica quietly fell asleep thinking of a line from a familiar song, one that had become a way of life for her: *Alone again, naturally.*

At 2 A.M. Jessica gave up any hope of sleep. Insomnia, that old devil, stalked her anew. With the full discomfort of inability to find restful sleep, Jessica turned to Father Jerrard Luc Sante for help, hefting his self-published book *Twisted Faiths* onto her lap where she sat up in bed.

She read halfway through the opus and determined that while Dr. Luc Sante's conclusions lived an inspired life unto themselves, and while he went way out on the cutting edge of a psychotherapy few people dared discuss much less examine at so close a range, his style and choice of words were too often uninspired.

Still, the conclusions seemed inspired by some suprahuman voice seemingly not of this Earth. Actually, the book's many conclusions surpassed anything she had ever read in psychotherapy journals or volumes.

At the same time, she clearly understood why Luc Sante could not find a publisher for his work. No one would pay money to read the convoluted thinking of what some might assume to be a mad priest gone on verbal rampage against the evil among us. Throughout her reading, she was forced to stop and reread for clarity, and, frankly, she found Luc Sante's crippled prose generally wooden and lacking in luster.

While she was no editor or grammarian, she judged his sentences as awkwardly constructed, his phraseology too often linear and syllogistic, while his annoying terminology-laden, for-psychotherapist-only approach stuttered every step of the way over the rhetoric of his own field: *religion*. Still, his "truths" were fascinating: Satan lives in the human breath and organs. Evil flourishes in the disease vials we call our bodies. Evil flourishes in our weak and hopelessly ruled brains, and yet we have children whom we teach and inspire. How many of us inspire hatred, racial prejudice, ignorance, poverty, and murder? We are Satan. Satan is us. And from generation to generation, we propagate evil through our children, and will continue to do so until the cycle of Satanism is broken and until psychotherapists join with religious leaders to both recognize and combat evil in its purest form—mankind. The same mankind that crucified Christ.

All the same, only occasionally on paper did Luc Sante's magnificent speaking voice come through. Consequently, the pace of the book became as turgid as a pollution-choked industrial canal. Still, the book filled Jessica with dread shivers. It held much rare information doled out like so many golden nuggets, she thought, all on a subject seldom to never touched on. Luc Sante's running thesis said: *True evil as it is created in society among people, as it is given life and breath in this world, is altogether so mundane and day-to-day as to be all but invisible to us, and in being so invisible, it gained in strength and cunning thanks to our blatant ignorance of it.*

She believed what Luc Sante said to be clearly correct in a sense, fitting into of her own experiences with twisted minds. Jessica began to believe that perhaps evil did indeed infest and infiltrate and find succor in the most mundane of human hearts and minds through the genetic makeup. That much of the pitiable state of the human condition, and the ferocity of the creature called man, was predetermined through a fate as biochemically fundamental as the DNA of apes, despite the outward veneer of civility, progress, and technological marvels.

Certainly mankind remained, throughout the ages and present day, an incubator for evil experiments as well as all manner of disease and disability. She imagined a world in which the worst of mankind, the most evil among us, were subjects of a cloning experiment, that had, in the later part of the twentieth century, blindly and unwittingly cloned its own dark side, so that the modern-day serial killer could indeed be explained. She imagined that nature had done the cloning for us with the hand of Satan in the mix.

She pulled back, short of putting full stock into the religious man's words.

"We've had the messages in the bubblegum wrapper defense, we've had the Devil-made-me-do-it defense, the talking dog from Son of Sam, and now we're to have the DNA-made-me-do-it defense?" she asked the room.

Still Luc Sante's book had one fine result: *It had put her under.*

She had fallen asleep at last, with his compilation of dark and sinister thoughts on her lap, and she dreamed of the many guises of evil he'd so elegantly described in his comprehensive work on the nature of evil and the duty of every psychotherapist to engage the diabolical, all malfeasance and malignancy wherever he or she found *it*, and to struggle in real-time combat with *it* at every turn.

"We fight the same enemy." Luc Sante's voice wafted over her dreams. . . .

• • •

Lawrence Coibby, used car salesman, loner, without a friend in the world, having never actually been buried, had spent the last few weeks in storage in a stranger's freezer in a garage in Kensington. Jessica was told this with such calm that she marveled anew at the ability of the British to understate any situation. Consequently, there having been no actual burial, due in part to the absence of burial sites, there was no true *exhumation* of the body. However, over the last twenty-four hours, the "hunt" for Coibby's body had continued, and once properly identified and located, the cadaver had been taken to a nearby hospital, St. Stephen's Parish Hospital, where Dr. Coran oversaw the evidence gathering—specifically the evidence gathered from under Lawrence Coibby's tongue.

Staring through the high-powered magnifying glass brought in for the job, Jessica found the tongue in remarkably good shape due more to the deep freezing of the body than to the embalming.

"There it stands, gentlemen," she told Sharpe and the others, Copperwaite, Chief Inspector Boulte alongside Dr. Schuller. "Have a look, Richard. It's the same message, letter for letter, word for word."

Sharpe eagerly took her place at the magnifying glass, finding just the right focus for himself. "As if the killer has a brand, and he keeps using it over and over."

"Two out of three, technically," agreed Copperwaite.

"It's clear enough."

Jessica took a last look at the message, inscribed in the flesh, burnt into the flesh by a micro-brand. "I confess, I've never seen the like of it before," she told the men.

"It's clearly the work of a serial killer now, one wishing to taunt police with a hideous method of torturous death for his victims," suggested Chief Inspector Boulte. "We'll keep this out of the communiqué you wish to forward the media, Richard."

"We'd like a good deal more said about the killings, Chief Inspector."

"I've reviewed your suggestions and those of our American colleague, Richard. I'm sorry, but it all seems a bit premature at this time to alarm the public with this information about . . .

about the tongues being seared on top of all this other nasti-
ness, you see?"

Jessica took several deep breaths of air, allowing her disappointment clear vent. Sharpe bit his lip and nodded to his
superior, saying, "Whatever you judge best, Chief Inspector.
It is, after all, your show."

Sharpe abruptly turned from his superior and rained com-
pliments on Jessica. "You've done a fine job for us, Dr.
Coran, in the startlingly brief time you've been on the case."

Copperwaite eagerly added, "Yes, she's already proven her
worth to the case quite dramatically, I'd say."

Copperwaite's compliment hardly left his lips when Sharpe
laughed aloud. Whether Copperwaite knew it or not, he'd hit
upon the true reason why Chief Inspector Boulte did not wish
to go public with this information. It had come not from the
Yard's efforts or findings, but from the American, the colonist, Jessica Coran.

Boulte only showed a politically correct smile and agreed
with his men, saying, "Yes, Dr. Coran, your contribution to
the case, thus far, has been most impressive. Keep up the good
work."

Dr. Karl Schuller, however, remained displeased, his dour
expression as frozen as the dead Coibby's, and he left without
a word to anyone. Boulte followed after him.

"Where do we go from here?" she asked Sharpe.

"How about lunch?" he replied.

"Bonzo," agreed Copperwaite. "I'm starved."

"There's a little pub not far from here, called Groton's, if
it's not full. Old favorite," said Sharpe. "Let's have a go at
it, shall we?"

"We shall," Jessica agreed.

"Over lunch, we can talk about our next move. *If* we have
one."

"What do you mean by that?" she asked. " '*If*' we have
one?"

"Chief Inspector Boulte's pushing for a new investigative
team to come on."

"What? What kind of thinking is that?"

"Administrative."

"Is that how New Scotland Yard works? If so, it smells like yesterday's fish."

"Boulte used a fishy metaphor as well," replied Sharpe, a bit amused at her anger. "Says we're rowing a leaking boat."

"He's always saying crap of that sort. 'Gain on swings, lose on roundabouts,' he says ten times a day," reported Copperwaite as they continued to the bar. "Gawd 'elp us. The man doesn't know the geography of his own house."

Sharpe laughed uproariously at this, leaving Jessica to wonder what she'd missed. He quickly explained, "It means he can't find the john in his own home."

She joined in their laughter. "I've a *Geordie* friend from Tynsdale knows more than that man," said Copperwaite.

"Boulte doesn't rise to the level of a Geordie, a George perhaps. . . ." Sharpe's summation brought on more laughter. Copperwaite explained for Jessica that a *George* in Britain meant the automatic-pilot mechanism on an airplane or the cruise mechanism on a car. "Let the hamster onto the wheel," added Sharpe, chewing now on an unlit pipe.

"Still, isn't it rather a bit premature to call in a new investigative team at this point?" she asked.

Sharpe shrugged. "Oh, I don't know. He has to have someone to play the goat. Short of having someone in the greenhouse—ahh, the lock-up—he has to point a finger in some direction. To be fair, he has a hell of a political Rube Goldberg balanced on his shoulder right now, and—"

"Ahh, you're daft, Sharpie. You make too many excuses for the man."

Sharpe ignored Copperwaite as they continued along a tree-lined street, children playing in nearby yards. "Boulte's right about one thing. We haven't amassed a thing on the killer, and now we may simply have to wait for the killer to strike again before we can learn any more about him or *them*. This is a sorry state of affairs, but it happens to be the circumstances we're now faced with, as you know."

"We're just to sit about like bumps to wait for a . . . another killing?" asked Copperwaite.

Jessica complained as well. "That's a bit like the tail wagging the dog, don't you think?"

"What steps then would you have us take?"

"Use the *Times* and the BBC. Get word out on this killer. Tell the public what you've found, what to look for."

"That might flush him out," agreed Copperwaite.

"Or send him packing," suggested Sharpe.

Jessica looked into his eyes. "Either way, don't you think people should be forewarned? If there's anyone out there who knows anything about this branding for instance, it could lead to a break in the case. As it is, you have no suspects and no direction. Sometimes you need to manufacture a direction."

· NINE ·

The hungry sheep look up, and are not fed, But swoln with wind and the rank mist they draw, Rot inwardly and foul contagion spread . . .

—JOHN MILTON,
LYCIDAS

While at Groton's Pub, Sharpe's beeper hailed him, and after making a phone call, he returned to the table with a grim look in his eye. "Afraid Stuart, Jessica, . . . before anything regarding the crucifixion deaths and the fact the victims had all been branded can be released to the press, another body, in the same condition, awaits us at the Serpentine."

"The Serpentine?" asked Jessica.

"A large lake, rather serpentine in form, if one uses imagination, bordering Hyde Park and Kensington Gardens," replied Copperwaite, placing a polite hand over his gaping, yawning mouth. "Rather a distance from the other bodies, wouldn't you say, Richard?"

But Sharpe's mind was elsewhere. He hardly heard a word.

"Ahh, of course," Copperwaite's light came on. "Not bloody far from where your ex and your children live, is it, Richard?" asked Copperwaite, knowing the answer.

"Let's get over there."

The ride to Hyde Park felt like a funeral procession marked by extraordinary solemnity. Sharpe brooded, looking like one of the ancient gargoyles atop so many London cathedrals. Obviously, the Crucifier had struck too close to home for Sharpe's comfort. Jessica followed Stuart Copperwaite's lead,

Copperwaite appearing to respect his elder partner's need for silence.

"Body's been snatched from the water. No telling how much evidence has gone lost before we were notified," Sharpe finally said, breaking the quiet. "First thing you'll want to examine, Doctor, are the wounds to the extremities and the tongue, of course."

"I'll have a look, of course," she replied.

"And if it's the same, we'll know that much."

"And if it's not?" asked Copperwaite.

"Then we'll have a bloody copycat killer to add to the mix, now won't we?" Sharpe's response came terse and angry.

Silence once again ruled the rest of the trip.

On arriving at Hyde Park, they turned off Baywater Road and cruised through Westbourne Gate onto West Carriage Drive which led them to water's edge at the Serpentine Bridge. Again, the body had been discovered washed up below a large bridge over a sizable body of water. A psychic could make hay with this repeated scenario, Jessica thought, as psychics invariably told authorities to "look for the body to be located near a large body of water, possibly near a bridge."

It so often became true because it was true to begin with; many a killer wished to wash his hands of the deed, and what better way than in a lake, at a river's edge or some other body of water.

When they came on the body, they found some ten or more men standing about in various poses ranging from awkwardness to confusion. Two of the men, hair and clothing drenched from having dragged the body out of the Serpentine, looked up at them as they approached, Jessica with her black valise in hand. She'd dragged it all about London in what Sharpe called his *boot*, the trunk of his car, and now she must utilize its contents.

"Stand back, all you chaps," Richard directed the others. "Dr. Coran here is a forensics expert. She'll have a look at the victim now. Stand aside, please."

Jessica appreciated his choreographing of the moment, tak-

ing charge as Otto Boutine, her FBI mentor, would have done
were he alive and standing alongside her.

Jessica immediately saw that the nude victim was female.
"Another A.N. Other," she heard someone say. Like the other
victims, this one was up in years, perhaps forty-five, perhaps
more. Impossible to be absolute at this point, but Jessica saw
the specificity of the wounds to feet and hands, the work of
large spikes.

Copperwaite, swallowing a gasp, exclaimed, "It's another
one crucified, all right. Look at the wounds to the hands and
feet."

Jessica and Sharpe had already seen and deduced the evidence of crucifixion. Like Sharpe, she suspected a copycat,
this murder having come so soon on the heels of Burton's
death. The only way to be certain lay beneath the victim's
tongue.

She located a pair of tweezers from her black valise as a
cricket clamored aboard the body and found its way across
the woman's dead eyes, which stared blankly out at Jessica.
She'd seen that same serenity about the features in both
Coibby and Burton's faces. It was as if these deaths meant to
defy her, as if their spirit remnants shunned her with a wry
grin.

Jessica shooed off the cricket even as she pushed her dis-
concerting thoughts away, concentrating on struggling into
her Latex gloves. Next she began fishing for the dead
woman's tongue using the sort of prong-ended tweezers sur-
geons preferred. She yanked and pulled at the dead tongue,
and brought it as far out as it would come, which in death
was two to three times further than in life.

All about her, men looked on, all but two wondering what
in God's name her interest in the dead woman's tongue could
possibly be, except the eccentric fetish of yet another eccentric M.E.? Jessica felt their combined stares as a mix of both
the curious and disgusted all at once.

"Give me a little light over here, will you?" she asked her
Scotland Yard colleagues.

Copperwaite grabbed for his penlight and shone the beam

down over Jessica's shoulder and onto the tongue held by the tweezers.

"Has she got it?" asked Copperwaite.

"Shhh!" cautioned Sharpe. "You'll tip off the lads." He indicated the others, but it was too late. One asked, "Got it? Has she some sort of disease we should be knowing about, Inspector?"

"No, no!" assured Sharpe. "Nothing of that nature, I can assure you."

"What then's with the tongue?"

"Dr. Coran examines every inch of the body," he half-lied, leaving out the rest.

Sharpe leaned in now, and saw what Jessica and Copperwaite stared at. A branded tongue with the exact same words, *Mihi beata mater*, staring back at them.

"Poor woman," moaned Jessica. "Such an awful way to die."

"Amazes me how these fiends think of such grotesque methods of torture and debauchery," Copperwaite bemoaned.

Sharpe asked the men standing about, "How was she found?"

"Facedown in the water, floating like a log."

"She bloody looks at peace," commented Copperwaite.

Jessica silently agreed with Stuart's assessment. The woman appeared restful, peaceful beside the lovely Lake Serpentine, and Sharpe appeared the agitated one. He began pacing in catlike circles before venturing off, down an incline toward the water and out of earshot.

"Sharpe's ex-wife, Clarisa, and his two young daughters, Milicent and Kimberly, live within sight of here, one of those lights up there." Copperwaite pointed to the nearby buildings and windows that circled about Hyde Park and the gardens. Copperwaite volunteered more, seeing that Jessica remained interested. "Imagine, this killer has been walking the same paths, visiting the pond where his little girls play and wade. It's really almost too much for anyone, even a stalwart chap like Colonel Sharpe there."

Jessica imagined the few short blocks that Sharpe could walk from here to see his two children. Those few blocks must seem a mere stone's throw from this bloody path taken by the Crucifier.

When Jessica had first met Sharpe, she could not have imagined him ever being anything but rocklike, unswerving, unshakable. Here he had definitely been shaken and shaken badly, given the proximity of the crime to the flat where his children lived and played. Sharpe's veneer had dropped and fear had replaced the inscrutable eyes, a fear of loss, a fear for the harm a maniac like the Crucifier could do to his children.

Jessica and Copperwaite drifted toward the water, as if drawn by the enormous Serpentine, or merely as subconscious steps to move away from the death at their feet. Copperwaite's reference to Richard as "Colonel" Sharpe surprised her a bit. Something odd in Copperwaite's voice, or perhaps in how Jessica interpreted the tone. Was it a sneer? Something about the sound of it made her recall Dr. Luc Sante's theory, found peppered throughout his book, might well be true: *The least suspicious among us, often turn out to be the most evil among us.* The thought made her flash on the bizarre possibility that Stuart Copperwaite had somehow arranged to hurt his partner, Sharpe, in this fashion. That the maniac hiding deep within Copperwaite had killed three others in this horrendous manner, just to bring home this fourth to his partner's doorstep, all done out of some twisted desire to see Richard Sharpe quake.

Jessica just as quickly dismissed her mad notion, and returned to the body, knowing her job was to concentrate on the evidence and not speculation. She returned to taking samples, expecting Schuller to arrive, and in his typically bombastic manner, take over the evidence gathering at any moment, but so far, she was the sum total of the evidence gathering team. She wondered at this, curious for a moment, but then her eyes shifted to where Sharpe stood at the water's edge with the two men who had dragged the body from the water, one a civilian, the other a police officer in uniform.

Jessica examined the victim's nails and found them perfectly clean. If she had put up a fight, the water left no trace of flesh or blood beneath her nails. This had been the same with the other victims. She imagined the same drug—Brevital—would be found in the victim's bloodstream, making resistance unlikely.

She glanced time to time from her work to where Richard remained at water's edge, joined once by Copperwaite, but now alone again. His eyes scanned Lake Serpentine in what appeared deep concentration.

"If you can suspect Copperwaite of so foul a crime, to unnerve Sharpe," she told herself in careful whisper, "then why not suspect Sharpe himself? Sharpe was behind getting you here, Jessica. Maybe, behind that veneer of respectability, he's just another madman anxious to test your mettle against his."

She instantly cursed herself. Had she become so jaded, she wondered, as to trust no one on the planet ever again? Evil had a way of overcoming the evil-fighter, and was she not being evil in her very thoughts now, first toward Copperwaite and now toward Sharpe?

She gasped when she realized Sharpe now stood over her and the body. He was speaking to her, saying, "I spent a number of years in the British forces, saw a lot of the world and evil at every turn, Jessica, but in all that I never once felt fear as I do tonight. Can you imagine that? I stand here so near my children, and I feel fear as I have never experienced it in my adult life ever. I'm reduced to a child by this madman."

"It's understandable, and quite frankly, I just finished up trying to imagine it. This maniac has hit quite close to home. Anyone would feel the same, Richard."

"I'm going to go see them."

"Now?" asked Copperwaite, exasperated with Richard. "Don't be a fool, Richard. That's all old Boulte will need to hear. He'll have your job f'sure."

"My children, Stuart. This is about my children. You're the primary investigator on this one, Stuart. You've earned it. Tell him that, should he bother to show up." With that he stepped away from the crime scene, resigned to whatever fate lie ahead.

Jessica watched him disappear into the gloom and fog that

had—like a secret everyone but Jessica shared—come in over the area.

She cursed. "I need more light. I can't do any more out here without field lights, Stuart."

"What more has to be done?"

"I guess you're right. I suppose we should get the body to the crime lab."

"I'll call for the ambulance. They've learned to come only when they're called. Maybe, if we act fast enough, no one will have to know about Richard's having left the scene. It could go bad for him."

"No one will hear it from me," she promised.

"Nor I, if I can at all help it."

Copperwaite took himself aside and made a call on his cellular phone for the police ambulance. He called back to her after several minutes to say, "Seems Schuller's wife fell ill and Boulte's been at some gala event for the city, some charity affair or other. They've neither one any knowledge of victim number four, our Miss Another. Perhaps Richard's got away with it after all."

"Are you talking to Schuller's assistant, Dr. Raehael, or someone else on call?"

"It's the Egyptian's day off, I'm afraid. They're overtaxed tonight, and say since you're on hand to leave it at that."

"We *are* fortunate, then, aren't we?"

"That we are."

Jessica looked in the direction Sharpe had taken. Upward in the distance, she could still make out the blinking lights of several tall buildings along Hyde Park Gardens and Baywater Road. They were a far cry from the discovery sites in the three other murders, all of which had been along the Thames, one within striking distance of Lombard Street—the City, as it was called—the principal street for banking and international finance. "The Big Four," Sharpe had told Jessica, "the major banks, National Westminster, Barclays, Lloyds, and Midland." "Giants," he'd called them. Jessica imagined them now, all the icons of London, among them Westminster Abbey, the Tower of London, and Big Ben, now with murder lurking in the shadows cast by each.

"Why?" she wondered aloud.

"Why what?" asked Copperwaite.

"Why bring the body so much further away this time?"

"From the Thames and Victoria Gardens Embankment, you mean?"

"From the more central locations the first three were found at, yes."

Copperwaite considered this. It had been the reason Sharpe had believed it possible the fourth victim could be a copycat. It didn't fit the geography of the other crimes.

"He knows we're watching the bridges about the Thames," suggested Copperwaite. "He's no fool this one. Rather clever, actually, if you think about his movements. The way he's kept us all guessing and on our toes, wouldn't you say? Smart bugger, he is, this one . . ."

"Yes, he knows we're onto his MO, at least how he disposes of the bodies."

"So he motors here with the body in his boot."

Jessica said, "Yes again."

"So our killer is quite capable of moving about the city, quite mobile."

"It appears so."

Copperwaite snatched out a breath mint and laid it neatly on the end of his tongue. "The bridgeman said he saw a car parked nearby but had thought nothing of it."

"Exactly how long has he been divorced?" she asked.

Copperwaite, befuddled by the sudden shift in her questioning, at first replied, "The bridgeman?" But he immediately regrouped and said, "Richard? Oh, yes. Three, three and a half years now, I believe."

"And has he someone he's seeing now? Has he moved on?"

"Dunno. He never speaks of anyone, no, but for a time he was seeing someone. Quite hush-hush, he is. I never knew her name. Puts his effort into his police work mostly. That and his children. Sees them fairly regularly. Gets on fairly well with the ex as well. She simply couldn't handle being a policeman's wife. Old story, really."

"Very," she agreed.

"He cut quite a dashing figure in his uniform. I've seen

photos. Looks like your GI Joe, really. Made rank of colonel, you know, in the military, I mean."

"Is that so?"

"Aye, it is."

"He seems a remarkable man."

"Remarkable, yes. James Bond we call him at the Yard."

"When you're not calling him 'Sharpie,' you mean?"

"Sharpe he is. Lives up to his namesake. An ancestor who fought in the Napoleonic wars. His great-grandfather or some other fought ferociously for the Crown and won honors in battles in Spain and France, but he didn't come from nothing like royalty. It's partially why he and Boulte can never get along."

"I see, I think."

"Richard's just your ordinary British blood, born of common stock as they say, which isn't bad, really. Richard himself was born within the sound of Bow Bells."

"Isn't that where the first victim was found?"

"Aye, true enough, Doctor."

"Just coincidence, like this . . ."

"Beggin' your pardon, mum—Doctor?"

"Tonight . . . being so close to Sharpe's home, and—"

"Former home," Copperwaite corrected Jessica as if defending his partner.

"—and that first killing being in the sound of Bow Bells, so close to home—Richard Sharpe's home, I mean."

Copperwaite suddenly stared quizzically at her. "Whatever are you gettin' at, Doctor?"

Jessica shrugged. "Oh, nothing really. Just funny how coincidental things happen in life, and how small the world actually is, even in an enormous city like London."

"Coincidence . . . occurrences. I could tell you scores of stories about my uncle Thomas that would curl your hair for the coincidence in that man's life."

She smiled at this. Then the sound of a siren signaled an end to her crouching over the body in the cooling evening, in the now dense fog of Hyde Park.

Somewhere out over the Serpentine, a swan bellowed a mournful cry, like some forlorn mother in anguish over a lost

child. Other swans answered the first to call out. Soon, like
dogs roused in a neighborhood late at night, a cacophony of
swan calls exploded like fireworks all across the lake. The
noise it made created a poor mimicry of the ambulance wail
as the little automobile screeched to a halt, kicking up dust.
Its siren went silent only when the driver came to idle, the
spiraling red lights creating a mosaic of shadows in all directions.

The huge-shouldered driver, his shiny bald head reflecting
the emergency lights, displayed the forehead of a Neanderthal
where he stood after climbing from the cab and striking a
match to light a cigarette. In London, smokers enjoyed their
cigarettes everywhere, regardless of the known health risks
the habit posed. So here the man stood, leaning against his
meat wagon like a New York longshoreman, daring anyone
to tell him what to do. So he rested, obviously not anxious to
lift the ponderous cargo he and his partner had come to collect. The partner, unlike him, his opposite in fact—a petite,
long-haired, blond female—raced to the rear of the van to
enthusiastically haul out the stretcher on her own. At the same
time she frantically searched about for the direction of the
corpse, until seeing Jessica, who waved them over.

Jessica didn't see or hear again from Inspector Richard Sharpe
until the following morning while at autopsy over the latest
Jane Doe. "Still no word on her identity," he whispered in
Jessica's ear. Most people whispered around dead people, as
if speaking quietly were a requirement, some sort of Miss
Manners rule number seventy-nine that stated, "Thou shalt be
tranquil and silent in the face of death." Perhaps they thought
that to go into rancor at it would only upset the demons. But
Sharpe's serenity seemed greater than the usual silence about
the morgue and crime lab. He appeared genuinely refreshed,
as if anxious to attack the problem of the Crucifier as never
before.

"How are your girls?" she asked.

"Gonzo, actually. Lovely creatures, the both of them."
Sharpe had a disposable cup filled with black coffee in his
hand, the steam caressing his cheek.

"Does you well to see them, I can tell. You look refreshed."
She wondered if he'd gone to bed with his ex-wife and had
gotten himself into a totally relaxed state this morning. It did
seem so, she silently mused.

"Absolutely, yes. Seeing the children, well it's like taking
a drink from that fountain of youth everyone throughout the
ages has searched for."

"Perhaps there is where it lies, in our children."

"Have you any? Children, I mean?"

" 'Fraid not."

"Pity. But then, you're young and have time." He sipped
at his coffee.

She smiled, thought of Jim Parry and his wish for children
and wondered if men felt as much a need to have children as
did women. In the sense that they wished to carry on their
DNA, to make little clones of themselves, perfectly suited to
the male ego.

Jessica returned her attention to the dead woman on the
slab before her. Schuller's young assistant, Dr. Al-Zadan Raehael, remained all the help she had. He seemed capable and
a good deal more at ease knowing that Dr. Karl Schuller
would not be barreling through the door at any moment.
Called back from his day off, he appeared sullen.

"I've found nothing to distinguish her," Jessica informed
Sharpe, her eyebrows raised in mock supplication. "No birth-
marks, no earlier fractures or sutures. Very little dental work
has been done. It will be hard to ID the woman."

"I've spoken with Paul Boulte. Fortunately, he never knew
of my stepping off the task last evening. Copperwaite covered
my bases, as you Americans are fond of saying."

"Not all of us are fond of baseball metaphors, Richard."

"I do wish to apologize for my behavior of—"

"Not at all."

"—leaving you and Stuart in the lurch."

"We managed just fine, as you can see."

"Well, do accept my sincerest thank-you."

"Accepted."

"And should you care to see more of London, I do happen
to be free this evening, say for dinner?"

"There's a great deal of the city I'd still like to see, and you have been so generous with your free time. Well, I'm both pleased and overwhelmed. You make a terrific guide." Their eyes met and held for a moment, as they had the first time they met one another, back in Quantico, Virginia.

He smiled wide, his eyes flaring silver sparks from the deep green irises. "I'll take that as a yes, then."

"Yes."

"Another scare for Londoners," Sharpe said, indicating the body before them.

"I saw the news photos. They must have paid the ambulance drivers. I never saw any press at the scene, nor at the crime lab when we got here."

"Imagine the usual *Geordie* out there, opens his morning paper to find *her* dead eyes looking back up at him from his *Gazette* or *Times*," ruminated Sharpe. "To find a photo of the victim in death on the front page. Turns out that Stuart put the other victims' photos out there, and he likely did this one as well, to shake the tree, so to speak. It's a general call that's gone around, for anyone recognizing the woman to step forward, you see."

"And you agree with the tactic?"

"Not altogether, no. Stuart and I had words about it."

She nodded, biting her lip, wondering what "had words" in Great Britain meant. She certainly knew its American cousin. She finally said, "We're apt to utilize the press often in such cases in the States, but it's usually a step not taken lightly, much argument of the pros and cons with each case. You have to weigh everything in the balance, and often you weigh up all wrong anyway."

"Press pressure," he confided.

"Ahhh, yes, we've certainly got that in the States, too. It's a so-called *legitimate* duress."

"Serial killers here are rare, so the press is all over it. Actually, it's becoming all too common, as if . . . as if . . . Well, I'm not a bloody philosopher, but as I said, the closer we get to 2001, as was the case with the year 2000 as well, the more madness and deviltry we find ourselves embroiled in and surrounded by. Course, you know more about that than I."

"The millennium? The madness? Or being surrounded and embroiled in deviltry?" she asked.

"Quite possibly all three. Oh, we have our share of terrorists, what with the IRA and Hamas and other organizations sworn to destroy us. That's madness enough, but this sort of thing, someone killing a string of people out of some blind rage or cult blindness. . . . No, I've not come across the like of this crucifying thing before."

He tossed his empty cup into a trash container. "Nor has anyone, I assure you. But you've faced monsters, human monsters, before, and that's what we're dealing with here. Not a man with a misguided political cause, but a man with a fantastic plan that boggles the mind and dares you to decipher the meaning."

"Yes, in that regard, I guess I have had some experience. And perhaps you're right to work a theory connected with what the popular press is calling the turn of 'true millennium.' I know we Americans are overanxious about it. The teen suicide rate more than doubled at the turn of 2000. I shudder to think it will triple with the turn of 2001. Teens are routinely carrying guns and other weapons to schools, many out of paranoia. Unfortunately, we often downplay the force of change—especially technological change—and the anxiety it breeds. But also this fear of a major shift in time."

"People are struggling, searching to make sense of a fundamentally unsteady world, a changing, evolving world," Richard agreed.

"What you said about the millennium is perhaps more true than you know. Historically speaking, any major event brings on a certain return to fundamental fears in mankind. Any turning of a century brings out his fears and frailties. He falls back on the primal urges, the primitive brain mechanisms that aren't so different than those of lizards, alligators, and other carnivores—those flee or fight mechanisms. And if that's true of the usual, run-of-the-mill turn of the century, then it's likely to be exacerbated by something as momentous as the new millennium. It's even exacerbated by the fact that nothing momentous occurred New Year's Eve 2000. So now the prophesies and millennial fears logically flip-flop to the year

2001, which experts tell us is in fact the actual turn of the thousand years."

"You realize there's a great deal of meat on that mutton. We must pick at it a good deal more to get to the bone," he agreed. "Historically speaking, the turn of any century sees an intensified unrest with panics, revolutions, and wars."

"You think the Crucifier is acting out of some reaction to the new age, the year 2001, then?"

He nodded several times, his jaw set, eyes stern and penetrating. "I think it quite possible, yes. I've read some history, and I've spoken with Luc Sante about the possibility. As it happens, since at least the 1490s, the century ending has normally meant speeded-up events, history and consciousness in the Western world."

"And the added religious and cultural dimension of this being the millennium to Christianity . . ." she mused.

He picked up her thread of thought and added, "Should triple if not quadruple the impact of the year 2001. Just as for so many cults and cult leaders, the year 2000 itself fueled fantastic beliefs and practices. We had quite a show of them in London, as reported by the tabloids."

"Predictable enough. Anyone could claim psychic powers who has studied the history of mankind and its mistakes. Those ignorant of history are doomed to repeat its mistakes. We in America, too, were innundated with millennial madness both approaching and at the turn of the year 2000. Considering history—and the compression of this period in time, 2000 to 2001 . . . Well, we're certain to see an intensifying of the end-of-world, apocalypse-now, end-of-century pandemonium multiplied."

"As I said, it's been true of past '90s, from 1490 to 1890. There's ample evidence in the history books that turn-of-the-century fears have brought on revolutions and wars, or have accelerated wars, as in both the 1690s and 1790s. The French Revolution began in 1789, and by the 1800s had turned into the Napoleonic wars. Early twentieth century wars from St. Petersburg and Constantinople to Vienna and Berlin began in the tumult and terrorism of the 1890s."

"Luc Sante told you all this?"

"No, he simply got me thinking, and I rummaged about my memory of what I've read. History's something of a fascination for me. It's so littered with stress—anxiety in general but characterized mostly as panic before the turn of the century."

"We've already seen plenty of tumult and terrorism in our own wounded, hurting decade," she readily agreed. "The 1980s to the 1990s have been filled with horrors of all sorts." Jessica looked deeply into Richard's sea-green eyes, losing herself there for a moment. She thought how he proved as sharp as his name. In the light of day, even where they were in the morgue below the crime lab, Jessica felt her fleeting suspicions and doubts surrounding Richard were so foolish that she wished to die at having ever entertained them even for the flashing moment. She wondered if there could ever come a time in their relationship when she could jokingly tell him about her paranoia. She rather doubted it. She also wondered what it said about her. How had she become such a suspicious shrew?

"I shall hope to see you at end of day, then. It appears you have your hands rather full here," he said, looking on as she had lifted the viscera from the rib cage.

She half smiled and said, "I'll look for you after I've closed."

"And I shall look forward to it." And he was gone.

James Parry could take himself and his newfound love and go to hell, she thought. At the same instant, she chastised herself for the uncharacteristic thought. Once again she thought of lines from Shakespeare's *Mid-Summer Night's Dream* and how rankled and insane love had made her. Still she did not wish Richard Sharpe to be "revenge" for Parry spurning her. She wasn't about to play that part. In fact, her mind actively fought the notion. She simply wanted to appreciate Sharpe's company. Richard Sharpe, a former colonel and a Scotland Yard inspector, courting her. Now *that* was something to write home to her therapist about. A smile serenely danced across her lips, for the thought made her momentarily dreamy-eyed: just long enough for Schuller's man, Raehael, to quizzically wonder what had gotten into Dr. Jessica Coran.

Jessica determined that her affinity for the Scotland Yard inspector to be completely genuine, and not some facile remnant of anger toward Parry. In fact, she felt nothing glib, cursory, trite, superficial, or insincere with regard to Sharpe; nothing elementary, apparent, simple, or obvious. Instead, a plethora of complex and confusing feelings proved to culminate in a pleasant acceptance of her admiration of Sharpe. She quieted her thoughts of Richard, returning attention once more to the fourth victim of the Crucifier's cross.

As she did so, Jessica wondered if new DNA testing with laser light to detect trace elements of DNA left on the victim's body from someone in close contact might be of help here. It had recently been shown that humans indeed secreted far more DNA through touch alone than believed, leaving trace elements of DNA on telephones, pens, desktops, anything they touched. She asked Dr. Al-Zadan Raehael if he had the capability at the Yard to run such a test, supposing they could locate and lift the killer's DNA off the dead woman's hands or feet, where the killer had held them down to stake them, or on her lips, for example, where the killer, using the micro brand on her tongue, would have left DNA traces, had the killer failed to use surgical gloves. The killer knew about Brevital and he used precision. Might he be a doctor himself?

"We have the laser equipment and the DNA testing equipment, yes. DNA testing began in Leicestershire County, not far from here, Doctor. Where that fiend killed all those little girls in Narborough, Littlethorpe, and Enderbury."

She recalled the famous case. Author Joseph Wambaugh chronicled it in his book *The Blooding*, which not only recounted both the discovery of genetic fingerprint testing through DNA analysis in Dr. Alec Jeffreys's laboratory in 1986, but the first official use of genetic fingerprinting to resolve a murder investigation and put a killer away for life.

"In that case, let's test her hands, feet, and lips for any traces of DNA not hers."

"At the point of each wound, that's clear enough," replied Dr. Raehael.

"How soon can the tests be run and results had?"

"We'll put it on first burner. Several days is the best we can do, but even then, without a matching—"

"Oh, I realize that. But if and when we determine who the Crucifier is, we'll have it on record to nail him—no pun intended."

"*If,*" Raehael cautioned Jessica. "Big if, like you Americans say. . . . If he's left any DNA on her."

· TEN ·

*If evil were easily recognized, identified, and
managed, there would be no need of forensic
medicine.*

—FROM THE CASEBOOKS OF JESSICA CORAN

After dinner at the Savoy, Richard, with tickets in hand, announced that they were going to take in *King Lear* at the
Globe Theatre.

They drove to the theater, located at a wide bend on the
River Thames on the opposite shore to that of St. Paul's Ca-
thedral between the Southwark Bridge and Blackfriar's
Bridge.

The air felt thick with an electric intensity as the crowd
grew and took on a rambling, monstrous life of its own. The
madding crowd, Jessica thought. The public anticipation of
the performance in the open-air, outdoor, Tudor theater had
created an intensity in the impatient audience. Jessica took in
the replica of the Globe Theatre, a painstakingly reconstructed
edifice down to the oaken steps leading onto and off stage.
Even the bard himself would recognize the theater as his
home. The place did, in fact, represent an exact likeness of
the theater in which Shakespeare's plays had been performed
in his day. The only change Shakespeare would feel was that
of time, for almost four hundred years had gone by.

"It's been a boondoggle, some say, reconstructing the great
Globe," Richard informed her. "Not everyone is happy with
her."

"Give me one reason why," Jessica protested, staring at the

beautiful stage, its circular shape and the two-story, surrounding building.

"It opened in 1997 at a cost of forty-six million of your American dollars. Having remained closed since 1613, purist and taxpayer alike didn't relish paying for it."

"Then it came into being through government funding?"

"Matching funds for a wood and thatch construction on the south bank of the Thames, some two hundred yards from the site of the original? Imagine the fire insurance alone."

Jessica's eye wandered to the concession stand where plastic pullover raincoats could be had for two pounds, about three dollars American.

"The original wooden *O*, as many call it, as Shakespeare himself called it in *Henry V*, was built in 1598 or '99 by a pair of well-to-do brothers, Cuthbert and Richard Burbage, using timbers from a failed theater in nearby Shoreditch. They wanted to place the *O* centrally, you see. Later, Shakespeare himself became a shareholder."

"I suppose the original, being made of thatch and timber, rotted of old age?" she asked.

"Fate has never been too kind to the Globe, no. In 1613, the thatch was put alight by two cannons fired during a performance of *Henry VIII*. King Henry's ghost's revenge on Shakespeare for depicting him as he did, some say."

Together they laughed at the jest.

Since there was no assigned seating at the Globe, further simulating Shakespeare's day, they made their way toward the stage, to locate seats as close to the action as possible. Richard now added, "History books say no one was hurt in the fire, except for one poor chap who, and I quote, 'Found his breeches afire so that it would have broiled him if he had not, with benefit of a provident wit, helped himself to some bottled ale to quench the flames.' "

Jessica laughed even harder at this image.

"The theater was rebuilt sometime after the fire, but again it came under destruction when in 1642 the Puritans, finding it offensive, demolished her as the breeding ground of the Devil that she is, you see." Guiding her to her seat, he added, "If you look closely, the reconstruction is not entirely complete. There's still scaffolding at the rear and some finishing touches are being applied. Only last year did the plywood stage get replaced with the oaken one we now have. Still, even unfinished, the theater has enticed some 150,000 visitors annually, a figure that is expected to triple by the year 2001."

In a balcony built overlooking the stage, an actor began hurling insults at the audience, his own patrons. "Ya've paid full fair to sit on a wooden bench to hear buffoons wail out their sorrowful lives here? Are ya' daft, ya' citizens of London? 'Aven't ya' a telly for that, the telly and soap operas? Are ya' daft?" he venomously shouted and tossed confetti at the front rows.

A female, acting as his wife, came out on the balcony to scold him, telling him to leave the paying customers alone and to come away with her, to help her prepare for the show.

"Ya're all daft!" he called back. "Ya' could be sittin' at the Coat of Arms down the street having a pint!"

"Shut that big hole of yours!" replied the wife.

"I'll not be aggrieved by ya', woman, not in public and not in private!"

And off they went, arguing, only to be replaced by an aged man with a white, flowing beard who talked to himself about the alignment of the stars, the heavens, and the meaning of life there on the balcony.

"It's a tradition with the Globe, the stage balcony rows," explained Richard. "Keeps the audience entertained and in a good mood before curtain rise."

"How many people does the theater seat?" asked Jessica, curious.

"To cover the cost of an opening, ticket sellers have to fill the seats, some 1,394. Five pounds buys the rights to be a *groundling*."

"A groundling?"

"See those people up front, all on their feet in the pit ahead of us?"

She nodded.

"Groundlings. They have a right to space on the floor, standing or sitting. We, by comparison, have tickets for a seat

in the terraces, a bit more costly at sixteen pounds, but well
worth it for these seats."

They had found their seats and settled in. Richard said in
her ear, "The season began in May with the Globe ensemble
of actors performing four plays in repertory. Performances run
till late September. Playwrights other than Shakespeare are
performed here from time to time as well."

"Such a splendid idea . . . to revive the Globe."

"We Britons can't take all the credit in reviving the Globe,"
Richard confessed. "One of your American actors, Sam Wanamaker, established a trust to raise funds for the project. Construction began in 1993, the year Wanamaker died at age
seventy-four in fact."

"I've seen Wanamaker on the screen and on TV." Jessica
pictured the ruddy-faced, tall Wanamaker.

"The project is still several million dollars short, and was
ten million short when the Globe opened in '93."

As if hearing Sharpe, and as if on cue, a new character atop
the theater at the balcony yelled down to the patrons to open
their pocketbooks. "You critics among you who said the theater would never survive! You dig the deepest and pay treble
for those seats you now have! Come along, out with it! There
are jars and wretched fellows milling about who will take
your donations!"

"We're still paying for her, but she is grand, isn't she?"
asked Richard. "Right down to her Norfolk reed roof, the oak
beams, the hand-turned balustrades."

"Yes, it's a fantastic recreation," Jessica agreed when suddenly thunder roared all around them, yet the source could be
traced to crude sounds being created behind the stage.

"Even the sound effects are authentic to their time," he
explained. "That's heavy metal shot, cannonballs, rolled about
in a metal washtub to simulate the sound of an approaching
storm."

"So there's actually no sound equipment?"

"None but what human hands and minds can create.
There's no electricity, no lights, actually. Look around you."

"So that's why we're here so early."

"The performance ends with nightfall, just as in Shakespeare's day."

"It's a totally 'rough' experience."

"Exactly. The only thing not authentic is that we, the audience, aren't allowed to bring in overripe fruit and vegetables to throw at the actors."

Jessica's behind already felt sore on the hard wood "terrace" seats. Taking her mind off the lack of creature comforts, Jessica noticed other buildings standing about, also with Tudor construction and thatch roofs. "What goes on there?" she asked, pointing.

"Just opened the final phase of the project, two museums, or rather one an educational center, and a three-hundred-seat small theater designed from blueprints left by Elizabethan architect Inigo Jones. Plan is to have them all operational by 2001 and have a gala millennium party alongside the 401st performance on the Globe stage at the same time."

"What an undertaking! It's magnificent," she conceded.

"The theater itself is fully operational now, and will support the cost of its operation. I firmly believe that, as a member of the board of trustees."

"Ahhh, no wonder you know so much about it."

"It's become a passion, something to give myself over to so that I am not wholly swallowed up by my job, as in the past."

She thought momentarily of how her own work had swallowed up relationships, such as her and Jim Parry's irreconcilable problems, which prompted her to say, "Something all of us in law enforcement must . . . guard against."

"Something indeed . . . When I allowed my job to consume me, well . . . for my troubles my wife gave me my walking papers."

"Divorce. I'm sorry."

"You see, too much time devoted to my work, not enough to the ones I love."

"I'm so sorry for any pain you've been put through, Richard."

"Pain, depression, you can say the whole gamut came down around me. Had to take some time off, get back my focus, regroup. The Globe project, when it came along, well, it worked as a lifesaver for me."

Jessica settled in comfortably, excited at the same time. Then the curtains, faithful to history, were hand-pulled back to reveal the opening scene in *Lear*. She soon learned that Richard hadn't exaggerated in the least about the method of "special effects" here. Sounds and sights were indeed faithfully reproduced, even the firing off of a cannon like the one that burned down the original Globe.

King Lear had always held a great fascination for Jessica. Especially interesting to her was the tragic tyrant who, when he had eyes, could not see, and when blind, could see. The play, she believed, actually represented a metaphor for all mankind, the blind lives we all lead.

At the close of evening, walking from the theater, Sharpe asked if she'd like to see the Thames from Blackfriar's Bridge. She accepted, and they made the short stroll to the center of the bridge overlooking the river and nearby massive St. Paul's Cathedral by moonlight.

While there he reached out, took her hand in his, telling her, "You are an extraordinary woman, Jessica Coran. I've not met anyone like you before."

"Funny," she replied, squeezing the hand that he'd placed in hers. "I've been thinking the same thought about you, Richard Sharpe."

"Perhaps we should do something about our feelings?" It came out as a question. He added a warm smile.

She dropped her gaze from his. "Perhaps. If you feel it won't jeopardize our working relationship."

"We won't allow it to."

"Are you sure? It often changes things."

He kissed her under the pale lampposts of Blackfriar's Bridge. She eagerly kissed him back. It had been a long time since a man had made her feel light-headed, giddy, and wanted all at once.

"Let's go to my place," he suggested. "I can make you breakfast there."

"Why not enjoy the York? We'll order room service," she countered.

"I have no other reply than . . . Yes, why not?"

• • •

With Richard Sharpe's deep, rhythmic breathing a soothing anthem alongside her, Jessica studied his peacefully dozing countenance. Unfortunately with her evil friend insomnia also in bed with her, Jessica took only fitful breaths of air; at the same time, she brought back the images and the wonder of Sharpe's and her intermingling. They'd meshed effortlessly, naturally, intuitively in their lovemaking; the two of them in sync, in symbiosis. How truly free and extraordinary.

Unable to sleep, Jessica cautiously pulled herself up to a sitting position, not wishing to disturb Richard. She sat contemplating the feelings within her, stirrings which Richard had left rummaging about inside her. Jessica carefully brought her legs over the bed. She searched through her purse on the bedside table, and from it, she pulled forth the last letter she had received from James Perry.

Both she and James had tried to hold on to the unraveling shreds of a long-distance relationship. Trying to make love work from across oceans and continents was hard to do in any time zone, and in any historical era. Was it an impossibility in the late 1990s, she wondered, or simply an impossibility for the likes of Dr. Jessica Coran? At any rate, *their* long-nurtured, long-distance affair had proved impossible, no matter whose fault, hers or Jim's or theirs.

Perhaps, she simply hadn't the determination required to maintain *any* close relationship. "So what do I do?" she muttered to herself. "I intentionally seek out relationships divided by continents and pernicious seas. Ultimately, safer that way," she finished with a disdainful moan. She then stared down at Richard, whose catlike serenity irked her; she so envied it. A part of her, a large part of her, wanted to simply cry her eyes out, here and now. She wanted to cry for James, cry for the death of their love, cry for the confusion she felt, cry for Richard and herself, for what they had now undertaken together, cry for the future of their obvious long-distance relationship—the one that could come of this night, if she let it. She wondered if it would simply be a great deal easier and wiser and cleaner and better if she told Richard they had no future whatever together. That he must immediately forget any thoughts along those lines. She wondered if she ought not to simply lie to him, tell him that she could never love him as she did James. "Would certainly make things simpler," she mumbled aloud.

She wanted to burn Jim's last letter, burn it in effigy to their several "reconciliations" and get the anger out. Instead, she sat rereading it, reminding herself that her intuition, upon reading the letter the first time around, had told her the relationship was over. She'd stubbornly and foolishly ignored the information from within, denial being the predator of all reason, the predator of all who failed to heed their own inner voices.

Jessica realized now for the second time, that all the signals had been given her then, and they were vivid, huge signals, like billboards in the sky. Signs she had simply chosen to ignore; signs she unconsciously shunned, like an insistent dream that one ignored only to find it coming to full-blown life.

"And me with my handwriting expertise, learned the hard way on the job," she muttered in a whisper. "If only I'd subjected this letter to the same analysis I would a criminal's letter." *If only I had paid attention to the handwriting, the hesitation marks that skitter between the lines*, she thought now. But like a motorist on an interstate, she'd been moving too fast to read the fine print on the billboard.

She imagined that if she closely examined his last several letters, she would find signs of the impending doom that had befallen the two of them. *Love makes you blind,* she told herself. She told her shadow self, the one keeping her awake, something altogether different. "Love's a war, a battle for one's soul, and in the battle pieces are lost, scars won, mostly scars bearing the appearance of defensive wounds. Love's poison. Love's a bitch. Love's a killing offense."

Richard—half asleep and in what appeared a muddled nightmare—crinkled his forehead and mumbled something about a bastard, stakes, and crosses. Jessica imagined his personal nightmare of the moment filled to overflowing with the spirits of menace in a place thickly populated by demons. A pained gasp for air made her wonder if he were dreaming of his own crucifixion death, pinned to a cross, unable to move or to fight back. Then as suddenly as the darkness had swept over his brow, the dreamer smiled a grin similar to those she'd seen on Coibby and Burton, one of contentment, peace.

Obviously, Sharpe lives, breathes, and sleeps his work, she thought. *Just as I do.* The conviction grew the longer she stared down at his prone figure. Still, he was older than James, and retirement for him loomed on the near horizon. He'd be free to come to America. They could both live in the Quantico area where he might buy a large farm—no, a ranch with horses. She loved horses and horseback riding, and when he would call for her to come out on a weekend, she'd drop everything and be there and . . . Her dreams ran a bit rampant for a half second, her eyes fixed on Richard Sharpe lying alongside her, her "alongsider" friend and lover.

Their lovemaking rivaled any lovemaking she'd ever known, and she sensed it the tip of the iceberg with this man. They had been cautious, yet passionate with one another, halting yet fulfilling each other's needs. Jessica knew that she could grow to love this man.

She reread the letter for the eleventh time. James had desperately tried to make it come clear to her, clear that she either choose her career or him, clear that he could no longer accept the status quo: the burden of the long-distance love affair they'd established had fallen squarely on her shoulders—typical of the male of the species.

Checking the time, realizing it is after twelve noon in Hawaii, Jessica impulsively telephones James. She checks the digital figures on her bedside clock and while she realizes the hour puts him at work, she calls nonetheless. Her toe begins tapping at the air where it dangles alongside the bed, and she mentally taps her thoughts: He will be at his desk, she *assures* herself, pacing, wondering if he'd done the right thing, calling off their relationship, worried sick about her. On the fourth ring, he *answers*, acting surprised to hear from her again, when in fact he is not in the least surprised. When he speaks, he spews forth venom, telling her, "Jess, damnit, it's over now! Now, please never call here again!"

In the background, she hears someone softly asking if

everything is all right: a female associate. Jessica throws the telephone through a nearby mirror where it is swallowed up. Her eyes open, and she finds, found, located herself in time and place, found herself being held against Richard Sharpe's powerful chest, listening to the beating drum of his heart, feeling the power of his grip on her back where his hands and fingers massaged while his voice soothed her pain.

Sharpe had grabbed her, holding on, telling her, "You're all right, Jessica. Your nightmare is just that, a nightmare." His voice flowed like fine wine, strong, firm, reassuring, solid.

"Sorry," she softly apologized, awake enough now to distinguish dream from reality, to assure him that she was no infant in need of coddling.

"Lamenting the death of an old relationship is never easy," he replied, holding up the letter from Jim Parry.

She snatched at the paper, tearing it even as he welcomed her taking it. "That's private!" she shouted, realizing that this moment could end their relationship with one stroke, that it represented one of those escape exits from a relationship that Dr. Donna LeMonte, her psychiatrist and friend, had so often told Jessica she grasped at like straws. She could so easily overreact, sending Richard out into the night, screaming at him for daring to touch her letter from Jim. She could easily accuse him of having read her private correspondence, of finding the act vile. Or she could hold on. Hold to the moment, hold to Richard, *hold*.

"I quite well know and understand the depression and horror of a long-term relationship falling apart," he calmly said, his hands still massaging her back.

"None of my relationships have any chance whatsoever, thanks to my . . . This obsessive drive to be the best forensic scientist I can be." She found herself confessing and not knowing why. Sharpe brought it out in her. She wanted to share everything with him, including her darkest moments and her every mole.

"To be the best at something. No better desire or goal on the planet. And you are, you know, the best M.E. I've ever seen at work. You don't have to keep proving yourself to me.

Boulte, yes. Me, no." He said it with the rich, lusty laugh which he'd trumpeted at the theater.

"God, you're a wonderful man," she told him.

"That's the nicest thing a woman, any woman, has said to me in a long time."

She bit on her lower lip, pouting. "So, you've found me out, and quickly. I found you irresistible from the start, from the moment I first saw you in my office."

"I had no idea."

"Nonsense, Inspector. You're both too observant and too fast for that, Sharpe."

He countered, saying, "I find you keenly quick—intelligent, capable—and as to your obsessions, well, I rather fancy them admirable obsessions. Far more so than those of women obsessed with hair, lipstick, and ornamentation."

She smiled at this. "Will you find it so admirable once I've returned to the States?"

"We're both adults, Jessica. We've both been in prior relationships, both good and bad. I have no wish to put any yokes on you. Besides, it's a great deal closer to London from Washington than it is to Hawaii."

She looked peculiarly at him. She hadn't explained to him anything about James Parry or ever mentioned Hawaii to him, not that she could recall. "Then you did read Jim's letter. How else could you know it was Hawaii?" she asked, point-blank.

"You said so, in your sleep."

"I did?"

"You repeatedly said the words 'paradise' and 'Hawaii' amidst a gibberish about spawning whales. I could not follow. I tried waking you before you toppled the phone, but—"

"Toppled the phone?"

He pointed to the floor beside the bed. She realized now that the buzzing in her ears was the phone off its cradle where it lay on the floor beside the bed.

"Perhaps you're not quite over this fellow in Hawaii, in which case, I feel that perhaps I ought not to have stayed."

"No, no, Richard. I'm glad you and I, that we . . . that we have had this moment. It's been . . ." She wanted to say therapeutic, but she feared he'd take that description badly.

He reached her mouth with his and covered her halting words, taking her breath away, feeding on it. She responded with quick energy, returning his probing kiss, feeling the heat and passion rising in Richard Sharpe again, feeling her own passions well up and boil over.

"It's been a long time since I've enjoyed a woman, and never one so beautiful as you," he continued the none-too-subtle flattery, and she loved it.

"It's been a long time since a man has lied so well to me," she countered.

"Lie!" He laughed and repeated it. "Lie? Me? Inspector Richard Sharpe of Scotland Yard? Lie to a lady? Never about such matters of *importance*."

"Shut up. Kiss me." She kissed him, James's letter falling in a crumple on the floor beside the bed with the phone still off the hook.

They made love for the second time, and the second proved better than the first time. Jessica's thoughts and memories of James Parry dissipated and faded as Richard's touch opened her mind to new possibilities. She particularly enjoyed hearing Sharpe laugh in complete and total abandon when he came in her.

They enjoyed a shower together and a large breakfast via room service the next morning, and Richard, having no change of clothes, left ahead of Jessica to swing by his flat to find what he needed. They both felt a euphoria about the step they had taken in forging a personal bond. Neither felt obligated to the other, and yet both wished to get to know the other at a still deeper level. They had parted with this feeling strong between them. Jessica had stopped just short of telling Richard how awful she felt at ever having, even for a moment, suspected him in setting up the Crucifixion murders to further his career. The nasty, *vulture-atop-a-tree* suspicious mind she had cultivated over the years, so rich in its cynicism, so capable in its bullshit detection, had simply kicked in prematurely there in Hyde Park when Richard had stepped off the crime scene so abruptly, leaving her alone with Copperwaite. Now she rather admired his having simply dropped every-

thing—all of his duties and responsibilities—to seek out his
girls in an effort to reassure himself of their safety.

Still, she thought better of telling him of her foolish suspicions during that fleeting moment in Hyde Park. The suspicion had come and gone like a bird flying in through an
open window and out another. No big deal. Funny, really.
Perhaps, one day, she might tell him, so that he might see
clearly and exactly the bad sort he'd become involved with.
But not now, not here. She feared spoiling what they had only
just found.

The phone rang, and Jessica found Chief Inspector Boulte
on the other end. "I've gathered together every available detective, policeman, and investigator in and out of Scotland
Yard who has devoted any time at all to the case, and it has
amounted to some one hundred and fifty chaps and ladies, all
of whom I wish for you to speak to this morning."

"Speak to . . . today?"

"As soon as you can get here, yes."

"About what we've uncovered thus far about the Crucifier?

"Exactly."

"You know how very little that is, Chief Inspector."

He cleared his throat before replying, "I do, but our chaps
need some guidance, and that is what you are here for, correct? Haven't you developed a complete picture—profile—of
the killer as yet?"

"I have some preliminary notes, but—"

"Good show, then read from your notes. See you in half
an hour, then?"

He hung up before she could protest with another word.

Jessica quickly dressed now in a lime green two-piece suit
with a forest-green blouse. The colors accentuated her auburn
hair and set off her smooth, tanned skin and hazel eyes. She
located her black valise and keys and set off for the stroll
from the York to the Yard.

The morning air felt crisp, clean, and brand-new, and the
sun felt like the life-giving source that it was. All around her,
life appeared bright, teemed full with promise, and Jessica
realized that her dream of telephoning Parry had been a com-
pensatory dream. Compensating for her true feelings of relief

that it was finally and cleanly over with James. While she
cherished their most intimate and fun-filled moments together,
she, too, had felt the weight of their relationship like heavy
chains of late. Her entire body now felt airy. Still a lump of
remorse stuck in her craw, a set of smoky, mirrored images
of James and her together in past moments, embracing; images of them in an imagined future. This sad and wasted hope
conspired with her unease at presenting what little evidence
they had against the Crucifier at an open meeting at Scotland
Yard. It proved enough to make her feel nauseous. Her stomach felt as if someone had left a hot poker inside her.

She tried to concentrate on her surroundings, ban the ill
thoughts, doubts, and fears. This area of London displayed
wealth and pomp on every corner, at every hotel door and
lobby, even down to what the doormen wore. Public pounds
kept this area of the City clean day and night. The vagrants
were kept out, leaving tourists with the impression that Britain
suffered no homeless problem, no poverty, prostitution, or
drugs. All social ills locked away or kept at bay, just beyond
the tourist-dollar districts.

Jessica watched London cabs and buses and people bustle
about the streets. Each had a purpose, a sure destination; while
she, like a rank tourist, stared at all the wonders of the City.
Suddenly a strange, odd, eerie twinge of fear struck like small
lightning down her spine, as if the Crucifier were close by,
damned near within touch, simply observing her out of mor-
bid curiosity, having learned of her presence on the case. Yet
when she stopped to look in every direction, staring down
one cabdriver, she found no one stalking her, no cameras
pointed.

She dismissed the notion and continued on to Scotland
Yard, finally coming within sight of the revolving cube-
shaped sign. At the entry, she flashed both her FBI badge and
her temporary Scotland Yard ID and was allowed to pass by
the armed security guards.

She didn't relish the idea of speaking before the huge
crowd Boulte had assembled, and she wondered where in the
building such a crowd might be stored. She stepped back to
the guards, asking advice.

One of the pair, in his late twenties to early thirties, said she must take the elevator for the top floor. "Entire top floor is a theater with a stage," he told her.

When the elevator opened on the top floor of the building, she found people in suits milling so thick that she had to fight her way off the elevator before the doors closed on her. She'd found the meeting room, a large lecture hall with a microphone and chairs set up before a table at the front.

Richard Sharpe, Stuart Copperwaite, Father Luc Sante, and Paul Boulte sat at the panel table, all of them looking sharply up at her as she entered. There was an expectant look on Boulte's face, like a pit bull before feeding. Luc Sante gave her a professional nod and a beaming smile. Copperwaite bit his own lower lip, and Richard dropped his gaze, as if pretending no interest in her whatsoever.

Just as it should be, she thought before plunking down her valise at her feet and a small notebook on the table.

"Good, Dr. Coran," said Boulte. "Glad you could join us. I've informed Dr. Coran that we wish to share all we have with the citywide task force, including but not limited to the information Dr. Coran unearthed regarding the tongues, and the meaning of the words found on those brands. We may proceed now, gentlemen and ladies."

"I would first like to make a call to Dr. Raehael," Jessica interrupted. "I have put him to work on creating some slides from the wounds. They may be helpful here."

"Time being a factor, I took the liberty. Here are your slides," replied Boulte, who with an upturned finger signaled someone in the dark rear of the room to bring up slide number one. Instantly, the murmurs and scattered discussions among the assembled police authorities fell to a dying *hush* as everyone stared at the seared flesh and lettering found on the fourth victim's tongue, the best impression they had been able to get. The words, large on the screen behind Jessica and the panel, reading *Mihi beata mater* held an eerie quality about them in their grand scale.

The room fell silent, seeing for the first time the words of the Crucifier.

·   ·   ·

No one had anything to say, not a single question regarding the tongue brandings. So Jessica, after asking Dr. Luc Sante to explain the meaning of the words to everyone, moved straight into her profiling of the killer or killers.

"The suspect or suspects will most likely be white, a man or men who live in the Bow Bells district, and most certainly London, and if he does not have a Messiah complex, it will be just as twisted or just as closely linked with one." She stopped to let this sink in. The response from the audience was one of whispered heckling, as if what she said must be obvious to all present. Some brave fellow finally said, "Really now?"

Another asked, "Is that an absolute certainty?" The tone alone ridiculed.

"The killer may have developed some interest in St. Michael, patron saint of the exorcists, and so as you can imagine, he likely spends a great deal of time on religious matters. Still, he may exhibit an emotional age of late teens to early twenties. He likely lives or works within close proximity to the crime scene, or in this case the dump sites. He may have recently acquired some knowledge or a psychological jolt to his system, some shocking news, as in the death of a close family member, the breakup of a long-standing relationship, perhaps a divorce or loss of income." She unconsciously stopped and eyed Richard. Then she hurried on, adding, "He may be a spontaneous person with a quick temper. He may take great pride in his vehicle." She read her own notes and paused, not sure she herself believed this one. The typical profile may not apply here, she reminded herself. "Might brag about his van or truck to others, might even joke about how many bodies it can carry. Having left the scene in disarray, we believe him to be a youthful offender, inexperienced at killing. He is known to have been in the Victoria Gardens Embankment–York-front area between three and four in the morning of the first discovered body. Now since the fourth killing, characteristics the killer may be displaying are: a change in eating and drinking habits, and personal hygiene. Inappropriate or obsessive interest in the crimes. The killer may frequently initiate discussion about one or more of the victims and the crimes. Anyone acting like a different person, and anyone who may have suddenly left the area."

Finished, Jessica asked for questions from the floor. She received many. Some seemed oddly repetitious, and she found herself having to repeat herself.

She pushed on. "The crucifixion deaths, Sharpe and I surmise"—Jessica paused to stare out at the detectives and beat cops from all over the city—"may have all to do with the coming millennium! As if the year 2000 were not enough, now we face 2001, and together, we'd like everyone to explore this possibility."

"Explore it how?" came another British-accented question from the group.

"Yes, how do you mean that, Doctor?" came the confusion.

A deep breath and she replied, "Primarily, we're asking that you be attuned to it."

"How do you mean, precisely, 'attuned to it'?" came back an instant response from the seats.

Damn but some of their questions seem of the idiot fringe, she nastily thought, then calmly said, "Read up on the coming 'true' millennium, the actual, honest to goodness one: 2001. Any deaths by cult members, any suicides relative to a cult practice and the beliefs associated with this notion we are at last on doomsday's doorstep. And don't forget anything to do with St. Michael or a St. Michael's cult you may stumble over."

"I see," replied the last questioner. "Like your Hale-Bhopal thing in America?"

"Hale-Bhopp," she gently corrected.

Stuart Copperwaite cleared his throat and helped Jessica out. "There's enough evidence to imply that our man, or men, are engaged in some sort of bizarre ritual surrounding the events that took the life of Christ. In the year of Our Lord's two thousandth birthday, 2001 . . . well, gentlemen and ladies, figure it out."

"So, it's as we thought before we got outside help," Chief Inspector Boulte said rather caustically and clumsily.

"Except that now we 'ave *four* victims of crucifixion murders, instead of three," said a female inspector from the floor.

Another woman chimed in with, "We've got ourselves another freaking Jesus freak, that's sure."

"Agreed, our killer has a Messiah complex," Sharpe softly added.

"Not just any old Jesus freak," suggested Copperwaite.

"A far more dangerous one this time around," cautioned Jessica. "One who indeed acts on his fantasy, and as we all know, religious fantasy—even in the hands of the supposed knowledgeable 'authorities' such as the Inquisition, this sort of perversion of religious beliefs can be absolute in its madness. We can't worry ourselves with a motive that only the killer comprehends."

"So what do we do now?" asked a heavyset detective, between moments of working a toothpick from one side of his mouth to the next.

"Yes, you want us to be on the lookout for hippies and skinheads or just what?" came the questions from the floor.

Jessica gently urged, "Be in tune with the killer as much as possible."

"And precisely how do we do that, mum . . . ahhh, Doctor?" asked another in an aggrieved tone. "What do you think of this, Sharpe?"

Jessica held a hand up to Sharpe before he could answer, and said, "You have to climb into his head. *Be* him."

Sharpe said, "Dr. Coran has made extreme strides ahead in the investigation, helping us out tremendously in a short matter of days. We expect to follow up on the leads she has provided."

Boulte put a prompt end to Jessica's question and answer period when he called upon Father Jerrard Luc Sante to take the podium to discuss the killer and his profile from Luc Sante's point of view. Jessica picked up her paltry notes and the forensic reports she had yet to complete and made her way to her seat. She herself felt great interest in what Jerrard Luc Sante might add to the picture.

Luc Sante clambered to his feet with a cane in his hand, which he used for pointing at the slide still displayed on the wall behind him. He repeated the words, *"Mihi beata mater,"* jabbing each word with the end of his black cane. "It's a grave

morning to you all, lads, gentlemen, ladies of the law," began
Luc Sante, his eyes giving away that powerful light of energy
that Jessica believed marked him as a passionate individual.
"I pity you your profession. What you must deal with on a
daily basis. You are the vanguard, the army set against evil
in this age. Now, today, we must explore this possibility that
Dr. Coran has spoken of, this cult slant to the crime. Cults
and cultism, I fear, are all too real. Throughout the Bible and
throughout history, cults have thrived among us as freely as
disease and domesticated dogs, and the more dangerous the
cult is can be judged by how often and to what degree the
cult threatens the life of its own followers or members of
society at large."

He allowed this to sink in. His intonation, his rich, redolent
voice, filled the room. Once more Jessica felt a strong affinity
with the wise old one.

"Many interesting human traits are put to the test at a time
like this, at and around the turn of the ordinary century, but
this . . . None of us knows of anyone who has been 'stressed'
by a coming millennia—twice if you will, given the millennium readiness first made for the year 2000, and now for
2001. Still, we already know that millennia mania and cruel
phobias surrounding this portentous time are rising out of control, beyond anything we've seen before."

Luc Sante had the undivided attention of every man and
woman in the room as he discussed the possibilities in some
detail. "The killer or killers may be fixated on the coming of
year 2001." He separated each word for emphasis. "And the
possibility the killer or killers are trying to hurry along
Christ's Second Coming is hardly out of the question." He
banged his cane down and it sounded like a gunshot.

This was met with murmurs, a general disquiet, some snick-
ers. Jessica tried to imagine what a police precinct in Chicago,
L.A., New York, or Miami would do with such "news" from
this expert.

Luc Sante judged the level of suspicion and disbelief, and
then he added, "Belief in a millennial experience that will
bring Christ to reign again on Earth, ladies and gentlemen, is
based on the Resurrection story and the Bible's own *Book of*

Revelation, and this belief recurs throughout the history of Christianity. Hedging their bets, the Catholic Church has made the year 2001 a jubilee year, as they had 2000, and the Adventists and several other conservative, evangelical groups take it even more seriously."

"Pardon, Dr. Luc Sante," interrupted Boulte. "Father, are you saying what I think you're saying?"

Luc Sante pushed on, adding, "Christ's Second Coming has always been just over the next horizon. Well, the actual date of the millennium is one hell of a horizon, my friends."

At eleven in the morning, Boulte called a halt to the meeting, encouraging everyone with a quip, "Do keep a sharp lookout for anyone impersonating Jesus H. Christ, lads."

The assembled investigators, some 160 of them, filed out of the largest room in the Yard's facility, in abject silence or confused murmurs.

Boulte took Luc Sante's hand, shook it vigorously, and turned to Jessica and Sharpe, while Copperwaite stood a bit off to one side. Boulte said simply, "I've put all my trust in you people, Dr. Coran, Dr. Luc Sante, Sharpe. Get me some results and quickly."

Sharpe simply nodded. Luc Sante simply smiled. Jessica said, "We'll end the career of the Crucifier soon, Chief Inspector. He will make a mistake. He will slip up sometime, somewhere."

"Soon, I pray." And Boulte was gone in search of his office.

"I have paperwork to my eyeballs," Sharpe said, "and Stuart has some phone calls to make, and we have some interrogations to take. Getting some anonymous tips, mostly bogus, but we have to follow through."

"Dr. Coran is in good hands, Inspector," Luc Sante assured Richard. "We have much to discuss, don't we, Dr. Coran?"

"About our year 2001 theories? Yes, we do."

"Good, then share a cab with me back to my humble cathedral. I must get back to my office on time or my secretary, Eeadna, will have my head."

Before she could answer Luc Sante, Richard interrupted, extending his good-bye, which Jessica thought sweet. Then the somewhat subdued Copperwaite followed Sharpe out the door. Copperwaite's body language told Jessica that somehow he knew about Richard and her. It might account for his awkward standoffishness.

"I want you to come back to St. Albans with me, Dr. Coran," requested Father Jerrard Luc Sante again as they climbed aboard the elevator and pushed for the main floor.

"I really can't, not just now. I have far too much awaiting my attention in the lab this morning," she countered, "but I do wish to pursue this cult notion and the millennium question with you. Perhaps later?"

He smiled and nodded. "I certainly understand how very busy you must be, Dr. Coran. Forgive me my persistence, and yes, perhaps later. Call me, but for now, do walk with me out to the cab stand. I must share my views with you."

"Absolutely," she agreed as the elevator doors opened. Jessica walked him past security and through the glass doors.

Outside, the stark sun burned their eyes. Luc Sante hailed a cab with his black walking stick. He opened the cab door but hesitated getting in. "I do wish to consult with you on this madman you and Sharpe are pursuing."

"Your input is much appreciated, sir, really."

"Oh, you needn't stroke me, my dear. I'm beyond having any ego whatsoever when it comes to needing a compliment fix. No, what I need from you is a sounding wall, a confidant. You see, I've been having these hellish, nightmarish dreams of late, all having to do with this maniac. I see him as a shadow, quite vague, but quite clearly intent on a mission, a religious test or quest if you will, to please God and Jesus and the Holy Ghost and the Virgin Mary, all of it. To set right what is wrong in the world. Does that sound foolish?"

"Not at all, Dr. Sante."

"Luc Sante," he corrected her. "It is said as one name."

Jessica felt agreement between them on the killer's motives and fantasy, but when she brought up the notion that there might be two killers rather than one, Luc Sante quickly shook his head and said, "No, not two. But perhaps an entire congregation, a cult following, along the order of any church, you see. . . . There is always a congregation."

"Yes, that would make sense, but convincing that many

people that crucifying innocent people is a good approach to . . . to—"

"To inspire the Second Coming, yes. There is literally no limit to the numbers on this planet who would gladly involve themselves in a ritual designed to reanimate Christ, my dear. My God, look at what else people involved themselves with during the year 2000. When December 31, 1999, gave way to midnight, Iceland lit bonfires, England gave a nationwide pealing of bells, and your New York turned Times Square into a circus; an extravaganza of TV screens and lights, showing festivals and feasts in all twenty-four time zones, but the suicides and the cult ritual deaths followed in the news as did the orgies."

"It stands to reason that, thanks to the *X-Filing* of America, most Americans will be expecting Christ to descend over the New Jersey Meadowlands in the mothership again come this January 1, 2001."

"Right you are. The psychological countdown began long ago, and the psychological fallout from the enormity of the disappointment—should Christ not show up, should the world not end or be punished . . . Well, imagine it. All those religious leaders marching their followers off to seaside shores, mountaintops, holy lands, and valleys. All those survivalists in your Utah and Idaho mountains for the Day of Judgment. It may well be devastating to us all, I fear. My French grandmother had a term fitting such extravagances, *fin de siècle*, now a synonym for the 2000 bridge to the 2001 disillusionment."

"*Fin de siècle*? End of a cycle?" she guessed.

"Quite."

The cab stood idling, the driver growing anxious to move on, anxious for the next fare, "Father, I'm dyin' here," he called out, sounding more like a Brooklyn cabdriver than a British one.

Father Luc Sante ignored the rude ruffian, gently reached into his inside pocket, and from deep within the folds of the cloth, he brought forth his business card, extending it toward Jessica. "Do ring me up when you can, dear. We have much to discuss."

Jessica nodded and tucked the card away in her own pocket. She shook his hand again and felt the warmth and energy coursing through his hand to hers.

She waved to the old man as he ambled into the cab, fighting with his knobby black walking stick. She wondered at the dedication of such a man, after so many years, that he should still enjoy his work, after seeing so much of the dark underbelly of humankind. This gave way to the fleeting thought that the old man himself must hold enormous fears for his clients and congregation both in the church and in his psychiatric practice. The old priest must also behold the turn of the true millennium with great trepidation, as did Jessica.

ELEVEN

If evil is an illness, then why fear approaching it as an object of scientific study, as with any mental illness?

—DR. ASA HOLCRAFT, M.E.

After a long, disappointing day in the laboratory in which she found herself in a holding pattern—waiting for the results of tests from experts on matters such as the DNA findings—Jessica felt bored and anxious. She kept returning to Father Luc Sante's words both at the meeting earlier today and from his findings in his book, which she had as yet to finish reading. Richard and Shakespeare had taken up all of her time the night before. She gathered an inward, delighted smile at the memory of her enchanted evening with the dashing, handsome inspector and former colonel. He proved to be a caring, kind, gentle man. When she'd brought up his children he had gone into a kind of beatific reverie, speaking of their beautiful faces, moments of happiness snatched with them between job and visitations. He had nicknames for the two girls, Pixie-snow and Pixie-cream, he called them. "Enchanting creatures, both with diametrically opposed personalities. Neither of them are the least like me. Sweet, the two of them. Bloody treacherous we have to bring such innocence into this world."

She hadn't pried into the causes of his breakup with his wife. She could imagine the underlying reasons, what had caused the underpinnings of the relationship to be removed. Most likely his story would prove similar to how she and James Parry had drifted apart. *At first in subtle ways that go unnoticed, and then came the wrecking ball at the end of a chain,* she thought.

Shaking herself from her reverie, Jessica scanned the victims' files once again. She looked up at the clock and found that time had become fleet-footed as usual. It was pushing four in the afternoon. She felt a twinge of pouting come over her, combined liberally with a dash of anger that Richard hadn't made contact. Her eye fell on Father Luc Sante's professional card which read beneath his name, *Minister and Psychotherapist of the Jungian School.*

Not all therapists declared themselves so openly and blatantly Jungian. This meant that Luc Sante believed in the power of the subconscious mind, that the voice of dream held potent sway over individual lives and decisions, and that—if dream therapy was right—dreams foretold, foreshadowed, and reexamined events of the waking world. Jessica knew from her own reading in the area that Carl Jung had believed dreams to be a kind of god-voice, the overseer of personal protection and good, not unlike votive god statues in primitive people's homes, not unlike praying to rosary beads or a statue of the Virgin Mary or to Christ on the cross. Jung believed the dream-god-voice to be the god of truth spoken of in the admonition "to thine own self be true." This god was also known as intuition and instinct from within, the one voice that never lied to the individual. The voice spoke in highly charged, loaded symbols. Many of them were archetypal symbols from avatars to zoo animals, from fish, water, and womb to the death's head. Nonetheless, if the dream could be decoded as one that denied or confirmed, then the individual could safely interpret the dream one way or the other.

Jessica had never heard of a shrink who so openly displayed his basic approach to psychotherapy by exhibiting it on his business card, but then how many psychotherapists were also ministers? *How many are as eccentric as Luc Sante?* she asked herself. Below the name and title, the address loomed large as St. Albans Cathedral, Marylebone Street.

On impulse, Jessica felt a need to really converse with Dr. Luc Sante, to delve more deeply into his feelings and hunches about the Crucifier. Perhaps his insights could kick-start the investigation back on track.

To this end, she telephoned Luc Sante, and after getting the nod from his proper, prim old secretary, Luc Sante came on the line, delighted that she had called. He had been thinking of her all day, as if picking up some psychic reading, he said and then laughed so loud it hurt her ear.

"I'd like to come over to talk about the case in more depth with you, Dr. Luc Sante."

"Hurry over, then. I will have Janet prepare us afternoon tea. Have you had afternoon tea?"

"Well, no, not today."

"And crumpets. I'll see we have something to nibble on as well. Delightful. Do come over. My calendar is always clear after three of the day."

She took the cab to his cathedral under a sky that had become menacing with roiling clouds that changed in hue and expression with each passing moment. The weather had turned cooler, the light dimmer, the day more dreary, making Jessica recall a time, as a child, when she didn't understand the clock or the passage of time. She had been in kindergarten when a storm had blown over her school with the sky a charcoal black only to grow even more deeply dark. The storm had intensified with sleet and crackling hailstones; the view through the sleek, storm-blackened window had represented a hole she might tumble into, like Alice had fallen into from the story they had read that day. The sky had turned to a blackness as shiny and fascinating as the coat of a black stallion. The blackness had felt impenetrable and forever, and as a child without understanding of time, young Jessica had assumed it was the blackness of midnight. She could not understand why her father and mother had left her at school so late into the night. She feared they had left her there forever. It had mattered not a wit that all the other children and teachers were also there with her.

The cab ride over to St. Albans took her into areas of the city not meant for tourist consumption. She saw the degradation and desolation that was part of any urban community.

All of London this morning, like Jessica herself, had been

seeking answers, not only to the current rash of killings. Londoners, and Jessica, wanted spiritual answers that might in some way help them to cope with the hideousness and horror that human beings perpetrated in this world. She also felt a need to find some personal and spiritual guide here in the City, where she felt somewhat disconnected as the newcomer. Perhaps Luc Sante might be that guide, like the old shaman she had met in Hawaii several years ago, the one to whom she had gifted her cane so as to begin to walk on her own two feet after having been maimed by a brutal serial killer. Now she hurried to see another shaman with a cane, seeking answers. It felt right, like a circle, like his French grandmother's saying, *fin de siècle*, full-circle.

Paying the cabby and standing in the threatening world that seemed to come in around her here, she again noticed the worn, gray stone gargoyles atop little St. Albans Cathedral, each blended in with its surroundings, camouflaged against the gray granite niches they inhabited. Their eyes stared cold and vacant. Their talons and teeth bared against evil, for as evil as they appeared, their ferocious demeanor portended a far worse evil, that which gargoyles historically did battle with—Satan himself. At least that was one theory set forth for the existence of the stone dogs atop cathedrals across the globe. Another said that each gargoyle represented some hideous aspect of human nature, and that this aspect had been overwhelmed and overcome by the church that struggled against the beast within mankind, finally displaying the beast in its true demeanor and ugly passions as an abject lesson to all who stare at its countenance.

She recalled Luc Sante's young, good-looking protégé, Father Martin Strand, and how he had referred to Luc Sante's psychiatric practice as the work of a "trick cyclist," and this made her smile anew. The two of them, old shaman and new, each in the robes of the church, seemed to have a strong bond and a fine working relationship.

When entering, Luc Sante was bellowing out, "I see no damnable reason whatsoever that I should move my practice from St. Albans *simply* because I am retiring from the pulpit!"

Jessica could not see with whom he tiraded, but she heard

the high-pitched voice of the secretary reply, "You do not, *Sire* Luc Sante, *own* St. Albans. It belongs to the church, and if the church wants you out, then you're out! Simple as that. Are you looking for an order of eviction or excommunication, Father?"

"Hmmmph!" he blew out air. "You still have fight left in you, you sweet old darlin', don't you? Write to the Pope, if necessary. My patients will need me whether I am ministering the gospel or not!"

Jessica tried to make herself apparent. Clearing her throat, she stepped through the open door, calling out, "Dr. Luc Sante. I've made it back to St. Albans."

"Jessica, can you imagine it?" He waved a letter overhead, one which had been mangled. "Apparently, some fool somewhere has complained of my using church property to do my psychiatric practice! And now, with my retirement looming, they're ordering me entirely out! Like last week's garbage, like stale fish! Out! Out on the street! Do I look as if I can afford an office on Picadilly Lane or Fleet Street? Besides, all my long history of files are housed here. The work is also done here, under the same roof where I have for so many years administered the sacraments to this congregation. By God, it's my being a Jesuit priest, it is. Some discriminating old bast—"

"Careful of your tongue, Father!" warned old Miss Eeadna. Jessica noticed that the lovely painting of the parish in the wood had been taken down from behind Father Luc Sante's desk. It lay now against his desk at Jessica's knees, apparently removed by Miss Eeadna, who had also begun boxing up books, in a befuddled effort to help out. She held a few of his precious books in her hands now. Jessica noticed that the parish painting had a metal emblem inscribed "Gloucester Parish."

Luc Sante settled somewhat at the sound of Miss Eeadna's shaky voice, but he continued pacing and speaking. "And apparently the church is somehow made embarrassed by me, by my good works . . . Getting bad PR flack, as you Americans say."

"I'm sorry they're giving you grief over it, Dr. Luc Sante," she put in sincerely.

"I bloody intend to battle."

The old secretary gasped at his cursing, and crossed herself. "And here in St. Albans," she muttered and quaked.

"I see no reason why the church can't allow me the luxury of low overhead. And besides," he continued, "people come more readily to my psychiatric practice for their spiritual needs than their intellectual needs. Wouldn't you agree?" he asked Jessica. "And it's convenient to the area people. Most of my clients live in the shadow of St. Albans. Don't you see the logic of it, Dr. Coran?"

"Yes, in fact, I do." She felt somewhat unnerved by him, as though he had seen the emotional turmoil she had had brewing within her for so many years, and as if he were speaking about this and not his usual clientele at all.

Still, she genuinely liked the old minister. Not knowing why, she felt he, and his insights into her, were strangely comforting. Similar again to the ancient seer she'd met once in Hawaii who had "foretold" her future so accurately.

Luc Sante didn't slow his pacing or his verbosity. "People find comfort in the aroma and aura of an old cathedral like St. Albans. It is a place to *heal, and how many places are there left in this world to heal*?"

Finally, he calmed when his ancient secretary promised to type a letter addressed to the Cardinal. She said, "I won't bother the Pope with such trifling problems, but those Cardinals, they haven't a great deal to do anyway."

"And the Bishop. Write my old friend the Bishop, but before you become involved in the letter," countered Luc Sante, "please, Miss Eeadna, bring in that tea and crumpets for my guest and me, in my inner office, please."

"Yes, sir, as you like, but I may not get that letter finished by quitting time."

"That will do, Miss Eeadna . . . Janet."

Over tea and crumpets, nestled in Luc Sante's luxurious old office, surrounded by lamps and leather and warm browns of every hue, Jessica felt encircled by books that had enlightened a life. Jessica finally found the opening to ask him directly, "Dr. Luc Sante, what is your personal take on the crucifixion killings?"

"My personal *take*? Ahh, you Americans and your American English. You mean, what is my personal viewpoint, my feelings and thoughts on the matter?"

"You must have formulated some personal feelings about the killings, the mimicry of Christ's death each victim is put through."

He pursed his lips, tapped a toe, shuffled a bit in his seat, and finally said, "Engaging case, really. Impassioned killer, well acquainted with the nature of evil."

"So close to it that he, or they, have become it, you mean?"

"Excellent, yes."

"Tell me more, please. Go on, Doctor."

Instead of replying to this, he asked her how her trip to England had been thus far. Intentionally, the old man held her at bay, as if testing just how sincerely she wanted information from so old a warrior on a battlefield that had decimated so many before him. Jessica held the image and wondered what kept him so firmly on that field, how he kept his armor in one piece, how he kept his footing amid the gore and gruel and horror of it all: all he saw as both minister and psychotherapist; all he had chronicled of depression, mania, madness, murder, and mayhem done in the name of Christ and God and church as it filtered through twisted minds. Still, like a gothic warrior with shield and sword in hand, stood the white-bearded, white-headed old soldier. How? She wondered if she could be so strong at his age.

He repeated his first question and added, "So, how do you find England? London in particular?"

She sensed she had to play his game. "Is the weather always so . . . dreary?"

Luc Sante laughed heartily. "No, not always, but when C. S. Lewis depicted hell, he described it as a gray British Midlands city." He again laughed and added, "A terrible dreariness indeed."

Jessica knew of the theory that weather patterns—especially weather that sits atop a region for long periods of time, as when the sun fails to show for three and four weeks at a time—caused depression, irritability, some forms of physical illness, and some forms of violence, generally domestic violence.

"Are you saying that whoever did these killings is perhaps bored with life as it is, bored with the prevailing winds?"

"Perhaps. More importantly, evil takes as many disguises as a Shakespearean villain, so . . ."

"So, I'm to draw my own conclusions . . ."

"Despite their pretense, the evil among us are the most insane of all. Evil is the ultimate disease. The stage upon which evil struts, my dear Dr. Coran, may be as brilliantly lit as, say, your Las Vegas with all its pretense and glitter and tasteless neon lights, all designed to hide C. S. Lewis's depiction—the very same terrible dreariness that is our lives."

"I'm not sure I follow what this has to do with—"

He pushed on. "Imagine a hell in which people mindlessly and forever yank at your one-armed bandits forever and ever and ever and ever on, all below the colored spotlights of a Siegfried and Roy production, while their children, infants to teenagers, mill about the casinos at two and three in the morning, sleeping in the lobbies, waiting for Mommy's and Daddy's addictions to abate."

"That would indeed be hell."

Miss Eeadna entered with tea and crumpets laid out on a silver tray. She silently and expertly served them, accepting Jessica's thank-you with a curt nod and smile before leaving, a ghostlike figure, Jessica thought.

After sipping her tea, Jessica asked, "So, you've been to Vegas?"

"I had the questionable pleasure, yes."

"I came away with sickening feelings myself."

"As I said, evil comes to all lands, in all lives in one form or fashion or another. To deny evil is to deny breath, life, beauty, its opposites."

"Are you saying that Satan is crucifying people here in London?"

"In the broadest possible interpretation . . . yes. And if not he, then Christ."

"Christ? Really?"

"There is a war going on in cosmic spheres of which we have no control or understanding."

"Ahhh, I see, and Satan oft masquerades as Christ, does he?"

"You've read my book closely. Was it not Satan disguised as Christ who prodded the Grand Inquisitor to create the infamous Inquisition? Was not Hitler a guise for Satan purporting to be the voice of God?"

"And, of course, he can take the form of a serial killer," she added. "One who thinks himself doing the work of Christ?"

"Precisely." He settled back in his chair with his tea and took several long sips, the steam rising to his eyes.

"Evil is grandiose," she muttered, tasting of the pastry in her hand, watching helplessly as the sugar-dust sprayed her lap.

"*It*, evil that is, likes to think so; *it* likes to think big."

Jessica had long believed that evil and Satanic behavior originated within mankind alongside superstition, fear, ignorance, cruelty, and the like, and not from some supernatural force. Father Luc Sante apparently believed in a living, breathing Satan that infused evil into humanity. Perhaps the two notions were not mutually exclusive.

Father Luc Sante, his eyes going to one side, his body language telling of fatigue, added, "But most times, *it* fails, and *it* embodies or insinuates *itself* into quite ordinary people in quite ordinary circumstances as well. So ordinary, in fact, that *it* goes by unnoticed and unheralded. Not all evildoers can be a Hitler, certainly no assassin has reached his level."

"So evil comes on many planes?"

"Yes. You *have* read the book, haven't you?"

She smiled. "Approximately two-thirds through."

"I'm impressed. Most people don't get that far! But getting back to your question, you want to ask this: Are serial killers manifestations of him, of Satan? Are spree killers him? Are mass murderers, bombers like your McVeigh and your Unabomber, are they manifestations of the same *it*—the Evil One?"

"Yes, good question."

"Aren't serial killers just that in the end, little men with little identities, whom no one thought to fear, whom no one recognized as pure and primal evil? Aren't they Satan gone undetected among us? And yet they display all the signs of the Evil Thing which so oft comes on little cat's feet, silent in the night, not so loud or grand a thing as a Ghengis Khan or Vlad the Impaler or Hitler."

"I can't argue with you there," replied Jessica, thinking how true Father Luc Sante's words were. Quoting from Luc Sante's book, she said, " 'And what are we to do with evil when their masquerade of sanity is so damnably successful, their destructiveness so . . . so . . .' "

"Bloody *normal*," he finished for her.

"Exactly."

"They take on the roles society provides—the evil elves of Satan become the fathers, the mothers, the providers, the loving caretakers for the world to be lulled into a sense of faith in them before they strike. Like the faith we all put in a uniformed security guard, and yet half a dozen killers in as many years have worked at one time or another as security guards."

She thought of the helpful young security guard at Scotland Yard that morning. The thought he might be the Crucifier as well as anyone flitted through her mind. "So, relating this to the Crucifier . . . ?" she asked.

He stopped to again sip at his tea, the tinkling of the chinaware a counterpoint to their conversation. "Whoever is doing these killings, he's grown up as a twisted soul, but also as a well-trusted soul. Mark my words . . ."

She gulped her tea, thinking deeply about what his words entailed. A twisted monster whom the community at large believed in, put their faith in, trusted wholly and completely. "What do we do then, Father?"

He sighed heavily, putting his tea and half finished crumpet aside, the noise he now made a staccato aberration of the earlier tinkling sounds. "First we must stop buying into the masquerade, allowing ourselves to be so easily deceived by the pretense. Question is, can we do that?"

She raised her shoulders. "Can we?"

"Will we ever learn to detect the pretense of the cunning and clever? Of the evil among us?"

"In your book, if I've interpreted correctly," she began, "you're of the opinion that although evil is antilife, it is itself a *form* of life."

"Precisely. A form of life that must itself be destroyed, but in the destroying of that life"—and here he held up an accusatory finger—"evil though *it* may be, we destroy something of ourselves in the destroying of *it*."

She bit her lower lip and then replied, "I've heard that argument."

"As someone who has taken life, don't you agree?"

"I don't kill for sport."

"No, only as your means of livelihood?"

She grimaced.

"I don't mean to pick on you, Jessica, but don't we all temper our own evil with words of justification, even denial? Society does so when it executes one of its members. And for the brief moment the switch is thrown, and people feel safe, insanely so, in their homes at night. When in fact, in your country and this, a minuscule percentage of death-row inmates are actually put to death, and most men on death-row are far safer there than in the neighborhoods where they once lived."

She had to nod in agreement to this fact. "And if we *sane* intellectuals can justify a killing . . . If *we* can justify a killing, it makes it all right in our soul of souls. Apparently, that is what the fellow this morning's newspapers are calling the *Crude* Crucifier has done."

"Crude now is he?" Luc Sante smiled.

For Jessica, Luc Sante's words on the nature of evil brought back images of the fiery end of the madman she'd chased just the year before, a maniac who had had frequent conversations with Satan. Jessica told Luc Sante the story, finishing with, "Satan was his justification for murder," she explained. "Satan spoke to him, told him to kill nine people, the ninth was supposed to be me."

"Apparently he missed his mark."

All of the conversation led to a supposition in Jessica's

mind, one which she now shared with Luc Sante. "Okay, suppose our killer here in London is hearing voices, too, but not Satan's voice. No . . . Rather, he's hearing Christ's voice. What if he's following some prescription laid down by the voice in his head, and the voice is that of Christ so far as he is concerned?"

"Imagine the power of such a voice if one believed wholly in it," replied Luc Sante when a knock preceded young Martin Strand's peeking through the door, asking if Father Luc Sante would excuse his rudeness. "I have those books you wanted, sir." Strand stepped through and put four books on the old man's desk. "Is there anything else I can get you before I leave?"

"Why don't we ask Strand?" Luc Sante replied to Jessica. "Strand, sit a moment. Listen to this."

Strand was then subjected to Father Luc Sante's wilting scrutiny. "Martin, my boy," the older priest began, "do you suppose that this killer who is crucifying people in our city, do you suppose that he may be listening to some prescriptions from God or Christ? Or that he thinks himself Christ, and is in an effort to decipher how to reinvigorate himself in order to make a second appearance before us all, to create his own Second Coming?" Luc Sante laughed at his own irreligious remarks, while Strand rocked a bit nervously in his leather chair, feeling doubly awkward at the old minister's words.

"Strand is confused by the question," attacked Luc Sante. "Still, he buckles to it, tackles it, grapples with it up here." He pointed to his head. "As he might a question of theology. Quite serious young man. Right, Martin?"

Strand returned to his feet so as to tower over the old man. He rocked a bit on his feet, then began pacing and finally erupted with, "Well, if we attempt to understand the killing mind—"

"There you're already wrong, man." Luc Sante verbally shook his protégé. "We're all carrying about in our pea-brained heads the killing mind. It's not something apart from you, Strand. That you must attempt to understand from afar. Look in the bloody mirror. Part of our makeup, our nature, Strand . . ." He lost his concentration, showing further signs of the fatigue and pain in his joints, but he didn't want to give up the floor any more than the office, his ministering, or his psychiatric practice. Hence his cutting of poor Strand left and right and back again. "We must," Luc Sante started anew, "we must ask after his motivations, his rationalizations. If they are religious in nature, then perhaps it is a religion of one and taken to extreme, as history has shown us: Evil can evolve from too zealous a nature, and as anyone knows a Christ complex is too zealous."

"I think it's time for you to retire for today, Father," Strand said to him, emphasizing the word "retire" ever so slightly, but enough to pinch the old man's ego.

"Strand did not help me to write my book," he countered. "Can you tell?" he asked Jessica. Then back to Strand, he directed a new barb. "Too bad, Strand. Such a book attracts lovely young ladies here to my lair, someone as beautiful as Dr. Coran, here, at St. Albans. See what you miss?"

"Father, I truly feel you've overtaxed yourself, today," Strand said. "Won't you rest before dinner?"

Luc Sante laughed a light laugh. It sounded like resolve escaping him. But he ignored Strand's request and the hand the younger man presented him. Instead the old man turned to Jessica again. "Well, to return to your earlier question, Dr. Coran—or was it my question? Ahh, either way, if *we* do-gooders kill evil people, do we not ourselves become evil in doing so? And so by definition killers ourselves?"

"Evil is in the eye of the beholder," she countered. "When McVeigh was given the death sentence, some called it justice, others called it a gross evil."

"And where did you stand on the issue?" Strand asked her.

"On the side of the children McVeigh wantonly murdered, on the side of justice served. I've seen too many serial killers and mass murderers on death row and in asylums where they are treated like celebrities to wish to see another situation like Richard Speck occur. Actually execution is too easy, too good for McVeigh's kind. He should be maimed and allowed to slowly die in agony, as did many of his victims in the rubble of the explosion he set off. A bombing like that, to me, is the most cowardly act of all."

Strand's voice rose in reaction to this. "But if our only way to deal with evil is to destroy it, then we end up destroying ourselves—spiritually if not physically. And isn't that where you are at this moment in time, Dr. Coran? Wondering what particle of soul you've been able to salvage over the years of your career?"

She bit back her lower lip, contemplating Strand's incisive words and the sharpness of his characterization of her. She also saw that Luc Sante's half smile said that he agreed with his junior partner. Did Luc Sante mean to hurt her as much as Strand's words did? she wondered.

She then spoke to the room, her whiskey voice filling it. "Sometimes, I fear that I've overstepped . . . That is stepped over the line . . . I mean that who we are becomes who we were, what we've said and done, where we've been and how we've gotten there, and how we've acted and reacted becomes us."

"That the current self is an amalgam of our past selves, perhaps?" asked Luc Sante.

"To destroy evil necessitates a destruction of self, of ego," added Strand. "That much I've learned in the ministry and from Father Luc Sante. No, I didn't help him to write his book, but I have read it more than once."

"Yes," she agreed with the two ministers, "destroying a man, even a maniac like Mad Matthew Matisak and some of the others I've killed, yes, it chips away at the block of one's humanity. That's without a doubt." She thought about Jim Parry, the life she would never have with him, about children she would never have, about a home she would never know.

"Well, I have much to do tonight. Bingo night, you know, and the Houghton sisters are at it again. Must go play referee," said Strand, smiling before he disappeared the way he'd come, hardly conscious of what his words had done to Jessica.

Luc Sante took Jessica's hand in his, squeezing warmly, and said, "You are essentially a good person, Dr. Coran."

"Thank you."

"I dole out no absolution to anyone. Despite what the church says, I don't believe in that sort of nonsense. But I am here, if ever you wish to talk, for to kill another human being does, as you say, chip away at all mankind's care and concern for the essential nobility and quality of existence. Still, certain evil out there cannot be ignored, either. Father Strand and others, myself included, we all sleep better at night thanks to the fearlessness of people like yourself. Fear is our first weapon against evil, courage our second, instinct our final defense. And you . . . you must trust to your instincts."

"Even blindly so?"

"Blind instinct is better than no instinct."

"Well said, sir."

"Still, in killing the evil that climbed from the primordial muck with us, we are likely to take down the innocent with the guilty."

"So, you believe our killer or killers here in London are at war with Satan on this ground, here?" She pointed to her own head.

"Precisely. Doing battle, grappling with our most ancient enemy in an attempt to resurrect the Son, Satan's greatest nemesis. Your killer fixates on the victim, sees the mark not of Cain on the forehead but that of Christ in the eyes, or some such manner, and then proceeds from there in his attempt to resurrect the Chosen One to walk anew among us. But, of course, he keeps missing his mark, and the resurrection hasn't happened. Until it does, he will, I fear, go on killing."

"In the name of God."

"And the Son."

"Theology student perhaps?"

"Who knows, but since the so-called true millennium is upon us, your killer likely believes this is the time of the Second Coming. He damned well wants to be a big part of it, hasten it along, just as others want to be a part of the biggest millennium party that will be thrown."

"Some kind of twisted thinking. How did you arrive at it?"

"Confessionals."

"Confessionals?"

"As I've said, I've had a great deal of experience in confessionals both in the booth and in my psychiatric practice, in this office."

"But you said you didn't believe in granting absolution."

"I don't. I merely hear confessions."

"But if you listen to confessions, you must . . . must say something to your parishioners."

"All right, I tell them I absolve them, but I don't believe it. I don't believe I have that power. I don't believe any man has, no matter the robes he wears. Absolution must come from within one's own heart, not from some formalized church ritual. I know, it's a wonder I haven't long ago been defrocked. I have had *my* disguises throughout my life as well, Jessica."

"What about your psychiatric patients? They seek a sort of absolution, too, don't they?"

"It's called absolut—vodka—there." He again laughed. "Seriously, though, one in every twenty or so patients I see, or confessions I hear, are nowadays about some grand-new beginning. Lately, concern and fear center around the doomsday prophets and soothsayers of the final end, Armageddon, all balled up with the new millennium. The fact that Armageddon or Apocalypse did not occur when the bell tolled on New Year, 2000, has only fueled the belief in the year 2001 as that of the final judgment, the final flood if you will."

She easily agreed. "Fear . . . Fear of the end, not hope for the beginning is typical of human nature, unfortunately."

"Not unlike every mental breakdown, every divorce situation, every loss of a loved one I've handled in my psychiatric practice, for instance."

"And such fears fuel phobias and manic depression, insomnia, and psychosis, as well as psychotic behavior, especially religious psychosis, right?" she asked.

"I think you've answered that one yourself." Luc Sante took her chinaware from her and stacked it on the tray left by his secretary, called out through the door left ajar by Strand, but no answer returned. "Where the deuce is that woman?" he asked Jessica.

"It's well past five. I think she may have gone home for the day, Father."

"What time is it?"

The bells of St. Albans answered the old man as if on cue, ringing six times.

Luc Sante grumbled about his secretary and Strand, "Both long gone by this time, having had enough of the old man's stubbornness," he spoke of himself in the third person.

Ignoring his obvious fatigue, Luc Sante now walked Jessica down the huge back corridors of St. Albans Cathedral. The ancient marble hallways clicked with the rhythm of Jessica's heels to counterpoint Luc Sante's more subtle step. To Jessica's right, the length of the otherwise dark corridor ran with beautiful stained-glass windows; but the images, relying as they did on sunlight, had grown dull, faded, hidden within the blotted colors as darkness had come to the world outside.

Luc Sante grumbled about the lost beauty of the panes, saying, "The new buildings all round us now blot out the sun more and earlier. I used to close up, make this walk, and fill my soul here in this corridor, replenished by the resplendent artwork you see there now in the darkness. All things bow to progress as they call it. Change, I suppose."

Jessica felt a sudden sadness for the old, wise man's loss, and she felt a sudden amazement at how much time had flown by while in Luc Sante's presence. This fact decided for her that she genuinely liked and admired the old scholarly Jesuit shaman. His appearance and crustiness reminded her of a later-day George Bernard Shaw. With his knowing hand grasping mankind about the throat to check for a pulse, Father and Dr. Jerrard Luc Sante found just cause for cynicism, despair, and hope all in the same breath and heartbeat.

All these thoughts flooded her mind as they continued down the seemingly endless corridor. The thoughts continued at the great oak doors—the entrance to the cathedral. Like Shaw, she felt Luc Sante a voice in the wasteland—T. S. (Thomas Stearns) Eliot's Waste Land, yes, but Eliot's wasteland had only become cluttered with more disaffection, more disenfranchisement of the human soul, more searing, jagged-edged alienation or other modern ailment since his poem had been written in 1922. And all of the ugliness of alienation of the soul had been eclipsed by an enormity of fear too great for the collective soul of man to bare up under.

Yes, an eclipsing fear in the late 1990s created a wasteland of the soul that mankind had never known before. Mankind collectively stood on the brink of the coming new millennium and teetered there, one foot in the abyss on a slippery slope that led to the end of a particularly black and empty hole, unless . . . Unless mankind and womankind turned the emptiness inside out, examined it, and came to terms with it. Unless people began to heed their own spiritual voices as had Luc Sante and others like him.

Jessica admired the old man's juggling his dual roles as priest and psychotherapist, his abilities in both fields, and his intellect and calculation that told all who came within his sphere that religion and science sipped from the same vast ocean-sized teacup of the unknown, and that both fields of human endeavor had much to offer the human psyche, and that both could and should cohabit down here on Earth together. The two, religion and science, did not negate one another; the two were necessary for understanding of the human spirit.

Luc Sante turned to Jessica, facing her now at the entranceway to the corridor, the streetlights filtering in through the windowed doors, bathing him in a green glow. Jessica stared into his warm, glowing, and rich blue eyes which spoke along with his voice. "In order to survive to the next level of evolution, mankind and womankind must not only stare deeply into the abyss that is *ourselves*, our human nature, our souls, my dear. But we also must fully accept and understand our most hideous aspect, our ugliest gargoyles, that *we* are indeed the beast we fear most, for we are the beast of our own nightmares and our own making. As unpleasant as it is. Well, you of all people understand the wisdom of it. But beware the beast, for it is busy, at this moment, calculating the most advantageous instant it can take hold of you and tear you from the slippery edge you stand on."

"Then you concede that Satan is of our own making, and not a separate entity from man himself?" she asked.

"I concede nothing of the kind. I tell you it, he—whatever you wish to call evil and the maker of violence—is both within us and without us. No less than the love of Christ is within us and without us."

Jessica felt a startled recognition at his words. She won-

dered if this shaman were a mind reader, or simply quite
clever and cunning at picking up nonverbal cues. Still, she
could not fathom it. *How does he know that I have spent a
good deal of my life on that brink, looking over the edge of
a slippery slope, wondering these exact thoughts. It must be
a lifetime of working with troubled people*, she concluded.

Jessica momentarily thought of the few truly close friends
she had in this life: Donna LeMonte, who had seen her
through psychotherapy and had become one of her closest
friends along with psychic FBI agent Kim Desinor. There
remained her friend and boss Eriq Santiva, and her associate
in the M.E.'s office, John Thorpe. She had few contacts outside her work, and whenever she did, the relationship seldom
survived for long. That had been the case with James Parry,
although she'd managed to hold on to James, and he to her,
for six years. Some kind of record. She wanted to add Luc
Sante to her list of intimate friends.

It was no coincidence that her best friends were in law
enforcement. Even the men she chose to love were in law
enforcement. She knew from experience that to ask anyone,
who had not been there, to delve so deeply into the rings of
hell with her, was asking too much.

After calling for a cab, Jessica shook Luc Sante's hand.
Each of them knew that the other had indeed stared into the
eyes of Satan and had come away from the experience
scarred. Somewhere, somehow, someday she would get the
story out of him.

She sensed, with the lingering handshake, that he again
knew what thoughts ran fleetingly through her mind.

"Your help, Father, has been invaluable."

"Bit premature to say so, Doctor."

"It *will* prove invaluable then, I am certain."

"Thank you for the compliment, and good night. I see the
cab you called for is here. Go with God." He waved her off,
and then the huge oak doors closed. She felt like Dorothy
being put out of Oz.

When she had taken a few steps from the cathedral she felt
some innate voice tell her to stop, turn, and stare, as if someone were at the door, watching her. She looked for Luc

Sante's fatherly eyes to be upon her, but he had vanished within. She felt a bit foolish, imagining what she looked like standing on the steps, retreating from the gothic old place like a "Pauline in Peril" character depicted on the cover of a raggedy little paperback book. She needed only to bite her knuckles to complete the image.

"Well, to hell with that," she muttered and consciously felt for the bulge of her Smith & Wesson in her shoulder holster. She dismissed her moment of uneasiness. Just being foolish to feel a buzz of intuition telling her that a healthy fear of this place and time might just save her life. Just being foolish, yet the same buzz of fear had saved her life on more than one occasion, and she'd learned to listen to the gift of instinct over the years.

This time she tried to shrug it off, but with each step toward the cab, the insistent intuition that most women felt in moments of danger made her glance back again. Again, there was no one at the door windows. Still, she felt the stare like a hot poker. Her intuition insisting someone indeed must be there. Stillness. She looked overhead at the huge edifice and saw hundreds of gilded and steepled windows staring back like sinister eyes. Someone could be at one of them, staring down on her retreat. Far above these many eyes of the edifice, she saw the stares of twenty or more bug-eyed gargoyles, concrete eyes all glaring down on her.

Her intuition proven right, she now stared back at the creatures of the subconscious sitting atop the cathedral, ostensibly to protect mankind from the far worse creatures that dwelled in even darker shadows at even deeper levels of the human condition. Ironic to fight fear with the images of fear, yet it felt right here in London, and it felt right here at St. Albans, fitting in with Dr. Luc Sante's message that the thing we should all fear most is ourselves.

In a glint of reflected moonlight and stars, one of the gargoyles winked directly at her.

· TWELVE ·

Given the physiology and the psychopathology of the truly evil among us, there appears no time in the history of mankind, nor in mankind's future worlds when they—the evil among us—will cease to thrive.

—FATHER JERRARD LUC SANTE,
TWISTED FAITHS

When Jessica arrived at her temporary home at the York, she found messages awaiting her attention. The hotel clerk flagged her down at the elevator, telling her there'd been two telegrams and a delivery of flowers.

She loved flowers, and guessed they were from Richard. She lingered at the desk long enough to collect flowers and messages and thank the clerk.

Going to the elevator, a reporter who had staked out the hotel helped her get the elevator. The young woman, her hair in her eyes, quickly introduced herself as Erin Culbertson, reporter for the *Times*. "I'd just like a few words with you."

Jessica had been waylaid by reporters before, especially reporters out to make a name for themselves by scoring on a big crime story. And in London, at the moment, the Crucifier was the biggest story going. Jessica replied with caution holding rein at the back of her mind. "And how do you know who I am?"

"The flowers."

"The flowers?"

"I use flowers often to get an interview."

"You bought the flowers as a way of telling who I was when I returned, and you've staked out the elevators since?"

"Clever, wouldn't you say?" she asked.

"Diabolically so."

"Will you have coffee with me? Answer a handful of burning questions about the case you're working on with the Yard? I learned of your coming on the case, made mention of it, but until now I haven't gotten your side of it, Doctor."

"Well, you have gone to a good deal of trouble. I can't divulge anything that is too sensitive, you realize."

"But you'll talk to me?"

"After I put these," she indicated the flowers, "in water. You have lovely taste."

The reporter laughed. "They weren't cheap, I can tell you that."

Later, in the dining room of the hotel, Jessica had a meal while Miss Culbertson drank a pot of black coffee and grilled her on the progress of the case.

Jessica candidly told her that she hadn't had much to do with the first three killings, as the autopsies on these had been done by Dr. Karl Schuller.

"Yes, I've gone the merry-go-round with that one, I have," she replied, a light laugh following her words. "What an old codger."

Now Jessica laughed. It felt good talking to another woman, and getting her perspective on Schuller couldn't hurt.

"What about the tongue brandings? I believe that was your discovery, wasn't it?"

"Yes, but that information wasn't released to the press. How did you find out about it?"

"I'm a reporter, a crime reporter. Facts like that do not remain boardroom or station house secrets for very long."

Jessica shook her head, knowing this to be true. She then told the reporter what she could of the autopsy on the latest Jane Doe.

"The one found in the Serpentine?"

"That's the one, yes."

"Number four. Oddly close to where Richard Sharpe once lived."

"Right." Jessica didn't so much as blink, but she wondered how on Earth this woman had gotten that piece of information. A closer look revealed that Culbertson had a sort of elegant panache about her and that she was, in Jessica's estimation, a pretty brunette. Since Richard had said that they had been close friends at one time, intimating that they had slept together, Culbertson likely knew about where his ex-wife and children lived.

"What do you think is the significance of the words found on the tongue?"

"Some sort of cult ritual? Part of the process of crucifying the victim, sending them over to the other side. . . . properly armed, symbolically speaking."

"Her name's been discovered, you know. She had a name."

"You know her name?"

"I told you, I'm a reporter, and I'm damned good at it."

"Apparently."

"She was a thirty-nine-year-old, a Marion Woodard, looked a good deal older. Must have had a rough life of it. A paralegal secretary at Hass, Stodder, and Weiland, a law firm on Fleet Street."

Jessica silently mused and she said to Culbertson, "Victim's age is far younger than the previous three. What does that tell us?"

"That your killer does not discriminate on the basis of age?"

"Frankly, I prefer to not know their names and ages, the number of children they left behind, their favorite hobbies, interests, or restaurants until I'm done with the autopsy."

"Really? I should think the more information you have on a subject—"

"Corpse, not subject. You reporters do interesting things with words. You hounded Lady Di until she was Lady Dead. Then the same people who lusted after this image you all created of a rebellious whore suddenly in death became Snow White. So she lived a lie created for her by the press and the public, and she died a lie created for her by the press and the public."

"I see. Well, you do have a low opinion of the press."

"Not everyone in the press, but yes, generally speaking, there are few people in the press who have my respect."

"So, you didn't answer my question. The information on the victim?"

"Knowing too much, too soon, can make me less than effective in my work."

"Clinical objectivity, you mean?"

"Precisely."

"But isn't that alone sort of working blind?"

"I must remain objective in doing my job, which is to examine the body for signs of trauma. Later, some information about the dead person or his past may be relevant." She thought of Tattoo Man back in the States. A corpse without any background, a good example of the need for information on the deceased's life. The reporter knew the answer to her question before she asked it. She wondered why Culbertson felt it necessary to beat about the bush. "What the forensic team does is to take a step-by-step approach, leaving nothing to chance," Jessica finally said.

"You do have a clinical air about you," Culbertson sharply countered. "Sorry, didn't mean that the way it came out."

The hell you didn't, Jessica thought. She knew when she was being sized up, and when someone had a hidden agenda. She guessed that Culbertson's agenda must be at least as personal as it was professional. Had she come to cash in on Jessica's reputation? To get a story she could sell to the tabloids? Was she mining for dirt? Jessica thought of Richard, and how vulnerable he might be to such a predator as the one sitting across from her right now. "Look, it's been a long and fatiguing day. If you don't mind, and if you've got your questions answered—"

"One more, and I'll be gone, I promise."

"All right."

"Has the old priest, Luc Sante, been of any help to the investigation? I've read where he has helped solve cases for the Yard in the past. I've been thinking of doing a straight profile on the man."

"That's a wonderful idea, and yes, he has provided invaluable insights into the thinking of the killer or killers through both his meetings with us and through his book."

"Killers? Do you think there are more than one?"

"It's fairly obvious that this is a likely scenario, yes."

"Do you mind if I report this?"

"And if I said I did? Would it stop you?"

"No." She smiled when she said it.

They parted with Jessica urging the reporter to do a piece on Luc Sante and his book. It would do wonders for the old man's ego, she thought, and it might divert the hungry young reporter away from herself, and so away from Richard.

A momentary scenario of Richard in a British courtroom defending his right to visit his daughters burned across her mind like a match being struck. Jessica stared after the young reporter whose hips swayed like a ship at sea as she stepped through the revolving door exit in the lobby of the York.

Dr. Raehael, his eyeglasses being used as a battering ram, held out the report he had made on Burton's corpse and said, "You were right, Dr. Coran." He spoke loud enough for the entire room to hear, but primarily, she surmised, for Dr. Schuller's benefit.

Jessica now stared in earnest at the results of the tests Dr. Raehael had rushed through on Burton's health prior to his death. In bold, Dr. Raehael wrote: **Colon cancer had eaten away most of the man's intestines and stomach. If he hadn't died as he had, he would be dead within days.**

"How could his doctors not have known?"

"He went to Switzerland for diagnosis, to keep it hush-hush."

"I see. And no one knew of his condition?"

"No one, not even his shrink."

"His shrink?"

"A Dr. Kahili, works not far from here. Police questioned him, but he refused to divulge anything about Burton, invoked doctor-patient privilege."

"Kahili?"

"Iranian."

"I wonder if Luc Sante would know of him."

"Possibly. You might ask."

"Thanks for the workup, Dr. Raehael."

"Here also are my findings on the Woodard woman. Particle and fiber evidence, but nothing strikes me as particularly useful, I'm afraid."

Raehael handed Jessica the lab work on Marion Woodard, and answered a call from Schuller who, apparently, had begun working his own angle on the case and isolating himself from Jessica. Schuller appeared none too pleased with his little Egyptian assistant, and the two men muttered some angry words between them before Raehael returned to his own corner of the busy lab where men and women in lab coats worked investigations other than the Crucifier case. In fact, the place appeared as busy, noisy, and buzzing as her Quantico, Virginia, lab back home.

Jessica found an unoccupied seat next to a microscope. She sat and leisurely looked over Raehael's findings on Burton, imagining the pain the man must have been in, and how the pain of the crucifixion death might mask this death from within, just as the gross scars and obviousness of the crucifixion murder had masked Burton's condition on the autopsy slab from Drs. Schuller and Raehael.

Jessica then began to look over the Woodard report Raehael had handed her. More of the same. No fingerprint evidence whatsoever. Brevital in the system. All particle and minutia from hair to carpet fibers creating a long list of useless information. But then she saw one unique item in postmortem number four, causing her to sit up straight. Coal dust, blackened wood fibers, and beetle dung embedded in the nails of Marion Woodard.

Suddenly, the Scotland Yard Crime Laboratory that was filled with the noisy, bustling business of investigating fraud, accident, and murder, all vanished and silenced around her. The coal dust had come from Raehael's having pried particles from beneath victim number four's long nails. The particles were so long embedded there that they had not been washed away by the waters of the Serpentine. Coal dust made up a good portion of the particle evidence. Could this be a significant factor in the fourth victim's death? What of the others? She recalled nothing about coal dust, wood fibers, or beetle leavings in the other reports. Most likely, the finding meant little or nothing.

Even in her excitement to further examine Raehael's findings, she found an unbidden, uninvited, unwelcomed thought of Richard Sharpe weaseling its way into her consciousness. The same Richard who had disappeared from the crime scene one night and made love to her the following evening.

"A phone call for Dr. Coran," someone in the lab announced. Jessica took it in the office turned over to her.

It was Sharpe, asking, "May I come over for a visit, or perhaps you'd care to visit me?"

Jessica instantly knew visit meant something more, another British euphemism for sex, she imagined. "What's really on your mind, Richard?" She wanted to make him plead a little.

"Actually, I wish to apologize fully for my standoffish behavior of earlier."

To apologize fully, she guessed, another euphemism for passion? "But you have nothing whatever to apologize for, Richard." *Play dumb*, she told herself. "Besides, I've had an exhausting day of it here in the lab, and I have autopsy results to slave over tomorrow, so I don't think a visit or an apology a good idea, not tonight at least. Perhaps you can apologize another night?"

He caught her drift, saying, "You may wager on it."

"Besides, I fear a certain green-eyed reporter may still be staking out the lobby of the York. It wouldn't do for the two of us to make your London tabloids, now would it?"

"I see. Erin Culbertson, you mean. Certainly. Well then, if your mind is set, I'll then see you at the Yard tomorrow. But if you later should change your mind, and you wish a visit, that is a get-together, to see one another, I'm quite sure I can find your room without anyone's taking notice."

She smiled at his persistence and his persistent euphemisms for making love. The terms most people used for making love were usually crass, and even the formal *fornication* sounded crude to Jessica's ear, much more pleasant to hear *visit*, *get-together*, and *apology* instead of the usual harsh terms that had become commonplace in America. Jessica found the British needed euphemisms to keep the world bright and cheery. Perhaps all mankind did, but the British were most adept at it. The British speaker substituted kinder, gentler words for the ugly, cruel, crude thousands that abounded in the language—words they considered irreligious or sacrilegious; words to stave off bad manners, ill-feelings, and anything smacking of sex, or to do with death, murder, or God's name taken in vain or in curse. Anything to flesh out a good Christian curse would do so long as one spared God's name being made a part of it. To her delight, Richard proved no exception to this truth.

She suspected that Richard and Erin Culbertson had, at one time, been lovers. How long ago she did not know, and mentally shrugging, she wondered if it mattered to her, and the more she thought about it, the more it did.

She begged off, thinking the nosy reporter might well cause irreparable damage to Richard's standing here, and possibly to the investigation, or to both. She imagined the spurned woman lying in wait for Richard to visit Jessica's bed. For oddly enough and in direct conflict with the British staid exterior, euphemisms not withstanding, an old-fashioned, juicy scandal drew no quarter and no soft substitution of terms. The typical Londoner's use of euphemisms and his or her desire to remain aloof did not extend to a rollicking good scandal, and Brit society delighted in the downfall of the great and powerful, the famous and influential. This passion rivaled anything Jessica knew in America. She wondered if it were human nature to want to see leaders and authority figures disgraced. Either way, she had thought it prudent not to see Richard tonight, so she claimed—and rightly so—fatigue, exhaustion, and headache while gently letting him down with her own set of euphemisms.

After hanging up, she felt good about protecting his standing and reputation, knowing the newshounds would have a field day with the fact of their lovemaking in the midst of the investigation into the horrid crucifixion murders. Still, she knew that her shrink friend Donna LeMonte would only laugh at her feminine "gallantry" and call it a lie. Jessica felt hurt by Richard, who might have warned her about the reporter-stalker Culbertson. But she didn't want to go there, part of her fearful of the hot coals she'd started across with Richard Sharpe. They had come a long way in a short period of time.

How had this man come to mean so much to her so suddenly? So much so that she stood here jealous of his earlier relationship with Erin Culbertson.

Jessica stepped away from the phone and out of the office, and back into the lab. There she mentally shook herself, vigorously pushing away any thought of Richard and his former girlfriend, forcing herself to focus on the test results of the minute particle evidence before her. She read without enthusiasm, her sleepy eyes glazing over when the words *coal dust* amid hundreds of other words leapt out at her.

She saw again the report prepared by Dr. Raehael; the two words, coal dust, seemed to clamor for her attention. For a moment, she thought it a brain tease amid the fatigue, nothing important, but the words continued to stare back at her, insinuating themselves in her mind's eye like little live things under a microscope. She thought it a significant item that she hadn't seen on any of the other autopsy reports, or had she simply overlooked these findings earlier?

Jessica returned to the other reports, bringing them up on the computer screen, clicked on Edit and word searched for coal dust. A hit on O'Donahue, next the same with Coibby, and with Burton. How could she have missed the significance of it before? How had Schuller and Raehael been so blind? And how significant a find was this?

She ran a computer search for any mention of black wood fibers and the beetle droppings. In both cases, she made hits. All of the victims had all three of these connecting remnant details, and while the dots were tenuous, they were dots in the maze. In fact, Coibby's body had a dead beetle caught in his hair.

She cursed them all for fools, not forgetting herself. At the same time, she breathed in a deep sense of relief over the fact that they had something, even as minute as it was, to zero in on. That thought filled her with a small hope like a lighted candle. All the victims had had coal dust particles found on their bodies, either in the sticky residue of blood and oil or possibly scraped from their nails, she guessed. It had to be significant, along with the wood and beetles.

After allowing herself a moment of exhilaration over the

new discovery, she earnestly wished to share it with Raehael
and Schuller, both of whom were laboring over a series of
tests in the Woodard case. In fact, Schuller had ordered a full
report on Woodard's health condition before she died—precisely the point Jessica had made in the Burton autopsy.
Schuller, a depressed man according to the rumor mill here,
a man hurting in his personal life from what she'd been able
to gather, took her comments as censure. He meant to prove
himself *not guilty* of negligence or incompetent work in the
Burton case.

Schuller appeared a fragile man this morning, she thought.
She worried how he would take the coal dust issue, if it might
not be the last straw for him. She struggled with how best to
approach the other forensic doctor on this.

She stepped to within whispering distance of Dr. Schuller,
asking, "Can we talk in private, Dr. Schuller?"

Raehael, beside them, overheard and looked up from his
microscope. Schuller promptly replied, "Al-Zadan and I have
worked together for three years. Whatever you have to say to
me, you can say to us, Dr. Coran."

She took a deep breath and said, "It's the report of coal
dust findings on the Woodard woman."

"What of it?"

"I did a check back through all the victims, and they all
show trace elements of coal dust. I think it significant, sir."

"Coal dust and beetles?" Schuller asked with an arched
brow, and then he exchanged a long stare with Raehael before
he said, "I give you my blessings. Pursue the beetle and the
coal to whatever end you wish. It's in the reports, and if and
when we can locate a killing ground, then perhaps we will
have some explanation for this trace evidence. Use whatever
you wish; our lab and our people are at your disposal."

Schuller put it in perspective for her, saying loud enough
for all to hear, "Coal heating remains one of the primary
sources of fuel consumption here, despite every effort that's
been made to end its use in the City. Nearly every flat in
London has a coal bin below, and the City is liberally dusted
with coal. Not to imply that all of us Londoners have coal
dust under our nails. But you will be hard-pressed to pinpoint

a killing ground in this city with coal dust and mites alone."

She tried to salvage something of it, saying, "In America, coal dust particles would have significantly different characteristics, helping pinpoint the killer's lair. Are you sure there might not be something worth—"

"No, forget about it, Doctor. Every city dweller in London has coal dust under his nails. It's miasmatic. It's endemic." His tone was sarcastic.

"Making coal dust the most ready substance in the city," added Raehael with a nearly imperceptible shrug to say he was sorry for Schuller's unprofessional outburst.

What had seemed so clearly an enormous clue immediately took on the attitude and character of dust mites—so abundant as to be useless, unless this coal dust had some significantly distinguishable characteristics buried within, like those minute differences found in layers of dirt at an archaeological dig.

She put the coal dust particle results aside along with her pride. Another bloody dead end, Richard would call it.

She moved along, searching the results of fiber evidence, hair evidence, blood and serum tests. Everything came up identical to the previously murdered victims. The Crucifier had left no trace of himself behind. Gloves and caution, she surmised.

One of the few remaining clues as to the Crucifier's identity remained his use of the drug Brevital to control Marion Woodard and the three other victims. It showed up in the blood work, found in large enough quantity to have put her under for some time and certainly to have subdued her, making her helpless against the god-awful attack she had suffered.

Schuller then stepped away and disappeared down the hall, a lightness in his step that hadn't been there before.

"Bastard," she muttered.

Frustrated, the police scientists at the Yard, along with Jessica, continued the entire day to sift through the minutia of evidence left by the Crucifier, with the result being about as large as the few clues left them. This being the state of the case, Jessica expected that at least Chief Inspector Boulte would feel good—or at least *vindicated* on his assessment of bring-

ing the American Colonist in on the case. Vindicated to the
degree that he had been wiser than Sharpe in the matter.

All the same, a nagging intuition, a kind of blind instinct,
forced her to ask Schuller, "Can we get this beetle that came
with the coal dust carbon dated?"

"Carbon dated?" His wide, questioning, gray-blue eyes told
the story of incredulity. "Do you have any idea the expense
of time and man hours that will put us to?"

"Carbon dating is the only precise way to know the age of
the specimen, the only exacting method to be precise."

"To what bloody end, Doctor? Beetles abound in London,
as I am sure they abound in America."

"Humor me, Dr. Schuller. Suppose it came with the coal
dust, and suppose it suggests—"

"Carbon dating a beetle found in Coibby's hair."

"Don't forget, we found beetle leavings on all the others,
in their nails, along with the wood fibers, and the wood fibers
appear to be from some ancient structure."

His tone clearly indicated the madness of such a time-
consuming step. "That would be a waste of our time here.
Regardless of what you and Sharpe and the others might
think, there are other, ongoing cases that have to be dealt with
here. Carbon dating trace elements of beetles, really."

"G'damnit, Doctor," she angrily retorted, "do you have the
capability to carbon date here? Or do we farm it out, and if
so, where are the bloody forms?" Jessica realized two truths
even as she said it. One, she hated the pettiness of having to
shout; and two, she'd managed to pick up something of a
British accent during her short stay in London.

Schuller responded by pacing and then exploding, "I will
not be ordered about within the confines of my own laboratory by anyone, Doctor. If you wish to pursue a blind alley
in this matter, you will get no help from me!" He stormed
out, leaving her to be stared at by all remaining in the lab,
most of whom were uninvolved in the Crucifier case.

Raehael came quickly over to her. "I will see to the dating
of the material."

"Carbon dating," she insisted.

"I am aware what you wish, Doctor. But such tests, it will

take time. Please, allow me to express apology for Dr. Schuller. He has been beneath great stress these many days."

She assumed *these many days* meant since the Crucifier had gone to work in London. "Thank you, Dr. Raehael." She could not read his black, inscrutable pupils. Like a pair of grapes, the seeds glimmered deep within.

"You see, Dr. Schuller's wife, she is in hospital. Not expected to live too much soon. You unders-stand?"

Jessica closed her eyes on the revelation. It explained a great deal of Schuller's behavior toward both her and others around him, and it certainly explained his absences and his short fuse.

"I'm sorry," she told Raehael. "I had no idea."

"He is a stoic man. How you Americans say, a man of stone outside only."

She thanked Raehael for the information. He took the beetle debris and particles—so much smudge lying at the bottom of a small vial as to be near invisible. "I will personally see over this matter for you, Dr. Coran. And as well, I have DNA tests, which you may now like to see some result?"

She nearly gasped at the suggestion. "You have some results?"

He held up a DNA scan sheet that reflected back the overhead fluorescent lights, making the tiny black marks on the oversize slide, like an X ray of minutia, shimmer and dance about before her eyes.

"What have you learned?"

"I rule out my own self as secretor. I rule out the investigators next, you and Dr. Schuller, of course next, so this will take time. But this . . ." He shook the DNA strand that had been scanned and duplicated onto an acetate sheet, and it made a small thunder in response. "I believe we have DNA from heavy secretor, and intuition tell me it is from the killer. Take time to look is lesson you have taught me, Dr. Coran," he said.

"I appreciate your kindness in saying so. If you don't mind, I'll also warn you not to smudge what you have there with your oily fingerprints."

He smiled. "Yes. I am secretor, too, heavy."

She stared at the smudge of patterns on the acetate sheet now thrown up against a viewing light pedestal. She tempered her hope-against-hope feeling that they were actually, scientifically marking the footprints of the killer, that they had indeed come into his cursed wake. Still, they remained a long way from proof and providing that proof to a jury. She must remain cautious, careful.

"First, rule out the DNA of anyone and everyone who has come remotely near the body, including the ambulance people and anyone here in the lab, including Dr. Schuller."

"He won't like it," warned Raehael.

"He understands the protocol."

"Heavy secretor," he repeated. "Very most likely to be, in any case."

They both knew that approximately eighty percent of the population secreted blood type indicators in their body fluids—saliva, semen, and perspiration. Not even soap and water could completely wash secretions away. A match could be made to the killer in all probability, if they ever made an arrest.

Jessica recalled Martin Strand's having wiped his brow twice in her presence, but she swiftly dismissed this as any kind of evidence. Still, she wondered why she so easily and quickly put the words heavy secretor and Strand together.

Luc Sante had dabbed his brow in his office, too. The place had felt stuffy and humid the entire time Jessica spent in the cathedral offices and corridors. The windows weren't exactly fashioned for AC units. For that matter, she had seen Sharpe and Copperwaite each break out in perspiration at the scene of the last murder. Secretions in perspiration were, in effect, everywhere.

"I will complete work of ruling out the investigators and doctors. Later, if we find some unusual markings, matches," said Dr. Raehael, his clean-shaven chin in hand, "then all will depend on arrest. If we find a match, this man will be the Crucifier."

Jessica watched Raehael's small, deft fingers nimbly place possibly the only single bit of evidence of the killer into its glassine slip. Raefael then found a home for it in a manila file folder and labeled it with the case number.

Jessica lifted the phone on the desk that had temporarily become hers, and she telephoned Quantico. While she had little to report, Chief Santiva had been leaving messages that he wanted to know any progress on the case. The case meant much politically to his career. It also meant an opening up of relations between the two most famous and powerful law-enforcement agencies in the world, the FBI and Scotland Yard.

Jessica, with little to add to the picture for Santiva, embellished what they had on the Crucifier and spent a good deal of time telling Santiva about Luc Sante, saying, "What a remarkable find he is! You really must consider putting him on as a consultant, Eriq. Our man in Britain. He's really top drawer."

Eriq Santiva expressed only his interest in the case, and how it was going. He was upset with her for not having kept him apprised. She'd failed to answer his last communiqué. He began to rave somewhat, when she stopped him, saying, "I've had my hands full, Eriq."

"Well, from here on out, I want a full report every other day from you, Agent Coran."

"Why're you so angry, Eriq? And why all the formality?"

"Short of that, e-mail me here. Do you understand, Agent Coran?"

She realized now that he was not alone, that he spoke for an audience there in his office, all likely on the speakerphone. Damn him and his bosses for their little dishonesties. "Nasty business here, Chief, really," she played to their audience. "No significant clues left by the killer. A diabolically clever fellow intent on our not having the least lead. But just this morning we've uncovered some new evidence."

"Fill me in."

She told him of the coal dust, the wood fibers and the beetle, and he hemmed and hawed over this for some time, saying only, "Interesting . . ."

"I'm having the beetle carbon dated, and analysis should

show us something. We've also found the killer does something unusual to his victims' tongues."

"Tongues?"

She had them. She told them all about *Mihi beata mater*, informing them she'd tried to keep the exact wording in-house, but that authorities were not cooperating with her desire to do so. "If you can apply any pressure along those lines, it would be greatly appreciated."

"Remember, e-mail or phone, but keep me informed," Eriq finished.

I don't have that kind of time, Eriq, she wanted to scream but dared not. "Absolutely," she lied.

"I want constant updates on this one, Jessica."

"All right," she grumbled into the phone. "Can you put me through to John Thorpe in the crime lab now?"

"Sure. And Jess, be careful over there."

"Thanks. I will be."

"Wouldn't want to lose you to Scotland Yard, either."

In a few moments, John Thorpe came on the line, saying, "Yes? This is Thorpe."

Jessica breathed easier talking to J. T., knowing she could fully trust him. She told him about her conversation with Santiva. J. T. grumbled one single word, "Typical."

She again brought J. T. up-to-date on the killings in London. "Whoever this lunatic is, he's giving away very little of himself," she finished.

"Sounds dire," he replied, "and you sound tired. Getting any sleep? How's that insomnia problem?"

"I'm bearing up. What news in Tattoo Man's case?"

"Some progress. Some surprising twists, in fact."

"Really? Go on."

"I met with one of the so-called giants in the art, at a convention in Memphis, Tennessee. Since he was such an expert, I showed him the artwork, you know, the autopsy photos, in an attempt to nail down the artwork and the artist it belonged to."

"And?"

"And turns out our boy, Horace, paid big bucks for his

illustrated body. The guy knew the artist, admired his work. We were right—a disciple of H. R. Giger."

"Congratulations, John."

"The actual artist who worked on Horace lives in New Jersey. I'm driving to see him tomorrow. He keeps records in his head, though, so keep your fingers crossed."

Jessica replied, "Will do."

"So, where do you go next on the Crucifier case?"

Again, Jessica found herself speaking more about Luc Sante than the case. She filled J. T. in on the man and his theories, using J. T. as a sounding board, and then apologizing for it.

"Don't be silly. If you were here, or I were there, we'd be bouncing ideas and thoughts off one another, wouldn't we?"

"Right you are. Strange how many seeming parallels there are between the two unrelated cases," she now said.

"Such as?"

"The amount of preparation the killer goes to, for one. Quite meticulous attention to detail, wouldn't you say?"

"Absolutely in my case. Whoever prepared Tattoo Man for murder went through a great deal of ritual, and at any point along the way might have backed out. Imagine the patience required to infect six dogs, then the safety required to handle them."

"Murder is easy to talk about, a great deal harder to carry out," she agreed, "especially if your murder requires elaborate stage props and preparations. Believe me, our two killers have a good deal in common, at least on that score."

"Is that right?"

"Our killer here is into preparations, to say the least."

J. T. found himself being paged, another call coming in. "Could be about the case, Jess. Best go. You take care, and get in some R & R while you're over there."

"Gee, I hadn't thought of that," she joked before saying good-bye and hanging up.

· THIRTEEN ·

We may easily fail to pity the sociopath and psychopath for their ghastly evil, but we must surely pity them for the unremitting lives of apprehension they lead.

—FROM THE CASEBOOKS OF JESSICA CORAN

The following Monday, Jessica joined yet another general meeting called by Chief Inspector Boulte, this one limited to Scotland Yard detectives alone. Every single detective on the force had long before been put on alert regarding the case of the Crucifier, but now with the additional information concerning new findings in the autopsy reports brought about by Dr. Jessica Coran, findings which could not be ignored, Boulte wished for his entire team to be "well-versed and further enlightened by Dr. Jessica Coran herself."

Why am I getting the idea Boulte hates my guts? she asked herself. At Sharpe's request, the man had contacted her superiors in D.C., who had in turn contacted Quantico, who had in turn contacted Eriq Santiva, who had contacted her. Obviously, Boulte saw her competence as a personal rebuff to him. In his zeal to demean her, he had pushed professional courtesy to its limits. Either that or worse. Perhaps he'd gotten wind of the budding personal relationship between her and Richard and he didn't like it. Worse still, he saw it as an opportunity to hurt Richard.

Still, Boulte remained in charge when he now asked Jessica, "Will you share further profile information, anything developed by you and Sharpe, for instance, with the rest of us." His tone made clear that he knew the two of them had slept together, and somehow she'd become yet another prize in the continual battles of the two men. Just how Chief Inspector Boulte knew remained a mystery, but Jessica suspected Erin Culbertson. Damn her.

Jessica nodded, taking the podium, and after saying good afternoon to some sixty or so assembled inspectors, she listed the likely characteristics of the killer again, adding, "*He*, first of all, we believe to be a *they*—at least two men. They have a religious fixation, an obsession with the crucifixion, likely find replicas and paintings of it everywhere they spend time. They will likely lead exemplary lives, purporting to be model citizens, even religious experts or leaders among their acquaintances. They will likely be in their mid-twenties to upper-thirties, and are most likely white men. They will be married, working steady jobs, likely lower-income, blue-collar, raising families and/or caring for aged parents, all the duties of sons, fatherhood, and husbands part of their facade, and part of the pressure they live under. We've also developed some threads of connection among the victims. The victims are middle-class for the most part, white—one reason we suspect the killers to be white. Each victim led a life generally uneventful, devoted to an effort at finding peace and comfort in organized religion and within themselves. They had little else in common save religious devotion. This doesn't tell us much, but it does suggest that they may have met their attackers in their quest for religious answers."

A characteristically wry Falstaff-looking British detective interjected, "Not exactly *lookin' for love in all the wrong places*. But perhaps looking for *God* in all the wrong places? Heh, Doctor?"

"You could put it that way, yes." Her smile relaxed.

"So, we seek out any and all bizarre-o cults in London? That's a gargantuan task in itself," said one inspector.

"Take us till bloody doomsday," added another.

Jessica went on the defensive, her tone firm, saying, "Actually, sometimes, if a law-enforcement official shows up at the doorstep of a guilty person, he automatically confesses and asks, 'Why'd it take you so long? I've been waiting for you.'"

After the meeting, Boulte said to Jessica, "A news conference is set to go. I'd like you to be beside me when I inform the press of our most recent findings."

Near her wit's end, Jessica exploded, "My God, Chief! Another meeting?"

"Meet the press time, Doctor," came his simple response.

"You don't intend to give them the details surrounding the tongue brandings, do you?"

"That bit of news may shake someone from apathy, may open someone's mind to the possibility of a neighbor's strange habits and lifestyle."

"It could also jeopardize a conviction, if and when the killer's apprehended. We need to keep some information in-house."

"We owe it to the public to be open and honest with them at this point, and . . . well . . ."

"And that's the image you wish to portray, but that information isn't news! It must be withheld. It could prove invaluable as a tool in interrogating viable suspects later, and it can certainly rule a suspect out quickly, if skillfully used to—"

"We need to tell the press something now, today, and it has to be something new, Dr. Coran, and it has to be concrete evidence."

"I see. Then no amount of persuasion on my part will change the course you've chosen."

"No, it will not."

Jessica followed alongside Boulte, Sharpe, and Copperwaite to the news conference. Surprisingly, Stuart Copperwaite appeared animated over the prospect of cameras and microphones pushed into his face. She chalked his enthusiasm up to his youth, his inexperience with the press. He'd soon enough learn the pitfalls of dealing with the "free press." Sharpe, by comparison, appeared sullen, perhaps angry. She wondered if he and Boulte had already had it out over this matter. The two men, obviously, were not speaking to one another at the moment.

Suddenly Richard said to Boulte, "This is shoddy police work, sir, and I choose not to participate in your little circus."

Sharpe stormed off to Boulte's, "You come back here, Inspector, right this moment, or I will be forced to take sanctions against you for insubordination. You force me to remove you from the case and it will be on your head, Richard! Richard!"

"Do that!" Sharpe shouted over his shoulder.

"Damn that fellow," bellowed Boulte at Copperwaite. "You'll have to buck up, Stuart. You are, for the moment, the lead investigator on the case of the century."

Copperwaite blanched and didn't smile, but he almost saluted and he might have clicked his heels, Jessica thought. "I shall do my level best, sir."

A far cry from his back-stabbing comments of only a few days ago, Jessica thought. *Now Copperwaite's lapping at Paul Boulte's boots.* She momentarily wondered if Sharpe had been given Copperwaite to mold and fashion for some insidious purpose such as his keeping a close eye on Sharpe's activities. It fleeted past like a shy shadow, but the intuitive feeling certainly sat squarely before Jessica now that Boulte nodded appreciatively at his junior inspector and said, "I knew I could count on you, Coppers."

Copperwaite's lips pursed in an unassuming smile, while his eyes sought out Jessica, sending a silent and unspoken message that clearly read: *What else am I to do? Storm off like a child, like Richard? What will that accomplish?*

Copperwaite read nothing in Jessica's return gaze. She allowed nothing to be transmitted. Still, the coldness of her gaze, the neutrality of it, brought about a painted smile that flit birdlike across Stuart's countenance, gone almost as suddenly as it had come.

As the press conference began, a pencil-thin, sharp-edged woman calling herself the new public prosecutor promised the usual political improbables. But Boulte worked the center ring with Copperwaite to one side of him, Jessica to the other. Since her way to London had been paid for by Boulte's department, she felt she must do as the man requested of her. But she volunteered nothing. Reporters had to pry the new forensic evidence from her with one leading question after another.

Jessica finally and reluctantly told the press about the branding of the tongues, only at Boulte's insistence. However, the exact wording was withheld and would be kept internal so that investigators could know when a suspect is viable or simply a crackpot wishing to confess to the crime.

Boulte seethed, his gaze piercing hers, for she said it in such a way as to make it sound like Boulte's order. Then in the sea of faces before them, Jessica saw the reporter who'd questioned her at the York. She glared at Erin Culbertson, wishing to stake the reporter to a cross even as the other woman asked Jessica a pointed question. "Are you and Richard Sharpe" . . . hesitation, pause . . . "Are you in agreement on the question of whether the Crucifier is one killer or two?"

"We suspect there are at least two men doing the killing, yes."

"Have you any idea *why* they crucify their victims?"

"We fear it is a religious fixation, a zealotry, possibly an attempt to reawaken in the general public an awareness of Christ, the cross, God's word, all that, but we are only speculating. It's difficult enough to climb into the head of one killer, much less two at once. But, yes, there does seem to be a pair-mentality at work, and some of the physical requirements of actually spiking someone to a cross might well require at least four strong hands."

"Thank you all for coming," said Boulte, bringing the press conference to a close. Jessica stepped behind a curtain, out of sight of the cameras and reporters, but she watched from her vantage point to see what, if any, contact Culbertson made with Boulte. To her surprise, there appeared none whatever.

Jessica felt good about having kept the exact wording of the killer's message and the *coal dust and beetle long shot* to herself. No one but she and Dr. Raehael knew of its possible significance. She secretly seethed now, knowing that the information on the tongue branding, and most likely the precise wording, would soon become newsprint fodder, plastered across every television in the city. Like America, the press in England, inadvertently or otherwise, made antiheroes of serial killers. The Crucifiers would make great copy for many days, possibly many months, to come. Even if caught, their story would continue through pre- and post-trial footage, and these psychos would be held up as "criminal geniuses" for young people to "worship" when in fact they were anything but.

Jessica saw that the Culbertson woman had remained behind, fixing her makeup, combing out her hair, preparing it seemed for the next interview, the next story. On a dare to herself, Jessica stepped from behind the curtain to confront the woman. Moments before Erin Culbertson was about to step away, Jessica intercepted her and asked, "Can I have a private moment with you, Miss Culbertson?"

"Absolutely, Dr. Coran. You're the hottest topic in London today. What can I do for you?"

"You can tell me what's transpired between you and Chief Boulte."

"Whatever are you talking about?"

"Don't play games with me, Miss Culbertson. Richard's told me all about you," she lied.

Erin Culbertson held back sudden tears and found it difficult to meet Jessica's gaze. She fell into the chair she'd occupied earlier. "I'd hoped it wasn't over, not completely, between Richard and me. . . . Have for some months now, but when I learned . . . When he told me about his attraction for you, I knew that it was."

"So you went to his superior, getting him into trouble with Boulte out of some female need for vengeance? That really sucks, lady."

"What? No . . . I would never hurt Richard."

"Well, you did. Boulte has changed toward Richard. He seems to know about Richard and me."

"Not from me, he doesn't! Perhaps you and Richard ought be more discreet, Dr. Coran. Given the circumstances, the fact you are involved cannot be healthy for the case, now can it?"

"That's not your call."

"But it is Boulte's."

"It might be, but Boulte isn't being direct with Richard or me. No, he's biding his time like some spider spinning a web. He doesn't want to cripple Richard. He wants to crush him, wants to figure a way to press him into early retirement.

I thought *you* with your press badge might be Boulte's trump card."

"I swear to you, I've said not one word against Richard or you to anyone, Doctor. Now, I am leaving. You can be assured that I love Richard, and I would do nothing whatever to harm him in any fashion. In fact, I would do all within my power to protect him, if I could. Good day to you, Doctor."

Culbertson stood tall and straight and proud as she quickly stepped away, leaving Jessica to wonder if Culbertson *wasn't* feeding Boulte salacious gossip, then who?

Twenty-four hours later

"We did it. Him and me is what did it," said Jacob Periwinkle, pointing again to his roommate and so-called partner in murder, Sheldon Hawkins. Periwinkle and Hawkins had said the magic words that might catapult them into the dark and infamous fame of the pantheon of antiheroes and Antichrists who, over a half century now had dominated world news— the serial killers. They meant to join the ranks by claiming to be "team" Crucifier.

Sharpe conducted the interrogation of the self-confessed duo, while Jessica stood behind the one-way mirror alongside Chief Inspector Boulte. While at ease for the moment, Sharpe had been extremely agitated by Periwinkle and Hawkins. Nearby, rocking on the back of a chair that *tap-tapped* the brick wall, Stuart Copperwaite looked sternly on, not asking any questions, content to allow Sharpe on his feet and pacing, to speak. Only occasionally did Copperwaite break silence to hammer a question home to one or the other of the suspects.

The information imparted at the news conference had spread forth like a fiery cancer, the result a shocking string of confessors claiming their place in history as the crucifixion killers. Most completely mad, but one pair claiming to be "The Crucifier Crew" or "Team Crucifier" must now be seriously examined, as they voluntarily came in, in tandem, both alleging to be the crucifixion killer "team" as touted by the press.

"They were on their periods, the women, weren't they?"

Jacob Periwinkle told them as he asked the question. And it had been true *according* to one news account. Jessica had volunteered to search all the news stories to understand fully what a confessor might pick up in the media to use to convince authorities of their claims. Facts, details of the crime scene, exacting times, all went into a believable, bankable lie. Between Periwinkle and Hawkins, they had already managed to repeat, verbatim, all they'd seen on TV and read in the newspaper. Bad news and a salacious appetite for it by newspeople in radio, TV, and print happened so frequently nowadays that people, jaded to the horror of murder, accepted it as a commonplace, and here in Interrogation Room A—the sweatbox Sharpe called it—the informer who used too many details, told too many exacting stories about how he did what he supposedly did, invariably lied. The truth-tellers, as Sharpe called them, had only one thing in common with pathological liars, and that was the simple matter of "Where do I go from here? Are you taking me to jail or not?" There the similarities died. The false-claims people told an interrogator more than what he asked for. As sure as "dabs"—fingerprints according to Sharpe—body language sent its own message to an experienced interrogator who could read each type, liar and truth-teller. All that is necessary is we show the confessor the *dabs* and tell him the prints came from the bloody crime scene, and he'll give it up one way or the other, usually. It hadn't been so with the two confessors today, who claimed they used surgical gloves throughout their tormenting and disposing of the bodies.

Sharpe stepped out of the interrogation room for a time, needing fresh air and a moment to collect himself. Seeing Jessica, he said, "I can tell from the change in expression which way an innocent man and a guilty man will react— whether the crime is his or not. These two are bogus, ingenuine article . . . despite their revelations, none of which my little six-year-old could not have plucked from the tabloids and the legitimate press."

Knowing most certainly now that Sharpe disbelieved this "tag team" crucifying couple, Periwinkle created a show, clamoring to his feet and making an attempt to grab Copperwaite, who'd remained inside. Sharpe took the opportunity to rush back inside to lash out at the foolhardy man, while warning off the tattered-looking Sheldon Hawkins. Sharpe almost broke Periwinkle's arm, releasing the man only at Copperwaite's intervention.

In the same instant, Chief Inspector Boulte muttered, "There's Sharpe for you. The real man. Take a clear look. He pops off like this more often than not. Not surprised his wife left him."

Jessica didn't need to hear this coming from Boulte. She wanted to run away from the man. She thought him as dull as a bolt, that Copperwaite had properly surmised all that there was of the chief and his talent.

"It's unfortunate that Richard's time is taken up by these false claimants to the Crucifier's throne."

"You think so, do you?"

"Yes, I do."

"For your information, Doctor, several promising leads have already opened up as a result of our cooperation with the press."

"Really? And I thought it just the opposite, that we're wasting our time interviewing subjects for the latest Ripley's museum or book of the odd and delusional."

"Still, you must admit that these two birds, that they are . . . That is, they make a strangely frightening couple, wouldn't you say?"

"What's strangely frightening, sir, and I mean this with all due respect, is how much time we're willing to waste on the usual suspects when this case is not about the usual in any sense of the word. These two men were mental cases before the Crucifixion murders. The press stories actually feed their delusional tendency, legitimizing them, so to speak. Now we are validating them by giving them our time and attention, and then the press will give them the attention of stars, celebrities."

"All well and good, Doctor, but you work out of a laboratory. The rest of us don't have the luxury to work in a vacuum, as much as we'd like to pretend otherwise. We are held accountable for progress or lack of progress on solving murder cases, and often the cases are, like this one, extremely high profile. We can't duck the press on such sensationalism. It's their bread and butter, and if we fail to cooperate, they crucify us. Ironic, but true."

"No, the real irony here, sir, is how we've tied our own investigative teams' hands to their backs, as if conditions aren't bad enough to begin with. It's a *catch-22* in which the soldier, scraping his knee on landing after jumping from the airplane, whines, moans, and complains about the scraped knee while ignoring the fact his entrails are lying on the ground next to him."

"What are you implying?"

"Implying? I'm not *implying* anything. I'm saying outright that we're wasting valuable time on nonsense that will only prove itself nonsense. It's like the proverbial camel—a horse created by committee. The results are not what you *want*, so much as what you *get* in the end."

"Are you making a joke?"

The man's thick-headedness drove Jessica insane inside, and she had no place to put the rage. She tried once more. "Take the last couple claiming to be the one and only Crucifiers. A man and woman team in a common-law marriage, who explained in vivid detail why they crucified their first victim, how they got a charge out of it, and seeing the hubbub around the discovered body, they claimed to have blended in with the tourists to take the ferry at the bridge."

"They sounded so convincing at first," Boulte muttered.

"Yeah, until they got on the ferry. Said they watched from the ferry out on the water while the Yard men were still looking over the body. That has to be a lie."

"How so?"

"Sharpe and Copperwaite had the ferry traffic held up for over an hour when they arrived, and a thick fog covered them. Finally, neither Sharpe nor Copperwaite or any police remained behind once the body was carted off, so how did the so-called killers see them from the ferry as it pulled from the dock? I'll tell you how: through gross imaginings."

"Quite," agreed Boulte.

"That single detail in error is large enough to tell anyone

those two were lying, that they were not in the proximity of
the corpse, the boat, or anything to do with the killing since
they quote 'watched from the ferry as it left the dock to see
how the detectives treated the body.' "

On hearing the lie during his interrogation of the confessing
pair, Richard Sharpe had quickly asked, "Oh, you must, of
course, mean the return ferry, just coming in, since we held
up the outgoing ferry."

"Yes, yes, that's the one," volunteered the confessor.

There had been no incoming ferries from across the
Thames that time of morning. Even the ferry that Sharpe had
heard that gloomy, fog-laden morning was the ferry crossing
downriver at another bridge.

When this was pointed out to the confessing couple, both
pleaded to be executed together. They wanted the Crown to
kill them. That had been their intent all along.

Now this second murder duo of males, Periwinkle and
Hawkins, a pair of seedy losers, had become altogether mad,
angry, and frustrated in their sad little lives. Jessica, listening
in on the interview from behind the one-way, realized immediately that the press, while useful if constructively involved in and committed to the ending of a serial killer's
career, failed often to serve a case for a number of reasons,
not the least being that a little bit of information in the wrong
hands or head, could lead too many people down the primrose
lane. Offering a reward often resulted in the same end. Except
in this case the reward meant national attention, great noto-
riety as when *People* magazine editors chose to splash can-
nibal Jeffrey Dahmer's face across a cover.

"I'm going in there. I have a few questions for these two,"
Jessica told Boulte. He did not question her motive, even
though she'd just told him that interrogating these men represented a gross waste of time and a wrong direction for the
investigation to take. Just as she left the observation room,
the thin, dark-haired public prosecutor entered via another
door, and Boulte's entire attention went to her. "Ellen!" he
falsely beamed.

Once inside the interrogation room, Jessica saw Sharpe's
eyes, at first disappointed, as if throwing up a barrier to tell

her *This is no place for you; it's not safe or right for you to be here.* This he quickly replaced with a quick nod, a half-smile, and an urging for her to come in. The moment she entered the interrogation room, she felt the palpable evil here, perhaps the reason that Richard wanted at first to stop her at the door. Evil in all its most excruciatingly toady ugliness resided in one corner in the pockmarked face of Periwinkle, who leaned over to whisper in the cauliflower ear of Hawkins. It were as if they shifted the evil back and forth between them, as if it were a salacious animal or insect. The sensation of it as a palpable, breathing entity here riveted first her sense of smell. Evil cast a noxious odor. It permeated her mouth where it tasted foul, and then found its way through the canals of her ears. Rude and disquieting words were coming from each of the desperate men. Each asked crude questions regarding Jessica's body and presence: "Why is the bitch here? Who is this whore kidding? We know what she wants, four wangs in the room. Wants us all to do her here and now while some other wang the other side of that mirror watches. Don't-cha, whore, bitch, cunt? Answer me, you fucking sweet-and-sour whore bitch."

Sharpe lashed out at Periwinkle, threatening bodily harm if he didn't *"Shut up!"* Then he warned Hawkins, followed by a chair he threw across the room.

Jessica now felt the present evil crawl along the epidermal layer of her skin. It crept everywhere about her body at once. It made her feel like the victim in some sickening horror show, and the sight of the two men claiming to be the Cru-cifiers disgusted her, brought up in her a twisting, coiling hatred. Hissing hatred. Hatred wanting to unleash its venom on them.

Jessica wondered at the sheer depth of her own rage: un-reasonably wild, natural, blind, primal, pure, dark, and fatal in the end. Such hatred existed as a natural survival signal for Jessica and other law-enforcement people, but it formed a *reason for living* for such monsters as Ted Bundy, Richard Ramirez, and countless others, including the Crucifier.

She wondered how many good and faithful so-called Chris-tians felt this sort of viperlike hatred toward those who did not practice their belief. Wondered if the real Crucifier had this in mind, to bring the nonbeliever into believing, to teach by demonstration and by example, the example being the crucified remains of those who mocked his religion, whatever vision of that religion existed in the killers' heads.

In any event, she felt the cold, hungry, animal hatred pacing Interrogation Room A. It permeated the room. Perhaps part of it belonged to Richard, part of it to Copperwaite—as well as being part of the two men they interrogated. Perhaps hatred fed off all of them, one and the same cowardly jackal, growing in strength as one man's hatred matched the other's, until the jackal became a two-headed, winged beast with horns and hooves and talons. "We become the thing we hate, if we chase it long enough." How often Asa Holcraft had warned her, and recently Luc Sante had said the same thing to her. Nothing new in the old belief, dating far before the character of Van Helsing in Bram Stoker's *Dracula*, going back to biblical story and the beginning of time: Pursue evil long enough with enough determination, and you become it, and doesn't it become you? she darkly jested somewhere deep within the regions of her multilayered soul. For part of the evil crouching in the corner resembled Jessica herself.

"I like driving in the nails," said Sheldon Hawkins, drooling over the image as he spoke the words. "Ja-see, that's my job. Jake here, he bleedin' prays over 'em, after we do 'em. Curly bastard, that's what Jake here is."

"Prayer wounds all heels!" joked Jacob Periwinkle, a small, obnoxious weasel whose body odor, something akin to hair and hide of the rat, preceded him. Hawkins's most prominent feature filled his face—an enormous beak nose, falconlike in size and appearance. Jessica thought them stark caricatures of the sort that Jim Henson's company portrayed in the Muppetland Band. Both men needed bathing, scrubbing, and grooming. They were like a pair of stray dogs who'd learned to live with their own lice.

"What is the purpose behind your crucifying people?" she asked them. "Why kill people in so brutal a manner? If, in fact, you two committed these horrible acts."

"Acts? Acts is it, all right, look it up in the Acts of the

Apostles six something. Says it all right there," replied Periwinkle.

"Bloody curly it is, too," replied Hawkins.

Jessica put it to Perwinkle. "Why don't you educate us, Mr. Perwinkle? Elucidate."

"All right, I will. Says there in Acts, why's it so hard for you to believe that your God can raise the dead? We wanted to see if God could . . , raise the dead." He barked out his laughter. "Come to find out, The Old Fellow wasn't inner-rested, I bloody guess." He laughed more.

"Keep a civil tongue, you animal!" shouted Copperwaite.

"In the name of Christ," said Periwinkle with a facetious tone as his hand did a flourish and his head gave a slight bow. "That's why we done what we done, right, Hawkins?"

"Codswallop and bullshit, Jake, bullshit. Tell them the real reason," shouted his partner.

"We don't reveal secrets God 'imself has provided."

"God speaks to you, then?" asked Jessica.

"Not exactly God," corrected Hawkins.

"Who then?"

"It's 'im, the bloody one on the cross, it is," shouted Periwinkle.

Hawkins shouted, "Christ, it's from Christ, you damned fool cuntie! Like to see *you* all done up on the cross, dearie!"

"Shut that flapper of yours, Hawkins! One more foul word, and I swear I'll strike you dumb," shouted Sharpe, approaching menacingly with fists clenched and the veins popping out of his neck like taut rope.

Hawkins ignored Sharpe's gallant attempt to spare Jessica foul words. He let out his own shout. "He's coming back! He's *come* back. He's here, among us now! And this world ain't seen no havoc like what He—the Son of God—will bring down round us all, that's what." He'd so lost his breath that his last words came out as mere tire-screech utterances.

Rat-boy had begun screaming over Beak-nose, chorusing the words, "Shut up! Shut up, Hawkins! Shut your hole!"

"Christ told us to do it. Christ wants revenge on the Jews for what they did to 'im. That's why we did Burtie Burton. That's it, pure and simple, and He's come to show us what goddamn revenge is really, really like in the first order, I tell you, the revenge of God! The revenge of the Son of God is coming down on all of us, so you'd better stand on His side, whore and whore no more." He ended with his eyes ablaze and burning into Jessica's eyes, Jessica matching his stare with her own intensity.

"Ten Commandments take on a whole new meaning for you now, don't they, slut?"

Sharpe, acting before Copperwaite could, struck like a snake. He had reached across the table where Periwinkle sat and nearly dragged him across it, shouting, "Shut up your ugly remarks to Dr. Coran! You want to see what revenge looks like up close, you bloody little pipsqueak!"

Copperwaite and Jessica pulled and pried Richard and Periwinkle apart while Sheldon Hawkins laughed maniacally at the scene. Jessica saw now the hatred had firmly rooted itself in Richard's eyes. He let go of Periwinkle and turned from her gaze.

Boulte, tiring of the verbal jousting and circles and anxious to get on the six o'clock news with results, stormed into the room now with the armed guards. He told the guards to take the prisoners back to the holding cells. "It's time we closed this down, Richard. Stuart." Boulte paced the room now, and even with the two confessors gone, the anger and hatred permeating the interrogation walls, breathing in and out of the very pores of the concrete, had remained behind with the stale and rank odors that had wafted in the wake of the two confessors.

Boulte said outright, "I, for one, heard enough to put those two psychotics away for life."

Richard stood in his face. "You're drawing at straws, Chief Inspector."

"Fairly sturdy straws at that. Look, Richard, seems to me we have two viable suspects here, certainly worth pursuing." Boulte turned to Copperwaite, now leaning against the wall, and Boulte's finger, like a thick-shafted arrow, now pressed into Copperwaite's chest as the chief added, "Get a warrant for the flat, the car they drive, all of it, Stuart."

"These two are not the killers," Sharpe firmly said, again

inches from Boulte's face. "They're a pair of sorry liars who couldn't tie their shoes if asked to. You turn them over to the cameras, make 'heroes' of them and yourself, sir, and I guarantee that you'll be making an enormous mistake."

"I'll take the heat in the event we're wrong about them. Get the warrant, make the search."

Jessica, Stuart, and Richard all knew Boulte needed someone to publicly "hang," no matter the truth of guilt or innocence. The two men not only filled the bill, they fit the costumes: They walked and talked the parts given them by the press. Obviously, Boulte had chosen to overlook the ready clues in their so-called confession that made their tale as farfetched as the "ferry boat" detail in the other confessors' tale. The biblical detail, however, may have proved just the right touch so far as Chief Boulte cared. Never mind the nonsense clues Richard had spent hours digging for, the clues that told them all that the entire confession could be characterized as bogus.

"They tell a compelling story," Boulte said to the others. "They know all the names of the victims, their histories, their backgrounds, their religious leanings, and where each body was dumped and found. And that remark against the Jews and Burtie Burton. . . . It all fits."

Sharpe argued, "They could've gotten all that from the press, and so could my six-year-old daughter from turning on the telly."

"We'll give them both lie-detector tests, if you are still uncertain," Boulte determinedly replied.

"While it's obvious that these two people are disturbed, it's not so obvious they committed these crimes," Jessica put in. "Speaking to them, interviewing them, Luc Sante would say we have just interviewed the Devil at play, but—"

"Luc Sante, Luc Sante," Chief Inspector Boulte lamented. "I knew you should not have involved him on this case, Richard." Jessica read into his words, *And you shouldn't have involved this lady doctor from America, either.* "Luc Sante's managed to so brainwash you two with his little sermons on evil that you don't recognize it when you see it before you!"

Jessica tried to reason with Boulte who stubbornly and tenaciously held to his tunnel vision. Finally, Richard said, "These two buffoons are *convinced* that they are the killers whom all of Scotland Yard, the press, the public, and the prime minister have sought now for weeks and weeks. Such a conviction lifts their mundane lives and low opinion of one another and self to a higher plane."

"Now you're a psychotherapist, too, Richard?"

"Of course, they can lay claim to this enormous ripple effect they've caused in society's pond," agreed Jessica, immediately coming to Richard's defense, understanding his point. "It's alluring to them, and it is quite real. Real enough in here"—she pounded her heart—"that no lie detector test designed can help out here. They are themselves convinced that they are the killers. They are convinced of their own guilt, the guilt of murdering the innocent. Yet they've provided no key evidence here, and their eyes bugged out when we asked about their victims' tongues. They first said they cut them out, and later they chose burning the tongues. They know nothing of this!"

Richard again added to the argument, "You see, Boulte, they are convinced beyond all reason and rationale that they are indeed the Crucifiers whom the world seeks. It makes their miserable lives worth a few pounds to think it so."

Jessica laughed a hollow laugh. "In becoming the Crucifier with a capital *C*, they take shape, form, and they become something larger than themselves, something the press has made larger than life, as it so often and thoughtlessly does in America with such madmen as Cunanan, Manson, Bundy, Gacey, Speck, Oswald, Sirhan. As your historians have done with Jack-the-Ripper. Rather than turn the cameras away from these desperate and dangerous sociopaths, the press has given them a stature in death or in incarceration that they never possessed in their miserable little lives. They have elevated them to the status of godlike monsters, capable of great feats of daring and genius, when in fact they are pathetic remnants of passing evil."

"Now you really are beginning to sound like Luc Sante," complained Boulte. The Chief stared several times at the two-way mirror, telling Jessica that the public prosecutor had been listening in on them all. "You've been talking too long to that old shrink. Look, we have the finest lie-detector men in the world here."

"And they will tell you the same as I have. Despite even hypnotism, the subject, if thoroughly convinced on this conscious plane of existence, he remains so on the subconscious level of existence as well. Lie detectors detect subtle nuances in honesty and truth, just as a hot blade burns the dry tongue of the village liar when the witch doctor lays the knife on. If the truth is subverted or overtaken by a rock-solid, all encompassing, life-altering *delusion*, if you are dealing with an abnormality that is the normality of existence for this person, an aberration that is cause for celebration in this individual, no truth other than the *delusional truth* will be forthcoming in such a test."

Boulte squinted, half-smiled, and asked Jessica point-blank, "Are you deliberately trying to confuse me?"

Jessica erupted with laughter. It careened off the walls, out the door, and down the long corridors leading to Boulte's office.

Sharpe grabbed her by the arm, taking her aside, saying, "Dr. Coran has been working extremely hard. She hasn't eaten today, either," he excused her behavior. To her, he added, "Why don't we have a bite to eat? I know a pleasant place just around the corner, a pub where we can have a pint and a sandwich, since I'm off duty. What do you say?"

"I'm famished and I'm buying, but we haven't finished here. We must convince your chief of—"

"His mind is set, was set before he spoke to us, and he'll remain immovable. We're both wasting our time and energy on the man. Walk away from it, now."

And so they did, together, leaving poor Copperwaite to deal with Boulte.

· FOURTEEN ·

Among . . . crippled legions—the mass of suffer-
ing humanity—the evil reside, perhaps the most
pitiable of all.

—M. SCOTT PECK,
PEOPLE OF THE LIE

"Old army saying, Doctor," Sharpe said in her ear, taking her
arm and gaining access to the other side of the busy, downtown intersection. "If it moves, salute it. If it doesn't move,
clean it."

"Is that where you feel the investigation is? A standstill?
Or are you saying that you've washed your hands of it?"

"I don't know a blind thing about it. . . . The man on the
street in bloody Bloomsbury knows more about the case than
I do. Says so in the *London Times*. Damn all."

"Isn't that Erin Culbertson's newspaper?"

"She's not to blame."

"I've met her, you know."

"Really?"

"Twice now."

"She's bright."

"Agreed, and pretty."

"From Bloomsbury," he finished.

"Bloomsbury?"

"West Central London. I should hang it all, go to the BM,
perhaps."

"The BM? As in bowel movement?"

He laughed. "British Museum. I should step out of it and

leave it to the whole boiling lot of them, and place myself in a fucking museum is what."

"What's happened?"

"They're after me, pure and simple."

"The press you mean?"

"No, the department, the Yard. Boulte in particular. I'm certain of it now."

She joked. "I hadn't noticed any animosity there."

This made him laugh. "You realize that sometimes paranoia is dead on, but sometimes we do nothing about it for too long a period before heeding its advice, and intuition often knows more than we do, but then it's too late."

"I'm sorry you're having problems, Richard."

"Simple matter really. Boulte doesn't want to take responsibility for a botched job, and since I'm nearing retirement, why not put me on the outs? I should just bugger off to Brighton seashore and put my legs up a bit there. I swear, I didn't know that Stuart Copperwaite wore brothel-creepers."

Jessica tried to slow him, to get him to explain, stopping him amid the bustle of the London streetcorner, asking, " 'Brothel-creepers'? Copperwaite?"

"Sorry, they're crepe-soled suede shoes. No bubble or squeak to them. How to blindside a fellow inspector, all that, and when I think of how much I've taught that young pup . . ."

"Whatever did he do?"

"I have it on good authority that he's buttered his eggs with that bumble!"

"Bumble? Buttered eggs?"

"Bureaucrat, Boulte. They're having crumpets and tea together, and have been regularly. His put-downs against Boulte have been a ruse. He's been put on me from the beginning as a watchdog!"

She immediately realized that it had been Copperwaite then and not Erin Culbertson who had informed Boulte of their affair. "Have you talked to Copperwaite about it?"

"I did."

"And?"

"He denies it, of course, but well, this may be a lot of *bumf*, but my theory is that Boulte and the public prosecutor—"

"The public prosecutor?"

"Lady you met when Boulte rammed Periwinkle and Hawkins down our collective throats."

"Oh, yes . . . I recall."

"Prosecutor and Boulte want to dispatch me from the Yard altogether, and they're mucking about the garbage to do so . . ."

"Perhaps, then, you should confront your superiors."

"That's bloody candyfloss, and you know it."

"Candyfloss?"

"A flimsy idea. Look, the cat's among the pigeons, and if the powers that be wish to catch you out, then they will manufacture it, if they must. In my case, they needn't manufacture a thing."

"Thanks to me," she muttered.

He immediately grasped her hands and shook his head in a vigorous denial of this. "No, not at all. Certainly it's hurt Boulte's ego to learn that you and I, that we . . . However, there's no law says we can't fraternize in the fashion of two consenting adults. There's no standing rules in the Yard against it, either. We modernized along with the Catholic church recently, you see. So he can't touch me there."

"But he could put it out for the court of public opinion."

"Yes, well, he may save that up as his trump card, but I rather doubt he'll take that gamble."

Jessica looked past him, her head spinning until she finally focused on a chimney pot, a pipe added to the top of chimneys. They were everywhere, all over London, ubiquitous for city dwellers whose homes spewed the remnants of their coal-burning fires, in shops and in homes. But this particular one had a red-legged crow sitting atop it, and at first Jessica thought it an ornamentation, but then it cocked an eye at her, flapped its wings and gracefully, thoughtlessly eased skyward.

Sharpe followed her gaze as she watched the bird, now a black dot in the distance. "A chough, we call them," he informed her. "So, where shall we go for a bite?"

"I thought you had a place selected?"

"I want to be democratic. That way is Fleet Street, where

the pubs are filled with newspeople and photomakers. If we stay put, the pub we enter will be full of bankers. And that way"—he pointed in the opposite direction—"will take us to Grub Street. Just the opposite—where starving artists, actors, and writers live in garrets and fill the pubs by day. If we walk out of the City, this way"—again he pointed—"then we can go to where I had planned."

"I'll risk your judgment."

Jessica had learned that the *City*, as Londoners called the financial district, was roughly the equivalent of Wall Street in New York, with some five thousand residents during business hours scrunched into one square mile of territory.

"This is one hell of an unholy dog's breakfast. This thing with Copperwaite being sucked into becoming a stoolie for Boulte and our Miss Prosecutorial Bitch. . . . A true unholy mess," Sharpe muttered, as much to himself as to Jessica, as they picked their way through the crowd. He was holding her hand now, taking charge and going straight for the place of his choosing. "Doom perhaps for me and the case, unless you stand firm, Dr. Coran. Doom . . . how ironic. Did'ya know that the painting of the Last Judgment over here is called *Doom*?" He laughed hollowly at the thought. "Are you sure you want to be seen with me, Jessica?"

"Don't be silly."

"He who sups with the Devil, must use a long spoon."

They passed pedestrian walkways, went through lights, crossed into narrow lanes, rushing past fascinating, quaint little shops she would have loved to browse, until they found a lane so small that Jessica could not imagine how cars passed one another until she saw some do so.

Another step around a corner and they found a quiet, even peaceful shop-lined street with outdoor cafes and art galleries.

"Maybe it's Copperwaite that bothers me most. The fact someone you trust can so quickly be at your back with the cutlery."

"I've had it happen to me. I know the feeling," she commiserated, still wondering if it were true.

"*Cupboard love*'s what we call it over here, Jessica—sucking up. Sucking one's way to the top. But perhaps the whole thing's a blessing in disguise, heh? A real curate's egg."

She'd heard this expression before—something both good and bad at once.

"I'd been giving some thought to retirement anyway. Copperwaite can have the damned dead man's shoes. You know that's what Boulte feared most about me, that I'd run for his job. Well, now Copperwaite or some other fool can just wait to inherit it when Boulte kicks off."

"Crumpet—getting any crumpet?" said a man lying in a vagrant's pose in a doorway to a vacant shop.

"Watch your vile tongue, rogue!" shouted Sharpe, just itching to thrash the man. Instead, he pulled Jessica past the hobo, saying, "Just a brainless *come-day, go-day*, that one. I pay him for information on the street from time to time, which explains his being so familiar."

"Why would he take me for your whore, Richard?" she said and jabbed him in the ribs. "Lighten up, please," she teased. "At least you are getting some *crumpet*."

This made him laugh and kiss her there on the street.

Jessica felt the traffic in the small back lanes here lighter and more willing to give way to pedestrians. Something about London, its small streets and compact alleyways, made her feel comfortable and at home, made her feel like an oversized Alice in this wonderland, and even made her feel important, large, and of consequence. Jessica held on to Richard's arm as the traffic halted for them to cross.

"There's the pub. The one I think you'll find both quite colorful and authentic," he said, pointing, but an entire array of pub signs stared back at Jessica from across the tiny street. They read: LION HEAD, THE SILVER CROSS, THE ROUNDTABLE INN, THE CAPTAIN'S GALLEY, and THE BOAR'S HEAD PUB.

"I had thought Stuart a smart fellow, you know, and it's a shock to learn that a man you called friend turns out to be dim as a Toc-H lamp, which he is, but worse yet, he's betrayed our partnership."

At the end of the street Jessica saw a flashing road sign which read in bold letters: **DIVERSION**, meaning detour. For some reason both sign and meaning stamped themselves on her brain with the force of a psychic vision, but she quickly dismissed the thought.

The unclean man who'd been lying in the street moments before suddenly limped up alongside them. "I got my leg banged up the other day, Inspector. Need some attention given it, but I got no green. I 'ave information for you. Can we do business? I got word on that Crucifier thing."

This made Sharpe stop, and with him Jessica, who truly looked at the man for the first time.

"Dot'n Carry's what they call me, mum . . . Steve's the true name, Steve Savile. Family migrated here from Sweden. Made of me a Londoner without they give me a choice, what."

"Whyever do they call you Dot and Carry?"

"Mostly on account-a-this game leg. When I walk, the wooden one goes dot, the other carries me. Got it in the war's what. It's why Sharpe and me can have some common ground, right, Colonel?"

Sharpe ground his teeth. "What've you got on the Crucifier, D.C.?"

But Dot'n Carry, or D.C., addressed Jessica instead, asking, "You must be that lady FBI woman Sharpe hired on for the case. Read about you in the papers. Think I can't read? I read good when I can find a paper left behind by somebody."

Sharpe grabbed him up by the lapels, and he dropped a walking stick which had so become a part of the man that Jessica hadn't noticed it until it bounced on the sidewalk, making two distinct *pings*.

"Word is, the Crucifier's really a good guy, Sharpe. What they call a benign killer. Only kills people who are in suffering, kinna like Robinson Hood and Sherwood's Forest, you see. Only he don't rob from the rich and give to the poor, but takes troubled lives and frees 'em."

"If that's so, then why hasn't he done a damned thing for your sorry ass, D.C.?"

"Must figure I don't 'ave it so bad. Still got my sense of humor. Ain't suicidal or depressed, Inspector."

"Get outta here, D.C."

"But Sharpe, Colonel, I need something. Please, man."

Sharpe tossed several bills down, grabbed Jessica's arm, and led her toward the Boar's Head, apologizing to her.

"What did he mean, Sharpe?"

"D.C.? He's full of it half the time and a no-opinion the other half. The man's double Dutch in his tongue and double-gaited elsewhere! Forget it. If you let him, D.C. will tell you everything opens that shuts and everything shuts that opens."

Jessica guessed that Sharpe meant the other man spoke with "forked" tongue.

"Filth!" D.C. called out from across the street.

"Common term for cops in England," explained Richard. "I think he knows I'm trying to get him on charges as a fire-raiser—an arsonist—even as I use him. Interesting past, the man has, actually. Just after returning from the service with his gimp leg, he tried white-collar crime. Was put away for his trouble."

"Arrested for what exactly?"

"Got 'im for fluffing the books, accounts."

She and Richard moved on, going right past the Boar's Head. They located a place called the Clockwork Arms, which Richard pointed out had been renovated from a building housing a clockworks and separately an armory. Now an eatery, the place made the most of the brick exterior and solid oak beams.

"The weather this time of year? Is it always so balmy and beautiful?" she asked.

"Luke's little summer," he replied, smiling, helping with her chair.

"Luke's what?" the noise of the crowd and the music from a live flutist in one corner whose melodic Celtic music touched something in Jessica's core, running along her spine, made it difficult to focus on Richard's words.

"St. Luke's summer. I suspect you call it Indian summer where you're from," he explained. "Look, if you don't mind, I have to see to the geography of the house," he said, and promptly left the table, leaving Jessica to wonder whatever he meant. Then she remembered an earlier comment and realized that he was going to the men's room.

While alone, Jessica took in the sights and sounds of the

pub. She caught snatches of conversation and found herself matching oddly strange Briticisms with the word or phrase that might be its counterpart in America. British English and American English proved two entirely different animals.

She overheard people in the pub referring to such things as "between whiles" at Billingsgate Market—a fish market, as famous for its foul language as its fish. She heard some men talking about her at the bar: one called her "an attractive bit of goods." She heard multiple requests for what appeared the national drink—bitter beers. She heard one woman complaining she hadn't been to Blackpool in decades and wanted to go there to ride the switchback—the roller coaster.

Jessica found something fascinating in every small word and thing and person, and in all the quaint places and place names everywhere she went in London. Even what she'd learned from hanging about Scotland Yard fascinated her. Fingerprints were *dabs*, handcuffs *darbies*, police cars—which were blue and white in color had become *jam sandwiches* or *panda cars*, while extortion was *demanding money with menaces*, and rape or criminal assault was euphemistically called *being interfered with*. A police beat or patch in America here became a *manor*. *To catch a packet* meant to stop a bullet. Ever the stiff upper lip people, the British didn't get their walking papers, but rather their *marching papers*. While American cops were cited for bravery, British cops were *mentioned in dispatches*.

Gin was *mother's ruin*, and denatured alcohol in Britain became *methylated spirits*, and *meths* were the unappealing derelicts who drank it. While the Mets in America meant baseball in New York City, *Mets* in London referred to the London police. And a pedestrian walk equaled a *pelican crossing*. A speed bump posed in London as a *sleeping policeman* or *rumble strip*.

In fact the British, aside from being a nation of shopkeepers and the "pudding nation," had come to be world renowned as the most euphemistic race on the planet. When speaking of being taxed, they put it as *suffering an assessment*. It appeared they would say anything to keep from cursing, even to abbreviating "God blind me" to *blimey*. . . . and "God's truth" to *'struth!* They much preferred a phrase such as "the best of British luck" said with irony. Even "bloody fool" was abbreviated to *b.f.* so as to avoid the cursing. She thought it rather hilarious. As a result of the euphemisms, many a word that passed British lips, while not a curse, stood in for one just as well. They had literally hundreds of words that kept them coming up short of calling God's name out in vain.

He's up *for the high jump* now formed a grim echo of the hanging days, and a mortician in London became a funeral furnisher.

Meanwhile, a *penny dreadful*, often called a *shilling shocker* stood in for a dime novel. The false issue of a red herring, ubiquitous and obligatory in any mystery story, here became a *Norfolk capon*. A literary hack such as the infamous Geoffrey Caine here might be called a *nasty* or a *devil*, but so, too were law apprentices.

When Richard returned to the table, he began a tirade about the two arrested as the Crucifying Duo. "A pair of comic book characters if ever there were," he said, spouting venom.

Jessica tried to get him off the subject, off work altogether. She asked him about the British Museum, what she might find there, but he ignored her, going on about the twosome under arrest for the Crucifier's sins.

Giving in, she said, "I particularly hated the one who led the other by the nose."

"Oh, that creep Periwinkle is a real Geordie."

"Geordie? Explain that again, please."

"A native of Tynsdale—raised with the pigs, maybe. A coal miner for sure."

"A coal miner? That's rather coincidental."

"Not at all. Everyone in Tynsdale goes to the mines for work. I've seen their like before. One is a Geordie, the partner a George."

"A George?"

"Automatic pilot. One's the planner, and he's a weak-minded bastard if ever there was one, and the other goes about on automatic pilot. A Geordie and a George, true criminal masterminds those two, truly fit your profile of the killer, as well, wouldn't you agree?" he facetiously asked. "But then in dealing with Boulte, one must take in the *Paddy* factor."

"Well, they are the right age, and they do live with their mothers." Jessica had heard the term Paddy bandied about in police circles here, referring usually to IRA terrorists, but it had an ethnic edge to it. It meant that the criminal mind often meant the stupid mind, and Paddys—a common Irish name— were criminally stupid. "Is Boulte part Irish?"

"If he is, he wouldn't admit to it."

London, despite its diverse population and the international flavor of its makeup, remained a haven for racial prejudice, just as Hawaii and other beautiful places around the globe Jessica had visited harbored racial disharmony. Sadly enough it appeared a global fact of life. Here a British racist was known as a *racialist*. Even now, she could hear *Paki* jokes being told at the table over her shoulder between calls for the waiter to answer the questions: "Where's the other half." "How 'bout the other half?" Both meant the speaker wanted another drink.

"Paki" formed an unpleasant racist connotation in its compactness. Hearing the term several times, Jessica asked Sharpe about it. His reply was off-handed, his shoulders shrugged as he said, "Paki-bashing. It's an extremely unpleasant activity here. At its most benign, it begins with jokes. At its most vicious, it ends with roaming gangs—usually a rat's nest of *Paddys*—looking for and usually finding Pakistanis to beat up."

"*Past a joke* is another British expression, meaning something's not funny anymore, but rather intolerable. Most Mets in London simply don't want Paki-bashing on their little patches."

Someone entering the pub and passing their table said hello to Richard, asking, "And how are you, Sharpe?"

"Not so dusty," replied Sharpe. "And you?"

"Gain on swings, lose on rounds, you know? Take all due care." And the man disappeared into the crowd at the bar.

"Drinking friends," said Richard. "Cricket metaphors . . . Sorry, they're rather like your baseball metaphors in America. Endemic here, really . . ."

"You needn't apologize for it."

"Everything in this blasted country has ties to the national sports. It's become part of our thinking and speech."

"Like it hasn't happened in America?"

He shook his head and bit his lip at once, disagreeing. "Here we say at close of play, bat a brace, bat first, boundary, bowler, duck, cap, fieldsman, batsman, play a straight bat, knock for six, get one's eye in, maiden over, night watchman, off one's bat, off the mark, pitch, rot, run out, run up, sticky wicket, stump, take first knock."

She laughed at his rendition.

He added between sips of dark beer, "For a time I played with the Marylebone Cricket Club, but I must admit, the game's become a fantastic obsession for the population here."

"In America we've got sports metaphors all over the language map, too. We talk about bush-leaguers, rookies, getting to first base, stepping up to bat, having something on the ball, making a hit, being off base, stealing home, pinch hitting, rain checks, check swing, strike outs, curve balls, and so . . ." She stopped to stare into his eye and to raise her own pint to her lips. "Anything you've got in the way of problem clichés from being cricket-obsessed, we've got tenfold in the Colonies with baseball- and basketball- and football-obsessing fans. Trust me."

"Even the police jargon uses cricket terms," he countered. "We *play in* a witness or a suspect before any serious interrogation begins. As we did with the rat brothers back there today. We began with the weather, the cursed traffic, the latest on the Royal Family and the current political crisis. Then the suspect plays himself in, as it were."

"We do the same where I come from. It's called reeling him in, from fishing expedition to having baited your hook to landing the big one."

He challenged on another front, a smile lurking behind his countenance. "At least your government has its house in order," he said, making her instantly laugh.

"Are you kidding?"

"To some degree, yes, but look here, our government can make a far greater muckery of statesmanship than yours any calendar day of the week."

"A muckery? Do you mean mockery?"

"I said muckery, and I mean muckery. The British government makes a muck of everything it touches."

"In about the same way the U.S. government makes a mess of things?"

"I hope you're not suggesting there's any room for comparison? Your American politicians might mess around, but ours muck about. They muck in places they have no business mucking. They pretend the exercise is a mental one, but we know what total mucks they are, despite the cloak of words they spew forth. They need to muck out Parliament and start over. They need to put every single one of those Parliamentarians in a muck to sweat and off their duffs. They spend their lives on the never-never. The whole business of government here has become an idle nonsense like . . . as in Alice's Wonderland."

"Are you through mucking over Parliament?"

"Aye, I mean, yes."

"What's a never-never?"

"An installment plan, and in the case of politicians, a never-never is a committee to study the problem. They have a committee to form committees. Lewis Carroll was right, you know, about us, aye."

She laughed. She knew he felt relaxed. He used "aye" instead of yes when he relaxed, reverting back to the "sound of Bow Bells"—the easy slang of his upbringing. She liked knowing he could relax around her.

"They have a saying in Ireland: 'Will the last person leaving the country please switch off the politicians?' "

She laughed uproariously in response. She then asked, "You seem to be coping with divorce well? Copperwaite tells me it hasn't been that long."

He laughed hollowly in response, shook his head, sat up taller, and took in a deep breath. "Well, I do have a potted lecture on the subject, anyone cares to listen. Frankly, I had so many inquiries about the divorce, the children, how I was holding up, how she was holding up, that the standard talk had to be formulated, as defense. I mucked the divorce up as I mucked the marriage up, I suppose. Very parliamentary of me, really. Spent some time in therapy, and while it's now off the boil, as they say, at the time, I felt parboiled. I felt pain in my being so intense, a depression so deep, I fear going near that part of me ever again."

She laid her hand over his. "I'm sorry. Didn't mean to open old wounds or to stick my nose in."

"Oh, you've hardly opened any wounds, and as for being a prodnose, well, that's another term here for detectives. And since I work with the lot at the Yard, there's little hope for privacy on the issue, really."

"But you still have wounds. A divorce is a war no one walks away from unscathed."

He nodded, but stiffly. "Wounds remain. Tell you one thing about a divorce . . ."

"Yes?"

"Only one who wins is the Old Lady of Threadneedle Street."

"Threadneedle who?"

"Bank of England. It's on Threadneedle Street." His eyes shifted. He brought her into focus and suddenly changed the subject entirely. "Copperwaite's somewhat upset with us— the two of us—but mostly me. He believes me over the moon about you, in raptures."

She blushed and lifted the menu to cover her face, pretending hunger and thirst, but asking, "Is Copperwaite right?"

"Right? I can't say, just yet."

She quickly returned to her menu and asked of a drink, "What's a pink gin?"

"Gin and bitters with water added. Would you care to indulge?"

"Only if you'll join me. But perhaps another beer, or a pint as you call it over here, would be wiser?"

"I'm off the ticker. Either way is fine with me. As for a pint, if a Briton asks for a pint, he means a pint of bitter. It's a unit of liquid measure, the pint in question is an Imperial pint, twenty ounces."

"A beer in America is only sixteen ounces!"

"Half a pint is ten ounces. That may be what you want to

order. It's what I carried over here for you." He indicated the now empty glass in front of her.

"I see, I think . . ."

Jessica gave him a bemused smile which he took to mean "go on," which he did. "As for whiskey or scotch, when you want a decent drink in London, you must ask for a double, but not even the bravest or thirstiest lad would dare ask a British bartender for a triple."

She laughed loud enough to alert the tables around them. He continued on, "If you want to go easy on yourself, you might try our vintage cider. Goes down too easily, actually."

"Really?"

"With the consistency of good sherry and at least as strong."

Row after row of glasses in two sizes, pint and half pint, gleamed in the light just above the bar, tethered upside down on hooks like crystal bats.

"Next," Richard continued, "you must decide between ordinary bitter and best bitter, when ordering a pint."

"What's the difference? Which do you prefer?"

"The best, of course. It's stronger, aged longer."

"Is that what we've had already? It was delicious."

"Yes. So what will it be?"

She settled for the pink gin. He called for two.

"So, I take it that Boulte doesn't like you, Inspector." Already, the half pint of bitters worked to slur her words and thoughts.

"Boulte would like to make me a points man."

"Meaning?"

"A policeman on point duty is a traffic cop."

She asked him about his time in the military. He evaded the question, beginning a spiel on England's pubs instead, pointing about the place as he did so. "Pubs—public houses— like this one are an institution in England. Everyone in Britain has his pub. Some call it the local. Each pub has two bars, generally, the public bar and the private or saloon bar where you're apt to find a carpet on the floor and linen tablecloths on the tables. Drinks in the private room are a bit pricier, of course, but the dartboard, the billiard table, and the shove-halfpenny board you'll always find out here. If you want, tonight, we could do a pub crawl, that is make the rounds as you Yanks say. In fact, we could go to Clubland."

"Clubland?"

"St. James's—an area of London that includes the palace of the same name. Houses many of London's most famous clubs."

"And you wish to do this for me? With the express purpose of getting the both of us loaded?"

"Stinking. Boulte and the public prosecutor would love to learn of it. They might well have one of the Q-Division staring at me right this moment for all I know."

"Public prosecutor? Q-Division?"

"A division of the Yard, internal affairs. As for the P.P., that'd be Ellen Sturgeon, what you would call the district attorney. You met her briefly at the meeting of all the citywide officers, didn't you?"

"No, I didn't. No one formally introduced us, but I do recall a stern-looking broomstick in the corner."

"That's her. She's moving so fast on the rat brothers, you'd imagine the Thames is at Floodgate Street. Boulte and she have it all worked out, you see, and if they can control me, then they haven't a bother. Typical upper-level thinking usually means no-thinking."

"Then perhaps we should go to a museum instead of doing a pub crawl, is it?"

"I say we rave-up. Take in some dancing. Either that or a drive into the regions?"

"The regions?"

"Home counties, the provinces. See the countryside."

"Sounds lovely. I'd like that."

"So, what looks good on the menu?"

She stared down at a list of sandwiches, soups, and meat pies. Coming across one called Spotted-Dog Pie gave her the strangest image of Dalmations all skinned and cooked in a stew. She pointed it out to Richard in a half-singing voice, "See spot run, see spot die, see spot as a Christmas pie."

"The dog is rather tasty, actually, a dessert pudding. It's a roly-poly pudding with suet, raisins, and currants, and *not* a

Dalmatian, I assure you. May I suggest number thirteen, however?"

She glanced quickly to the number and read aloud, "Resurrection Pie . . ."

"Apropos, I should think," he finished.

"What is it?"

"Resurrection . . . created from leftovers, you see."

She flashed on a mental image of the leftover lives of the many victims of the Crucifier, wondering if the rat brothers could be considered victims in this bizarre case as well. "Suddenly, I'm not so hungry," she pleaded.

"Fine, then let's have at the shove-halfpenny."

"But I don't know how to play."

"You're quite better off not knowing. It's quite possibly *the* most frustrating game in the world."

Soon they were shoving well-polished old halfpennies with the flat of the hand along a board separated into horizontal sections, each with numerical value, a kind of miniature shuffleboard. With each halfpenny came laughter from them both.

As they played, Jessica began telling Sharpe of her last visit to Luc Sante and their conversation. She felt inept, however, in restating the man's words. She feared her retelling of his remarks on the Crucifier fell flat.

"Slut's wool," he replied.

Taken aback by this, she asked, "Whatever do you mean?"

"It's the stuff collects under the bed, behind the bureau, and other hard-to-reach places. Half or more what the old shrink says is slut's wool. I know. I went to him when I'd become depressed over my divorce."

"Really?"

"I had worked with him on many occasions. I learned that he was good with divorce, and he was, but he also likes to hear himself talk."

"But I thought you thought him of excellent reputation and help in police matters."

"Of course he is, but I'm on my way to being smashed tonight, so there you have it."

• • •

Freshly cleaned and scrubbed and prayed over, the holy cross awaited its next supplicant. All about it and all around the pulpit placed here by their leader, the followers of the Church of the New Millennia and the Second Coming, bowed their heads in prayer and supplication. They did so amid the squalor and degradation of a church that must shun the light of a society that condemned it, in a place where rats infested, where an ancient floor lay buried, and where a long forgotten mine shaft and a putrid, unclean canal sat dormant for generations.

The unclean water meant they had to take the bodies elsewhere for cleansing, which was part of the ritual. They had to be cleansed in God's lakes, ponds, and rivers.

Below their feet, Roman stone floors reminded them with each footfall of the persecution they would face, should they too soon make known their teachings and practices, should they step forth into the light without the Son of God clearly beside them.

At the moment, however, they felt a collective and profound disappointment. It proved so deep that for some time they in sum felt a sense of loss: loss of direction, loss of identity, loss of purpose, loss of rationale, loss of meaning, loss of self and God. All they had done, they had done in the name of Christ for the greater glory of God. So why had they failed?

"It's a test, a cosmic quiz, my friends. Not unlike God to create His own brand of dark humor, now is it? His design, we cannot know, cannot ever hope to touch or so much as stand near. He is inscrutable, the enigma of all enigmas, a mystery within a mystery within a mystery added to a grand mystery more complex than any puzzle mankind can ever hope to piece together. There we shall not attempt. There we shall not go. We know only what His Son gave us in His word. That He would send His Son once again to purge this horrid world we ourselves have created, purge it of all the evil, all the ugliness, all the inhumanity, and all the humanity required to cleanse this Earth."

The leader wore the heavy ancient robes of the early church, something one might expect to see dangling from a wax dummy in the historical fashion section of the Victoria and Albert Museum. The heavy vestments, dark and grim, gave their leader the image of large and powerful shoulders, a straight and tall appearance, and a solidness he would not otherwise have had. The coat made him appear stout and oaken, wooden like the huge cross beside him.

"We must not fail. To give in to despair now is certain to lead to failure, assuring that the Second Coming simply will not be in this millennium, and then what is mankind left with but another thousand years of darkness and ruin? We must not lose sight of our collective will and purpose."

"But we've sent four innocent people over. We've crucified the wrong people. We've made mistakes fourfold!" replied the most vocal of the followers. An Iranian named Kahilli who had brought Burton, one of his patients, and more of the Brevital they required.

"None are innocent, and all who went before our final choice went as sacrifices to a greater good. Burnt offerings, you might say," countered their leader from on high at his enormous oak pulpit, where he stood above them all.

"Their sins washed clean," muttered another of the fold, a weak old woman.

"When do we make our next selection?" asked another elderly female.

"Soon, very soon, this temple shall come into the light, and soon, very soon, a new history of mankind will begin and this world will never be the same after. . . ." replied their leader where he stood in the hidden cathedral where stagnant water stood unmoving like a snake without life.

One of their fold, no longer with them now, had once asked where the water came from. No one could tell him. Then he asked where the water might be leading to. No one could tell him this, either. But their minister had assured him that what must be most important is the here and the now of a thing, that their concern must be on the small strip of water in their temple, and not its source or its confluence. "God grants us but one view of the whole," their leader had said to the wayward member whose questions seemed never ending—until he was silenced altogether.

Others in the fold recalled those questions now, because a sudden rumble and gurgle and bubble below the surface of the water rose up, and the silent strip of green liquid, like ancient lacing around a giant Christmas package, rippled and belched almost on cue to what their minister spoke.

"It is time," their leader pronounced. "It is time to select a fifth Chosen One."

· FIFTEEN ·

Evil creates labyrinthine power, layer upon layer, and begins to weave bonds of dominion over its followers, creating a web of monstrosity from acceptance.

—GEOFFREY CAINE,
BLOODSTREAMS

Richard's hangover had him in the bathroom, praying to the porcelain god, while Jessica, sympathetic but exhausted with her own headache, tried to recall just how many pubs they had crawled to and from the night before. Sharpe had been in a foul mood, and his anger and sullenness came out in this manner—drink and everything else be damned. But he proved to be fun and even hilarious when, in a crowded pub, he drunkenly and loudly explained the game of cricket to all "foreign-born immigrants and tourists." Climbing onto a bar and bellowing out the explanation of the game, he had said, "It's all quite simple, really! You have two sides, one out in the field, one in. Do you understand so far? Good!"

"So far, yes," volunteered someone from the crowd.

Richard continued, adding with a flourish, "Each man on the side that's in goes out, and when he's out, he comes in, and the next man goes in, until he's out. When they're all out, the side that's been out in the field now comes in—they come in, you see? And the side that's been in goes out to try to get out those coming in. If, however, the side that goes in *declares*, then you get men still in, not out. Then, when both sides have been *in and out*, including *not outs*, twice, that's the end of the match. Now do you comprehend?"

The crowd, Jessica included, roared while Sharpe shouted,

"What? Don't you get it now? Shall I explain again?"

"No, no!" Jessica had pleaded.

She had watched Richard Sharpe put away an amazing amount of booze, his mood and the occasion calling for it. She had once been there herself. She sympathized with his need to wash the images of the victims, whom he feared to let down, from his brain.

Jessica had come with Richard to his home, a chalet-bungalow, basically a one-story house with an extra room in the eave-space. The exterior brickwork recommended it as a pleasant place, but the interior felt as dark and cramped as a cave.

Jessica feared her friend and lover was on the edge and teetering there. She knew she could not count herself a friend, if she failed to talk to him about it. These thoughts bombarded her now to the chorus of his nausea.

When Richard emerged, his eyes shone bright, his smile pervading the room. He showed not the least sign of injury or suffering, but rather appeared refreshed. A mask, a disguise, she thought.

"Richard, are you aware you are an alcoholic?" she asked point-blank.

His response came out as a hefty laugh, and he asked, "Are you the least hungry? My cupboard is near bare, but I have some breakfast cereal, some breads, a handful of eggs. Do you care for an omelet?"

"I don't think I could eat right now, no. And I don't know how on Earth you could. No, thank you."

"I hope you won't mind if I throw something together for myself."

"After what I just heard? You must have a cast-iron stomach."

"Speaking of which, I am given to understand you are pursuing a lead regarding coal and dung?"

"Dung and beetle, but how did you learn of that?"

"You forget. I am an inspector with Scotland Yard. I know how to get people to talk," he said with a smile. Then he freely added, "Heard you took a resounding ribbing from Schuller on the topic."

"Is nothing sacred?"

"Not in questions of murder, no."

She nodded, knowing this old truth of seeking the truth. "All right, yes, I've got the lab looking at any and every minute clue we have. The fact her hands, even after the water soaking, had the coal dust in them, got me to wondering, and it all tickled Dr. Schuller's funny bone."

"And rightly so, my dear Jessica."

"But suppose she and all of the victims were kept hostage somewhere before their being crucified, and suppose it was an underground someplace where coal abounds?"

He gave this a moment's thought, and brought his shoulders up before he replied, "England and London in particular are dotted with old coal mines, but only a handful are still in operation. Most have gone under."

"I see."

"Literally used to be hundreds within the city itself, if you consider the city one city; you see, London is in fact a sprawling bear, and all the separate little villages about the city proper have been swallowed up by the bear with each new bridge and roadway built over the years. But at one time, each small municipality had its own coal mine. So, there's the problem."

"Problem?"

"Even if you were certain the coal dust under Woodard's nails—"

"No longer just her nails. We went back for a closer examination, and Raehael and I found coal dust embedded in her wounds as well, in the palms and feet."

He slowed to digest this fact. "Even if it had come from someplace she had been held hostage, where do you begin? Not likely at the few still in operation. And there are hundreds not in operation, you see?"

"There ought by now to be results on the carbon-14 dating. Let me ring the lab." She knew Richard meant only to humor her.

To her dismay, she found that the phone lay off the hook. She picked it up, rested it on its cradle and frowned, realizing that they had been out of touch with the investigation for

nearly fourteen hours. Saying so to Richard resulted in a mutter of indifference from the man.

"I only hope nothing's happened and no one's missed us,"
she replied, wondering now if he'd intentionally taken the
phone off the hook.

She telephoned for Dr. Raehael at the Yard's crime lab,
her face giving way to surprise, which Richard read as, "Another body's been found, hasn't it?"

"No, no," she reassured him. "Yes, Dr. Raehael, I did hear
you. Thank you, and please, let's keep this bit of news between us, please."

Richard stood over her as she dropped the phone onto its
cradle. "What news have you?"

"Raehael dated our dung beetle sample back to Roman
times."

"My word . . . my word . . . So it was formed in Roman England."

"Now where shall we begin?"

"You sound like Alice-through-the-looking-glass, Jessica."

"And you, my Mad Hatter, have you the time?"

"It's late, it's late," he sang out an alteration of the rhyme,
"it's very, very late."

"And have you a direction?"

He gave a moment's thought to this, his hand rising with
an *aha* notion playing about his features. "You know, there
is a little frequented museum, an industrial history museum
inside the RIBA. Rather buried in the basement there. A—"

"Where?"

"Royal Institute of British Architecture near Regent's Park
in Marylebone area on Portland at China. They—RIBA, that
is—built all that stands in London, you see, over the years.
They're quite proud of their bridges, railways, mines, the
tube—underground rail lines and their daft factories. They
might have something on the mines, and perhaps someone
there might be expert and helpful."

Jessica only half heard what he'd said beyond Royal Institute of British Architecture and Portland Street. "I was once
a member of the elite army corps of engineers of which we
British are so proud. That makes me a tad more familiar with

how London is laid out, and where all of her underpinnings and underground niches, nooks, and crannies lie. Still it's a complicated mess. I need to locate a moldy old institution dealing with the layout of the city to find my own way about."

"We haven't left yet? Let's give it a shot. Who knows? Perhaps we can locate an underground kill site, a site from before the time of Christ."

"Well, actually, Marylebone is quite the ancient district."

"Marylebone?" She thought the place sounded grim.

"Aye, where the Royal Institute stands moldering. Not many visitors there. Out of the way, off the tourist treks, you see . . . Has one of the oldest cemeteries in the city, and there's actually an Epicurean statue in a park there of the Madonna and Child. The home of the fictitious Sherlock Holmes isn't too far from the area, either. But it is on the bus routes, I can assure you."

"Twenty-one Baker Street? Really? How interesting."

"It was loosely based on twenty-one Baker Street, yes." He returned to his cooking in the kitchenette, calling back to her over his shoulder, "And so . . . what do we hope to locate in this ancient mine, should we ever find it?"

"I have as much clue as Alice, but like her, I am curious. Get your breakfast. I'm going to shower and dress. If you don't mind, perhaps you could take me by my hotel for a change of clothes, and then we can bugger off to this RIBA place, is it?"

"Bugger off," he repeated. "Now you're getting the language!" He'd returned to her, took her by the shoulders, and firmly kissed her where she stood in his robe. He kissed her again, attempting to rekindle the passion they'd shared the night before, but Jessica pulled away, saying, "Bugger off, yourself! We haven't time. It's already near nine. Get your breakfast, now!" she ordered, and he wandered back off into the kitchen, a smile creasing his features.

She went toward the bathroom but found herself stopped before the bed, her eye falling on a book he'd left under the bed. It's flap winked at her where she stood. Crouching and lifting the book, she saw horrid pictures of various visions of hell. Closing it, she read the title: *A History of Hades and*

Crucifixion Motifs in European Art. She rummaged through and found the words *Mihi beata mater* highlighted on a page he'd marked. It gave her a chill. Apparently, the words appeared on many paintings and depictions of both Hades and the crucifixion of all crucifixions.

Suddenly he stood over her, staring down at the book in her hands. "So, you've found me out," he said with a sour frown.

"Light reading?" she asked, attempting to mask the shakiness she felt, not wishing to sound at all unnerved by her discovery.

"A prize from the library."

She noted the spine, seeing that indeed it was a library lender's copy. She opened it, saw the date stamp which placed it at before her discovery of Burton's tongue art.

He lamely explained, "Been doing my homework."

"How long have you known the meaning of the inscription?" She wanted to hear him admit to it.

"From the moment I heard you pealing them from Burtie's tongue, I realized I had seen the phrase in my reading. I went back to the book later to confirm it."

"Why lie about it? Why didn't you tell me outright that you knew?"

"I played dumb on it in order to get Luc Sante involved. His being a linguist would suit my superiors, you see, and we'd have him to consult with. You have no idea the budget constraints we work under."

"Actually, I do have some idea. We have the same problem in the Bureau." But a glimmer of disquiet remained with Jessica. Hadn't he called Luc Sante's words slut's wool? "I'm going to get that shower now."

"And I that breakfast. Certain you don't want some?"

Without answering, she closed the bathroom door and locked it behind her, hoping to sort out her nerves, her suspicions, and the facts under the rain of warm water.

Later Richard showered while Jessica dressed.

After having showered, and after having accepted Richard's explanation for the book and his prior knowledge of the Latin

phrase found on the dead victims' tongues, Jessica made haste
to dress and start the day. All the while nagging doubt tugged
at both her brain and heart. She had slept with this man. Her
judgment could not be so impaired, she promised herself. She
could not be so blind as to sleep with a serial killer, or someone involved with a cult of serial killers. Impossible, she kept
promising herself over and over.

A quick call to Scotland Yard, she felt, was in order. She
asked to be put through to Stuart Copperwaite who came on
instantly, asking, "My God, Doctor, where have you and
Sharpe been?"

"We were missed?" was all Jessica, feeling guilty, could
manage.

"We've had another crucifixion death."

"Dear God, not another."

" 'Fraid so, Doctor. Discovered in the wee hours again,
with the cadaver disposed of in a body of water, St. James
Park, and I can tell you now that if the Royals weren't taking
an interest before, they bloody well are now."

"The House of Windsor, you mean?"

"The Queen Mother herself, along with Parliament, the
Prime Minister, you name it. Where's Sharpe?"

"In the shower."

"I see." *Cozy*, she thought she heard him mutter.

"Where is the body? Has Schuller and Raehael done an
autopsy yet? Of course not. I spoke with Raehael only fifteen
minutes ago, and he said absolutely nothing about it."

"Most likely Dr. Raehael didn't know at the time, but he
does by now. There appears a rift growing between Schuller
and Raehael, one you may know something about?"

"No, I don't know anything about any problem between
them," she half-lied.

"In any case, the postmortem is being held up, Doctor, for
your attention. We . . . that is, Scotland Yard, the Crown, are
paying well for your expertise."

Something definitely icy in Copperwaite's tone; perhaps
Richard had him pegged right after all. "I'll be right there."

"And Sharpe is requested in Boulte's office."

"I'll pass that request along to him. Thank you." She immediately hung up. Sharpe, stepping from the shower, looking into her wide eyes. Her mouth agape, he momentarily thought she might be gaping at him, until she divulged the facts, saying, "The Rat Boys, as you call them, will be released today."

"Then there has been another killing!"

"While we ate and drank, while we made love, while we slept."

"At least you know I'm as innocent of the crimes as the Rat Boys."

"I never suspected you, Richard!"

"Don't lie to a detective, Jessica."

"All right, I felt a strange sensation come over me when I saw that book, but I never truly entertained the notion you might be the Crucifier."

"Not even one of them? Forget it. I'd be disappointed in you if you hadn't a healthy suspicion after seeing that book below my bed. So, tell me, has the Yard been beating the bushes for us?"

"Indeed they have. Boulte wants you to report directly to his office this morning. They're holding the body for me to do the postmortem."

Richard dressed solemnly, and she nibbled at the food Richard had burned on the stove. Soon, together, they were pressing for Scotland Yard, Jessica without time for a change of clothes.

The latest victim, thought by some in the Yard to be a copycat killing—and hoped to be one by P. P. Ellen Sturgeon and Chief Inspector Boulte—had all the markings of the real Crucifier at work, down to the coal in the nails and the branded tongue.

At half-past three in the afternoon, Jessica declared the body, that of a slim, pathetic, silver-haired old woman, to be the fifth victim of the Crucifier. Without an identity, Jessica had to tag her toe as A.N. Other. Boulte had come down to the autopsy room, hoping against hope that Jessica would find cause to declare the latest victim a random copycat crime in which someone, wanting to kill another, masked his crime by mimicking the ongoing series of murders. Jessica's findings proved otherwise, proved that this was indeed the work of the Crucifier.

This meant that Periwinkle and Hawkins had to be set free. The press would report the foolishness of the Yard in making the grandiose statements of the day before, which had declared an end to the crucifixion murders in London. The Rat Boys were returned to the streets, likely to do mischief to someone somewhere for which they might legitimately find the sort of twisted fame they sought.

It had all made for a long and tiring day. Now Jessica said good night to Raehael, who had, unlike Schuller, stayed till the very end of the postmortem examination. Raehael and she discussed the strange findings with respect to their Roman beetle. Dr. Raehael told her, "I informed Dr. Schuller of all result, which he do not at first believe until he look over my findings—that same coal dust was embedded into the wounds of the victims, not just Woodard—and that he should look for himself. I told him then, Doctor, that he owes apology to you."

" 'Fraid I got none."

She thanked Raehael and they shook hands, and he waved her off to what he hoped would be a good night. Alone now in the scrub room, she stripped her surgical gloves and gown away, reached over and tore off paper booties protecting her shoes from blood and fluids, tossed all recyclables in one bin, all garb in another, and stretched, using a yoga position that relaxed her back and neck muscles. As she turned to leave the operating theater, she came face-to-face with Luc Sante's disembodied head framed in the surgical doorway. "Goddamnit," she cursed inwardly at her sudden fright.

He smiled in at her and waved her forward.

"I came as soon as I could get away," he explained. "Tragic, a fifth victim. Is it possible he is planning to kill seven? Seven is often a number people fixate on, given its biblical connotations, its mystical history."

"At this point, I haven't a clue, and I'm extremely, extremely tired, Dr. Luc Sante."

"Obviously, yes, and with good reason."

She almost thought he meant something by the remark, that

he'd heard of her tryst with Sharpe and was attempting a small, secular joke. But no, her mind told her to think better of his remarks than that. Then she recalled Richard's words about trusting one's own intuition and sense of jeopardy, that the subconscious often knew more than the conscious mind, and this led her to recall the remarkable workings of FBI psychic investigator, Kim Desinor, who would not allow a red-legged crow, a DIVERSION sign or any other "signal" to get past her conscious self, because a psychic like Kim Desinor kept in tune with her subconscious.

"You must be anxious for a shower, something to eat. I have my car. Allow me to see you to your hotel, and there I will wine and dine with you, my dear Jessica."

She could find no reason to say no. He offered precisely what she needed at the moment, and she had truly wanted to speak with him again regarding the latest aspects of the case.

"Yes, yes," she told him. "I would like that, Dr. Luc Sante, Father."

"Good, very good, indeed." His smile left a small gap in his teeth, and his teeth were yellowed from years of smoking, which he'd obviously given up. Likely due to doctor's orders. His wispy hair flew about his cranium where he stood below the air duct in the surgical scrub area. He reminded Jessica of Scrooge, looking as if he'd stepped out of that bygone era, despite his modern cloth and the cut of his vestments.

"I am told the latest victim was left like the others, in water?"

"Yes, St. James Park."

"Dear me, close to the Queen's little cottage. This will have a ripple effect, indeed."

"Let's get out of here, Father."

Before leaving Scotland Yard, Jessica dropped off her post-mortem report in the ops room with Copperwaite and Sharpe. The two men now were working under a cloud. She told Richard of her plans to spend the evening with Father Luc Sante, and after an initial frown born of disappointment, he accepted this, wishing her a good night. Copperwaite added a "Cheerio," while still studying her autopsy report.

Once back at the York Hotel, Jessica scanned a brief message left at the desk for her by first Richard Sharpe, saying he missed her terribly, and one from J. T. in America, which simply read: *Tattoo Man's case heating up. Call you when I can.*

Jessica, with Father Luc Sante waiting in the lobby, needed her own heating up, so she showered to cleanse the sad postmortem of the day from her fingers and nasal cavities as well. She very much wanted to enjoy her time now with this fascinating "Father," and she felt a desire to confess to him, or at least to bare her soul to him. She felt some senseless worm of guilt eating away at her regarding this case, the fact that it seemed to be moving at a snail's pace. Not to mention that while she and Richard had made love, another victim had been staked to a cross somewhere, her body thrown into a lake.

Still, if she could tell anyone of her painful doubts and fears, it would be Father Luc Sante.

As she showered for the second time this day, she decided that Luc Sante was a man of great magnetism and charisma, due in large part to the kindness of his eyes and the kindness with which he imparted information, even on the most gruesome of subjects. In fact, his eyes stroked those he reached out to help.

After showering and dressing in evening wear, Jessica met Luc Sante in the lobby, the priest telling her that he'd already taken the liberty of booking them into the York's exquisite lounge. "My treat this time," he assured her.

Quickly seated, they soon found themselves sipping a fine rosé wine, a 1979 vintage, something Luc Sante had selected previous to their having actually been seated. "They know me here," he whispered in her ear.

After a few sips of wine, Luc Sante asked pointedly, "Why do you seem so melancholy in this place? We have comfort, wine, music, good company . . ."

She instantly apologized, realizing he must have read the melancholia from her features. "I am sorry, Father. It's . . . it's just that . . . Well, it would appear that all my scientific

skill has been of little help in actually pinpointing these killers, Father."

A waiter stood in a nearby corner, and from time to time
he rushed the table, refilled the wineglasses, and disappeared
again. Something of a faceless, nameless penguin in his black
and white, she thought.

The elegant restaurant at the hotel filled with music from
a piano now being played by a gifted young black woman.
She played Chopin, moved to Bach, and then settled on one
of Beethoven's lighter moods.

"I do not mean to mock or disparage your attempts or what
you do for a living, Dr. Coran, but . . ." He hesitated.

"But?" she encouraged.

"But experience has taught me." Luc Sante's voice, so
deep, rich and full, rose above the music. He spoke around
sips of his wine. "What is paraded as scientific fact is quite
often mere *rhetoric*."

"Rhetoric?"

"We know what we know. We don't always need a scientist
to tell us what we *already* know."

"All right, but we—*people*—don't always know what we
need to know." She tried to counter his logic with her own.

"So they need *you*? They need to be told what is what?
They need to follow the precepts of some current belief held
by a mere handful of scientists searching for truths beyond
the scientists' reach in the first place?"

"Not unlike our investigation, you mean?"

He lightly laughed. "I hadn't thought of it in quite the same
terms, but yes, you might say so," Luc Sante added, snatching
up the roll of bread between them, offering her first a piece
and then taking one for himself. "Perhaps, it is time to abandon your scientific goggles for a pair of intuitive eyes. Your
instincts have saved you in the past, and they will again in
the future if you let them," he attempted reassurance. "If you
get out of the way of your own instincts, Jessica Coran."

"Maybe it's this place, London. It's dizzying and roman-
tic."

"Thank God for romance! But Jessica, we both know you
are gifted, and you must feed your gift at all times."

"But I trust in science, and—"

"Blindly? To the detriment of answers, solutions, truths? I should hope not."

She continued to argue, "Well . . . as for current belief, we scientists—as blind as we may be—"

"Call it tunnel vision rather than blindness. Comes from staring down too many microscopes, perhaps," he joked and chewed down his food in barbarian, hedonistic fashion, like a man who'd just stepped from the thirteenth century. He saw her staring at him. His hands and his mouth were full of bread. Choking it down, he laughed like Falstaff in Shakespeare's *Henry IV*. "My table manners, I should warn you, are atrocious, but then I have the excuse of being French!" He laughed more. "In France, everyone eats with his hands and his heart. You should try it! Handle your food and it tastes supreme. I have spent my life in service here in England, but I spent my youth in France. I return only for the air nowadays."

She laughed at this. "You really need not apologize to me, Father."

"Then let us return to the subject at hand."

She nodded, saying, "All right. We scientists do require some sort of current belief to make it—"

"To make life palatable? To make chaos orderly? To create the next best toothpaste?" He again laughed boyishly at his own words, causing her to smile.

"To make connections. In seeing the connectedness of things, we learn. We can only learn when we see—own—the relationship between and among things. And one generation guides the one after. And what's wrong with that? Some singular scientist generally leads the way. Remember Galileo? Newton? Leonardo, Michelangelo, Einstein, and—"

"Newton was a fool!" He did not stop to explain this. "I don't abhor science or scientists as a rule, really, dear. But we mere mortals become too easily impressed, too easily swayed and convinced by the *magic and incantations*, the smoke and mirrors of it all. We are too easily accustomed to regard scientific knowledge as Truth with a capital *T*, when in fact what scientific knowledge is, is the best available approximation of the truth in the judgment of the majority of scientists in a specified field."

"Touché," she offered.

He continued, and she thought about Luc Sante's detractors who said that he loved to hear the sound of his own voice. Then again, so did she. "This is so whether it's paleontology, psychology, or pathology, or any other-*ology*, you see?"

"Do you include ideology in this overstuffed basket of approximations of the truth?" she asked.

"Aha, now we spar and parry. Have you ever fenced, my dear?"

"Coincidentally, I have recently taken lessons."

"Fencing with words can be just as diabolical and can cut just as deeply. As to your question, yes, most ideologies are as insipid and leaky as any sieve."

"But hasn't it always been true and necessary that throughout the history of mankind's search for truths, that with each step, we require some railing, some bedpost, some lamppost to hold on to? In order to further the search for understanding, growth, learning? That each science or philosophy must suffice us, in order for us to move on, to nurture growth to the next level of being and light and godliness, that place where our young generation today points us toward, absolute understanding and coexistence?"

"Of course, you are right, my dear, but not to the degree that science be taken as a Holy Grail, child."

Calling her child made her smile. Coming from anyone else, it would have been insulting. Coming from Father Luc Sante, it felt comforting.

"I simply ask that you not allow science to overtake your faith, my dear." He continued sipping his wine, the waiter continued filling their glasses. "And if you dispute me, my stand is shared by every psychotherapist worth his fee." He stopped to acknowledge her furrowed brow before going on. "And make no mistake about it, psychotherapists are in fact 'faith healers' in the sense they restore one's faith as much as anything, for their concern is not with science but the soul of a man and the innocence of a faith often lost in childhood."

She nodded boisterously. "Most scientists want to prove

some truths exist in a world in which the ultimate truths are always going to be elusive. I think that's what you're saying. That while such things as blind instinct, blind faith are viable, they have no identifiable variables or mathematical equivalents or formulas attached, that blind faith is the ultimate in freedom of choice. That's just the way it is. Reality's a *bummer* for the scientists as well as the rest of us."

He took her hand in his again, smiling as if she were a student who now fully and finally understood. "Indeed, truth is not something that we are born with. It is not something we possess, but rather a goal toward which we strive."

"Well, I understand that we scientists are little more immune to jumping to an unsound conclusion than anyone else, but in the absence of any other physical—"

He threw up his hands, waving her down. "We are simply too anxious and too content to let our scientists and anyone in authority do our thinking for us, Doctor. We are too easily led, too readily compartmentalized and departmentalized and happy to do it. Happy to live the life of ants scurrying across gingham tablecloths without the slightest notion of the whole. Seeing only that part of the floating opera of life confined to one's limited, single perspective, a world of colloquials. We accept that the business of God, time, and space are all questions best left to those in charge whose job it is to explore these testy areas. So we can go about doing our mortal accounting and following the one precept of God's which pleases us most—bearing children."

"Whoa, now hold on. Not everyone on the planet is—"

"I tell you, there is a profound tendency in the civilized world to make our scientists 'philosopher kings' whom we ask to guide us through every intellectual labyrinth, when indeed, they are just as lost as we are. The blind king leading the blind cave dweller out of the cave and into a larger cave— the life of a cerebrally unmotivated, uninterested, disinterested peasant. . . ."

"But Father . . . Dr. Luc Sante, you're a scientist. How can you say we've not progressed from the cave one step in all these many years on this planet?" pressed Jessica, defending with her own verbal joust. "There've been tremendous strides in psychotherapy alone."

Luc Sante cut himself a thick slice of cheese that had been brought to the table. He chewed and spoke all at once. "Oh, we in the *brain factory* have indeed progressed, so true, now that we're through bandying about Freudian terms and have at very least begun to convince people to acknowledge the existence of the sun-conscious—sorry, sub—*sub*conscious mind and its power."

"I agree, but—"

"God smile upon us," he interrupted her again, "we've even got people taking responsibility for their unconscious minds these days!"

Jessica laughed at his runaway enthusiasm, so rare in the aged, even more rare in the young these days, she thought.

"You laugh, but this taking of responsibility for our dual nature, it may well be the portal to the way of true salvation for this race of ours, Doctor. Listen to Beethoven." He stopped to let the music waft over them. "There lived a man who instinctively knew. Perhaps due to his own personal dualism, his deafness, and his obsession with harmony, sound, reverberation."

"Taking responsibility for our dual nature? Really? Through educating the masses about their own unconscious minds, you mean?"

"Think of it, a return to intellectual responsibility—all this time, the seed to our salvation turns out to be our own damned subconscious minds." He giggled at his own summation of the origin and end of the problems of the world.

"The blossoming interest in the subconscious will lead us back to God? Is that what I'm hearing?" she asked.

"Absolutely."

"Why didn't this revelation play a part in your book?"

"It will, in the sequel, you see. My thinking is ever evolving, never static; besides it's not The God but the godliness within us."

"You've only recently come to this conclusion?"

He shrugged. "It has been as elusive as the smallest of butterflies, yet there before my eyes the entire way. Think of it. Dreams are gifts of God, our subconscious is the voice of God working through us. We don't always recognize the voice or understand the symbols, but there you have it."

"Interesting notion."

"Nothing new, really. Nothing new under the sun, really. The fact of it will, however, form the core of the sequel to *Twisted Faiths*."

Again she smiled at his enthusiasm.

"I already have it titled: *God's Signature*, the book I'm currently writing. Of course no publisher will touch it, so I will have to self-publish as with the previous title, but my practice allows me to indulge this passion. I wrote *Twisted Faiths* well before I formulated my conclusion on the true nature of man's subconscious mind. I tell you, man's own inner workings, his mind, if created in the image of God, imagine the complexities handed us, yet the instrument remains directly wired as a telegraph to the Almighty to—"

"Really, Dr. Luc Sante? I've never looked at it quite that way."

"It's just that some of us—most of us—have cut the wires, and often the optic fibers."

"So, when can I see your new work?"

"Soon. The wheels are always turning, you see." He winked and pointed conspiratorially at his forehead.

"Interesting premise."

He nodded. "Yes, indeed. You see, the interest and acceptance of the source of our darkest selves, our prejudices, hidden hostilities, irrational fears—"

"Perceptual blind spots," she added, "mental ruts . . ."

"Mental *rats*!" he exploded, "Scourging and scouring our psyche for morsels of meanness. The Devil at play on the switchboard, all that. Add to the predatory nature of our earliest ancestors, the primitive 'fight or flight' mechanism of the primordial brain which, by the way, still resides within our thick-skulled heads and—"

"And the ever-present resistance to growth."

"Exactly!" he shouted, arms waving. "The fear of change and evolution and awareness itself—well, I tell you, it's that first step on the journey of a thousand miles that Buddha spoke of."

Jessica considered his words with care and muttered, "The start of an evolutionary leap."

"English history, nay, world history, provides us with untold examples of hideous behavior and hedonism, murder and cruelty on a grand scale. Perhaps one day mankind will reach a level of mind in which one can perform the business of existence without hatred, fear, prejudice, mayhem, mass murder, but at the moment mankind slaughters mankind on the basis of a religious principle that says, 'You must obey the One God, and that is *my God*, whatever or whomever that god may be. Oh, and by the way, thou shalt not kill.' Are we getting mixed signals from God, or the lesser gods of our limited minds? And if so, how do we sift out the voice of God from the voice of selfishness and indulgence always at work in the human psyche, and if God created the human psyche, isn't *He* partially responsible for our nature? Or are we responsible for our nature and the outcomes we create, and does the answer necessarily come from another source, say as from Christ?"

"Christ? I had thought your diatribe would end with the Antichrist. I'll never live to see the day, but in a sense, it's what every caring human being is striving toward, to evolve into a Christlike figure."

"And who do we know who is striving hardest to attain that goal?"

It dawned on her that his entire discussion led her about in a full circle to one rhetorical truth. Her eyes widened and she bit down hard on her lower lip, waiting for his reply, which was slow in coming.

"Isn't that what our killer, the Crucifier, wants?"

Jessica realized that she had been had by the old man, whose exercise in logic and syllogistic wisdom came clear: Socratic method, pretending ignorance on the subject, asking questions of her, so she might arrive at the conclusion on her own, once again the shaman of psychotherapy and religion opened her eyes.

After a most pleasant dinner, he insisted she return with him to the church. "Strand is there late tonight with his alcoholism group. We won't be alone altogether, so you needn't worry about an old priest making any improper advances." He laughed fully and with glee at the thought of it. "You must know how very striking you are, my dear Dr. Coran."

"Thank you, Father. I'll take that as a compliment coming from you, but I am rather tired and would—"

"But there are some things back at St. Albans I must show you, relating to the case. I would not urge it upon you if it were not pressing, you must believe."

She wondered if anyone had ever said no to this man. She smiled. Standing in her full-length white gown, which she'd facetiously told the mirror looked *virginal* when she put it on for dinner, thinking it appropriate for her night with the ancient minister, she now nodded and said, "All right, but I must be home before the carriage turns into a pumpkin."

"Absolutely," he agreed, his smile radiating love, tenderness, and caring, even as the candlelight flickered across his countenance, cutting deep lines. "We both know one truth in this world undeniably."

"And what is that?"

"It's a procreating world we live in." He smiled, the wine allowing him license to go on. "Think of it. The sun procreates with the Earth by day, the moon takes her turn at night, the stars and the faraway planets, too, procreate with Earth, and she in turn procreates with all the known universe. Indeed, it is what you cops call an *effing* world."

She took only a moment to realize he was making fun of her, the known universe, perhaps even God. She laughed uproariously at his conclusion, garnering stares from other tables, and realized only now that they'd been getting stares all along, all night long.

"Shall we return me to my quarters at St. Albans?"

"Do you sleep at St. Albans as well?"

"Expect to be buried in the nearby cemetery, my dear. No, not often do I sleep over, but it's some distance to Hampton where I maintain a flat. So when I am late in the City, I stay at my room at St. Albans."

They stood, and many people in the room obviously recognizing Father Luc Sante, giving Jessica further explanation for all the stares. Luc Sante appeared to be a local legend.

· SIXTEEN ·

*No man can concentrate his attentions upon evil,
or even upon the idea of evil, and remain un-
affected. To be more against the Devil than to
be for God is exceedingly dangerous. Every cru-
sader is apt to go mad. He is haunted by the
wickedness which he attributes to his enemies;
it becomes in some sort a part of him.*

—ALDOUS HUXLEY

Martin Strand arrived with tea for Father Luc Sante and his
guest, explaining that he had seen them arrive from an upper
window where his group had just said their good-nights. Luc
Sante, pleased with the warm, rich ginseng tea, laughingly
replied in Jessica's direction, saying, "Ah, Martin, my first
convert! And the bonus is, he knows my every whim."

She shook her head. "I rather doubt that's true. I mean that
he is your first convert!"

Again, the old man laughed. "Indeed, that would be eons
ago. You catch me up."

"Where was your first church, Father?" she asked.

"Small, out-of-the-way hamlet, really. Nothing to speak of.
To the north and east of London."

"Really?"

"Bury St. Edmunds, wasn't it, Father?" asked Martin.

"Quite . . . quite right."

Jessica had heard the name of the town in connection with
someone else, victim number one, the schoolteacher. A coincidence? Great Britain was, after all, an Island Kingdom.
Martin Strand was pushing the plate of crumpets before her,
pleading with her to try one.

"Really, I'm stuffed from dinner. Filet mignon is so filling,"
she replied, taking only tea and sipping lightly. For a

moment, she caught the two men staring at her. Recalling what Sharpe had said of Strand's past, she blurted out, "I understand you worked hard to get to and through the seminary, Father Strand."

"I was determined, decided on the clergy at an early age, yes."

"Strand worked the roughest of jobs, on the docks, as a lengthsman. Mapmaker, too, weren't you, Martin?" The old man sounded proud of his young charge. "All with a single aim, a single determination. Not everyone can point to that, Martin."

"My word, Father, you'll have me blushing."

"Sorry, if I've made you uncomfortable," Jessica found herself apologizing to Strand. "People in my line of work are snoops. It's what we do for a living, and after so many years of experience, we get so good at it, that we upset people," she added, smiling.

"You're a bit off, however," he corrected Jessica with a smile of his own. He seemed an Adonis, handsome, strong, filled with light and energy. "You see, I worked to accumulate enough to follow my ambition. I never intended any other career choice. All else amounted to a part-time thing."

"You did wonderful work, however, Martin. I recall that letter you showed me from the RIBA people, the Royal Institute of British Architecture," Luc Sante explained. "Housed not too very far from here, actually, over on Portland."

"Right you are again," Strand said to Luc Sante. "The old boys' club, and the old boys want to keep their maps and information up to date. It was an interesting job, for the most part. Got me round the city."

"And past many a DIVERSION sign, I'm sure," Jessica added. "Would you know of any old mine shafts running below the city, say any ancient ones?" She pressed a metaphorical button, awaiting his reaction, but his expression could not be read, nor his body language. He gave nothing away.

"Just how ancient?" Luc Sante wondered aloud.

"My territory was confined, for the most part, to the Marylebone area, and no, I found no shafts you'd categorize as ancient, I'm afraid."

"How ancient?" again Luc Sante wished to know.

"Roman times ancient. Anything pre-dating Christ, say."

"No, I don't believe so," said Strand, laughing now. He then apologized with a compliment. "We seldom to never see anyone so smart or pleasant looking as you here, Dr. Coran, so you will forgive my staring back at you?"

Luc Sante instantly bolstered the apology, saying, "We deal in derelicts here mostly, aside from the regular congregation, made up of the usual good, simple, caring folk and the occasional politician!" He stopped to stomp a foot and to laugh. "If not physical derelicts, derelicts of the soul. Most of these have given in to some form of addiction or other. Hence Father Strand's near nightly groups. So, you must forgive our staring at a whole person such as yourself, Dr. Coran."

She snickered at the characterization of herself as whole. Strand interrupted, "There is the matter we spoke of earlier, Father, that is still left hanging, sir."

Jessica's antennae went instantly up and at the ready.

Luc Sante's face dropped in an enormous and sullen frown as he replied, "Later, Martin."

"It is much later now, sir."

Luc Sante smiled across at Jessica. "Church business," he explained.

"Bills," Strand clarified. He then said in as stern a voice as Jessica had heard in the building, "With all due respect, sir, perhaps, sir, if you weren't so busy with police matters—my pardons to you, Dr. Coran—your psychiatric practice, and book writing, then the bills would be paid on time."

The old man grimaced at Strand and smiled at Jessica in one fluid motion of the mouth, eyes and forehead, and then he asked Jessica, "Are you aware how the British preface with that phrase 'with all due respect,' Dr. Coran?" He pushed on. "It means, when translated, 'I have lost all due respect for you!' "

"Now that's not fair, Father," Strand immediately defended himself. "I am concerned we do not close our doors like so many others have had to do in recent times."

"The bills will always be with us, Martin. But how long will we have Dr. Coran's company?"

"Yes, sir. If you say so, Father." With that Strand left them alone.

"The boy worries too much," Luc Sante said with a spry grin. "Now, to the case. The hellhound is afoot, Watson," he teased in his best Sherlockian tone.

For the next half hour, he and Jessica reviewed every aspect of the case together, the old man giving her his perspective on the tongue branding, as well as the coal, the dark wood fibers, and the beetle scrappings found on the victims. He called the tongue branding a cult identity ceremony. "It likely marks her as a cult member. She may well have willingly volunteered to die for the cult."

Jessica thoughtfully considered this possibility. "The idea has, of course, crossed my mind that all the victims may well have belonged to some bizarre cult with strange rituals, but your confirmation means a great deal. Still, I had not, until you spoke of it, considered the victims of these serial killings as willing participants in their own deaths. . . . Yet it makes perfect sense, at least in theory. Still, I have trouble believing that a group of people could so easily be of one mind."

"The group mind is powerful, Jessica," he countered. "We know this! In fact, we humans are in possession of so much hard evidence about ourselves on this issue, but we fail to use it to improve our institutions and our lives."

"Are you talking about how the underlying assumptions of our institutions, our *groups*, are never questioned?"

"More than that. Nothing is *acted upon* even when it is questioned and found wanting."

"Knowing that groups control individuals, why can't we make the leap to a kind of scientific, objective stance that will allow us to . . . to . . . what?"

"To admit it—that our lives are controlled by the group mind! Examine it in all of its dynamic, and organize our attitudes accordingly."

"If we understand the animal, why can't we change him?" she asked, sipping more tea.

"Precisely. We can no longer have the luxury of simply

pulling out the underpinnings, the assertions and assumptions
that govern our species, but we must discuss them, notice
every particular of them, the main one being that we are gov-
erned by the *group mind*, a thing intensely resistent to change,
suggestion, addition or subtraction, a thing equipped with sacred assumptions about which there can be no discussion. Can
you forsee a day when this sort of irreverence to the group
mind is taught in schools? The school itself is founded on the
group mind, so no—never! Yet it is through our young and
those who constantly challenge the status quo that we progress, if we are to evolve at all as a *species . . .*"

He then laid out before her a series of ancient books with
illustrations of men, women, even children who, for the
greater glory of their god had accepted, blindly followed, and
willingly stepped up to an altar of sacrifice, to be beheaded,
to have their hearts torn from them, some to have their blood
drained, others pinned to crosses and burned at the stake.

"Even Joan of Arc, in the last analysis, sacrificed herself
to God in not recanting her faith. Our victims may have died
for their faith."

Jessica tried to imagine the five crucified victims as willing
accomplices in their own torturous deaths.

"It is a possibility," he finished, closing the book on St.
Joan of Arc.

"She listened to the voice of God in her head, too," Jessica
said.

"Or her subconscious, if you wish to think in more scientific terms. Either way, she held firm to her faith, however
blind it appeared to the authorities who burned her at the
stake."

Time growing late, Jessica said she must go. She hadn't
eaten Strand's goodies or finished her tea, and she felt a bit
woozy, exhausted from the long, tedious day and now the
exhalted conversations with Father Luc Sante. He called for
a cab, and she said she could find her way out, preferring to
wait in the open air. She'd suddenly begun to feel claustro-
phobic and warm all over, feverish. She knew she'd shared
too much wine with him.

On leaving, Jessica met a strange-eyed pair of creatures

with gray-and-orange hair whom Luc Sante, having followed Jessica out, introduced as recent converts, a pair of twins. The twin women, up in years, perhaps in their late fifties, smiled vacantly at Jessica who towered over their twisted frames. Luc Sante gave their names as Miss Caroline Houghton and her sister, Juliana Houghton, "Both of whom do volunteer work in the church, and both of whom are repaid in psychotherapy sessions," he explained, adding in light jest, "A bargain for both in the barter."

The two women each stared vacuously at Jessica as if she were a wax figure in London's infamous Wax Museum of horrors.

Luc Sante, after fondly bidding the twins good night, took Jessica aside to explain that the twins had been traumatized as children by their parents, actual witnesses to multiple murders, a case involving torture and sodomy. The children had been made to watch by their parents. "True evil," he tells her. "Forgive them—the parents, I mean, long since dead. Dying without knowing God. That is the ultimate purgatory."

While Luc Sante remained in mid-explanation of the strange twins, Jessica stared over his shoulder at the huge, beautifully sculpted wooden crucifix depicting Jesus mounted on the cross behind Luc Sante's pulpit. The eyes radiated a painful, suffering life, the color along the throat and torso draining before her. She imagined His death. The prolonged agony of the physical realities, yes, but even more so the prolonged suffering of realizing that he had been so absolutely and thoroughly betrayed, so ultimately alone, left there not only by His race and followers but by God Himself. Betrayed in the sense that even had God foretold the event, nothing could have prepared Jesus for the sense of abandonment at the moment of crucifixion. She wanted to crawl up onto the cross herself, right this moment, meld into the sculpted form and become Jesus, to see, feel, smell from Him, to touch and feel and hear from within Him, to fully and absolutely believe, comprehend, and embrace her faith. But that remained impossible; no one could become Jesus.

Her eyes trailed downward to the sculpted, bloody feet where Luc Sante stood every Sabbath to sermonize at the huge, gilded pulpit before an array of candles. She imagined the power and craft of Luc Sante's sermons, the sway he must hold over his congregation, wondered how different it was from the control the Crucifier held over his victims in the end. She felt compelled to tell him, "One of these days, I'm going to come to hear one of your sermons, Father."

"As well you must," he agreed.

Her eyes traveled back up to Jesus.

Luc Sante watched her stare, realizing she'd become captivated by the crucifixion art behind his pulpit. He stopped to stare up at it as well. "It was done in the thirteenth century, an obscure Italian artist . . . so realistic . . . Studied under Leonardo's disciples, but I think he went with a touch of Donatello, don't you agree?"

"Lovely workmanship, yes, and so large, overwhelming to the emotions. So . . . so real."

"Indeed. Step to your right, watching the eyes the entire time."

She did so and found the experience of Christ's eyes as depicted by the artist unnerving. They followed her.

"Now to your left."

Again, the eyes followed her.

Luc Sante, smiling, announced, "I know what you're thinking."

"You do?"

"That a replication such as this, seen by a madman, a maniac, such as our Crucifier, that such artwork could . . . Well, it could be the catalyst to move a man from merely fantasizing a thing to actually committing a horrid act."

"Such as murder by crucifixion?"

He nodded. "And you're right. But what would you have we churchmen do? Lay a canvass across every crucifixion scene in the city? Yes, the sick mind might contemplate such a work of art and begin to hear messages from it, hear Jesus' own voice telling him to go and take lives, to sacrifice life to the Son, but can we truly blame such an aberrant reaction on the artwork itself? I think not."

"The mind is already sick that looks on such art and takes away with it a purpose for murder. I see your point."

"You look extremely tired, my child. There are rooms in the building, if you'd care to lie down. I could secure a blanket, a pillow. You look a bit pale."

She managed a smile. "No, no. It's not far to the hotel, and you've already called the cab. I'll be fine."

After saying good-bye to Father Luc Sante, she left his cathedral and thoughtlessly leaned against one of the enormous stone buttresses supporting the cathedral wall, thinking Father Luc Sante right. She didn't realize how ill she'd actually felt until Father Luc Sante had remarked on her paleness. She looked down at her body, which seemed independent of her, and she realized that she'd dirtied her white evening gown thanks to the smut on the cathedral walls. The stain formed a small black bat, an awful, black smudge, like a coal smudge.

Without warning, her mind suddenly raced out of control. *Ruined-forever-stained! Nothing-to-wear or be-done; you-can't-salvage or restrain! Relinquish-any-now-moment with hindsight's 20/20, a-hole-in-the-whole-wonder-king-think-thing, but-useless-in-last-analysis-of-performance . . . Art, Arthur. Yes, her-smudging-the-virginal-gown-again . . . Against St. Alban's coal-grimed-walls . . . this exhaulted-body-soul-raiments and remnants and remainders to-level-of-performance . . . art. Art, Arthur . . . King Arthur and Knights of the Round Table, Knights, night's-Templers. She had become art . . .*

What the hell's going on inside my head? she wondered. *Why are my thoughts racing into one another, out of control*?

For some reason, she felt light-headed, dizzy even, and she recalled a warning from her friend, Donna LeMonte, before traveling here. Donna warned, "Careful . . . Watch out for the sherry. English sherry and wine are potent indeed."

She felt strands of her hair tickling each cheek. She'd done it up properly, and now it had come loose, and she feared she must look a fright, her long, auburn curls like snake ringlets. Then for reasons she little understood, she recalled Sharpe's having said that half or more of the older structures in the city still used coal for heating, and that much of London's famous or infamous fog came about via the accumulation of

coal dust hovering above London from the burning furnaces
and destructors—incinerators—in the oldest sections of the
city. She knew that St. Albans certainly fell under that category, being near Golders Green in the Marylebone district.

Still no cab. Who did the old man call? Did they have to
build the cab from scratch? *It's dark out here*, she thought,
one hand clutching the small bag she carried where her Smith
& Wesson comfortably rested. For some reason she could not
fathom, she felt a twinge of need, a twinge of fear—foolish
subconscious, intuitive thread of unreasonable fear. Yet as
Luc Sante said, the subconscious knew all.

She couldn't stand still. She felt an enormous energy battling a desire to lay prostrate here on the darkened church
steps where she might easily sleep. Between the insomnia and
the case, she hadn't been getting *must* . . . no *much* . . . no *any*
rest, and *toss*, no *turn*, no *push*, no *pile* on the red, red wine . . .
the blood of Christ . . . the crumpets . . . the wafer . . . the
body of Christ . . .

Holding firmly to the stone stairwell, feeling the eyes of
the army of gargoyles atop St. Albans like so many birds of
prey, waiting for her to stumble and become theirs, Jessica
forced herself down to street level where she paced catlike,
fighting her sudden disorientation and enormous desire for
sleep, until her pacing left her standing before an alleyway.
A noise in the alley alerted her. A look down the alleyway
beside the cathedral and the small noise became a train rumble, and then the pounding of mad hooves. In the cloak of
black shadow, a half block away, at the back of the cathedral,
a huge coal truck downloaded its contents onto a rattling
metal conveyor, the cathedral literally eating up the tons of
coal fed it.

"My God," she exclaimed aloud, her mind still at racehorse
speed, "the killers could be in any underground cellar in the
city. It's virtually impossible to pinpoint the actual murder
site. Certainly not without more clues." *Now the bastards
have me talking to myself*, she thought. Further had her asking, *Just where in St. Albans does the coal bin lead?*

Her mind suddenly settled, but her stomach felt a quivering
nausea. A cab turned a corner and slowly made its way toward

her. She mentally chastised herself for even momentarily suspecting Father Luc Sante and his grand cathedral of hiding the darkest secret in recent English history along with its coal.

She felt a surge of unremitting self-hatred, the disgust taking on a brilliantly red hue; she couldn't help being angry with herself for being so damnably cynical. Hadn't she formerly suspected Richard?

The cabby's sudden barking question, "Do ya want a ride or not, lass?" broke her from her reverie. She hurriedly climbed into the cab, inhaled its stale, cigarette-sodden interior, and asked to be taken to the York.

"Aye, just down from the Savoy," muttered the heavyset driver to himself as if to re-familiarize himself with the area into which he must forge. She looked back at St. Albans as the cab pulled away. In the darkness, the gargoyles had gone from their appointed posts, no doubt wandering purposefully in search of their enemies.

In the lonely backseat of the musty, smelly cab, even as she rolled the window down, catching London's damp night air, she recalled what Richard Sharpe had told her about paranoia: Sometimes a healthy dose of paranoia was called on by the subconscious for good reason; that sometimes those you thought were out to get you, were indeed out to get you. For some reason, this night, she had felt as if a thousand eyes had watched her, or one huge eye, the eye of some unknowable, mysterious, inscrutable god.

Then in an eye-blink, she learned why she felt she'd been watched all evening long when the cab came to an abrupt halt a block away from St. Albans.

"What's going on here?" she said, clutching the weapon in her purse at the same time.

"Easy, mum! The gent's with Scotland Yard. Pulled me over on my way to the church. Told me to bring you right to him."

Jessica saw the parked car across from them bring up its headlights and then switch them off. She then saw Richard Sharpe climb from the car and come toward the cab.

The bastard's been following me all night, she snarled to herself in seething silence. She didn't like it in the least. It smacked of stalking, possessiveness, control, all the things she hated in men.

He came to the window all smiles. "Thought you'd like to know. There's been another body discovered."

Relief flooded her. She'd just come from Luc Sante and she had seen Strand as well, and so she grasped at the notion that Father Luc Sante could not be involved in the crucifixion murders, despite her earlier suspicions. She had even begun to suspect that Strand and Luc Sante had planned to drug her with their blasted tea and crumpets. Once again she felt angry with herself, at the suspicious creature she had become. *Still*, her scientific side whispered, *this new victim may well have been dumped hours or even days before*.

"Another crucified body?"

"Regent's Park this time, actually not far from here. Come along." Richard efficiently paid the cabby and tipped the man who gave him a thumb's-up and said, "Right, Guv," and drove off.

Jessica realized now she stood amid a silent, black street with Sharpe who had obviously trailed her all evening, and she was about to climb into his car with him and go ostensibly to a crime scene in her smudged evening gown with no medical supplies and no flat shoes or aprons.

"Can we return to the hotel first, so I can change and get my medical bag?"

"I've got a change of clothes for you, jeans and a blouse, and I've got your medical bag—to save time."

"You went into my room at the York?"

"How else?"

"What is it you British call that?"

"Pardon?"

"Cheeky, damned cheeky of you, Richard, I'd say."

"I'm sorry if it offends you. I certainly didn't mean to."

"When were you in my room? While I was at dinner?"

"No."

"While I was at St. Albans?"

"I got the call when you were inside. I had no idea how long you'd take."

"And you've had me and Father Luc Sante under surveillance all evening. Why?"

"I can't explain it. I just felt I needed to keep you in my sights tonight, that it was important. Call it intuition."

She shook her head. "Take me somewhere where I can change." Her tone hammered him over the head, firm and focused and nail-driving.

He silently did as told, and soon she had changed in the ladies' room of a restaurant calling itself the Chicago Pizza Factory only a few blocks away from where they'd met on the street. From there, they raced to Regent's Park, north of St. Albans, the opposite direction of the Thames and where all the other bodies had been found discarded.

Regent's Park, already alight with police activity and equipment—dead stock, the Scotland Yard fellows called such things as generators and night-lights—buzzed with both the number of police and the crowd that had gathered. A small pond in the park marked the place where the body had been located. Jessica and Sharpe were waved over by Stuart Copperwaite who stood alongside the nude body of a man, a much younger man than any the Crucifier had discarded before now.

"They're getting younger in age," Copperwaite announced. "Perhaps a pattern developing?"

"Christ was only twelve, maybe thirteen when he began preaching in the temple," suggested Jessica. "Maybe you're on to something, Stuart."

Copperwaite nodded but let it go at that. He said a firm, if strained hello to Richard, who acted as though there existed no problem between them, Sharpe's entire focus already on the corpse, his professional acumen taking over.

After searching for clues and closely examining the body, Jessica looked up and into Richard's eyes. For a moment she flashed on the wonderful time they had had when pub-crawling London, and she wished they were at it again. After she and Richard had made love, she had slept the sleep of the contented. It had been a long time since she'd actually rested fully, and he had given her that gift. The sure knowledge that Richard could not be the killer, that he harbored no secrets from her that might kill her, that she could fully and unreservedly trust him felt like the greatest gift of all.

"What're you thinking, Jessica?" he asked.

"I'll have to tell you that later, when we're alone," she whispered.

He smiled a moment, relieved, she guessed, that she had not allowed her anger with him to linger. Finally, he said, "I mean about the body."

"Something wrong here," she announced, sensing it, feeling a resignation to wholly trust herself. "I think we may well this time have that copycat killing we've all been expecting along the spectrum; someone masquerading as the Crucifier merely to rid the world of this poor slob."

"Could be I agree with you. Nail marks haven't the usual pattern."

"First thing I noticed," she agreed. "Likely he was dead before the nails were driven in." She shone a flashlight on the palm wounds. "Notice the lack of coloration about the wound itself? Not the sort of reaction expected from the living. No bruising."

"How do you think he died?"

She closely examined the eyes, taking her time. "He isn't likely to have died of asphyxia but something else, likely a poisoning."

"Then the staking of the hands—"

"A hasty cover-up, an afterthought to what may have been a well-planned meal of rat poison, but only an autopsy can say for sure what he ingested."

He nodded agreement but said, "Still, why don't you have at the tongue, to be sure there's no connection."

She pulled out a pair of tweezers from her valise, yanked open the dead mouth, and pulled the tongue out while Sharpe flashed his light on it. No marks whatsoever.

Sharpe instantly said, "Put Raehael on this one. We need you focused on the real thing. This most likely involves the fellow's closest friend or relative, roommate or lover, someone who knew him well enough to hate him."

She thought of Tattoo Man in the States. Same situation, she believed.

After closing down the crime scene, Sharpe offered her

company for the night, saying, "We have some things to talk about and some things to nurture."

She realized that she didn't want to be alone tonight. Looking into Sharpe's strong, steady eyes, the glistening moisture of them sparkling in the blinding police lights, she nodded her assent, casting all her little doubts and fears aside like so much collected flotsam. She simply could not believe ill of the man.

Jessica dreamed dreams of creamed cream, floating furniture, floating lovers, rising to the ceiling while in embrace as in a Marc Chagall painting. She dreamed of warm places, soft touches, caressing fingertips; she dreamed of wonder and other worlds gone undiscovered in faraway galaxies with strange-sounding names, and at once she wondered how her faraway dream places could possibly have names if they were as yet to be discovered. She dreamed on for the first time in as long as she could remember, dreams of childhood and love, tenderness and morning, of fuzzy animals and milk shakes topped with cherries. She dreamed dreams she wanted to take firm hold of and never let go, dreams she could live as a lifetime, but the images, odors, feelings, sounds, smells, and tastes in this playground of the subconscious all dissipated as candle smoke when suddenly she awoke.

The morning light woke Jessica where she lay at the foot of Richard's bed, having fallen asleep there after the lovemaking had exhausted them both. She lay nude, recalling the night of passion they'd shared. The light filtering in bathed the bed they lay upon, but when she reached for him, where his leg ought to be, she found Richard gone. She looked about and called out his name. Nothing. The small place returned a deafening silence. No sign of the man, when suddenly the door clicked, the key turning in the lock to announce his return. He poked a head into the small bungalow and shouted back to her, "Are you up in there? I've brought us some pastries and coffee."

"Attention to detail," she said, standing in the hallway now, his white terry-cloth robe wrapped about her. "That's what I like in a man." If she couldn't have the dream, she'd settle for the Englishman, she thought.

"I suspect you received all the attention you could handle last evening," he replied, a broad smile coloring his features.

"I'm starved."

"Good. Soon as we eat and get out of here, we're visiting the RIBA. Should have found time to do so before now."

"And exactly when would that have been?"

"Eat!" he ordered.

· SEVENTEEN ·

Genuine demonic possession in the annals of church history is rare. Everyday human evil, by comparison, all too common.

—FATHER JERRARD LUC SANTE,
TWISTED FAITHS

At the Royal Institute of British Architecture, Jessica and Richard did indeed locate a large array of information on coal mines and coal mining in England and London in particular. A curator of the museum housed in the bowels of the place, both amused and confused over their interest in the area, became befuddled further when they told him who they were. At that point, he made a phone call and asked that Donald Wentworth Tatham come up from the subbasement to speak to the authorities.

Tatham, a bald, round little man with glasses, lit his face up for them when he learned of their interest in coal-mining history. He could hardly contain his energies, ushering them from his boss's office, a ranting and endless diatribe on coal mines spewing forth now as they made their way through a door marked EMPLOYEES ONLY. Down a flight of stairs and through a set of double-doors and out into a room filled with stacks of metal shelving completely full with boxes of dusty collections of decades and centuries-old junk, far more than the museum had display space for. The stacked metal shelving went to the top of a ten-foot ceiling, and this back basement room appeared as large as any assembly room in any factory.

Jessica marveled at the sheer amount of treasures and his-

tory going unattended and unseen here in the dimly lit, musty
backside of the museum.

Through the maze of stacks, they emerged on the other side
at another door, and through this portal they stepped and suddenly found themselves in the public exhibit on coal mines,
located in a dark, sepulchral corner of the little museum, the
terminus of an unlit, musty corridor for those ghostly few
visitors who dared enter here. The place and the exhibit
seemed a great anachronism, reminding Jessica of a little
whaling museum in the midst of Maui's towering beachfront
condos and hotels, a quaint little museum on Maui that saw
far more visitors than did this place. Jessica flashed on her
trip to Maui, meant as a rendezvous getaway that had never
happened, and even her vain effort to get in some diving had
failed when a call from a field chief in Honolulu by the name
of James Parry had come through. Parry wanted forensic help
on a bizarre case that plagued the city of Honolulu on the
island of Oahu. It all seemed like a hundred years ago now
that she and Parry had put away Lopaka Robert Kowona for
butchering native Hawaiian women.

And here she stood amid the beauty of London, again in
pursuit of evil. But this evil, an evil that used the raiments of
the church and Christ's death as a starting point for itself, for
its existence and reason for being, this evil rooted in Christian
values seemed a far greater and more twisted beast than any
evil she had faced before. Whereas Kowona's evil rested on
a pagan religion that sacrificed women to a god, the Crucifier's evil rested firmly on the rock of the crucifixion and
resurrection of Christ. Did the killer or killers believe they
could and had resurrected the souls of their victims?

They now stood before small-scale models and replicas of
mining operations in and around London. They stared at hundreds of sketches and photos of early mining operations,
framed and under glass. The detail abounded, as did diagrams
of whole mining concerns. Here the walls and glass cases
were littered with the paraphernalia of the coal-mining indus-
try in its heyday.

"Mind you, coal mining still goes on, but it's run by computers nowadays, all the romance, so to speak, completely

282   ROBERT W. WALKER

taken from it," said their guide, Tatham. His eyes shone like shiny large seeds, bright with the anticipation of speaking on his favorite obsession.

Already, Jessica had learned that there once had been 160 coal mines in operation all across England, "But this number has dwindled to only a handful about the city, only fifty all told across the nation in operation nowadays," Tatham added, his small grin growing with the intensity of his excitement about his arcane field.

"We're not interested in any mines outside the city," said Sharpe. "Have you citywide plans? Original specs of the underground caverns within the city?"

"We're also interested in mines that date back to Roman occupation within the city limits," added Jessica.

"My, that does narrow the field. London began as a Roman garrison, so we're speaking of quite some time ago," the museum man replied. "That must be the Marylebone Mine."

Sharpe instantly replied, "Marylebone?"

Tatham, in a world of his own, simply said, "Come, follow."

Sharpe gave chase, asking Tatham, "Do you mean Marylebone? Near the cemetery of the same name?"

"It's within walking distance, but sealed underground, you see. Is that important to you?"

"Could be . . . could be," muttered Sharpe. He drew Jessica aside, and after a studious look into her eyes, he near whispered, "Marylebone Cemetery also stands well within walking distance to St. Albans."

"Coincidence?"

"How much coincidence do you believe in one city?" he asked, his eyes never leaving Jessica's.

"I'll have to search the archives for any maps that might be of help, but don't hold your breath," Tatham told them as he began to desert them here.

Jessica, trying to catch Tatham, who seemed to be fleeing the museum, shouted, "Also, please search for any maps of the time when the mine was last in operation."

"Showing proximities, you mean?"

"That and anything underground."

"Underground? Like the tube lines, you mean? There *is* one such map on display, but you can't possibly have it."

"You must have copies, something," suggested Sharpe.

"We may, may not. I will have to search the archives and the shelves."

"Do that."

"While you wait, you may wish to study this display," Tatham trumpeted, his hands flourishing like a magician's. "My triumph," he finished, pointing at a huge display of the original mine shaft at Marylebone just northwest of Hampstead Heath.

They did indeed study the layout of the mine in its small-scale version. A series of shafts had been cut in several directions, one leading as far as the cemetery it appeared. Another led out to a canal, long since shut down and no longer in use, Sharpe told Jessica. A third one led off in a dead end in the opposite direction, but it opened on a huge, cathedral-sized room where, according to Donald Wentworth Tatham's reconstruction, huge oaken beams, thick as railroad ties, were stored along with any heavy machinery.

"Read the placard. I wrote it myself," he told them, caressing the glass covering the scale model. According to the placard, the Marylebone Mine had closed down in 1911, played out, no longer economically profitable or feasible, as there had been cave-ins. Few appeared to know of its existence below the streets of London, and even men like Tatham, who appeared to be obsessed by such arcane information, confessed that he had not ever set foot in the mine itself.

They were kept waiting a half hour before Tatham again returned, and further frustrating them, he'd come up empty-handed and apologetic. "It's as though some gremlin simply will not allow them out of hiding. I know we had books and blueprints drawn up by some of the early engineers when they reopened the thing in the late 1800s. It's as if they've been . . . I fear saying it . . . stolen. I can't seem to put my finger on the material this moment, but I will assiduously continue to search. You have my word on it."

"But wouldn't you have had need of the same information when you designed this display?" asked Jessica.

"That's right."

She reached into her purse and pulled forth her petite Nikon, set the automatic flash and was about to snap off a shot, saying, "We can remedy the situation with a single—"

"No . . . against museum rules to take photos of the exhibits." Tatham almost shouted. "You know, gift shop and all upstairs. Besides the flash, you know, causes deterioration."

"Take the photo!" ordered Richard. To Tatham he menacingly said, "Bugger the bloody rules, Mr. Tatham. We 'ave people being murdered by crucifixion. Are you at all interested in the killer's g'd-awful rules?"

"Yes . . . well, putting it that way," muttered Tatham as Jessica snapped three shots of the exhibit in order to get the entire thing.

"We'll have these immediately developed and blown up," she said. Turning to Tatham, she took his hand, shook it, and said, "You may well have helped us put an end to the Crucifier's career, Mr. Tatham. You must find reward in that."

"Well, yes, of course, but it's actually Dr. Tatham. I received my doctorate in museum affairs and history last month."

She smiled in return, again thanked him and asked if he could show them out.

"Hold on a moment," said Sharpe. "Have you a similar exhibit of the canals?"

"The canals?" asked Tatham.

Jessica asked in tandem, "The canals?"

"London is littered with canals. The maps're dotted with them, and many—most, actually—are no longer serviceable. Others are put in use only in times of storm, as runoff. I'm curious to know where this one, on your display, originates."

"Perhaps if I had the original notes on the project. They will surface, of course. If you took one peek into my office, you'd understand the . . . the disarray. I know the research is somewhere at hand, but this particular canal stuck out for me. I recall it from my research and the building of the replica."

"And why is that?"

"Associated with it, the canal, that is, is an ancient bridge, a clapper bridge."

"Really? And why hasn't it become an archaeological dig then?" asked Sharpe. "Too far from downtown to bother tearing up the streets to get at?"

Tatham gave a nervous laugh at Sharpe's joke. "Funding dictates everything in the archaeological and historical spheres, Inspector."

"All right, then, about your notes."

"Yes, well, when I can—"

"Locate them and fax a copy to Scotland Yard to my attention. The number is here on my card." Sharpe pushed the card at Tatham. "No unnecessary delays, man. This is of vital importance to the Crown, you realize. You could be saving a life, and in doing so, perhaps currying a bit of favor with the Royal Family could save your dark little concern here." Richard's eyes roved the room as he threw Tatham this suggestive bone.

Jessica only half listened, still wondering precisely what a clapper bridge might be.

"If you're actually onto his game, the Crucifier's that is," replied Tatham, his wheels within wheels behind his eyes now turning. "I suppose my helping you out couldn't hurt my career."

Sharpe breathed inward, taking a deep sigh with his inhaling.

"Can you get us back up to street level and out, Dr. Tatham?" asked Jessica.

"Of course, back this way."

Jessica, following in single file behind Tatham, Richard at her back, felt as if they were stumbling about in a confusing, crisscrossing, turning-in-on-itself maze, not only here in the pit of the ancient museum with its ancient artifacts and displays, but outside, in the real world above, on this bizarre case that she had signed onto; she feared that somehow Luc Sante, his church, the strange-sounding Marylebone Cemetery, the Roman mine, the canal, something called a clapper bridge, Father Strand, Richard Sharpe, and Jessica Coran had all come to this place and time in a preordained fashion, that somehow they must do battle against evil, to force it into the light of the millennium in order to see the true face of evil in all its ugliest manifestation.

They finally found ground level and sunlight from the waning day. Outside, they both breathed deeply of the sweeter air. They stood talking on the steps of the RIBA, feeling small below giant columns on either side.

"You keep coming back to this Marylebone Cemetery and St. Albans, Richard. That whole area."

"Aye, things appear pointed in this direction, yes."

"You can't seriously believe that Father Luc Sante is conducting some sort of bizarre cult ritual involving the crucifixion of men and women below the streets of London in an ancient mine shaft somehow connected to St. Albans, can you?" she asked Richard as they climbed into his car.

"All the dirty little cow paths keep returning us to the man's neighborhood, you must agree. Despite all that we know about the man—his cloth, his rational nature, his reputation. I keep finding St. Albans in the bitter mix of this atrocious stew. We all know appearances are often deceiving, and those who have their houses in order are often the messiest of beings in private."

"I can't believe it of Luc Sante. I simply can't."

"What then about Strand?"

"Yes, how much do we know about Luc Sante's apprentice?"

"Actually, I've done a deeper background check on Strand," Richard informed her even as he started down the stairs.

She fought to keep up, asking, "Really?"

"Didn't care for him when I met him at the church the other day. Don't know precisely why, but I gained an ill feeling just being in his presence. Too—I don't know—solicitous, asking about the case, seeking some sort of picture as to where we are on it. A bit too crowding."

Jessica knew the familiar cop thinking, that if someone—particularly a civilian—showed too much ready interest in the specific details of a case, suspicion bloomed.

Jessica stared back at the Royal Institute as Richard climbed into his squad car. Surprised, she saw that embedded within its ancient niches, high above them, gargoyles again looked down on her movements.

"Let's get out of here. See if we can't locate the terminus of that canal and an entry point," he suggested as Jessica climbed into the passenger seat. They sped away, carrying the map of the underground passageways, canals, and mine shafts of the Marylebone area with them, locked away in Jessica's camera. Richard had mentioned someone at the Yard, expert in handling photographic evidence, who would develop and enlarge the photos for them. But before returning to the Yard, they would have a look to determine just how difficult it would be to get inside that ancient mine shaft below Marylebone.

Richard drove for the area where Luc Sante's church seemed a focal point. A few blocks from the RIBA, Richard pointed out a cemetery nearly hidden by the urban streets and said, "There is Marylebone Cemetery. Odd that the Crucifier, if he is working out of this district, doesn't simply dump his bodies there, but then . . ."

"Then it would break with his ritualistic obsession. If he is attempting to resurrect his own victims, he needs to follow a strict regimen, which obviously includes a clean body of water."

Richard laughed. "Just try to find a clean body of water in this city."

"Pull over," she suddenly asked.

"What for?" he asked.

"I want to see the cemetery, up close. I love old cemeteries, and this one looks ancient."

"That much is true." Richard pulled the car to a stop, and Jessica climbed out, peering now through the gates of Marylebone. Richard trailed after with the map of the area in his hands. "Look here," he said, pointing at the opened map.

She did so, and Richard continued, "This cemetery stands as close to our Royal Institute as it does to St. Albans."

"It's a fantastic find, this place." Her voice took on the tone of a schoolgirl with a crush. "I love it."

Richard merely shrugged and Jessica began strolling among the headstones, many green with lichen and age, and she mentally read off the names and dates of the people housed in this city of the dead. While she did so, Richard continued on about Martin Strand. "I ran a second check on our choirboy, Strand, but he came back as polished as a schoolboy's apple."

"Which only makes you even more suspicious, no doubt," she replied, pulling her eyes from the grand old cemetery."

"Actually, he looks more suspicious by the moment, Jessica."

"What do you mean?"

"He worked his way through various jobs to gain enough money to go to seminary at Westminster Seminary for the Clergy."

"And?"

"One of his jobs was as a lengthsman."

"A lengthsman? And what is a—"

"A caretaker around damns, canals, regulating water flow. That sort of thing. He would have had keys made up. He would know where every canal and clapper bridge in the city lies."

"Clapper bridge?"

"They're bloody prehistoric bridges, built before recorded time some of them. The Romans often built over them, or rather demolished them and built new structures over them."

"Are there many in London?"

"Oh, no one knows for sure. Not so many in London as you will find in the West Country, actually. They're normally something in the area of six feet long by four or five feet wide and a foot thick, but only the carefully placed stone masonry remains, you see. The bridges were laid over boulders spaced two or three feet apart to get across streams and some remain here and there over canal junctures."

She seemed more intent on reading headstones than listening to him. He pushed the map of the area again into her face, making her halt, ending her stroll, and saying, "Look here at these areas I've circled."

Jessica stared now at the marked map, at the circled areas, indicating coal mines which once thrived in and around London. In her ear, Richard said, "Most will have associated with them canals for transporting the coal out. There is an exhaustive number, but I intend to put a surveillance team at every single one, to watch for unusual activity. That is, if I can sell this whole notion, half-baked as it sounds, to Boulte, of course."

"So Strand's job, the job that got him through seminary, would have been enough to make him intimate with the waterways here? He would know every body of water in the city."

"And the system of underground canals, like the one we saw in the replica of Marylebone Mine. He would know of the shortest and simplest routes to and from the mine."

Her mouth agape, her eyes staring out at the traffic and the world outside the cemetery gates, Jessica concluded, "Then it must be Strand. We have him. We have the nails to crucify the Crucifier."

"Hold on. We have nothing but a packet of speculative conjectures . . . *Strands*, if you will, strands of loose circumstantial facts, none of which the Crown prosecutor would take into a courtroom, I assure you."

"Then we've got to get the evidence we need against Strand."

"You're assuming Father Luc Sante innocent in this, but remember, we early on agreed that no one could be working this hideous circus alone."

Jessica tried to imagine the old man who spoke so eloquently on the subject of evil, who had devoted a lifetime to the scrutiny of evil, who wished to create a psychotherapy of treatment in cases of evil and demonic possession. She tried to imagine how Luc Sante himself might be taken over by the evil he combated. He had warned her of this very real danger. Yes, the possibility existed, but she resisted finding Luc Sante guilty. "It . . . it simply cannot be. Look, Luc Sante is an old man. This horror could be going on about and around him, and he might not know," she submitted for Sharpe's consideration.

"Perhaps, perhaps," he replied noncommittally.

"How do we get the evidence we need?"

"We could take what we have at this point to Boulte, and do a surveillance of the area, or better yet have a full-out mucking of this canal and approach it from all sides."

She readily agreed. "Every passage we can locate beneath the city that might converge on this canal running between here and St. Albans needs to be cut off."

"Definitely time we mounted an all-out effort, but we can't have this leaking out. The gossipmongers get hold of this news, and the Crucifiers are forewarned, and we'll find 'zip,' as you Yanks say."

"Perhaps we can enlist Copperwaite? Inform a few trusted others?" she suggested.

"Copperwaite can no longer *be* trusted."

"I suspected as much." She came onto a stone bench and sat, Richard joining her where bushes and tree branches reached out to them among the headstones.

"Stuart has his eyes on a prize extended before his nose. Boulte's filing a charge with our internal monitors to look into my recent conduct, as when I stepped off from the scene the other night. 'Fraid young Coppers got caught up when trying to cover for me. Boulte's known for turning his people against one another. Too many eyes on a crime scene to manage secrets, really. My fault really."

"Are you sure that Copperwaite is a part of this witch-hunt against you?"

" 'Fraid so. Can't blame him, really. It's his career on the line, too, and I put it there. He did at first try to cover for me. It's been a long time coming between Boulte and me, really. Not any worry of yours."

"Really?" she replied, offended, but he took no notice of her emotions.

"The public prosecutor's involved to her nipples as well. Pardon, but it's the truth. She's a spurned woman since . . ."

"Since you slept with her?"

"I made that mistake, yes, at a particularly low point in my life, I'm afraid."

"And that reporter who's so interested in you? How many women have you had since your divorce?"

"We call it grazing, but—"

"And is that what we've been doing—grazing?"

"No, never!"

She challenged him, asking, "Then what?"

"What we have is altogether new to me, beautiful and lovely. Please, you must trust me. I hold you in the highest regard, Jessica."

She managed a smile and a shake of the head, and then she asked, "All right, so how do we break this case and restore you to prominence at the Yard in the bargain?"

"To find a cult that is conducting the bizarre 'business' of crucifying people in some sort of warped sacrifice to God. Yes, Doctor, where to look? The million-pound question."

"We both saw those huge cross-tie beams in the old photos of the Marylebone Mine; wouldn't be difficult to fashion them into an old wooden cross. . . . And since coal dust was found embedded in the wounds of the dead, this mine shaft direction we've taken, it does make sense."

He nodded appreciatively, adding, "Yes, even the cross might be made of coal-shaft beams, in which case, they'd have long before become coated with the ancient coal dust that might have shared space with a Roman beetle."

"I fear any delay and we could have another crucified victim on our hands tomorrow. I fear they are going for seven victims."

"Quite right." He looked at the darkening sky, clouds having rolled in, his watch now telling him the time. "My Lord, it's already 5 P.M. We don't have much light left. Let's have out of here."

The entire trip to where the mine had been, Jessica tried to recall a single word, a single clue that might actually have been given her as to Luc Sante's possible involvement in murder, and while she recalled the entire picture of the man as a saint who fought against evil his entire life, she could not recall any single word or phrase he used that would implicate him in any such depraved and hideous wrongdoing as staking men and women to a cross to watch them die their slow deaths. She could not imagine the old man plotting with such depraved indifference to human life.

No, she simply could not accept the notion of Father Luc Sante as the leader of a cult bent on murder in the name of Christ, the Second Coming, or the True Millennium. They might just as well indict his elderly secretary, Miss Janet Eeadna. Still, strands of their last conversation, all about the group mind, began to insinuate itself upon her like some night creature, like an incubi come creeping over her to take her breath away. Had she been asleep throughout the investigation here? Had she been blinded by Luc Sante's apparent benevolence? She recalled the sensation of having been drugged on the tea Strand had served her.

When they arrived at where the mine once stood, they found nothing but paved streets and the Crown's End Bazaar, a place crowded with merchants and tourists who'd been brought in by the busload. Not a single sign of the old mine remained.

"According to the map we saw at the RIBA, it was here."

"Richard, the operative word is was . . . *was* here."

"But no more," he conceded.

She gripped him by the arm, sighed, and asked, "What now?"

"To the terminus of the canal. It spills out into a reservoir not far from here."

They drove to this destination, and once again located disappointment. If there once had been a thriving canal, like the mine, it had disappeared. Richard, frustrated, climbed from the car and began a foot search for any remaining sign of the canal. After scouring the ditches around the reservoir, he finally located a rusted over, weeded over grate, buried in the brush, a grate large enough for a man to pass through, but it hadn't been opened, he estimated, in forty or fifty years.

"No one going in and out of here," he resignedly said.

"Let's go back to the Yard, Richard, get the photos developed, have a closer look. Perhaps we overlooked something in the replica."

"This case leads from one dead end to another."

She attempted a hug to soothe his anger and disappointment, but he pulled away, saying it had grown late. "Let's be out of here, Jessica."

Across the city in the operations room of Scotland Yard, Chief Inspector Boulte had long before ordered Copperwaite to set up surveillance teams at every entry road to the Thames embankment, and every pond and lake in the city parks, using as many city patrolmen as required. Inspector Boulte, angry that his plan to prove Periwinkle and Hawkins the Crucifiers had failed, now determined to catch the killers as they disposed of their next victim. Meanwhile investigation into the copycat killing proceeded separately.

"Where the hell are Sharpe and that woman from America?" Boulte exploded at Stuart Copperwaite.

Copperwaite threw up his arms in defeat, explaining, "I've left messages all over the city for both to call in, but they've remained silent. Frankly, sir," Copperwaite said, "I'm somewhat worried about them. It's not like Inspector Sharpe to simply disappear and not—"

"Find them. Send them to me when you do."

Boulte strode purposefully from the ops room and down the long corridor to his office, his footfalls like clapping hands against the smooth surface of the floor, his face like a lantern smoldering in a haystack.

Copperwaite, when sure his superior had closed his door and was out of earshot, muttered, "Sharpie tried to tell you we had the wrong men in custody, you fart-bag, but you wouldn't listen, now would you? And that bitch prosecutor Sturgeon, she simply wants to embarrass Richard. Maybe now you'll pay more attention to the postmortem evidence at hand."

Copperwaite noticed other investigators staring at him, one jokingly calling out, "So, Coppers, it's finally come to this? You're talking to yourself, man."

Copperwaite ignored the jibe, grabbed up his phone, and eased into his chair. The Crucifier had stepped up the schedule of sacrifices he or they intended, and the Yard must be ready for the bastard this time. It would prove a long night, and he must amass an army of eyes, enlist them all in the hunt for the maniacs behind all this madness.

Copperwaite took a moment to assess his part in hamstringing and bringing Richard Sharpe to his knees. He admired and liked Sharpe, always had, but at the same time, he disliked Sharpe always being right, always in the know, always on top. When Boulte had made it perfectly clear that Sharpe had become the target of an internal investigation, it was whispered into Copperwaite's ear that he would do well to distance himself from Sharpe and to cooperate in any way necessary with the internal audit. Then and only then did Copperwaite begin to see Richard's flaws.

He must have said to himself a hundred times overnight, "Richard brought this upon himself. It was never my doing. So why do I feel so guilty and so alone?" And where was Richard now? And was Dr. Coran with him? Funny thought flitting in and out of his mind replied, *Hampton or Surrey, in a bed-and-breakfast, enjoying one another and the country-side on a getaway, perhaps.* Copperwaite smiled at the notion, wishing Richard well.

He returned to the business at hand, setting up surveillance teams all over the city to cover any and all large bodies of water.

· EIGHTEEN ·

The only power Satan wields is our belief in his lies.

—FATHER JERRARD LUC SANTE,
TWISTED FAITHS

Diamondback, Louisiana
At dusk, Sunday October 1, 2000

The squad car ran silent, no lights flashing nor siren roaring, the entire feel of the climax of Medical Examiner John Thorpe's search for Tattoo Man's roots coming to a "Blue Bayou" ending in this remote corner of the universe. Dry potato dust sand, kicked up under and around the squad car, heralded their arrival at what once was Tattoo Man's home, as all leads had brought Thorpe to this place.

"There ain't no way the family's gonna have known anything about this tragedy," moaned Deputy Sheriff Luther Whitney Frizzell, who continued to whine in an irritatingly nasally voice for which Thorpe thought he ought to apologize. "Kate, that po' woman; she's just a spiritless woman, older'n her years. Sanocre done that to her. Story is he'd lock her up, tied up, all night in their damned root cellar if she looked cross-eyed at him, but damned if she ever pressed a single charge, and ain't nothin' our office can do if the wife don't press no charge, Doctor. Well, you know that. But as for their knowin' he come to a bad end in New England—"

"New Jersey," Thorpe gently corrected the man.

"Yeah, New Jersey . . . ain't New Jersey kinda in New England?"

"Not technically speaking, no. Mid-Atlantic states."

"Gotcha, right. Anyhow, I don't think you're gonna find none a them clues you're lookin' for here if he was kilt way up there."

"But we can put to rest who he is, Deputy Frizzell, and that's a good portion of the battle won. We can have Sanocre shipped back here for burial, return the body to the family. That way, he won't be buried—"

"At taxpayers' expense," Frizzell finished for J. T.

"—in, I was going to say, a potter's field full of John and Jane Does. This way he can be buried at the local churchyard or wherever the family wants."

"Can't 'magine any church 'round here'd want his carcass stinkin' up the ground, not even the pet cemetery'd take him'd be my guess." He chuckled at his little joke.

"He was hated that much?"

"Hate ain't narry a strong enough word for what folks thought of Sanocre. He was Satan walkin', that man. I thought a killin' 'im myself once or twice, if you want the God's honest truth."

J. T. suspected that Frizzell had often wanted to make good on his thoughts. The lawman's sense of legality or fear or both likely held "Whitey" in check. He dared not ask the man with the guns, but he did ask, "Was there any saving grace, any trace of good in the man you might point to?"

"None by me. Certainly none by his family. Tell you what, Dr. Thorpe, when no one in your own family can stand the sight of you, maybe you ought to go off and get yourself killed up in New England, ahhh, Jersey."

"So you think my bringing news to these people about Max Sanocre's death and possible murder is a mistake?"

The deputy had been bitching, moaning, complaining, and whining the entire way out to the house in the cypress wood, the deputy's car now rounding a tight bend in the dirt road, red-rimmed and clay-colored, giving way to sand, loose and pulling. He whined about too much rain, the flooding in the bottom land, crop failures, something about a bovine disease and scrawny hogs this year, went on about too much humidity, not enough wind, the condition of Fords, that Chevys had gone "commie" and foreign trade would one day destroy all that America ever stood for. He bitched about the squeak in his right rear tire, the distances he had to cover in his work, the long hours, short pay, lack of help and understanding from the sheriff to his wife, and that he feared his wife hated being married to a cop. He bemoaned the fact he hadn't ever seen New Jersey or New York or none of them *New* places up North until he finally, winding up with an enormous sigh, wound down like a clock gone dead, his entire, hefty chest deflating in balloon fashion with a few remnant words: "Well, here we are. The Sanocre place."

Medical Examiner John Thorpe, riding in the passenger seat, had squirmed into the small Nissan and felt jammed next to the officer's thirty-ought shotgun, which the deputy nervously and often fondled. J. T. looked up now at the Sanocre house, a shack really. One could hardly call the place a house. Weathered clapboards put together like so many cards in the wind, it leaned to one side as if more fatigued than any living thing on earth.

Pecan trees intermingled with willows and cypress; Spanish moss tossed about like salad leavings everywhere, including the front porch and yard. A pastoral place for a lovely home if one were to build here, he thought. As J. T. climbed from the patrol car, he found himself out of his time, staring at the old shack of a home on cinder blocks and yes, about to topple, and then there were the Snuffy Smith characters arrayed on its peeling, cracking porch. FBI Agent and Medical Examiner John Thorpe wondered if he'd stepped out of the legal boundaries of the United States of America. Somewhere along the line of his trek to discover the truth about Tattoo Man, the flight he'd taken from New Orleans International airport on a private carrier, had landed in Gator Head Bayou—Home of Snoutnose, The Largest Alligator in captivity in America. All the clichés and nightmares J. T. had ever heard about or entertained regarding Louisiana proved true in this patch of place. From the single strip, dirt airport, they had taken the long, winding car ride into the interior of Diamondback, Louisiana. And wasn't Diamondback in America? Wouldn't a postage stamp cost the same here as anywhere? *Sure*—he silently answered his own thoughts—*if you could locate a stamp machine in Diamondback.* While J. T. amused himself with his own musings, Deputy Sheriff Frizzell continued the touchy-feely with his shotgun, his fingers displaying indecision on whether he should or should not unfasten the lock and take the hefty and quite visible weapon with him to the front doorstep of this place.

J. T. felt bemused by the local color, from the deputy down to the hanging vines, the huge cypress knolls and the gnarled and bubbled, toiled and troubled roots of trees here which he guessed the obvious residences of gnomes.

J. T. had asked on local law-enforcement authorities in New Orleans to pave his way. Frizzell had been waiting for him at the local airport. For all Frizzell knew, the people here at the Sanocre home might well be harboring a murderer.

J. T. had made clear his suspicion that someone who knew Max Sanocre had had a hand in his death, someone who also knew dogs, and from the moment they pulled up to the front yard of this place, dogs appeared and approached, some on four legs, some on three, some inching forward, some crawling on their bellies, some straight up and fast, while others held back in the shadows. It gave J. T. a strange feeling, as if the dogs lived here and ran this place, and the people on the porch were being held hostage by man's best friend.

Dog attacks being on the rise all across America, J. T. hesitated at the side of the car until Deputy Frizzell finally came out on his side, deciding to leave the shotgun, while unbuckled, on its pedestal between driver and passenger seat. J. T. noticed that the deputy had also unfastened his .38 where it rested on his hip.

"Are you expecting trouble?" J. T. asked.

"Always prepare with these kinda folk for any possibility. You learn that when you've been here for long."

"Then you're not originally from around here?" J. T. asked.

"Didn't *saya* that." The deputy pulled up his pants and started to part the dogs, a few of them growling, and Frizzell in turn barked like a madman at the dogs, laughing at their cowed response. He then told J. T. to follow him up to the porch.

"I 'spect one or more of them that's living in Max's old shack here's done him in. Is that what you boys in Quantico wanna hear?"

"No, we don't *wanna* hear anything."

"What you think, I mean. Is-at what ya think?"

"Yeah, some of us suspect family involvement in the murder, but first I just want a family member to ID the corpse from photos."

"If he had no identification on him, how'd you trace him back to here?" asked the deputy, his nasally twang reaching to the family on the porch, all engaged in watermelon and lemonade, it appeared.

Some children waved madly at the deputy, shouting that they wanted to hear the siren blast. J. T. heard the children shout at the deputy as "Uncle Whitey."

"You're related to the family?"

"I am. Something of a cousin to 'em. Kids I know from after-school programs, fund-raiser and like that."

J. T. felt suddenly vulnerable. If the entire town knew that Maxwell Sanocre had disappeared one night, then tacitly covered it up, and the helpful law agent is part of that conspiracy against the hated Sanocre, then what might they do to a stranger from "New England" to shut him up? A cover-up of a cover-up, the family secret growing ever deeper with J. T. six feet deep?

As if reading J. T.'s visage and understanding his thoughts, Deputy Frizzell quickly and firmly assured him, "I don't condone what happened to that animal Max Sanocre, but like I tol' ya, there come times I wanted to murder that low-life sonofabitch, I tell you. If someone was drove to it—and I'm not saying they were—well, I understand it. The man was the vilest thing walked on two legs in my experience."

The tallest, oldest looking man on the porch stepped toward them, waving in a friendly gesture, asking them if he could help the pair, nodding to his cousin the officer, and adding, "Some reason you're out this way, Whitey?"

"Got some news, folks," announced Frizzell in calmer tones

than Houston's command control during a satellite launch, J. T. thought.

Everyone on the porch stared hard at the stranger—John Thorpe. The deputy hastily introduced J. T. as "A card-carrying G-man in search of a killer, maybe two, maybe three." There were three adults in and around the porch, all standing and staring now like their small army of dogs. They all looked like they wanted J. T's blood.

J. T., through a thorough trek about the world of tattoo art—and gaining an education in the process—had convinced first one man to help him and then another until he learned of the signature artwork of Deltrace D'Iazetti, and he'd had to travel to Missouri to meet D'Iazetti who, after long searching in his files and mind, came up with "a guy more crude than Andrew Dice Clay and Howard Stern rolled into one who treated women like . . . like g'damn meat loaf." This identification led to Louisiana.

"Sure, I can clearly recall the artwork. Hell, man, it won me my first major prize," D'Iazetti had told J. T.

"Really?"

"At the state fair. Ever since, I've been highlighted in every major tattoo publication in the country. You kidding?"

"M.E.'s seldom kid around," replied J. T., "and when we do chide, you'll know it."

D'Iazetti had grimaced, asking, "Chide?"

J. T. pushed on, replying with his own question, asking, "What more can you tell me about this man."

"Such as?"

Man, this guy's stoned, J. T. recalled telling himself, wondering if it were a prerequisite of the artistic life to do drugs, or an affectation since Edgar Allan Poe's day. "Such as . . . such as his name," replied J. T. "Right now he's a John Doe, and will be buried as such if we can't learn more about him in the next twenty-four hours. His time on the taxpayers' dole has run out, you see, and as such—"

"Dog or Maddog or Mean's Hell or Tough as Bison or something like 'at is all I can rightly recall outta my head, because I do remember this guy was an ass, a real creep. Mean as hell, and he made *my* skin crawl, and ain't too many

can make my skin crawl, you know, but he was the best thing
ever happened to me when I *showed him* at the fair."

"Showed him?" J. T. flashed a mental image of the man's
body art being displayed at a sideshow carnival.

"Well, not him, not really him, closeups of the art, man."

"You have photos?"

" 'Sat what they call irre—irrefusable evidence, man?"

J. T. stifled a laugh at the pothead. "Does his name and the
date appear on the photos?"

"Name, date, time, you name it."

"We've got to find those pictures then."

"Be my guest." He pointed at sixteen shelves of photo records of his work. "Sorry, been in the business a long time.
Started when I was just a kid, and I'm a damn sight older
than I look. I think it's the small frame and height. People
think I'm Michael J. Fox, you know, the actor? Hardly looks
like he ages."

"This could take a while," J. T. said, staring at the books
of tattoo artwork representing an obviously disordered life.
There appeared no dates on the booklets.

"Take all the time you want."

"I could use your help. Your country needs you."

"My country? Hmmm. Never ever thought of it as my
country. Strange world we live in, Dr. Thorpe."

"Strange indeed."

"Strange, strange world . . . Are you telling me that this
guy's name is, you know, like a matter of like, you know,
national security, something like that? This guy plotting some
sort of McVeigh thing against the government or something?"

"Yeah, something like that." J. T. hated to lie, but he saw
no alternative. Already, the stoned artist had dismissed the
fact J. T. had told him the man was deceased, a John Doe. Or
perhaps the artist understood the term John Doe as little as
he did the word chide.

Deltrace D'Iazzeti metaphorically rolled up his sleeves like
a farmer at this point, saying, "OK, let's have at it. But be
forewarned, dude, records like CDs I can put my hands on,
but records for business, I don't keep so good, so it could
take a while."

J. T. offered to order a pizza and a jug of wine, if it would help. The artist liked the idea, and so they rolled up their sleeves and dug in.

They whittled it down to the approximate last time he'd done body art on "Horace" and the tattoo artist said, "That'd be the work I did on his ass. Can't be stoned when you're doing precision work, 'specially round the geni-till-ya area."

"Now you're telling me more than I want to know," J. T. replied, holding up a hand. "What exactly do you remember about him?"

"Disgust. Rock-bottom disgust, man. Guy disgusted me the entire way, man, and that's what I was thinking at the fair when I stood up to get the award, disgust."

J. T. could not help but smile. He wanted to laugh.

D'Iazetti continued, saying, "But, but, the dude paid in bread, real green, not like I get usual . . ."

"Drugs?" suggested J. T., wondering why in God's creation people allowed this guy anywhere near their bodies with a hot needle and ink while he was on PCP or some other potent drug.

"Sometimes drugs, yeah, but more oft than not, it's a damned Pomeranian puppy or a lousy canned ham somebody ripped off, a bottle of scotch, somebody's unused toys like once I got a fish tank for doing a big job."

"So, you do remember this man?" J. T. held up the photos of Horace on the slab, and the close-ups of the artwork.

"The face, the ass, the art, the disgust . . . sure, but not the name."

J. T. gnashed his teeth.

"It'll take the record to jog that back."

The artist, typical of his peripheral world, managed, stoned, to hold himself together long enough to locate a billing file buried beneath a stack of newspapers and magazines—*US, FAME, People, Fangoria, Scream Factory, USA Today*. D'Iazetti did this during the time that J. T. had begun on the photo collection. This collection of data he recalled after pizza and Pepsi. In the manner of an embarrassed teen, he showed the index cards to J. T. and said, "I think I found a shortcut. I try to keep the names and numbers of all my clients in here.

If I filled out a card on him, it should take you right to the number of the book and the page where his photos are, if . . ."

The cards saved J. T. hours, and they did lead circuitously to the photo shoot and photos. On the billing card came the name, phone number, and address of Horace the Tattoo Man, which read Maxwell Sanocre, Rt. 4, Diamondback, Louisiana. On the card, the middle nickname didn't read Dog or Maddog or Maniac, but "Abominable." "Abominable" Max Sanocre. Actually the nickname was far from any of those proffered by the spongy-headed D'Iazetti. But J. T. felt good, a sense of closure coming with this news, for finally, John Doe had an identity, such as it was.

Questioning of friends and neighbors in the small town of Diamondback had netted J. T. little information. The police station prided itself on the fact it was hardly needed and hardly the size of a pair of telephone booths stood side-by-side, and about as public. J. T. decided he wouldn't hold out too much hope of help here in Diamondback. The actual county sheriff's office lay some twenty-nine tarmac miles to the north, at the county seat.

However, J. T. puzzled together a broken picture of Sanocre's having "moved to Utah in search of open territory." The story was told and retold by anyone J. T. or Deputy Frizzell had asked. J. T. gained the impression that even the local schoolchildren had been tutored in the same story about "Abominable" Maxwell Sanocre who, it appeared, had terrorized this hamlet from the day he was born.

And so now, here they stood, Deputy Frizzell, his thumbs in his waistband, buried below his protruding stomach, and J. T., looking out of place from his Ralph Lauren glasses to his expensive leather shoes, marking him as a visitor from Mars, standing before the platform porch of the place where Abominable practiced being abominable the most—on his own family.

Now more young people, large burly men and boys, spilled from the doorways of the house, over the porch and into the yard, all wanting to know why their deputy cousin and uncle had come in the company of this obvious outlander. What had happened and what was going on telegraphed from every hang-mouth face.

Deputy Frizzell explained the situation bluntly and without fanfare. The news garnered no tears, but it did get a pair of whoops and yahoos and curses. One of the boys said, "Damned glad to hear it, Dr. Thorpe. Thank you." The implication being, "You can go now," J. T. thought.

Another of the sons asked, "But why'd you come all this way to tell us about it when you coulda' just phoned it in?"

"Did he ever make it to Utah? That where he died?" asked another of the younger boys who'd missed the earlier conversation about the mysterious death in New Jersey that had led J. T. to their doorstep.

One of the older siblings, a girl holding firm to a baby, brought her little brother up-to-date with a few choice words: "Don't be stupid, Kyle."

J. T. added, "You see, the body went unidentified, and it took a great deal of detective work, using his tattoo art, to trace it—your father—"

"Gran-pap," corrected the younger boy.

"Yes, of course, pardon."

"You think he was murdered up there in New Jersey?" asked the young woman with the child in her arms as she stepped forward, the baby cooing *mam-mam-mam!* in her ear.

"Matter of fact, yes."

"How was he kilt?" asked the older woman who hadn't budged from her porch chair.

"Are you Mrs. Sanocre?" J.T. asked.

"That'd be me."

"We need to talk."

"About?"

"Arrangements, return of Mr. Sanocre's remains."

"We don't want his cussed remains here," said one of the youngest boys.

"He were the Devil," said the young girl with the babe in her arms. "Ever'body knows-sit!"

J. T. saw it flicker in her eyes, the hatred, yes, but also the truth. "You killed him, yourself, didn't you, young lady. I read you like a book."

"She done nothing of the kind!" defended one strong-armed fellow instantly at her side who didn't have the same coloring or hair shade as the others.

"Your husband, Miss Sanocre?" asked J. T. of the man.

"Yes."

"Tell me, son. You own any of these dogs?" asked J.T.

"What's going on?" asked Mrs. Sanocre from the porch chair.

"That bastard broke my mama's legs, both of 'em, just outta meanness and evil. If he got killed, it was God put him dead, not us," said the young girl.

"Do you have access to a rabies venom, sir?" J. T. asked the man at her side.

"All right . . . All right, I did it. I killed that Devil, and I did it on my own. None of these folks here had anythin' to do with it."

"No, no, July!" shouted the daughter. "I ain't allowin' you take this on your head alone!"

"Shut up, Cassie! You know I done it alone, all on my own!"

The others were abuzz, some of them clearly confused, and the old woman shouted, "What're you all talkin' about?"

The daughter went to her maltreated, malnourished mother to comfort her, cooing that everything would be put right. The mother accepted her daughter's words as if they'd been spoken by an angel or God.

Deputy Frizzell said, "Cassie, July, I think we have a long night of talkin' to do down in Diamondback at the jailhouse. Come on."

Cassie handed off her child without a misstep or a tear, and she and July voluntarily found the rear of the squad car. Their deputy cousin did not handcuff them. Others in the family gave out threatening gestures, lifted voices, and banged on the car, but they did allow Deputy Frizzell to pull off with Cassie and July in custody.

Deputy Frizzell began to read the pair their rights.

It came off as simple as that. All they needed to see was an FBI expert in their front yard telling them that he knew they had done it, and the entire elaborate scheme fell away like a house of flimsy cards.

When the full story came to light, three others in the family, two of whom had raced off to become fugitives, were implicated in the conspiracy to kill Maxwell Sanocre, all of them his children, all full-grown adults. They had conspired to murder him in New Jersey where they sent him on a supposed reunion with his high school buddies. Before he ever got to the "reunion," however, he was fooled into visiting the junkyard for "great used Harley parts." There he was murdered by the rabid dogs which his daughter, married to a veterinary apprentice, had masterminded. "The beauty part," Cassie at one point in the interrogation said in chilling matter-of-fact manner, "was that we used his own damned, vicious pit bulls to get him. He made them dogs evil, same as he wanted to make all his children evil. Somebody had to put an end to him and his dogs. The rabies was for the dogs as much as him, and we figured since he was wanted in New Jersey, he'd die before he took hisself to a doctor, even if he could get over that junkyard fence. He was the Devil *his-self*! No matter what you think, Dr. Thorpe, we done the right thing . . ."

One son, a daughter, and a son-in-law, each of whom passionately hated the old man, were held over for trial, while two others remained at large. Clearly, Sanocre's wife, with little sense left, did not understand this sudden disintegration of her family, but she clearly laid it at her dead husband's feet. Perhaps, if the jury found any sympathetic thread in all this so as to understand the terrorizing and traumatizing abuse that even to J. T., an outsider, appeared rampant, then daughter and sons might find some mercy with the court.

J. T. wanted out of Diamondback as quickly as possible, and so he flew back to New Orleans, where he took some time to relax, see the sights and recoup before even thinking of flying on to Quantico, Virginia. From New Orleans, he dialed London, in hope of reaching Jessica to tell her that he'd wrapped up the case of the Missing Person known to them as Horace the Tattoo Man.

Proud of himself, pleased at his handling of the case, bursting to tell Jessica the news, he called the York Hotel only to find her not in, and in converting the time, he wondered where she might be at 6 P.M. British time, for when he tried Scotland Yard, she could not be found there, either. He couldn't opt to leave her E-mail because his terminal awaited his return to Quantico. He hated being out of touch, and gave some thought to that laptop he'd been thinking of purchasing.

His next call caught Eriq Santiva between meetings. Santiva gave him great praise at having so efficiently worked the case. "And all on your own," the chief added. "Enjoy New Orleans! Take whatever time you like."

They spoke briefly about Jessica's case in London, neither of them having heard from Jessica in some time now. Each promised to keep the other informed should they hear from Coran in London.

Sunday Evening, October 1, Scotland Yard

Jessica and Sharpe, skirting the peripheral corridors of Scotland Yard, found their way into the bowels of the building where Sharpe introduced Jessica to Ralph Crider, telling her that Crider knew more about film and film enhancement than anyone on the planet. Jessica left her film with Crider, who promised to have it developed and blown up to enlarge the map and scale models she'd taken pictures of at the RIBA. She lamented having had no time to take "normal pictures" here in London.

They carried on, as Richard called it, now past the computer archives to an archive predating the computer age, where hard-copy materials and microfiche remained housed in boxes and on shelves.

Still struck by the strangeness of the two "orphaned" twins named Houghton, Jessica insisted on searching the Yard's data banks on them, to see what might turn up. She again said to Richard, "I just know I recall something about a case dealing with a pair of twins from Gloucester."

They gained entry to the file rooms using Sharpe's identification. Soon their eyes marked the speeding trail of a microfiche tape machine, as the dates she was most interested in, the years between 1950 and 1960, sped by in a newspaper

history on the microfiche. The whining of the machine
sounded like a miniature siren wail as the tape sped past their
eyes.

Searching the index for the Houghton name in relation to
any crime or victimization, Jessica found several. She scrolled
first to one and then to another. On the third scroll, they found
the Houghton twins.

On the fiche a registration number told them where to look
for the police report, but here, staring back at them, was a
London Times article and pictures of the twins and their parents. Details of the case, while sketchy, came clearer and
clearer for Jessica as she read on, as they did for Richard,
who suddenly gasped, saying, "Of course! I now remember
the case well. Tragic, horrifying really. A real curler."

For Jessica, the veil had also been lifted, and she found it
strangely coincidental that the shocked, traumatized twins as
children were now hanging about St. Albans, getting spiritual
advice from Father Strand and Father Luc Sante.

While she scanned from photo to photo display, Jessica
thought of how little play the case had gotten in America. At
least in public America. But in police circles, the Houghton
case had caused quite a ripple and wave, especially among
forensics people. It had been a case in which the killers,
mother and father to the twins, almost escaped a just execution over a botched forensics trail of evidence, not unlike the
O. J. Simpson case in America in this regard.

Records clearly detailed the British case from 1954. Sharpe
began paraphrasing and reading aloud in her ear, saying, "The
father hailed from Gloucester, England . . . name of Frederick
Houghton . . . finally caught while burying a thirteenth victim."

"Literally caught in the act," she replied.

"Fifty-two-year-old Houghton confessed to over twelve additional murders, all of which his wife knew of and nine of
which she'd helped him to commit."

"Look here," she added, pointing at a buried paragraph and
saying, "the last victim's remains were located in someplace
called Finger Post Field."

"Some ten miles outside Gloucester, near the remains of

Houghton's first wife, his first victim," Richard read on.

Now, her memory jogged, Jessica recalled having read the details in Press Association, Britain's domestic news agency. Asa Holcraft had received the British news that way for as long as she'd known him. "Rosemary Houghton, the second wife, forty years of age," mused Jessica aloud now. "She had been charged with killing nine women, including her husband's own sixteen-year-old daughter, Heather."

Richard shook his head as though the gesture might ease the words he read aloud. "Houghton, a construction trade builder, was charged with killing the same nine women—Heather, a daughter from his first marriage and Heather's mother, his first wife."

Jessica read on in silence, Richard doing likewise over her shoulder, following her finger down the page.

Nine of the bodies were found below the Houghtons' house on Cromwell Street in Gloucester, some 110 miles west of London. Heather Houghton's body was discovered under the house of a former place of residence nearby. The eleventh body, that of the original Mrs. Houghton, Catherine Costello, had been located in a field in a place called Kempley, beside another victim, a former baby-sitter to the family who'd mysteriously disappeared some twenty years before.

"Amazing story, but where's the information on the twins?" she wondered aloud. "I remember twin little girls who lived in the house while all this was going on. There were other children in the house, too, but I particularly recall the twins for some reason."

"Read on," suggested Richard.

The thirteenth and final victim was yet another young baby-sitter, but in her case, the disappearance caused an uproar in the entire village. A search for her had gone on for weeks when Houghton, under pressure from his accomplice wife to rid the house of the "hot" body, found himself spotlighted by authorities, who had

begun to watch him on tips from neighbors about
strange goings-on in the Gloucester home where the girl
had baby-sat from time to time.

Something about the case which Jessica couldn't let go of:
The total devotion the killers had instilled in their children to
keeping the family secrets, as grisly and as gruesome as they
were. It harkened back to what Luc Sante had said about the
group mind, the power of authority figures and peer pressure,
the sort of brainwashing and conditioning, which in her estimation, never completely left a person, whether the conditioning was to the lifestyle of a survivalist, a KKK member,
a prisoner of war, a wrestling fan, or a child taught that murder, under the right circumstances, was all right; this mentality
or some remnant of guilt stayed with a person forever. She
pushed on with the article, reading:

There were five children living under the same roof
with Mr. and Mrs. Houghton besides Heather. When
Heather disappeared and next the baby-sitter, too many
unanswered questions went wanting. The additional
five children, two of them young twin girls, were all
taken into custody and placed in the care of authorities.

Jessica assumed these Houghton children had all been
placed in child welfare and protective agencies, and later
found homes. The two Houghton twins she'd met earlier, according to Father Luc Sante, were nowadays devoted to helping others in the cause of Jesus Christ, but each of the sisters
lived behind big, onyx glass eyes, glazed over at that. They
appeared drugged, at least on a mild sedative, she believed.
Perhaps, even now, they must continue on a regimen of psy-
choactive drugs to hold back the horrors of their childhood,
in order to *not* live a life condemning their own parents who,
out of a core evil that included abuse, murder, incest, and
forced sodomy on their own children as final insult.

Once again, Jessica must face Luc Sante as a possible suspect in the crucifixion murders. Obviously, he had access to
various drugs and would know how to use Brevital.

Jessica could not help but wonder just how traumatized the two grown children of parental abuse must still be, and just how long Dr. Luc Sante, as a psychotherapist had had them under his care and treatment. She further wondered just how far the two bug-eyed creatures might go to further their cause in the name of the Father, the Son, and the Holy Ghost.

She shared these fears with Richard, somehow relaxing them by putting words to her fears and sharing with another person.

The name Gloucester, too, sounded familiar, and a quick check of the birthplace of Theodore "Burtie" Burton came up Gloucester. Another simple coincidence? Britain was, after all, an island nation, and life popped full with synchronicity and coincidence every day here. Still, Jessica could hardly help questioning these two hounds, coming as they did on one another's heels, yipping away at one another.

Good Inspector Sharpe, too, had difficulty simply swallowing these two examples of chance at play in the fields of murder in one generation so unkind and cruel, and the crucifixion murders in this generation.

"What do we do with this information?" she asked.

"It all remains relatively circumstantial."

"Agreed. I've lost cases on more evidence."

They fell silent, each locked in thought for some time before Jessica blurted out, "I think it's time we got a search warrant for St. Albans."

"St. Albans? A church? You want a sanctuary for evil to—oops!—sorry, a Freudian, I suppose. Do you really expect that a sanctuary for any and all in peril—such as the Houghton twins—to be served with a search warrant? In London?"

"I realize this isn't the South Bronx or West Queens, but we are dealing with a radical situation here, and the timetable on the body count has risen and will only continue to rise if we don't do something."

"I tell you, getting a court order to raid a Catholic church in London, or anywhere in Great Britain, will not do. I'm afraid we've not progressed too far in that area since Henry the Eighth. But what we could do is approach from the bridge, the canal, the end of that labyrinthine tunnel we saw on the map. That's public domain."

"Are you suggesting we go it alone?"

"Everyone else is concentrating efforts elsewhere, looking in the wrong place, I fear. Convinced by Boulte and company that surveillancing the waterways is our best effort. It appears Chief Inspector Boulte has everyone out in force doing so. So, I'm afraid we're on our own."

"That could be damned risky. I don't have a desire to find myself spread-eagle on a resurrection cross, Richard."

"Do not tempt me. It presents a fairly juicy picture to this person, love."

"Stop that."

"I will not," he teased further.

"All right, as soon as we have the maps in hand, we go," she agreed.

Sharpe had not exaggerated Crider's gift for magic with film. The maps were sharp and clear and easily read. They took them in hand at 8:26 P.M. and left the Yard without anyone but Crider having known they'd been in the archives.

Sharpe made a detour along the route back to the Marylebone district, stopping off at the RIBA in search of someone familiar with the locks and canals of London. Someone who had the right know-how and tools to open a locked grate covering an ancient canal below the city, someone who knew a clapper bridge when confronted with one.

As luck would have it, Donald Wentworth Tatham turned out to be the ready "soldier" on the spot, as Sharpe referred to him. Together, Sharpe, Jessica, and Tatham traveled toward the far northern border of Marylebone, at the terminus of a canal no longer in use, serving only as a drainage ditch and locked away from the sight of men for some forty-eight-odd years.

Sharpe dug out large, powerful flashlights from the boot of his car, along with the Wellington boots he'd scavenged for the three of them. "The Wellingtons," he told Jessica, "are the same as used by veterinarians when mucking about pigs-tys and cow sheds. You'll be glad you have them."

Now they approached the silent, sealed grate which had grown over with vines, weeds, and vegetation for birds to build nests in. It took a good ten minutes for Tatham to locate the lock in order to insert the key, and even unlocked, the grate, sealed now with layers of rust and tightly bound by tenacious, stalky clinging vines, refused them entry.

"Bloody 'ell," moaned Sharpe. "It'll be dark before we're a foot through."

The three of them, using their combined weight and strength struggled for some time, standing in the drainage ditch, to pry the grate open far enough that they could squeeze through. Skittering eels played about them here in the water.

"Well done," gasped Richard. Turning to Tatham, he added, "Your job is done then. Off with you, Dr. Tatham."

"You'll be lost inside an hour and never find your way back without me," Tatham firmly declared. "Don't be a fool, Sharpe. I think I should accompany you and Dr. Coran to your destination . . . Which would be . . . ?"

"Where's the map?"

Jessica, who held the map out of the water, said, "Here you go, Richard."

"We want to come out below St. Albans, the church, somewhere about here, I should think."

"The church, really? You suspect the church somehow involved in the murders?" asked Tatham.

"Not the church, but perhaps a churchman?"

"Never. You can't seriously suggest that Father Luc Sante of St. Albans the Crucifier!"

"More likely his soon-to-be replacement, but again it's all speculation until we find some concrete evidence."

Tatham remained incredulous. "Such as?"

"Such as a resurrection cross, some large spikes, an altar of sacrifice perhaps, whatever we might find," Jessica impatiently filled Tatham in.

Tatham's eyes lit up like a Boy Scout's when he said, "Quite the expedition then, really."

Sharpe leaned into Jessica and whispered, "I rather wish Coppers was with us."

She couldn't agree more, and nodding, her flash indicating

her movement, as it bounced off the ancient, cobbled walls, blackened by shadow and age. The trickle of water, moving with their swaying step, reminded them all of where they stood. "Well, Guv', let's shove off then, shall we?" Jessica suggested in her best attempt at a Cockney accent. "Dr. Tatham, lead the way."

· NINETEEN ·

Has it become human nature for the individual to forfeit his or her ethical judgment (moral judgment, identity, personality, mind, and soul) to the leader, to the cause, to the fanaticism? Unfortunately, we are witnessing the result of this weakness in the human fabric with increasing numbers giving themselves over to cult beliefs.

—DR. ASA HOLCRAFT, M.E.

Jessica and Sharpe—now determined to literally look under Luc Sante's rug, to see if anything might be hiding below St. Albans—continued through the black tunnel, following the canal, sloshing the stagnant water ahead of them, sending vermin racing ahead of them as well.

"This dungeon passage looks like something out of a horror novel or Tolkien," Jessica complained.

"Watch out for the little people," agreed Sharpe.

"Gnomes have been known to inhabit underground passageways," Tatham joined the fun.

Jessica felt strange here, out of time and place, the very walls so ancient they must have seen the Dark Ages. In fact the air here felt sodden with age, perhaps the odor of time itself. Whatever she might label it, it felt palpable and alive and smelling like the grave. The odor mutated as they stepped deeper and deeper into this damp abyss until the stench smelled like rancid meat put over a flame. The odor clawed at her, choking her.

She hated their having to be here like this, skulking about below London streets for the subterranean regions below St. Albans. She hated herself for the fact she had to be deceitful and lying to Father Luc Sante, that she had to have such dark suspicions of the man she so admired. She genuinely liked this old man of the cloth, who held the hope that all mankind might read their own dream-talk in order to find solace and happiness in a pitiless world. She had earlier delighted in Luc Sante's presence, respected him, admired this follower of Christ and Jung, and yet there appeared something amiss, something afoot, something evil that passed for good wandering Luc Sante's church corridors, peering out the cathedral windows, making friendly with the gargoyles that perched over St. Albans.

The Houghton twins still disturbed her, the fact they were from the same town as Luc Sante's first ministry disturbed her. As Luc Sante's own admission had revealed, he had once practiced his ministry and psychotherapy at Bury St. Edmunds, the place from which Katherine O' Donahue, the first victim, had hailed. Sharpe agreed with Jessica that the coincidence could not be ignored.

"I made further inquiries into Luc Sante's past," Richard told her as they trekked onward through the dismal tunnel that appeared to be—*and felt as if*—it were on a slight incline, as the water level rose with each step, now spilling over the tops of their Wellingtons.

"So, what did your further inquiries tell you?"

"He has spent time at the parish of every victim on the list."

She visibly blanched. "Then we must be pointed on the right track. That's a bit more than coincidental, I'd say, as much as I hate to admit."

"And there's something more."

"Yes?"

"Father Strand . . . He's the one who prompted my inquiries to begin with, and believe me, just try to get information on a clergyman in this town. In any case, Martin Strand was born in Bury St. Edmunds, into the very parish where Luc Sante preached to Katherine O'Donahue. He was one of Luc Sante's choirboys."

"Then Strand has known Luc Sante all these years, even as a boy . . . How large a congregation might it have been at the time? Enough for Luc Sante to have forgotten Katherine O'Donahue?"

"Likely seven, perhaps eight hundred tops."

"He may not have recognized the name after all these years," she countered.

"And Strand? What excuse do you provide for him?"

She had none.

"Young Strand appears indoctrinated, I should hazard a guess."

"Or rather, Strand believes himself gone beyond the master?" she challenged. "Might he have gone from choirboy to prophet of the Second Coming?"

Richard stopped to stare into her eyes, bringing his light up to her face, asking, "What do you mean?"

"I've seen the way the two interact. Strand condescends to the old man. He's anxious to take over at St. Albans. Suppose . . . Might we not suppose that Strand, and not Father Luc Sante, is masterminding the crucifixions? As a student of Luc Sante's logic, Strand, twisting it, may well have taken the ultimate step in the ultimate search to . . . to . . ."

"To ultimately end all evil in the universe by working through a twisted faith?"

"You do see the possibility, then, don't you? The disciple, taking the words of his master, buckling them to his belief, his faith . . . twisted faith. And so enter the cult mentality. Hell, anyone might take Luc Sante's plan for a psychotherapy of evil to go seek it out and defuse it, but a minister of the Christian faith, believing it his mission, that certainly might put a spin on murder neither of us, Richard, have seen before."

"One for the courts, anyway," he mused. "Still, suppose the two of them, Strand and Luc Sante, are together in this? We know that it requires at least two men to hoist another onto a cross and nail him there."

"Two *able-bodied* men. Have you looked at Luc Sante, lately? He's failing, a weak old man, while Strand looks as if he'd just stepped off the pages of *Billy Budd*."

"Do you rank him with Billy Budd?"

"No, yes, not really . . . in a curious way, perhaps, but no," she finally decided. "But returning to my point, if Martin

Strand has a cult following behind him, he won't lack for muscle."

They came to a T-intersection. Tatham—who'd been earnestly listening to their conversation, which even when whispered, reverberated about the sepulcher here—stood deciding which was east and which was west toward St. Albans.

"This way," he finally said. The torches—as the two British men called the flashlights—bounced off the water and the blackened walls as they now entered what was once the actual black mine shaft. Their lights wildly reflected giant shadows ahead of them, dappling reflections and a startlingly black sheen to the walls. The shadows at play ahead of them startled Jessica, until Tatham pointed out that the black images would prove their own. Jessica thought it like watching one's own astral projection.

The silence and the chill of this place seeped into the living bone, feeding every childhood phobia and every adult irrational fear.

"Afraid the coincidences building against Luc Sante in this case can no longer be rationalized away or ignored," Richard commented as the floor beneath them began a sharper rise.

"Naturally," she agreed, but added, "however, being a cleric and being a psychotherapist, Father and Luc Sante is likely to be surrounded by the walking wounded, remnants of man's inhumanity to man, such as the Houghton twins, and possibly Burton, O'Donahue, Coibby, and others like them. Simple people leading simple lives that, for one reason or another became complicated lives, too difficult to handle alone, without professional help." She drummed her fingers along her cheek, thinking of a time when she, too, had found her life spinning out of control, when she needed the help of an outsider in the form of Dr. Donna LeMonte, now a lifelong friend and confidante. She wondered if it had been the same with Katherine O'Donahue, Burtie Burton, Coibby, Woodard, all the crucified victims.

"If so, if it were mere innocent happenstance, a weird kind of serendipity or synchronicity, why hide the fact he knew these people? O'Donahue, in particular, I mean."

Jessica considered the logic of it, Sharpe's logic, so tight and secure and sure. "It stands to reason that troubled souls, the ill and infirm, the weak and helpless, all the societal "victims" of a harsh world, victims of alienation, child abuse, rape, incest might flock to a man like Luc Sante for confession, redemption, salvation. His book alone would draw them near, not to mention his sermons and his practice," she said to Sharpe now as they arrived in a wide corridor where they could step from the canal water and follow alongside on a concrete levy. "To date the only single piece of evidence tying the victims of the crucifixion killings together remains the meager message left on their tongues, but what if it means far more than Luc Sante or anyone else has suggested or suspected?"

"Not quite sure I follow you," he replied, and for a moment, she thought she saw something sinister playing amid the flickering of the torch light and the light in Richard's eyes.

She shrugged it off, anxious for him to hear her fully, so on she explained, saying, "It would take monumental acceptance of a leader to hold out one's tongue to allow such a hot-iron branding."

"Then you've determined the branding occurred before death?"

"Absolutely. Dr. Raehael left the findings on my temporary voice mail."

"You forget the victims were drugged."

"No, I am not forgetting that. I'm saying that even in their drugged state, to stand and allow their tongues to be yanked outward and upward, likely by pinchers, then branded on the bottom side, that they—the victims—may have been *willing agents* in their own crucifixion deaths."

"That's astounding. An astounding conclusion."

"But altogether fitting with what we know about cults and the cult mentality, whole congregations checking out en masse—no pun intended. Add to what we've learned over the years about such cult thinking. Luc Sante makes the same point in his *Twisted Faiths*."

"His book, you mean?"

"Yes. It has been assumed the victims were either drugged or tied to the cross upon which they were crucified to have

their tongues branded, but suppose, like the bug-eyed sisters
I saw at Luc Sante's cathedral, that every cult member willingly stepped forward to be branded at some time or other
long before they were crucified, and if so, then they, too, had
become sheep, followers to a cause, and this meant only one
thing, that they were not victims so much of murder as they
were of religious zealotry and sleight-of-hand. And—"

"And what if the magician were none other than Father
Jerrard Luc Sante who masked his evil with his own philosophy of what evil in this life actually looks, speaks, smells,
and feels like."

Jessica took up his thinking, adding, "Suppose all the victims were anxious to follow in the footsteps of Christ by way
of the Father, Luc Sante? Or possibly Father Strand? What if
all were anxious to be the next 'Chosen One,' to be crucified
in the shadow of the millennia, to take on the role of the new
Messiah?"

"Sounds both preposterous and right for our century,
wouldn't you agree, Tatham?" asked Sharpe, who wondered
what a more impartial outsider to the case might make of such
talk.

Tatham gasped but picked up the pace of the discussion at
once, mumbling, "Your theory, Dr. Coran, when presented to
your superiors could put the two of you in the fun house with
my aunt Dee-Dee."

"Does sound far-fetched, even preposterous," agreed Jessica, "but it's exactly that kind of thinking which allows the
behavior of a Jeffrey Dahmer type to coexist alongside normal
people who don't murder and eat one another."

Richard nodded, saying, "Agreed. It's that counterproduc-
tive editing of our intuition that makes victims of us all. Think
of it! Each victim was quite religiously . . . mad? Would you
say, *over* the edge, insane with an obsession, to be the Chosen
One. At least obsessively driven in his or her faith?"

"Burton converted . . . Maybe so he could show his devotion to the cult."

"A cult catering to the aged and the highly religious who'd
given up on the usual, organized religion for something more
promising?" she suggested. "I'd have called your theory too

mad in itself, too outer fringe to actually be worth pursuing, but with what's gone on here of late," Jessica replied as they trudged on, "it rather rings plausible."

"Given the state of cults in the free world today, anything's possible," Richard agreed.

"Not sure anyone else would believe it, however."

"I'm afraid it's too much for me," added Tatham, "and it would appear we've come to the end of our journey. Look ahead."

Their combined lights illuminated a dead end, an impenetrable brick wall, lichen growing on it here in the blackness of this world. Scurrying rats made *pitter-patter* noises like the sound of miniature hooves over cobblestone.

"There's no way beyond it?" asked Richard.

" 'Fraid not from the look of it . . ." Tatham and Richard sought a crevice, a roundabout, but the area had been sealed many long years before.

"What about the canal? Where did it go?"

"Veered off in another direction somewhere behind us."

"Perhaps if we followed it."

"I don't think it would help, as it goes off away from the church. You wanted near St. Albans from what I gather, right?"

"Yes, yes indeed." Richard's disappointment resounded in the cavern where they stood.

"I see no way out but the way we came," Jessica said, even as she searched the walls here for a doorway, a set of stone steps leading up or down, any sign at all that they were not completely dead-ended. "We've managed to investigate our way into a blind corner."

"What about the other corridor at the T-section," suggested Richard, stubbornly hanging on.

"I tell you, it would take you nowhere near St. Albans," Tatham assured them.

"Why the deuce doesn't this wall show up on the specs?" shouted Richard, his voice bouncing off the slick walls.

"We're not dealing with specs. We're looking at it twice removed, from my replicas and maps made from the ancient maps, and then from your photo enlargements. We're lucky to have found our destination at all."

"Some destination," grumbled Richard.

She knew that to Sharpe, the wall represented far more than a wall below London's streets. To him it must mean an impenetrable barrier leading to an inglorious end to his entire career.

"Come on, Richard," she coaxed. "Let's get out of this vile place."

He finally nodded, indicating the way. "Yes, let's find the world. Why I ever let you talk me into mucking about here, I don't know."

"Richard, it was your idea."

"My idea, indeed!"

"You brought RIBA into it, remember?"

He frowned in Tatham's direction, Tatham saying just the worst thing in response. "Sorry, old man, things didn't work out as expected."

"Just lead us back to light, Dr. Tatham," Richard groused. Silence and regret marked their arduous journey back.

Their Wellington boots, dripping and smelling of the stagnant water from the out-of-use canal, Jessica and Sharpe drove Tatham back to the RIBA where they had enlisted his help, bidding him good-night and thanks. He waved them off and they drove back toward Victoria Gardens Embankment and the York.

"I desperately need a shower," Jessica said.

"Feeling a bit dirty from ratting around in the sewers?"

"You know it."

"Yes, I feel the same way."

"Your place is on the way. Stop over, pick up an overnight bag, and come stay the night with me," she suggested.

"Are you sure?"

"I'm sure I don't want to be alone tonight."

"I don't relish the thought, either. If you're quite sure."

"Quite, yes. And when's the last time you showered with a woman?" she asked.

He smiled and reached out to her, squeezing her hand

warmly in his. "You've made me care about things of that
sort again, Jessica, small things like touch and warmth. It's
rather true what Luc Sante says about the child within us all,
clamoring to surface, to be given attention. Somehow, with
you, when we're intimate, I feed that child all and more than
he ever bargained for."

She reached across, and tugging at her seat belt, she kissed
his cheek. "You've made London a beautiful place to be,
despite all the shadowland horror we're chasing."

He smiled. "You've made life a great deal more bearable
for certain, dear Jessica."

Again, they spent a warm, affectionate evening together,
indulging in fantasies, one providing whatever the other
wished, and then the other reciprocating. Jessica had always
felt that making love in the shower, under the warm spray, to
be the perfect place to begin a night of unbridled passion.

The following day, Jessica awoke to find Richard gone, a
note announcing that he had been unable to sleep, and so he
had gone into the office to get an early start on much ne-
glected paperwork.

Jessica prepared for her day, showering and dressing with
much thought given to what she guessed Richard would like.
She had learned that his favorite color on her to be blue, and
that he liked to see her hair held back by a band across the
front. "It's much softer than wearing your hair up always,"
he'd said.

She dressed for Richard this day.

She had decided that whatever came, whatever evolved
from their intimacies, she would accept. She'd become so
intensely focused on James Parry when she had fallen in love
with him that, in a sense, she had become a prisoner, a shackled person, shackled by her own emotions and fears and passions. She found she had as much, if not more feeling for
Richard, and yet, this love felt intensely novel, startlingly and
wholly unconventional, despite Richard's "conventional" veneer; in fact, this love felt freeing, liberating in every sense
of the word, delivering her from . . . she must wonder *from
what*?

Actually, she told herself, Richard Sharpe delivered Jessica

Coran from Jessica Coran. He made her feel completely free; his love was not measured in give-and-takes, compromises or restraining demands. His love knew no constraints and placed no constraints on her. She could never be the object of his love, for he did not treat her as an object. Rather, he treated her as his equal, and he asked for no ties, no commitments, and expected none to be hoisted upon him. In a word, Richard Sharpe turned out to be the most continental man she'd ever known.

Once dressed as she felt Richard would like, Jessica hurried out to Scotland Yard, hoping that today she and Sharpe would find a solution to the Crucifier mystery.

Just as she stepped from the door, however, the phone rang. Richard, she thought, and not wishing to miss his call, she returned to find an excited J. T., filled with good news about the outcome of the Tattoo Man's case.

She had to slow J. T. down, thinking he might hyperventilate on the other end as the story of Maxwell Sanocre unfolded. Jessica encouraged him to take it slow and to tell her everything.

J. T. told how he had located the dead man's family, and how it appeared from all evidence that members of his own family had first plotted and then killed the man.

"As it turns out, the dead man's own children arranged for both the dogs to tear him to shreds and for the rabies infection, to insure his death. The daughter in particular really hated the old man, and she had damned good reason to."

"What reason led her to kill him?"

"She had a child by him. Incest. Then she tries to get out from it, tries to marry a boyfriend, but the old man won't hear of it. Says nobody but him is 'good enough' for his baby girl. Sick, I know."

"Evil is what it is. A man deprives his own daughter of a natural life."

"The boyfriend, whom she did marry only days after her father was killed, turns out to be an apprentice veterinarian. He saw to the rabies, but the dogs they used, the dogs actually belonged to the old man. Family says he treated his dogs better than he did his wife and children."

"Sounds like one man who deserved what he got," she muttered.

"More I learn about the case, more I'm thinking the same, and we're educated doctors, Jess."

"So? We can hate with the best of 'em, J. T."

"The old man was infuriated at his daughter for wanting a normal life. Blocked her every avenue. I think the court will have to take in the circumstances, show some mercy. Sure it was a vicious murder, but in a sense, the girl was driven to it."

"And the accomplice?"

"Nice young man by all accounts, but premeditating with the rabies like that. It's not going to go down well. The rabies was his idea."

"How do you know he's not covering for her, that it wasn't her idea all along?"

J. T. considered this. "You're right. Could well be."

"Hell hath no fury like a woman scorned."

"You may have something there, Jess."

"Find out how long the boy and girl had been seeing one another. The shorter the time period, the more likely she hatched the whole show, putting him up to it."

"They'd been seeing each other for less than a month when they started planning the details and planning their marriage. The boy meant to raise her child as his own, and they meant to have children between them as well, start a real family, she told her cousin."

"Her cousin?"

"Her cousin's the authority in Diamondback, Louisiana."

"I see."

"Max Sanocre had only been missed by people in his biker gang, but word had been put out that he'd gone to Utah to allow both John Law and rival gang members to cool off, because he had—according to an elaborate story circulated by his children—somehow pissed both parties off, so that no one had the least suspicion that Cassie's father, Maxwell 'Abominable' Sanocre was even dead."

" 'Abominable'?"

"It's what he went by."

"Sounds like you did one hell of job on this one, J. T."

"Thanks. I am feeling pretty good about now. Chillin' in Naw'leens, right now."

"Great, but tell me, J. T., how'd you get all these people to confess down there in Diamondhead?"

"Back. Diamondback. And I did it by just showing up."

"Showing up what?"

"Just showed up on their doorstep. It seemed like the girl and the boy, they just expected me, and when they saw me standing there, they just gave it up."

"Maybe that's what I need to do on this case."

"What do you mean? You have a suspect, and you think if you just showed up on his doorstep that a guy like this serial killer Crucifier guy is going to just give it up? London's a far cry from Diamondback, and I suspect Londoners are a bit different than Diamondbackers, Jess, so I'd be a bit more cautious than—"

"Than you were? You could have just as easily disappeared in that remote area of Louisiana as not, J. T. But hey, don't worry about me. I'm not going to do anything foolish to endanger myself. Hell, look how long I've gone without any scars. I've got a record to maintain, and a pool to win back at Quantico," she joked.

J. T. laughed, finding this amusing, adding, "Hey, who do you think started the pool?"

They parted with good-byes and well wishes, and Jessica started anew for Scotland Yard, but at the cab stand, rather than walk over to the Yard, she made a detour.

"I'll just show up on Luc Sante's doorstep," she told herself. "See what gives if he knows that I know." The doorman hailed the next available cab in line to come forward to pick Jessica up. When she climbed inside, she announced, "St. Albans, the Marylebone district, please."

"Ahhh, St. Albans, a wonderful old lady, she is," the cabby said of the church.

"Yes, beautiful really," she agreed.

"Married me wife in that church, twenty-six years ago, God rest her soul."

Jessica tried to formulate what she would say to Father Luc

Sante, how to arrange the list of coincidences, the list of questions and suspicions so as to best checkmate the man. She feared she would botch it, but she realized now that the entire time they had spent together in the past, the old man meant to recruit her, to win her over and to make her his newest convert, that he indeed had some sort of strange power over her as he did over others, and that he ran some sort of cult following somewhere out of the light of the Catholic church, out of the light of all other judging bodies and out of sight of people he could not control. But what to say to this man, and how to say it . . . How to trap him in his own lair, using his own lures . . .

· TWENTY ·

The lie has seven endings...

—ANONYMOUS SWAHILI PROVERB

Slowly, Richard Sharpe had begun to win young Stuart Copperwaite over to the idea that somehow Luc Sante had been connected with the violent deaths of the crucifixion victims all along. Sharpe had spent the morning trying to convince Copperwaite of the weight of the evidence pointing to the old man and minister.

Together now, in a stairwell, Richard wanting no one else to overhear, he forced the issue onto Stuart who had raged at him for having disappeared.

Copperwaite could hardly believe his ears on hearing of the underground trek Richard and Jessica Coran had taken in the company of the RIBA man the day before. He could hardly believe that both Sharpe and Dr. Coran had, independently, arrived at the same conclusion, that somehow St. Albans and Luc Sante had become focal points in some sort of bizarre, twisted Second Coming–Millennium cult. He haltingly said, "I cannot begin to believe that the two of you, M.E. and inspector, as levelheaded as you are, have concocted this incredible theory—not from whole cloth but from cheesecloth, this 'fantabulous' idea," as he put it.

However, Sharpe persisted, laying out the number of bizarre crossovers and connections and coincidences involving Luc Sante.

Someone pushed through the stairwell door just below them, and Sharpe put a finger to his lips, not wishing for anyone to hear Copperwaite's pronouncements. When it became clear that they were alone again, Sharpe continued, saying, "He's bloody protected not only by his sterling reputation, but by the bloody church," Sharpe barked in ending. "But I've spent hours piecing it together, and there is a major organization behind all the smaller organizations to which each victim has left his worldly goods. It's St. Albans itself. With the help of computer sleuth Gyles Harney, I just got that piece of the puzzle today."

"That is remarkable," Copperwaite agreed, astonished.

"The organization and care with which the donations from the victims were masked, that took some expertise in computers, but Gyles managed to unravel it for me. No one can unravel like Gyles."

"And none can unwind so well as Gyles."

Sharpe managed a smile, the first he'd shared with Copperwaite since the falling out. "Aye, Gyles likes his pint."

Copperwaite bit back his confusion, gnarling on his lower lip. "And so, we're caught out. We can't bloody get a search warrant against St. Albans."

"Nor is it likely we'll get one for Saint Luc's house or office—being attached to the church—either."

"And in the meantime, what do we do? Wait until another victim shows up in another body of water somewhere around town?" asked Copperwaite, exasperated, pounding a closed fist into the wall.

"We take no bloody action until we can prove what we now merely think, Copperwaite," warned Sharpe. "Our hands are tied."

"Unless we can get Luc Sante on tape, admitting to his new cult following, and the fact he's involved in these deaths," suggested Copperwaite.

"And just how do you propose doing that?"

"He seems to've been working overtime to convert Dr. Coran."

"No, I won't endanger her, Stuart."

"You're bloody in love with her, aren't you?"

"We share a great deal. Love, I don't know that I would go that far." Sharpe's inner mind mulled the question over. It hadn't occurred to him to call it love. Certainly, Jessica had not ever used the word, and he had been careful not to, and it all seemed somewhat of a younger man's game, this thing called love. Still, he found himself thinking of her always, to distraction, he warned himself now.

"But it may be our only hope. Have Coran wear a wire, with us nearby. Suppose I'm right?"

"Right about Luc Sante's wishing to win her over to his new world order and religion. I can see that now. He's been building up to it all along, but I daresay she's given him no encouragement."

"She encourages by her very being, by her engaging him, returning to him, don't you see?" Copperwaite next suggested they walk up a flight for the exercise and so that they didn't appear too damnably suspicious here. Sharpe agreed, and they trekked up a flight.

"By God, Coppers, you are going to make a fine full inspector, one day. That's rather an insightful point you've made, perhaps one I've been blinded to, being . . . Since I've become so fond of Jessica."

"If you take it a step further, Richard, if what you suspect Luc Sante of, then it follows that he may well see Dr. Coran as . . . well, as a perfect candidate for crucifixion?"

"Thanks for that, Coppers. You've the target in the cross-hairs indeed."

"What will you tell Dr. Coran?"

"I'll tell her what she wants to hear, that we're going to move on Luc Sante, one blasted way or another."

"Then you will propose her wearing a wire device?" asked Copperwaite, standing still now at the top stair.

"Yes, if it's the only way. Can you arrange for the device, the surveillance van, all of it?"

"Consider it done, Sharpie."

"I must contact Jessica. See if she is willing to become the sacrificial lamb."

"She's not likely to say no to you, Richard. She hasn't so far."

"Curb your tongue, Coppers. She's every bit a lady."

"Meaning no harm, Sharpe."

"Good, keep it so, and get the surveillance team together, then."

"Right-o."

Copperwaite disappeared through the door to their right, while Sharpe took the stairs back down for another exit. He'd decided that Luc Sante had too many friends on the force, too many eyes and ears. He wanted the element of surprise to be on their side when and if he decided to arrest. "Arrest for what?" he asked himself now. "On suspicion of being the Crucifier? On the suspicion the man had wantonly killed five human beings? That he showed a depraved indifference to human life?" Precisely what could he make stick to a priest of Father Luc Sante's standing in the community?

Luc Sante looked up from his scribblings to confront the shadow that suddenly lengthened and scurried across his desk. He half expected to look up and into the eyes of Satan himself, for so many years his archrival and enemy, but instead he found a stern-looking, somber Dr. Jessica Coran firmly rooted before him.

"Ahhh, Dr. Coran, amazing you should show up this way. I was just wondering how I might entice you back through request or invitation. I have so enjoyed our talks, and you're such a wonderful conversationalist."

Flattery, she thought, *will get you everywhere you want to be, if the target of flattery is weak-minded, weak-kneed, feeble, or strung out on drugs. How many poor slobs had Father Luc Sante lured into his cult through the kind word?* "I hardly call what I did conversing, Dr. Luc Sante."

"And why would you not call our conversations conversation, my dear?"

"You delightedly talked, I delightedly listened."

"Are you suggesting that it was *tutelage*? I the teacher, you the student to be filled like some empty container? I hardly think it so."

"Tutelage perhaps? Perhaps persuasion?" she countered.

"My arguments are admittedly persuasive, practiced, I confess."

"Honeyed, sometimes wondrous," she characterized his arguments.

He only laughed lightly and smiled. "I masterfully led you, like a talented dancer, through the intricacies of my thinking, but it hardly can be called propaganda or an attempt to change you or your thinking, my dear, at least not without your consent."

"My consent?"

"Your absolute consent, for without consent, there is no truth in a gesture, be it making love or committing one's soul to the Almighty."

Any time now, she thought to herself, *any time now you can just spew forth your confession to me like the kids in Diamondback had done for J. T., but I guess I won't hold my breath on that score.* Instead, she crazily, insanely wanted to totally give in to Luc Sante here, now. She wanted to allow his verbal symphony on the eternal truths and the eternal battle of good over evil to manipulate her, to use her, place her as another pawn on his cosmic chessboard.

She resisted, however, in the deepest part of herself, and in turn she began to manipulate him, telling him, "I've actually come about the case. I've a theory you must hear and verify for its veracity."

"A theory of your making?"

"Yes."

"Go on."

"Perhaps the victims are not what they appear to be."

"A victim is a victim, how else should a victim appear?" he replied in caustic staccato.

"If a victim is a perfect victim, as in a willing victim, has she not been persuaded that in becoming a victim, that she, in some small measure, helps in God's cosmic plan for the universe? You see, Dr. Luc Sante, where I'm going with this?"

He looked confusedly across at her where she now sat in the big leather chair opposite him. "A willing victim, a perfect victim to this foul villain who is leaving a trail of blood across

London. You *are* speaking hypothetically, I pray?"

"Hypothetically, yes, but what do you think of the theory of the crime? That there are willing, perfect victims among us, and I suspect the Crucifier has found them in the sick, the feeble and infirm. My autopsy on Burton showed him to have colon cancer, and I suspect the other victims, too, were facing some sort of health crisis, and perhaps found leaving this world in the fashion they did easier than suicide. Suicide closes the gate on eternal life, but sacrifice, now that's another story altogether, now isn't it, Father?"

"Depends upon what it is your are sacrificing and to whom, I should think."

"Imagine if all of the Crucifier's victims were willing participants in their own sacrifices. It might make sense of this bizarre case."

"Yes, yes, of course, the literature of religion and cults is littered with examples of just that, yes. I suggested this early on in the case. Richard Sharpe knew of my fears along these lines. I suggested the victims could be participant members of a cult, or don't you recall?"

"Yes, well, the possibility's been staring us in the face for some time now, hasn't it?" She stared for a moment at the painting over his desk of the hamlet and small parish in the English countryside, a place of purity and innocence, the image of peace on earth, his former parish, he'd called it. Then she added, "Victims who voluntarily go to their deaths, imagine it. Imagine the impulse to be a major part of the Second Coming. Certainly, if convinced of this . . . Well, I can appreciate the longing, the need to be part of something greater, larger than oneself, can't you?"

"Yes, I can imagine it."

She wondered what she might say to get him to admit to one incriminating word, to state that he had been working overtime in his attempt to mesh with his God, to mesh with Jesus Christ, and in so doing, bring about the Second Coming.

"Do you believe, Father Luc Sante, that a person can be born into this world a victim, that his or her fate from the day of birth is stamped victim of murder?"

Luc Sante suddenly and forcefully disagreed, shouting

"No!", his fist coming down on his desk like a hammer. "A child is sent from God, and a child demands to be born, and we are all placed here for a reason, not some reason we fabricate, but a reason He alone fashions. We have no say so in it, and we must listen to our inner voice. No one is created by God for the express purpose of being murdered."

"What about created as a sacrificial lamb, then?"

He shook his head, considering this. "There is so much evil waiting here for the innocent. True enough, but innocence must face evil, do battle with it, struggle against it. Speaking of which, actually, I've recently had my eye on Strand," he said with a conspiratorial whisper, a finger raised to his lips as if telling her to keep it down. "Sometimes, I believe these old walls are filled with gossiping ghosts."

"What is your concern about Father Strand?"

"Strange business going on hereabouts, that is between here and the street bazaar that I've only recently learned of. You know, I fear that Martin is no saint after all, but the very sort of being I've spent my entire life combating, the sort that disguises himself even in the robes of the church."

She felt intrigued. "Tell me more of your suspicions, Father." She felt hopeful, that if Luc Sante could point her in another direction, it might prove him the innocent victim here, too.

"Well, I've my suspicions now that—God help us—that Strand could be involved in something sinister. Even that he could be this . . . this awful, godless Crucifier himself."

This came as a revelation to Jessica and a welcomed one. "What makes you suspect him?"

"I learned of some questionable bills. That's how my suspicions were first fueled. These led to even more questionable donations, death gifts, actually. As it turns out, Coibby, O'Donahue, Burton, all of them have left funds with St. Albans through roundabout means, and it smacks as suspicious as bloody . . . as can be, you see."

"How long have you known of this?"

"I only just uncovered the evidence. I was here writing a letter to Sharpe on the matter. Look, look for yourself."

She crouched forward and turned the paper he had been

writing on, and yes, in black and white, he had been asking Sharpe to look into his findings, to determine what connection Strand might have with the murders.

"I tell you I am now frightened to be alone around the man. But I did not link the problem at first with murder, of course, until I telephoned the bank. He's been forging my name to accommodate himself in whatever manner he sees fit. He made a major purchase from an antique store."

"What sort of purchase?"

"An altar of some sort, an altar I have not seen."

"Are you certain of this?"

"I inquired. The storeman I spoke to over the phone thought me mad. Said I had paid for it with my own personal check. Forged, you see."

"His own personal altar?"

"I've not seen or located it. I have no idea where it stands. But this and my curiosity about what he does with his evenings . . . Well, I'd often wondered over that . . . and so last night I followed him down to the bazaar near old Crown's End pub on Oxford Street, and there I lost him. You know how crowded Oxford is always with tourists, all the quaint shops there. He disappeared into thin air before me, somehow into the bowels of the underworld there."

"Underworld? What underworld?"

"There's said to be a series of catacombs and vaults, old cellars left over from Roman times down there below the bazaar. No one goes there of course, rat-infested, perhaps a few homeless living down there, but Martin somehow disappeared there."

"Shall we go have a look?" she asked.

"By all means, but shouldn't we call for what is it? Backup? As they say in police parlance?"

"If we find something, we'll call for backup. Come on. Lead me to where he disappeared."

"First, I want to settle your mind about St. Albans."

She looked queerly back at him.

"Don't deny it. I know you've come to suspect me in all this hideous affair. Rampant suspicion. Isn't it all part and parcel of what you do for a living, my dear?"

She sighed heavily, nodding. "Yes, I'm guilty."

He took her gently by the arm. "Now come along to our dungeons here in the cathedral, so you will put your mind at ease about Father Luc Sante."

At midday, Richard Sharpe pulled up to the York Hotel in search of Jessica, time seeping away from him like water through a sieve. He'd been unable all morning to locate her to even inquire if she would consider wearing a wire. He inquired with the crime lab, Schuller and Raehael. No one had seen her this morning.

She had left word with no one.

He then tried telephoning her at her room, but he'd been unable to reach her at the York, either.

He had a mad notion she might actually be in her room, sound asleep with earplugs in her ears, or in the shower when the phone had continued to blare. He kept telling himself that she could not be so foolish as to go into Luc Sante's lair again, alone.

He banged uselessly on the door even as he listened for the shower within, but no report of any noise whatsoever on the interior returned to him. Finally, he went back downstairs and demanded a key, flashing his badge, fearful she might be incapacitated inside her hotel room.

When he and the chief of hotel security, a friend of long-standing, entered the room, they found it immaculate, the bed even neatly arranged, he supposed so that the maids needn't work so hard where she might be concerned.

Richard searched the premises for any clue, any sign of where she might have gotten off to when his eyes fell on Luc Sante's book on the nightstand. "Can we trace her last call from here, time and destination?" he asked the security head.

"Absolutely. I'll just have to make a call," Harlan Nelson replied.

The wait felt longer than it was, Sharpe nervously pacing the empty room. Finally, Nelson read the phone number, saying, "The call was put in at 10:40 P.M."

"That's the Yard, CID, no help."

"Anything else I can do for you, Richard?"

"No, Harlan, but thank you. Will you lock up here? I must hurry."

"Certainly, Richard, and my best to your girls."

But Sharpe had disappeared through the doorway. In the lobby, he ran into Erin Culbertson who slowed him, saying, "Aren't you spending a lot of time here these days!"

"Out of my way, Erin."

"Cheeky of you, Richard, not returning my calls!" she called out after him. She then located her assistant who drove the van with all the equipment, and they tried to follow Richard Sharpe through the noonday traffic.

Driving as fast as he dared, Richard imagined all sorts of horrors for Jessica. He suspected that she had indeed gone back to St. Albans, knowing what she now knew, in an attempt to confront Luc Sante with the facts.

Sharpe feared such an act both brash and deadly. He rushed toward St. Albans, but he found himself hopelessly snarled in traffic, some accident ahead. He radioed for Copperwaite to join him at St. Albans, to stake the place out as Stuart had suggested, explaining that Jessica Coran had already returned there before he could get to her to discuss the wire device.

"Can you meet me there?"

"Where are you now?" asked Copperwaite.

"In traffic at a streetlight. Some accident has gridlocked me in. I'm abandoning the car for a few blocks' walk, and from there I'll catch a cab."

"See you a block south of St. Albans, then? On Exeter, maybe?"

"Fine, yes, do that."

Richard was off and running.

Using a flashlight, Luc Sante led Jessica to and through. "All the known secret chambers of the cathedral," as he put it, explaining that the crypt they stood in, at the very bottom-bottom of the church had, in the Middle Ages, become the burial crypt of the early priests who had lived their lives behind the walls of St. Albans.

Her penlight in hand, Jessica felt the breathing, staring walls closing in on her. They'd left the warmth and sweet-smelling incense of rosewood in the cathedral, left its familiar corridors. This place formed a dungeon mired in time, sodden with dampness. It recalled the mine shaft she and Richard and Tatham had traversed.

"You have a cemetery below the church. How . . . interesting," she managed. "I'm something of a cemetery enthusiast, and I've seen crypts and cemeteries in every place that I've ever visited, but nothing like this." The room opened on a secret chamber where headstones lay in rows on the dirt floor; beneath each a former priest lay at eternal rest.

"In ancient times, it was thought the only way the graves of the holy fathers would remain undisturbed," explained Luc Sante.

"They were robbed in those days by grave robbers, body snatchers, I know," she said.

"Actually, the holy men had their bodies hacked up and pieces sold to the superstitious who—"

"My God, why?"

"Oh, but a holy man's finger or even more so his penis could bring joyful bounty to a family who blessed it each night!" Luc Sante laughed. "Human idiocy, but there you have it. Imagine how much people paid out in funds for the purported bones of Christ over the years. His body has been sold over and over for countless generations like some of your swampland in Florida." Again, his laugh bounced about the silent sepulcher. He then pointed to the slabs with inscriptions. "My predecessors. Their remains still considered as holy as ever."

Luc Sante next opened another room, using a huge jail-house key on a large ring, and there he displayed a small crypt. Jessica saw the crypt here as an ancient, sealed stone coffin, like something out of a Robert Bloch gothic novel, where a timeless vampire might reside within.

Here, too, stood walls lined with torches that burned centuries before, now sitting silent under Luc Sante's modern, battery powered, handheld torch, the flashlight sluicing through cobwebs, creating a patina of flying dust particles everywhere. The walls were festooned with dust-laden cobwebs, appeared crumbling as did the stairwell leading to this place.

"I think I've seen enough," she confessed.

"Not at all. There are corridors on either side of this room. A regular mausoleum. What we hide here is fairly banal, of no interest, and certainly out of use."

"You've made your point well, sir."

"We may just as well take this path," he countered. "It leads full circle to where we entered, and it is no further, and along the way, you can decide for yourself if St. Albans has any other skeletons in her closet."

They continued along ancient corridors, the odor of earth and mineral-rich water, seeping through the rock face here, filled her nostrils. They passed several dungeonlike rooms, each of which Luc Sante insisted on opening, each sending forth a vile, stale breath like that of cadavers. Cobwebs and filth which appeared to have gone undisturbed for centuries met them at every turn. "Nothing whatever here," he assured her again. "Still, I can well understand both your suspicion and curiosity."

"How did you know I was suspicious and curious?"

"It's part of you, isn't it? In your genes, your nature? And me . . . I read people. Part of my genetic makeup to read and understand people."

Jessica felt a sense of calm acceptance and welcomed relief waft over her as a result of Father Luc Sante's simple gesture and his revelations here. She felt badly that she ever doubted the man, felt badly about herself as well, that she could be so stupid as to embarrass herself this way, and she readily discounted all the coincidences when Father Luc Sante said, "I fear my suspicions about young Father Strand, however, to be true. Do you know he brought many people here for solace, such as the twins, you know, the hapless pair you met the other day. He thought they could benefit from both his ministering and my therapy, and perhaps they have. They respond to me because I was once their minister, when they were younger, you see."

She noted his absolute innocence in admitting this fact.

"Father Strand knew this fact, and so he arranged to bring them here?"

"He did."

"And what about Father Strand. How long have you known him?"

"It seems forever. He was just a boy first time I met him. He readily joined our choir at Bury St. Edmonds at the time."

"Bury St. Edmunds?" she asked.

"No, no . . . Gloucester. Edmunds was my second parish. Had to pay my dues to find my way to a London parish.

"I didn't want the twins here, but Strand stood his ground, saying they had no other place of refuge, that the world was too big for them. He convinced me to take them in. They live nearby, but in practice, they live here at St. Albans."

"O'Donahue lived in Bury St. Edmunds," she told him. "And you never told police of your connection with her."

"I had none. If she were in congregation there, she did not make herself known to me."

"But you saw the police report saying where she had once lived."

"I did, but I didn't think it relevant. I did not know her."

She nodded, accepting this. "I'm sorry," she told him, "for ever having suspected you of . . . of being involved in such evils as . . . as I did."

"Nonsense, my dear. It is your job to cultivate a healthy, suspicious, and cynical mind. Without it, where would you be? Shall we go down to Crown's End, to the street bazaar, see if we can learn where Martin has been hiding himself away of late?"

"Do you think it might tell us something?"

"Me, perhaps. I know the young man has been doctoring books. I just don't know why, and this purchase of an altar? I know he's not set up a storefront church anywhere."

"I suppose it wouldn't hurt to have a look."

"That's exactly what I had thought."

"Where is Strand now?" she asked.

"I'm not sure. He comes and goes pretty much as the spirit moves him, especially of late."

"Well, then, let's have at it." It was a phrase she'd picked up from Sharpe.

On exiting the church, just before pushing through the doors, Luc Sante spotted Martin Strand getting into a cab. He pointed at the man in black and said, "It's him—Strand. He's likely off to the bazaar. We must flag down a cab and follow him."

Jessica rushed out ahead of Luc Sante and waved down a passing cab. They clambered into the cab and with Strand's cab long out of sight, the old man shouted, "Crown's End bazaar."

"Which end, east or west?" asked the driver.

"Either! Just get us there the quickest possible speed."

"That'd be east end, then," replied the cabby.

"Then do it, man! Do it!"

They soon found themselves deposited amid the street bazaar, a series of street hustlers in makeshift cubicles, many surrounding ancient buildings here which by day served as office buildings. Booths and open air stands invited tourists in, the booths three layers deep, some fixed up around ancient pillars. This, the east end of the serpentine bazaar, teemed with shoppers, mostly tourists, but somehow, amid the crowds, Jessica made out the back of Father Strand's head. She feared losing sight of him. Strand moved along briskly just across and down the street from where Jessica stood alongside Father Luc Sante. They froze for a moment, seeing the shadowy, distant figure of Strand looking about before disappearing again into the crowd.

"Where the deuce is he?" Luc Sante wanted to know, waving his cane.

"He's there!" she told Luc Sante, pointing. But Strand's visage, or rather his long golden hair, went in and out of a sea of others. "We need to get closer, or we'll lose him."

"I'm slowing you down. Go ahead, shadow him as you police people like to say. I shall come along behind you. I don't wish to lose him any more than you do. Go, go!"

She did so, putting all her effort now into keeping Strand in her sight. If anyone at St. Albans was guilty of serial killing, it must be the mysterious Father Martin Strand, she told herself as she became Strand's shadow.

She gazed back once to see if Father Luc Sante followed, and she could see him coming along, slowly but surely. People on the street engaged Luc Sante, called out to him, asked for his blessings. When Jessica returned her gaze to Strand, the man had again vanished.

"G'damnit," she cursed.

Luc Sante, catching up, gasping for breath, asked, "Why have you stopped? Where is he?"

"He's gone."

"Gone?"

"Vanished."

"Without a trace?"

"Like smoke . . . like a chameleon."

"Oh, and this is exactly where I lost him when last I was here." Luc Sante jabbed the sidewalk with his black cane.

Circling, staring in all directions, being jostled by the crowd, Jessica said, "Then there must be someplace he is disappearing to, right about here. He can't have stepped into another dimension."

"Oh, you don't know Strand. He's something of a magician, that one. Had me fooled, and I'm the supposed expert. Let's face it. For all these years, his choirboy looks have gotten him by. He simply is not what he appears to be."

Jessica began the search through this street-corner madhouse of electric energy, a kind of Sodom and Gomorra of bartering. Every item imaginable could be purchased here, and one of the shops Jessica now stood before must be where Strand purchased his ancient altar. At the same instant Jessica's eyes fell on the incredible array of oaken furniture made to appear ancient. Father Luc Sante, growing excited, pointed it out as well, saying, "This is the shop on the receipt for the altar I told you about, Jessica. This is where he purchased the missing oak altar."

On entering the shop, Jessica saw that it was filled with an array, indeed the entire spectrum of religious icons and paraphernalia, including crosses as large as the beams on ancient firehouse ceilings. She immediately wondered if Strand had also purchased an ancient cross here, with spikes thrown in to seal the deal? Jessica asked the question of Luc Sante who puzzled it out.

She followed with, "What about having a custom-made brand for the underside of the tongue made here?"

"There is a shop for every taste at this street bazaar," he assured her. "No doubt there is a shop where this sort of branding is routine, like tattooing now! Or body piercing. Trust me, on this street, anything can be had for a price."

Jessica could easily imagine it possible here from the evidence of her eyes. For here, staring from every tabletop and street vendor's booth, lay black market items from rhino horns to human skulls, ancient swords too heavy to lift to entire table and chair sets that appeared to have been taken from royal homes, the workmanship that fine and intricate. Here Jessica saw the arcane and archaic, the bizarre and fantastic, including a fellow whose entire stock comprised of *branding tools*! Branding irons, both large and small, even miniature in size to create ready-made tattoos without the wait for those able to withstand the pain.

Jessica wondered if the tongue branding iron had not come from this collection of knockabout junk. Jessica saw real family crests for sale, stamps of office, royal seals, extraordinary candles, canes, boxes, paintings, artwork, and sculptures from around the globe; she saw mantels, clocks, children's toys, portmanteaus, chests, armoires, cast iron stoves, kitchenware, pirate ware, fantasy ware, warfare ware, and pinned insects of the most exotic nature, followed by an array of colorful African, handcarved coffins, and beside these, Old World headstones made to order, all this and more within walking distance of St. Albans, and all the variety of wares displayed within feet of one another. Many of the outdoor salespeople had covered ancient doorways, alleyways, and stairwells leading up this way, inviting down that way. The street vendors had built their makeshift booths, like any flea market, wherever they found space, and this section, where Jessica and Luc Sante found themselves, sat squarely in a run-down area of old warehouses that had fallen on hard times many years before, long since abandoned. In other districts, partic-

ularly along the Thames, property in ill repair had become
fodder for real estate developers following the lead in America
to build condominiums and time shares out of old buildings via judicious refurbishing. But this blighted area would
have none of that.

So where had Strand disappeared to?

They came up blind at every turn. Every doorway locked,
every alleyway empty, every stairwell leading to yet another
locked door. Until Jessica found one stone causeway leading
gently downward. "This could be where he disappeared to,"
she suggested to Luc Sante.

"We should not attempt to go any further alone," Luc Sante
warned. "There's a dark side to Martin that I—forgive me—
fell blind to. Me! Me, the so-called expert on evil, and yet I
could not recognize it all this time in my presence in its pleasing form," lamented Father Luc Sante who suddenly looked
old, frail, small, defeated, sunken.

"Exactly right. I saw a pay phone about a block back. Go
there and call Sharpe and get the troops here. We may well
be onto something."

"I will not leave you alone here, and you cannot go any
further, Jessica," Luc Sante near ranted. "Do you understand?"

"I'll just wait here until you get back, in case he shows up
again."

"If you're promising me you will stay put, then I'll make
the call, otherwise . . ."

"I promise. Now, go!"

Jessica watched as Luc Sante disappeared into the crowd
around the bazaar. She turned back to the stone walls and
stairwell that so caught her attention and curiosity. It was
remarkably old, these walls, this stairwell going down into a
dark and gloomy place where there might be yet another
locked door, but one she could not see. She lifted her penlight
from her pocket, the same as she used in the tunnels with
Sharpe. She had used it at St. Albans as well, and now here,
but the light, as powerful as it was, revealed no door at the
long, downward spiral below her feet. Instead, it appeared to

be a bend, a cornering which meant the shaft continued onward in a zigzag fashion.

Luc Sante would be some time, she thought. He seemed as genuinely amazed at Strand's sudden disappearance in the area as she had been. He had been certain that this exact area had swallowed Strand up before when he had followed the man here yesterday.

Jessica wondered if she hadn't stumbled on a passage of Roman architecture in the city. She stepped down into the passage which led invitingly, hauntingly into a labyrinth of walls—still Roman in appearance. From here she located another passage going off in yet another direction with its own set of stairs. Strand could be anywhere among the dark corridors of this ancient place.

All the stone stairwells led downward into the bowels of this place. "Damn," she swore at herself, "why didn't I have Sharpe come along with me?" She continued one step in front of the other, while at the same time thinking, "I've got to go back, let Father Luc Sante know I'm all right and that these walls and stairwells lead somewhere."

She turned full around, taking a step back toward the direction from which she came, anxious to reenter the bustling world above, to return to street level and the life that abounded there, to see Father Luc Sante's kindly face searching the entryway for her, but a noise from behind distracted Jessica. It seemed the sound of a falling foot, followed by another. *Strand?* she wondered.

In the dark distance, she could barely make out the form of a man, his back to her, moving steadily onward, downward into this Stonehengelike place.

A rat scurried past, followed by another, each no doubt carrying enough fleas and disease to infect anyone they might bite. She returned to the lip of the opening where she had first stepped into the Roman walls, scanning for any sign of Luc Sante. On seeing the old man tottering back, his cane held high, she cautioned Father Luc Sante, pleading, "Please, remain aboveground and direct authorities when they arrive. Watch for Sharpe."

"I could only locate Boulte. Sharpe and his partner were

unavailable. Listen to me, young woman, you promised me you wouldn't trek down in there alone!" Luc Sante protested.

"No, I promised you I'd wait until you returned *before* I did anything else." She whipped out her .38 Smith & Wesson from her shoulder holster, and she felt the comfort of the more compact Browning automatic strapped to her ankle below her pants leg. The .38 police special alone should be enough to assure Luc Sante of her safety. She said, "I'm not entirely alone!" as she hefted the .38 between two fists for him to see. "I know what I'm doing. I'm a marksman."

The gun made the old man start, as if he suddenly saw her in a new light. Perhaps he had never thought of her in relation to a weapon, despite the work she did.

"I'm going ahead with my investigation," she declared. "Direct authorities when they arrive." She could hear Luc Sante behind her, still cautioning her to wait, cursing her for being so stubborn and impertinent, a cute word to use under the circumstances, she thought and continued forward into the gaping darkness that rushed up to meet her.

The stairwell dropped incrementally below her feet as she went deeper into the recesses here, and then the stone floor began a sharper spiral, and the walls narrowed in and in, as if moving in on her, wanting to crush her. Soon—her flash signaling each new step—the walls began scratching at Jessica's shoulders like ghouls reaching from vaults to tear at her clothing.

She could no longer see Strand or what had in the blackness appeared to be Strand, but she continued to hear noises, peculiar, odd sounds: the swishing of a robe, the scratch of a heel, the hum of some sort of machine, perhaps the reverberating noise from aboveground traffic, traveling through the rock here. She heard the distinct sound of seeping water, and for the second time today, she saw walls that bled with moisture. Her clothing had long been stained with the mineral-rich water.

The odors assailing her nostrils were those of ancient crypts and dungeons, stagnant places where only things requiring no light grew and festered, died and decayed. Her thoughts continued worrying her with each new step.

The noises coming from above and through the rock, like the pulse of electricity—like the blood fuel that drove all of London—calmed to silence now, but sounds rising from *below* her rose up like awakening gnomes. She imagined the walls coming to life; she imagined the stairwell turning to Jell-O, slick and thick and slimy. She imagined spiraling into an Alice in Wonderland world below her ankles or coming out on the moon and stars, finding herself inside a bell jar. But none of this happened. The walls and stairs held even as she slipped on the now slick surface.

If this is the way to crucifixion at the hands of the Crucifier, she mentally whispered to herself, then how did those older people make it along this passage? Were they carried, dragged along in their drugged state? She recalled no serious bruising that would indicate such a scenario, so then how . . .

A moan, human and low and guttural and pained escaped from somewhere ahead, and at her feet the inclined stairs ended, leaving her on a bed of rock.

Jessica, hearing distinctly human noises—the sound of more than one man—wondered whom Strand had met in this awful place? What was the meaning of the low, animal-like but human wail? Was she at last in the lair of the monster, on the Crucifier's ground?

She hesitated taking another step, but in the near distance, she saw that the tunnel opened on light, flickering, flaming, dancing light. She feared investigating further on her own, but she felt drawn to see precisely what lay at the end of the tunnel.

She inched forward, praying that by now Sharpe, Copperwaite, and an army of police were this moment taking direction from Father Luc Sante as to her whereabouts.

She believed now that she had long since left the rim of this peculiar hell, and that she now stood in the belly of the beast. This horrid place called to mind the rungs of hell in Dante's *Inferno*, the rungs to which a killer the year before promised to send Jessica. It appeared Satan had had his way with her after all, she now mused, for the Devil had brought her here, full circle, in a sense. Was the same evil that stalked her a year before still at her heels now? she wondered.

· TWENTY-ONE ·

*Man's latent talent for group evil is so attuned,
so polished and honed today, that we fear any
microscopic study of this uniquely human quality.*

—GLENN HALE,
DR. O

Richard Sharpe had waited for Copperwaite just down from
St. Albans, scanning for any activity in and around the church
as he did so, but the place appeared at this late afternoon hour,
silent, abandoned even. No one in or out.

With Stuart Copperwaite finally joining Sharpe, they together started for the huge stone stairs and the oaken doors.
Richard, familiar with the church corridors, went directly for
Luc Sante's office. Not even the secretary was present. He
called out several times for Luc Sante by name, gaining no
response.

He next tried Strand. After finding a speaker to the PA
system that fed into the altar and main congregational room,
he called again for Luc Sante and Strand. They waited to see
if this had any effect, but no one responded. Nothing moved
in the enormous church.

Richard wondered about Luc Sante's patients, but then it
was late. He wondered about the Gloucester twins, and as he
did so, he studied the painting of the Gloucester parish, looking closely at it for the first time and seeing the artist's name.
It read in spiking letters: **M.S.**

"Could it have been painted by Martin Strand?" he wondered aloud, pointing to the painting.

"Strand, the other minister?" asked Copperwaite.

"It's just possible he wants more from Luc Sante than St. Albans."

"Where to from here?"

"Get an army in here to search through the catacombs below. There may be something afoot here, and if so, it may be in the bowels of this place."

"But have we the right to defile the—"

"We have cause to fear for lives here, Stuart. That's enough reason alone. We're acting under suspicion someone may be in danger of life and limb. Now do it."

Jessica inched forward and found a small room with a Roman arch, light filtering through from ahead of this room. She found a series of such small rooms, before she came upon a wide open vault from which the firelight originated. The source of the light, torches in the walls, not unlike unused ones she'd seen in St. Albans' corridors.

No longer did the walls close in; rather, they expanded, and here a stagnant pool of water, part of a canal, similar to the one she'd seen in the company of Sharpe and Tatham the day before, lay like a fat, green, sleeping boa constrictor. Here she stood, circling, taking it all in when her eyes fell on the altar no doubt purchased with St. Albans' funds by Martin Strand, just as Father Luc Sante had said. She stood back of and behind a huge oaken cross, its front facing out to the cavern beyond. Then her eyes went beyond the wide beams of the cross to the huge, thick oaken altar, until a dull moan brought her eyes straight up to the cross. She saw first the feet, and as she inched closer, the length of the dying man's legs.

She gasped, standing now before the ancient cross—finally found—the killing ground of the Crucifier. To her astonishment, she saw someone still living, and not Jesus' carved image, squirming on the cross. He was nude and dying of his wounds, blood trickling down.

From her vantage point, below and behind the huge cross, she saw a scaffolding in nearby shadow, a scaffolding used to take the victim up to the cross.

Shadow played across the writhing figure on the cross, deep shadows thrown up by the fire burning in thirteen torches and one small fire at the altar where oil and incense burned; beside the incense fire lay the hardware for the branding of the tongue. Jessica moved toward this highly important piece of physical evidence when droplets of blood from the person on the cross stained her blue suit jacket purple. Realizing this, she looked up to see the nude man's form dangling there, chin on chest, struggling to breathe in the semidarkness.

Jessica wanted to call out to him, tell him to hang on, but then that sounded foolish in this context, and she feared being found out. She dared not shout, wondering where Strand might be, if he were watching her from one of the deep shadows across the cavernous hall.

Jessica haltingly raised her flashlight to the dying victim left here on the cross, her fear rising to a crescendo she had never known before. Her flash shakily played now over the features of the dying man on the cross, and she realized almost instantly that the victim returned a familiar image, that of a blond Christ with a familiar face: the near dead man, his eyes gaping back at her before rolling back in his head, was Father Martin Christian Strand.

"Oh, Jesus! Luc Sante!" she moaned just before something hard and flinty struck her in the back of the head, sending her into darkness.

"So now what?" Copperwaite had asked Sharpe after the cathedral was torn apart in an effort to locate Jessica, Luc Sante, Strand, anyone, but Sharpe's first instinct had been right, the place had been deserted.

It was then that Sharpe said, "Back to the clapper bridge."

"Clapper bridge?"

"Yes, I'll inform you along the way. Let's go!" That had been fifteen minutes earlier. The twosome now stood at the lip of the tunnel which Sharpe, Jessica, and Tatham had scoured the day before, finding nothing. By now, Sharpe had explained to Copperwaite what this place was and how they had come to find it.

"But if you've already searched it and found nothing, Richard," moaned Copperwaite, "why the deuce are we searching it again?"

"I know no other way to go than to attempt the other corridor, the one Tatham said would only lead us away from St. Albans, and perhaps it does lead away from St. Albans as indicated on the map, but then, we found no underground debauchery in the dungeons there, so perhaps the killer's lair has no direct connection with St. Albans, at least not the place."

"Did the RIBA guy tell you where the other tunnel led?"

"Toward Oxford Street and the tourist area."

"Old Crown's End bazaar? Good, I have to find a gift for my nephew anyway. So let's push on through this muck," replied Copperwaite, frowning at the horror and sludge before him. "Smells bloody awful."

Sharpe pushed through the grate and into the pipe that led to the tunnel, the water higher today but no less filthy and stagnant for it.

Copperwaite complained as he sloshed through in his good shoes, Sharpe's mention of three sets of Wellington boots in the back of his car not easing his suffering. "I just bought these shoes. Italian leathers."

"Best kind. They'll clean right up."

"But they'll retain the stench."

Sharpe agreed as he trudged ahead of his partner, saying, "Aye, that's-struth, all right."

"Cost me a week's pay on the black market."

"Quit your complaining, Coppers. I'll buy you a new pair, and you can resell these to the marketman."

"I just don't want this all to be for naught. And I'm worried about Dr. Coran."

"As am I . . . as am I . . ."

"She is the way!" declared Father Jerrard Luc Sante, pointing at the unconscious form of Jessica Coran where she lay on the cold, coal-blackened floor of the cavern. "I brought her here because I firmly believe that we must begin with another, someone not of our community, someone yet unborn and uninitiated, you see, a child whom Christ will take as his receptacle to rise from the death throes of an unborn innocent."

"You speak of her as if she were an unborn child."

"She is, in our ways, she is unborn."

"When did you decide this?"

"We've talked about it, that our selections must be younger, stronger in mind and spirit and body," he replied to his congregation's dissenters. There were always dissenters, he reminded himself now, doing his level best to remain calm and in control. He pointed at Martin Strand, saying, "I gave you my spiritual son for this purpose, convinced him of the wisdom of going before God in the ultimate sacrifice and there he stands. Wilt not you look on your Father Strand?"

Through the haze of unconsciousness, Jessica picked up bits and pieces of the conversation going on around her.

"Strand is younger than this woman."

"In body only. In spirit and in the knowledge of our Lord Jesus, Strand is the older of the two. I bring you a person who has fought evil her entire life. Who better for Christ to blow His eternal and blessed breath into, should He fail to use Martin's form?"

Jessica half-heard the voices as they bounced about the walls of the catacomb, and she heard the work of men who, like electrical pole linemen, worked to get Father Strand down from the cross. Strand was long dead now.

Someplace in her mind, her brain began to regroup and fashion some connections in its attempt to compute how Father Strand could already be dead if he had, in fact, been only steps ahead of her coming down into this hell. The timetable felt completely off. When she and Father Luc Sante had seen Strand get into a cab outside St. Albans, she realized now that what she had seen hadn't actually been Strand. She'd taken Father Luc Sante's word that it had been Strand who dropped into the cab for the bazaar. And at the bazaar, later, Luc Sante had pointed out Strand, but again, while Jessica had followed the back of a man's head and a pair of wide shoulders, she had not once gotten a good look at Strand. It followed that it had been one of Luc Sante's disciples disguising himself as Strand to lure her here in a carefully contrived plot to isolate her.

Jessica fought the dark interior of her mind where a part of her wished to remain in hiding, but someone saw her body stir and her eyes blink, and this woman screeched a loud, "She's waking up!" Jessica's single eye opened, focusing on one of the Houghton twins of Gloucester.

Jessica saw the little hole of the business end of her own Browning automatic, stripped from her ankle holster, pointed directly at her eyes. Luc Sante snatched away the gun from the Houghton sister who held it on Jessica, frightening the woman off by pointing it at her. Luc Sante also held Jessica's .38 revolver.

"Dear Jessica," began Luc Sante, "it will now be your pleasure to have a role in Christ's Second Coming."

"How could you be a part to these atrocious murders, Father? You!"

"Murder? No. It was never about murder, dear. This isn't one of your sordid, filthy serial killer cases, Dr. Coran. Look there, at Strand there"—he pointed to where others prayed over the young man's corpse—"he begged me to please accept him next, and—"

"Accept him? Listen to yourself, Luc Sante. You're playing God."

"He pleaded, begged me to take him next. As for playing God, the crucifixions always remained throughout a choice my followers willingly made, and the last time I looked, freedom of religion and freedom of choice remains legal." He indicated his flock of dwindling followers, perhaps forty, among them a number of familiar faces: the Houghton twins; Mrs. Eeadna, the secretary; Luc Sante's patients whom she'd seen coming and going; and in shadow, there stood Tatham from the RIBA, the man she and Sharpe had trusted. She half expected to see Copperwaite and possibly Sharpe step from the shadows to complete the nightmare.

"You," she said to Tatham whose stern glare replied in silent menace.

"Don't be so hard on Tatham. He was to be next until you came this way, Jessica."

"Me? I'm not here of my free will."

"Ahhh, but you are. You willingly chased what you perceived to be evil to this place, and in so doing, you have instead found benevolence and a love of mankind, a cabal bent on lifting our species to the next and greatest plane, the level of pure love, pure giving, pure religious thought— Jung's overmind."

"Put her on the cross," said Tatham, breaking his silence. "Else, the world finds out about us and we are all stopped in our efforts, Father."

Luc Sante solemnly nodded and simply said, "Take her."

Jessica put up a struggle, bloodying Tatham's nose, tearing loose, making a run for the direction in which she'd come, but she was roughly brought down when the others tackled her and dragged her back to the altar.

"I am sorry that you are fighting this so, dear Jessica," said Father Luc Sante. "In a manner of speaking, your whole life has led to this moment, and you should actually relish it, delight in it, for you die here for the greater glory of Jesus Christ and our Lord, and for the greater glory of all mankind, my dear."

Her lip trembling, Jessica could only pierce the old man with her sudden hatred and contempt for him. "All you stood for, all that nonsense you spouted about creating a psychology of evil, about combating evil at the source, and who is the greater evil than you, Luc Sante? You have become the thing you despise most."

"Then perhaps we are two of a kind. Perhaps I will join you after, and in the afterworld, we will continue this debate. But for now . . ." He jerked his head to one side, indicating that the others now could take her to the cross. "Tie her and prepare the drug and prepare her for the stakes," he ordered.

"What about the tongue branding?" asked one of the Houghton sisters, her question sounding like a curse.

"They all had their tongues branded to send them safely over," agreed the other sister, sounding balmy in the head.

"This one don't belong . . . isn't a believer!" chided Tatham. "She shouldn't be branded. We're needing to rid ourselves of her, and that's all."

"But isn't that . . ."

"Murder!" shouted Jessica.

"Inject her, now!" ordered Luc Sante, tired of the bandying about, not wishing to lose control of his meager following, nearly a sixth of whom had already gone over, willingly, *if* he could be believed. Jessica had seen the stark evidence of how powerful the cult mentality could be on her cutting room slab, and she recalled the Hale-Bhopp comet aftermath in America some years before.

Jessica saw the slight quiver of glee going through Tatham's body as he plunged home the drug that would sedate her. She tried to pull away, to physically fight them, but there were too many hands holding her, and so she fought mentally to stay sharp. She cursed herself for having come full steam ahead, and for having held so tenaciously to her faith in Luc Sante.

The drug's effect worked on her now, making her drowsy, weak and uncaring, disinterested in her own execution, but she fought, shouting at them, shouting, "This is not a willing crucifixion! This is an execution! Murder! An execu . . . exe . . . cue . . . cue . . . tion."

And Jessica's system shut down, and somewhere deep in the recesses of her unconscious mind, she knew that she would wake up dying.

Luc Sante brought her around gently, his voice breaking through the pillow clouds of her deep slumber. A throbbing pain pulsed at the back of her head, and she felt a dampness there where blood had soaked her hair. She heard Luc Sante's words as in a dream, the drug dizzying her. "This is how *we* intend to combat evil in the universe, my dear Jessica. First, we will annihilate it on this ground, on this holy cross." While she could not see, could not focus her dilated eyes, she imagined his bony finger pointing to the enormous and ancient cross where Strand still hung in the throes of mortal pain.

Strand's labored breathing made her wonder how long the man had been hanging here, hours, a day, more? Jessica kept her eyelids closed, struggling with how she might locate and take control of the .38 or her Browning automatic. Then she realized that Strand's labored breathing was not Strand's but her own gasping breath. She hadn't yet been staked to the cross, but she had been drugged.

She heard Luc Sante continue for his rag-tag army of followers, all of whom were in awe of the old man with the wild eyes and unruly shock of white hair. "Place her on the cross. Do it. Do it now."

Jessica struggled to her feet, lashing out with fists clenched at men in heavy robes and dark hoods, but two strong men grabbed her before she could get her bearings, stripping her to her bra and panties, discarding her clothing, some of it cast into the stagnant, standing water as they raped her of her identity. She now represented an object, a mere symbol, an obstacle to their continued obsession, an icon to religious fanaticism.

They dragged her, kicking and screaming, to the cross. Luc Sante's followers looked on as if in rapture. Luc Sante shouted, "Dr. Coran will now take the place of Christ."

"What about increasing the drug?" suggested one of them, the voice strikingly clinical and familiar, she thought. But Jessica had enough trouble focusing on the fact they had drugged her to worry about the familiar voice.

Luc Sante solemnly replied to the one man who stood up against him, "This time, no high dosages."

"But she must be willing, like the others were," countered another follower whose cowl masked his likeness. Jessica could not be sure of her sense of sight or sound as the Brevital continued to work havoc with her brain.

Still somewhere in her mind, Jessica held on to the fact that all of Luc Sante's victims had been, as the old man himself had admitted to her earlier, willing participants in their own crucifixion deaths. She must use this fact against him here and now. It proved the one truth from Luc Sante's mouth irrefutable, and if so, perhaps his followers might question her being forced and man-handled into this role.

Jessica fought to focus on the once empty chamber now filled with people of all sizes, shapes—all below heavy cossack-styled robes and deep hoods, cowls holding their features hostage in shadow. Colorless and of one mind, she thought.

Her own mind multiplied . . . multiplied the crowd before her even as it spun out of control. She saw all Father Luc Sante's converts closing in around her, all wishing to touch the icon before *it* departed; before being sent over to the other side. Now in the crowd, she saw the visage of Chief Inspector Boulte which made her gasp with a moment's hope, until she saw J. T.'s image as well, followed by Santiva, Donna LeMonte, Kim Desinor, James Parry, Stuart Copperwaite, and there, too, stood Richard Sharpe—dear Richard—all of them fooled by Luc Sante. All of them were pleading for the man to "take me next, take me next . . ."

"All the others volunteered!" Jessica shouted.

Some grumblings of response came from the crowd as Luc Sante assured them that Jessica *had* volunteered, even if unconsciously so.

"You sisters, you Houghton sisters!" Jessica shouted. "It's your turn. You've waited years upon years for this day."

"She's right, Father," said one of the Houghton twins in response.

Luc Sante's stentorian voice silenced them all with a shouting sermon. "A child came to me in a dream," Luc Sante told his followers now, "and in this vision, the child—neither male nor female—told me what to do. And this is that prophetic dream come true. Now we all know that dreams are the word of God incarnate, so to ignore the child's voice is to ignore the voice of God Himself."

"Tell us more of this dream," asked one follower who dropped his cowl, disclosing his face to Jessica, who believed her mind fevered on seeing Dr. Karl Schuller staring at her.

Luc Sante continued, pleased at this reaction. "I've concluded that she . . . Dr. Coran . . . must feel the pain as Christ Himself felt the pain to truly atone for her sins of which she has many, and in order for the subsequent resurrection to take place. You will see the resurrection of the child of God, Jesus Himself in due time! You will all be witness to the miracle of miracles reborn, returned to this Earth . . . and to this end, no more drugs."

A scaffolded stairway was wheeled forward. Two men pushed it into place before the cross, and they worked to take Father Strand down from his suffering. He appeared lifeless, without breath, and no sound came from him. The men holding Jessica now ascended the stairwell to the cross, guiding her into place. Meanwhile, the others, silenced by Luc Sante's words, looked on, awestruck and fascinated.

Jessica felt her body rising from the scaffold as the men lifted her to the cross, Strand's blood still wet at the extremities. Jessica felt a wave of uncaring and disinterest in her own death flood over her. *Who cares,* she told herself, the drug having firm control now.

They had now lifted her onto the cross by way of a scaffold brought to face it. When did they do that? When did they take Strand off the cross? she wondered. She found herself in a new perspective now, a new point of view, staring down on the congregation from on high where her hands and legs had been lashed to the cross, and she saw Strand once again. They had placed his body on a natural outcropping of rock on one wall that formed a stone bed. He looked for all the world like a blond Jesus Christ; he'd been wrapped now in linen. Only now did she realize that Luc Sante had won, that she had replaced Strand on the cross.

Jessica felt sensations, numb and distant as her arms, forced to each side, stretched outward to touch the ends of the crossbar, each wrist tied securely by leather tongs. She was here, on the cross. She felt cold hands on her ankles, felt her ankles likewise being lashed together with rough rawhide lines. She cried out for help, for mercy, but no one responded. Her cries might as well be silent screams of nightmare. No one above on the busy Crown's End bazaar streets could hear her, and no one down here could either. Here in his dark, underground pulpit, they only heard Luc Sante's voice.

They were a group mind listening to a promise, each in search of a hope that only Luc Sante might fulfill. The dying Burton, the old schoolteacher from Bury St. Edmunds, all of them had been filled with fear so great that facing an execution by crucifixion proved inviting by comparison. More than inviting, in fact, since Luc Sante's world held out an otherworldly hope to them. This hope came on the heels of hopelessness, and it proved a hope that extended to an afterlife in which they might touch God. And so dying like this, in Luc Sante's insane game of hide-and-seek with Christ, meant the greatest hope of all. True of Strand, of Tatham and of Schuller—people from all walks of life, anyone who'd lost all faith and hope only to discover Luc Sante's dream his or her dream.

Karl Schuller, yes. He stared grimly up at Jessica, his features imprinted on her mind as being real and present.

She saw the spike placed at her right palm, the other at her left, as each man in dark robes and cowls held firm to a thick hammer, readying to strike each spike simultaneously. She could not distinguish if it were dream or reality. This confusion proved short-lived, however, when the first blow of the hammer striking the stake, resulting in the stake striking through her flesh, startled her into a more conscious state, and she screamed, "What of my being bathed in oil and blood! What of my branding!"

This outcry halted the hammer wheelers. The desired effect.

"I demand it of you, Father!" she cried, thrashing on the cross like a pinned butterfly. "If you crucify me, I demand the ritual be followed to the letter."

Jessica knew this would slow the process, perhaps give Sharpe and Copperwaite time enough to locate her final movements in aboveground London, but she feared her hope a mere fantasy. They had no way of knowing where her last footfalls had brought her, now had they? She cursed herself for being a headstrong fool.

Her pitiable outcry for the ritual branding had stopped the spike to her feet. However, the blood rivulets dripped with each pulse now from her right and left palm over the stakes and onto the crossbar where each hand had been pinned. She felt no sensation to her hands, but she felt the weight of hanging there, felt the pressure on her lungs already building, and she felt the leather straps cutting both her wrists and ankles.

The collective debated the branding.

To brand or not to brand. The arguments flew. And in this simple act of calling for the ritual branding, Jessica had indicated her willingness to turn convert, to join the cult body and soul—to turn herself completely over to Luc Sante, to Jesus and thereby God for *reconditioning*, and the convert capable of standing before him and accepting the hot iron on the underside of the tongue had, up till now, she guessed, been the next to attempt to merge with Christ on the cross and die for his or her trouble.

It was how Martin Strand and all those who preceded him on the cross had lost their lives.

It all made perfectly logical, sound religious sense to everyone in the room—all Father Luc Sante's converts to this extreme devotion. It was, after all, a cult built on the faith they could hasten Christ's return in the new millennium.

At the urging of his followers, Luc Sante stopped the crucifixion process long enough for the branding. "Heat the iron and get the oil," he told his followers, who now went about doing so.

Jessica wondered now what she had gotten herself into: She was about to have her tongue branded, and to become the next crucifixion victim.

· TWENTY-TWO ·

While I see many hoof marks going in, I see none coming out.

—AESOP,
THE LION, THE FOX & THE BEAST

Between St. Albans and the Clapper bridge, Inspector Richard Sharpe had radioed in for a quick, factual background check on Dr. Donald Wentworth Tatham, asking dispatch to contact him immediately with where exactly Tatham hailed from. It was just a hunch, but it scored big, for the man had originally hailed from Bury St. Edmunds. Sharpe had run the background check on a hunch and out of habit. As a Scotland Yard inspector, he had learned always to know with whom you were dealing, and he passed this advice along to Stuart, who, now, trudging through the muck of this underground world, asked Sharpe one pointed question: "What else do you know of this chap at the RIBA who walked you to a dead end in the canal?"

"Are you asking whether or not Tatham knew it would be a dead end before we began?"

"Perhaps, perhaps not. Worth a look to see if he's any record when we get back, if we ever find our way out of here."

"A computer search should reveal if he's had any prior arrests or any problems in the past."

Inspector Richard Sharpe, having now little doubt that something strange was afoot, and that it centered around Luc Sante and St. Albans, felt extreme fear and frustration at having been unable to locate Jessica for the past several hours. He hoped and prayed that this search would not again become just another termination, another dead end. They trudged onward along the unfamiliar, bleak avenue that Tatham had called a useless waste of time.

It was but a thread to go on.

They concentrated their search here. Sharpe raced ahead of the others, Copperwaite having radioed for assistance. Sharpe found himself now in a winding corridor out of a nightmare, and from it radiated any number of mine shafts. The array of choices proved both frustrating and cruel. He must slow down, weigh each detail, and give orders to the men, give each his own detail. He did so, finishing by ordering them to "Report back to Copperwaite and me, should you locate anything the least suspicious. Do not attempt anything alone."

"Stuart, you stay with me. You other men are to remain in pairs, taking each tunnel," Richard ordered the others. Sharpe then watched the others disappear. He and Copperwaite now stood alone, their flashlights the only light here. "We'll take this avenue, Stuart."

"Lead on," came Copperwaite's ready reply. Once again alone with one another, the two Scotland Yard investigators felt the darkness claw at them, gaining in power like ink over ink with each step forward in this pit, when Sharpe suddenly stopped. Holding up a hand, he cocked his head to one side.

Copperwaite, too, suddenly made out the sounds of people ahead. Next they saw light, faint at first but growing as they inched forward. They doused their own lights.

Sharpe's ears detected clear, animate sounds and words now, voices chanting *Mihi beata mater* over and over, welling up like the sound of uneasy ghosts. Placing a forefinger to his lips, Sharpe called for silence and caution. "Careful. They're just ahead. We've hit some sort of pay dirt," Richard assured Copperwaite. "Go find the others. Bring reinforcements."

Copperwaite spoke under his breath, trying to keep their presence a secret, saying, "But Richard, I—"

"Do it! Do it, now," whispered Sharpe.

Stuart Copperwaite sighed and nodded before racing off after the other men.

Sharpe continued, guided by the sound of the voices. Soon, he located a stone stairwell that must be the way taken by the Crucifier and any victims he or they might have forced down into these awful catacombs—like the bowels of an ancient Stonehenge, an underground cathedral.

Sharpe thought of Jessica at the lab, about the CID building, at St. Albans, at her hotel, at his apartment, and his anxiety rose like a knife in his throat. He sensed Jessica near; sensed her, this very moment, in grave danger.

Now, Sharpe heard Jessica's voice, shouting and in pain, saying something about rituals. Now he knew most certainly that Jessica stood in harm's way, and he knew she was just beyond the next catacomb, just beyond the light, filtering from ahead, beyond his sight and reach, but the tunnel split again, two separate directions here, and he could not be sure which led to Jessica.

Richard heard raised voices now, angry voices. They chanted, "Brand her, brand her, brand her. *Mihi beata mater. Mihi beata mater. Mihi beata mater.*"

"Hold her wrists! Hold her tight! Control her!"

"Hold her hand still, so that I can stake it!" shouted another frustrated voice, one with a distinctly familiar ring, not Luc Sante's.

Frustrated and angry at the turn of events, Richard Sharpe again raced ahead of the others, taking the left tunnel in a headlong effort to save Jessica. He feared her in pain, a pain that might turn to a death at any time. He felt an intense hatred now for Luc Sante, wishing to mete out some pain to the Jesuit madman of twisted holiness. Obviously, Luc Sante had an agenda only Father Luc Sante fully comprehended.

Sharpe raced until he came to the end of a tunnel closed off by a grate, and staring through the grate, he could see the ritual in progress before his eyes. He saw Luc Sante conducting, and he saw Jessica with her hands staked, her feet tied, and that she hung naked from a cross. His heart filled with the horror before his eyes.

The men nearest Jessica had dropped their cowls, and

Sharpe recognized Tatham of the RIBA, a Dr. Kahili, Burtie Burton's shrink whom Sharpe had spoken to, and beside Kahili stood Dr. Karl Schuller. Sharpe could hardly believe what his eyes imparted. His mind worked to make sense of it all.

Those nearest Jessica prepared now to bathe her in an oil and blood mixture, the blood taken from a cut made in her right side. Others near her prepared to brand her tongue with a hot poker.

Sharpe screamed and kicked out at the grate separating him from these demons, the clattering noise riveting everyone's attention from Jessica to the intruder.

Luc Sante, using Jessica's Browning, fired and struck Richard a grazing blow to the temple just as Sharpe leaped down from the overhead tunnel. The gunshot knocked Sharpe back, while Luc Sante, over the noise, cursed, "The sanctity of our home is invaded, defiled!"

Sharpe fired back with little aiming. His army training as a sharpshooter took over. His single bullet created a neat, round hole in the old man's chest. Father Luc Sante sank to his knees, dying and pleading rhetorically, "Who will save . . . Savior know to . . . if I am not . . . here? Where will . . . I am, be? You fools . . . have destroyed any chance of . . . Second Coming."

Luc Sante's body went into spasms, his chest constricting, his throat filling with blood that he now gurgled and choked on. He amounted to a lump of robes now on the coal-smeared, ancient floor.

"He's. . . . *Father's dead!*" moaned one of the Houghton sisters who'd raced to the old man to tend his wound.

The others followed suit, falling to their knees over their leader. Schuller, finding the gun there, lifted it and found himself staring at the bore hole to Sharpe's weapon. Sharpe stood in the flickering light like some mad devil, bleeding profusely from his temple where Luc Sante's bullet had ripped a course through his skin and hair.

Other police and inspectors, along with Copperwaite, now rushed in to see Dr. Karl Schuller drop the gun, drop to his knees, and crumble under the weight of having lost all hope for the chance to be one of the *Chosen* to cross over.

In the end even Jessica, still in her drugged condition, saw the pitiful rabble of religious zealots for what they were. How all had been willing to step forward for the opportunity to create a moment in which the transmigration of their souls might link with that of Jesus Christ. All this bloodshed in order to bring Him back as promised in their Bibles and their addled, world-weary brains.

"Cuff them!" commanded Copperwaite. "One and all, and take them out of here."

Sharpe, his forehead and the left side of his face covered in crimson blood, stumbled to his feet, trying to get to Jessica. "Get her down at once! At once, do you hear? Take all due care with her!"

The men of the Yard did as Sharpe ordered, easing Jessica's weight immediately. Her stakes and leather bonds were next pulled from her, making her gulp with a last dose of pain. Richard tore off his coat and covered Jessica with it the moment she left the towering, intimidating old cross.

"Need to staunch the blood flow," Copperwaite shouted.

Sharpe took her in his arms, stroking her auburn hair, reassuring her as he wrapped each hand in handkerchiefs offered up by his men, while Copperwaite did the same for her feet. Sharpe imagined the scene as it must look to the others, as if it were a painting of the resurrection. Sharpe spoke reassuringly into Jessica's ear. "I've got you now, Jessica. No one can hurt you now. You're all right now, we've found you."

She cringed and cowered like a child in his arms, giving into her fear and loathing altogether now, sobbing uncontrollably. Out of the corner of her eye, she saw Luc Sante's lifeless body, and in the flickering light she thought he winked, and for the first time she fully appreciated her hatred for the old minister of twisted faith.

"Is he . . . Is he dead, truly?" she asked Sharpe.

"Utterly gone."

"We'll soon have these others talking," Copperwaite interjected. "Imagine it. Schuller among this collection of lost wretches."

Sharpe added, nodding, "I'm sure he's just like all the others. Did it all in the name of their Lord and Master and no more, so they bear no brunt of responsibility in the deaths of their kith and kin."

One of the uniformed policemen who'd entered behind Copperwaite shouted, "Over here! This one's alive!" He pointed to Father Martin Strand whose form stirred and partially rose, Copperwaite throwing his coat over the naked man's form, saying, "Hold on, man! Medics! Get medics down here!"

Luc Sante's followers, Schuller and Tatham the loudest, went into a paroxysm of religious frenzy on seeing the *resurrected* Martin Strand, calling out his name now as Christ! Chanting "Strand is Lord, Strand is Christ, Strand is the Holy One!"

Strand smiled a weak, broken, curled smile in response, but he could hardly move otherwise, his entire body going rigid as he went into cardiac arrest.

"He needs medics!" shouted Copperwaite. "Get some medics in here."

"Radios won't work down here, this far in!" came the response.

Strand died a second time, this time in an uncontrollable seizure as Schuller and the others crowded Copperwaite out, ignoring the orders and guns trained on them. Strand died in Karl Schuller's arms.

"Under and behind the cross," muttered Jessica to Richard. "A set of steps, goes out of here, to street level."

Sharpe ordered another investigator to have a look, and with the exit located, Luc Sante's motley crew of followers were marched up and out to street level, there met by police cars. They were ignominiously hauled off as coconspirators in the Crucifixion deaths in London. Strand and Luc Sante's bodies followed.

"Why didn't they just hide away the bodies down here?" Copperwaite wondered aloud.

Sharpe replied, "It was in keeping with the ritual, like the tongue branding, the blood and the oil—to bathe the dead in a clean body of water, water representing God's tears. The water in this place would hardly do. Besides, a part of Luc Sante wanted the world to know."

Copperwaite gritted his teeth, nodding his understanding. "You're probably quite right, Sharpie."

"Now help me get Jessica out of here."

"Thank you for coming for me, Richard," she said through the dull haze of the Brevital.

"Rest. Rest now," he said, his voice soothing her. "You knew I would find you."

"Yes, but I didn't know if you'd find me alive or dead facedown in a body of water. I'm still not sure you're real."

"Rest, dear Jessica . . . rest," he soothed.

Through the drug haze that hung about her brain now like gauze and film, she caught a flashback of Donald Wentworth Tatham's voice, saying coldly, *"Mihi beata mater!* In Mother Church and her Child lies salvation for us all." She saw Tatham as if from a great distance, and his eyes grew gargantuan where they remained glued on Luc Sante at the pulpit.

The religious frenzy among Luc Sante's followers had obviously taken on a life of its own, carrying Tatham, Schuller, the Gloucester twins, Miss Eeadna, Strand, and others along, propelling them to follow any order.

Again, she watched as two men with the huge iron hammers and stakes approached: faceless men at first, each encouraging the other with toothy grins, each exciting the mob to do as they chanted, "Brand her, brand her, brand her. *Mihi beata mater. Mihi beata mater. Mihi beata mater.* Hold her wrists! Hold her tight! Control her!"

"Hold her hand still, so that I can stake it!" shouted another frustrated voice. The stake looked and felt hefty, larger than before. Somehow she felt it in her hand. One of them, teasing her, wanted her to know its weight. The voices of those around her, driving the stakes home now, through flesh and rending bone, suddenly had familiar and then absolutely recognizable voices which brought their features into clear focus. One was Copperwaite, the other Richard Sharpe.

She woke up screaming in the London Memorial Hospital to where she had been moved since the cave with the cross that rose so high there seemed no top to it. Her screams woke Richard who had been sitting the all-night vigil with her.

Her hands were those of a mummy, both bandaged and wrapped. She felt no pain. She wiggled her toes, all to the good. She felt no blisters below her tongue. And she realized for the first time that not all her nightmares had come true.

"Jess, Jess, it's me, Richard. You've had a bad scare, I'm afraid, and God knows why. You're in hospital. They say you can walk out of here tomorrow."

"Oh, Richard, it was . . . It was horrible."

He grabbed her up in his arms. "I well know. I was there."

She saw that his shoulder was in a sling and his forehead bandaged from his own wounds. "Cut my shoulder badly going through that grate and—"

"Dear God!"

"—and Luc Sante nearly took out my eye with a bullet, but I'm doing splendidly now, seeing and hearing from you. You were in shock when they brought you in, and I was a close second."

"I walked blindly into his trap."

"Never you mind that."

"Never mind? I was so . . . He so charmed me!"

"Luc Sante charmed everyone. He could charm a snake."

"Thanks, I think . . ."

"What you did, Jessica Coran, was to singlehandedly put an end to the Crucifier club. Well done, so says the papers and Boulte and the Queen." He pointed to cards, letters, flowers filling the room.

"Well done? What well done? I acted foolishly and nearly got us both killed."

"Survival, that's what. You survived. Strand and five others did not, six if you add the copycat killing."

"That would have made me Luc Sante's seventh victim."

He nodded. "I truly believe the old man thought you the prize ring, Jessica. You must have touched something in him as well. You can be fairly charming yourself, you know."

"Shut up and kiss me, you Briton."

He smiled, bent over, and passionately embraced and then kissed her. "God bless you, Jess."

"And you, too, Richard, and you, too."

· EPILOGUE ·

Perhaps our failure to scientifically examine the phenomena of evil in all its myriad forms is our fear of the end results.

—FROM THE CASEBOOKS OF JESSICA CORAN

October 10, 2000, Heathrow Airport,
Boarding Concorde Flight #414
5:09 P.M. Greenwich Mean Time

Jessica's parting with Richard Sharpe proved miles different from those times she and James Parry had parted. While parting with James had proven Shakespeare's "sweet sorrow" theme, there too had always been the element of guilt that James managed to leave her with, that she should feel guilty at leaving him, at not instantly changing over her life to box it all up to fit into his neat little world there in Hawaii. Richard would have none of that, and he didn't shed any tears, actual or metaphorical at her leaving, but rather said, "I will make it my business to visit America to see you, Jessie." He'd taken to calling her Jessie James since the incident, and he had since shortened it to simply Jessie. "I won't let a pond as small as the Atlantic stand between us, not for long anyway."

It made her smile, hearing him say such words in so matter a fact a tone, as if no obstacles existed between them, because Richard wouldn't allow obstacles.

"You have a place to stay—a warm bed—anytime you visit," she assured him. "You've made my time here more valuable than any time I've spent on the planet, Richard. I . . .

I can honestly tell you now, I love you. I truly do."

This caught him unaware, and he audibly gasped. "I had no idea. You hold your cards so close to your chest, as you Americans put it."

"Hold on there, Inspector. You haven't said those words to me, either."

"I hadn't dreamed you could feel so deeply for me. I thought our relations . . . relationship purely a matter of . . . you see, physical attraction."

"Nothing wrong with that."

"I mean . . . I guess, I mean to say, I hadn't considered a woman of your intelligence and beauty to be all that, well . . . interested in a dull sot like myself, an aging fellow to boot, and—"

"Older men intrigue me. You've lived a life, Richard. And you do have more to offer than anyone I've known, Colonel Sharpe."

"Including Parry?"

She had told him all about her love affair with Parry, and he had been silent and understanding, and when she'd finished, he had told her all about his wife, Clarisa, and his two daughters, his eyes sparkling as usual when he spoke of the children.

Final boarding on the Concorde for America was called. She'd been given clearance to sit in the jump seat in the cockpit behind the pilot and copilot, and she felt extremely excited about the trip home, and nothing Richard said or did spoiled any of it. He remained focused on her the entire time of their parting, never once making her feel odd about leaving so soon, as she had decided, never once asking her to remain longer, but rather promising to see her sooner than she might like.

They kissed a final, long, passionate kiss, embracing as lovers, the world falling away from around them, dissolving into oblivion for they lived, each and the other, in this moment alone. He whispered in her ear, "We're good together, you and I."

"Yes, yes we are. I'll tell my shrink all about you," she teased, "and I'll ring you up as soon as I get to a phone. I must admit, I'm anxious for home, my place."

"I certainly understand that, but I rather doubt you'll be happy over there in the Colonies for long without me."

She laughed and socked him with a petting punch to the cheek.

"And I wager that I will ring you up long before I hear from you," he challenged.

"It's a wager I will take."

He breathed a great breath, his chest heaving. "Off you go, now," he quietly said, and she saw a moment's weakness flush over his features as he held her pair of bandaged hands in his.

"The bandages make my wounds look more severe than they are," she told him. "I'm really in no pain, though I wish more feeling would return."

He instantly controlled his emotions with a joke. "You jolly well better get more feeling back in those fingers. I want you, touch and all. Time you toddled off now, sweetheart." He kissed her a final, lingering kiss good-bye.

And toddle she did, staggering a bit under the influence of his intoxicating taste. She parted with him in harmony and in romance. All the way to the airport, he had spoken of working diligently to breathe life into the flame of their newly kindled relationship. She believed he meant every word, but she feared the distance, knowing what distance had done to Parry and her.

Heathrow Airport bustled about her and Richard where he stood waving her off. All she saw remained him, his smile wide and caring, all the rest of reality had faded, blurred, moved about her in slow motion. She thought of what he'd said to her the night before, after they'd made love for what might well be the last time. "I'm soon to retire," he had told her, "and I have always thought that a retirement to America might not be a bad idea." It had sounded like a fishing expedition, to see her reaction.

"I think it a marvelous idea," Jessica had replied.

"I'd do a bit of consulting, that sort of thing, perhaps even with the FBI, so I might live rather close to your area there, Quantico, Virginia? I've always thought Virginia a pretty sounding place."

"Are you serious?" she'd asked, beaming. "If you are, I could speak to a few people in key positions at the FBI on your behalf. I could start with my chief, Santiva."

"You'd do that for me?" he teased.

"You know damned well I would, Richard. It's so right for you. What else would you do in retirement? An active man like you?"

"Fish, hunt, trap wild game like you?" he joked in return. "I'd have to cultivate some bad habits and bad hobbies, for certain."

"Do you dive?"

"Dive? Do you mean like this?" he buried his head in her bare bosom, both of them laughing.

"Stop it! No, dive, as in dive the ocean?"

"No, but I've always wished to learn. Never found the time, you see."

"Then you must learn someday, and we'll do some diving together. There's nothing more fantastic aside from . . . aside from being with you, here, like this."

He had next gently kissed her, but she pulled away, grabbed a pad of paper, and began jotting notes to herself, plans for his retirement from the Yard and his moving to America.

"You are serious, and not simply making a fool of me, are you?" she asked, looking up from her notes.

He had laughed then at her enthusiasm and replied, "I don't want our relationship to end when you get on that plane tomorrow, Jessie, if that's what you mean."

"Good. Neither do I." And now they waved their final good-bye which was not supposed to be their final good-bye, but she feared it might be, feared how he would feel once she left. She hesitated a nanosecond before boarding, her fear of losing him overwhelming, sending gravel through her veins, freezing her to the spot, a nausea replacing the concrete mixture in her blood vessels.

But when she turned to look back, to tell him that she might simply stay another few days, she found that he had done the smart thing: He had disappeared. Out of sight, out of mind, but not really, not ever, she told herself as her frozen legs found movement again. She handed her boarding pass to the flight attendant who looked curiously at her bandaged hands. The hands made her feel as if she were attached to two balloons. "It looks far worse than it is, really," she assured the attendant.

"I recognize you from your photos in the *Times*," said the attendant. Then the young woman gasped before asking, "Would it trouble you too much to grant me your autograph for my nephew, Dr. Coran? He collects them, you see. Name is Nigel; Nigel Caulder."

Jessica managed a half smile and said, "Why would anyone want my autograph?"

"Oh, he's keen on all to do with criminals, criminal detection. You're a hero after that Crucifier thing that was all the rage in the rags."

With some difficulty, Jessica signed her name for little Nigel on the back of an envelope the woman extended. "Welcome aboard, then," said the attendant.

Jessica walked the makeshift passageway between the terminal and the Concorde, and there the flight attendant smiled warmly and showed her into the cockpit. She found the cockpit of the largest passenger plane in the air dazzling and mesmerizing. Her interest in airplanes and flight took center stage as she shook hands with the captain and his female copilot, both of whom remarked on her having helped out the Crown. "So you must expect to be treated here as royalty," Captain Carlisle warned, and there were laughs all around.

The takeoff, and her vantage point, seeing it from over the shoulder of the captain, proved one of the most exciting moments of Jessica's life. However, still weak from her hospital convalescence, she knew she would soon be at peaceful rest.

Some hours later on the flight, Jessica awoke from dozing in the cockpit. Her eyes went directly to the stars and the empty darkness that filled the Concorde's windshield. A physical pain like a hot poker, at once took her breath away and attacked her heart, making Jessica gulp, leaving her trembling at all she had been through, at the depth of horror and evil she had seen in London. It brought up a heartache and forlorn desolation like none she'd ever known, and the strength of this monster emotion's grip held her heart in icy fingers.

She knew the meaning of this; underlying her nightmare reaction to all that Luc Sante had done, she sensed the truth of her own inner demon. She felt a sense of overwhelming aloneness, coupled with waste and solitude, coming full upon her in the form of never feeling herself in Richard Sharpe's arms ever again. Never being in his embrace again. She feared something would keep them apart, that something would end or poison their love, that she would lose him as she had every man in her life: her father, Asa Holcraft, Otto Boutine, Alan Rychman, James Parry . . .

The plane sped forward through the blackness of empty sky that revealed only an eerie void—nothing out there . . . yet everything out there . . . and it all awaited Jessica Coran's return to America, to Quantico, Virginia—to home.